I don

What, oh <u>what</u>, was she doing?

The buzz of impending danger hummed in Mary's head, but it couldn't drown out the rush of her pulse, or the low, building heat in her womb. No matter how or why it was happening, this was her first real kiss not experienced between the pages of a book.

And she wasn't yet ready for it to end.

Later, she would burn in humiliation to think her first kiss had been delivered at the hands of an utter scoundrel, a man who had not even told her his name. A man whose hand had gripped her bum and pulled her too tightly against him, letting her feel his hard, unforgiving body. A man whose tongue had done wild, wicked things in her mouth and tangled her already vivid imagination into a great, hopeless knot.

But at present, she wasn't thinking of how she would feel later. She was thinking only of how she felt now. She had no experience with such things, but something told her he was a *very* good kisser. She opened her lips, wanting to feel the sweep of his tongue inside her mouth again, and he obliged as if he could read her mind.

It felt *so* deliciously depraved to kiss in such a manner. Had any of the books she'd read through the years gotten it right? She didn't recall reading anything about kisses beyond lips fervently—and quickly—pressed together. But this was a different experience entirely, warm and wet and *wicked*, an invasion of her very soul.

By Jennifer McQuiston

The Seduction Diaries

THE PERKS OF LOVING A SCOUNDREL
THE SPINSTER'S GUIDE TO SCANDALOUS BEHAVIOR
DIARY OF AN ACCIDENTAL WALLFLOWER

HER HIGHLAND FLING: A NOVELLA
MOONLIGHT ON MY MIND
SUMMER IS FOR LOVERS
WHAT HAPPENS IN SCOTLAND

Jennifer McQuiston

The Perks of Loving a Scoundrel

DISCARDED

THE SEDUCTION DIARIES

AVONBOOKS

An Imprint of HarperCollinsPublishers

THE PERKS OF LOVING A SCOUNDREL. Copyright © 2016 by Jennifer McQuiston. All rights reserved. Printed in the United States of America. No part of this book may be used or reproduced in any manner whatsoever without written permission except in the case of brief quotations embodied in critical articles and reviews. For information, address HarperCollins Publishers, 195 Broadway, New York, NY 10007.

First Avon Books mass market printing: October 2016

ISBN 978-0-06233514-2

Avon Trademark Reg. U.S. Pat. Off. and in Other Countries, Marca Registrada, Hecho en U.S.A.
Avon, Avon Books, and the Avon logo are trademarks of HarperCollins Publishers.
HarperCollins® is a registered trademark of HarperCollins Publishers.

16 17 18 19 QGM 10 9 8 7 6 5 4 3 2 1

*To my readers, for your enthusiasm and
unwavering belief I can do anything.*

It isn't true . . . but you make me believe it is possible.

Acknowledgments

It isn't easy to write a book. Neither is it easy to live with someone who writes a book, and so I must acknowledge my husband, John, for not only tolerating the crazy that seems to invade my body as deadlines loom near, but also for offering helpful advice, reading the worst of it, bringing me egg sandwiches when I am hunched over the laptop, and offering me bourbon to unlock secret plotlines. Thanks to my girls, who took their math homework to Daddy during most of 2015, realizing that they were far more likely to get the correct answer from the parent getting enough sleep. Thanks to my CDC co-workers, for imagining that I can write nearly anything. Thanks to my critique partners for their advice, camaraderie, and daily email encouragement, and to Georgia Romance Writers, for providing a safe place to learn about this crazy, wonderful writing world.

To my wonderful agent, Kevan Lyon, thanks for listening: my path is so much clearer now, thanks to you. A special thank you is needed for Tom Egner and his team in the Avon art department for gifting me with yet another incredible cover, the sort I can (and do!) stare at for hours. Finally, a heartfelt thanks to my editor, Tessa, as well as Elle and Jessie and Caro at Avon: you are truly the dream team that makes this process work . . . and I am grateful for and humbled by your support and enthusiasm.

The Perks of Loving a
Scoundrel

From the Diary of Miss Mary Channing
May 24, 1858

Eleanor wrote today. I should have been glad to hear from her, given that she is my twin sister and I love her dearly, but it would be untruthful to say the contents of her letter pleased me. Her new husband, Lord Ashington, has been called away on business and she's asked me to come to London to keep her company during the last two months of her confinement.

Can you imagine? Me, in London?

My family says I must get my nose out of my books and begin to live in the world around me. It is true I've never been further afield than a day trip from home, and that I have never slept a night outside my own bed. But why would I ever want to leave, when I have my books to keep me company? And a trip to London is not without its perils. I could very well end up like one of the characters in my beloved stories, snubbed by the popular crowd. Whispered about behind lace fans. Or worse . . . led astray by a handsome villain and then abandoned to my fate.

Yet, how could I <u>not</u> go? Eleanor is my sister, and she needs me. So I shall put on a brave face. Pack a trunk. Smile, if I must. But I can't help but wonder . . . which worries me more?

The many things that could happen in London?

Or the thought of seeing Eleanor, with her handsome new husband, and her shining, lovely life, and everything I am afraid of wanting?

Chapter 1

*T*he smell should have been worse.

She'd expected something foul, air made surly by the summer heat. Just last week she'd read about the Thames, that great, roiling river that carried with it the filth of the entire city and choked its inhabitants to tears. Her rampant imagination, spurred on by countless books and newspaper articles, had conjured a city of fetid smells, each more terrible than the last. But as Miss Mary Channing opened her bedroom window and breathed in her first London morning, her nose filled with nothing more offensive than the fragrance of . . .

Flowers.

Disconcerted, she peeked out over the sill. Dawn was just breaking over the back of Grosvenor Square. The gaslights were still burning and the windows of the other houses were dark. By eight o'clock, she imagined industrious housemaids would be down on their knees, whiting their masters' stoops. The central garden would fill with nurses and their charges, heading west toward Hyde Park.

But for now the city—and its smells—belonged solely to her.

She breathed in again. Was she dreaming? Imagining things, as she was often wont to do? She was well over two hundred miles from home, but it smelled very much like her family's ornamental garden in Yorkshire. She didn't remember seeing a garden last night, but then, she had arrived quite late, the gaslight shadows obscuring all but the front steps. She'd been too weary to think, so sickened by the ceaseless motion of the train that she'd not even been able to read a book, much less ponder the underpinnings of the air she breathed.

She supposed she might have missed a garden. Good heavens, she probably would have missed a funeral parade, complete with an eight-horse coach and a brass band.

After the long, tiresome journey, she'd only wanted to find a bed.

And yet now . . . at five o'clock in the morning . . . she couldn't sleep.

Not on a mattress that felt so strange, and not in a bedroom that wasn't her own.

Pulling her head back inside, she eyed the four-poster bed, with its rumpled covers and profusion of pretty pillows. It was a perfectly nice bed. Her sister, Eleanor, had clearly put some thought into the choice of fabrics and furniture. Most women would love such a room. And most women would love such an opportunity—two whole months in London, with shops and shows and distractions of every flavor at their fingertips.

But Mary wasn't most women. She preferred her distractions in the form of a good book, not shopping on Regent Street. And these two looming months felt like prison, not paradise.

The scent of roses lingered in the air, and as she breathed in, her mind settled on a new hope. If there was a flower garden she might escape to—a place where she might read her books and write in her journal—perhaps it would not be so terrible?

Picking up the novel she had not been able to read on the train, Mary slipped out of the strange bedroom, her bare feet silent on the stairs. She had always been an early riser, waking before even the most industrious servants back home in Yorkshire. At home, the cook knew to leave her out a bit of breakfast—bread and cheese wrapped in a napkin—but no one here would know to do that for her yet.

Ever since she'd been a young girl, morning had been her own time, quiet hours spent curled up on a garden bench with a book in her lap, nibbling on her pocket repast, the day lightening around her. The notion that she might still keep to such a routine in a place like London gave her hope for the coming two months.

She drifted down the hallway until she found a doorway that looked promising, solid oak, with a key still in the lock. With a deep breath, she turned the key and pulled it open. She braced herself for knife-wielding brigands. Herds of ragged street urchins, hands rifling through her pockets. The sort of London dangers she'd always read about.

Instead, the scent of flowers washed over her like a lovely, welcome tide.

Oh, thank goodness.

She hadn't been imagining things after all.

Something hopeful nudged her over the threshold of the door, then bade her to take one step, then another. In the thin light of dawn, she saw flowers in every color and fashion: bloodred rose blooms, a cascade of yellow flowers dripping down the wrought iron fence. Her fingers loosened over the cover of her book. Oh, but it would be lovely to read here. She could even hear the light patter of a fountain, beckoning her deeper.

But then she heard something else above those pleasant, tinkling notes.

An almost inhuman groan of pleasure.

With a startled gasp, she spun around. Her eyes swam through the early morning light to settle on a gentleman on the street, some ten feet or so away on the other side of the wrought iron fence. But the fact of their separation did little to relieve her anxiety, because the street light illuminated him in unfortunate, horrific clarity.

He was urinating.

Through the fence.

Onto one of her sister's rosebushes.

The book fell from Mary's hand. In all her imaginings of what dreadful things she might encounter on the streets of London, she'd never envisioned anything like this. She ought to bolt. She ought to scream. She ought to . . . well . . . she ought to at *least* look away.

But as if he was made of words on a page, her eyes insisted on staying for a proper read. His eyes were closed, his mouth open in a grimace of relief. Objectively, he was a handsome mess, lean and long-limbed, a shock of disheveled blond hair peeking out from his top hat. But handsome was *always* matter of opinion, and this one had "villain" stamped on his skin.

As if he could hear her flailing thoughts, one eye cracked open, then the other. "Oh, ho, would you look at that, Grant? I've an audience, it seems."

Somewhere down the street, another voice rang out. "Piss off!" A snigger followed. "Oh, wait, you already are."

"Cork it, you sodding fool!" the blond villain shouted back. "Can't you see we're in the presence of a lady?" He grinned. "Apologies for such language, luv. Though . . . given the way you are staring, perhaps you don't mind?" He rocked back on his heels, striking a jaunty pose even as the urine rained down. "If you come a little closer, I'd be happy to give you a better peek."

Mary's heart scrambled against her ribs. She might be a naive thing, fresh from the country, and she might now be regretting her presumption that it was permissible to read a book in a London garden in her bare feet, but she wasn't so unworldly that she didn't know this one pertinent fact: she was not—under any circumstances—coming a little closer.

Or getting a better peek.

Mortified, she wrapped her arms about her middle. "I . . . that is . . . couldn't you manage to hold it?" she somehow choked out. *There*. She'd managed a phrase, and it was a properly scathing one, too. As good as any of her books' heroines might have done.

A grin spread across his face. Much like the puddle at the base of the rosebush. "Well, luv, the thing is, I'm thinking I'd rather let *you* hold it." The stream trickled to a stop, though he added a few more drips for good measure. He shook himself off and began to button his trousers. "But alas, it seems you've waited too long for the pleasure." He tipped a finger to the brim of his top hat in a sort of salute. "My friend awaits. Perhaps another time?"

Mary gasped. Or rather, she squeaked.

She could manage little else.

He chuckled. "It seems I've got a shy little mouse on my hands. Well, squeak squeak, run along then." He set off down the street, swaying a bit. "But I'll leave you with a word of advice, Miss Mouse," he tossed back over one shoulder. "You're a right tempting sight, standing there in your unutterables. But you might want to wear shoes the next time you ogle a gentleman's prick. Never know when you'll need to run."

GEOFFREY WESTMORE—"WEST" TO his friends, and "that damned Westmore" to his enemies—sauntered down the sidewalk, still chuckling over the brown-haired mouse of a woman he'd frightened back into her house.

West hadn't recognized her, but then, Lord Ashington had only established his household there a few short months ago. West tended to sleep during the hours domesticated souls roamed the streets, which meant he had no idea who she was. Certainly not Lady Ashington, who was reported to be somewhat increasing. Although, could anyone be *somewhat* increasing?

It was really rather an all or nothing phenomenon.

This woman had most definitely *not* been increasing. He might still be drunk from last night's misadventures, but he wasn't so deep into his cups he had overlooked the lithe little form lurking beneath that virginal white cotton. Lady Ashington's maid, most likely, given the early hour. Probably charged with filling the vases with fresh flowers before her mistress awoke. No one who could reasonably avoid it would be up at this hour.

No one except him, that was.

He had yet to find his bed.

He sidestepped a lamplighter extinguishing the gas light flames along the square, then followed the vocal trail of his good friend, Charles Grant, who was singing loud enough to wake the dead, not to mention the good citizens of Mayfair.

> *"Ye Rakehells so jolly, who hate melancholy,*
> *and love a full flask and a doxy!"*

He found Grant standing in front of Cardwell House, pissing on an azalea bush. "Damn it, have a care where you aim," West growled, shaking his head in disgust.

> *"Who ne'er from Love's feats,*
> *like a coward retreats . . ."*

"Grant!"

But Grant was swinging into his favorite part of the chorus now, no matter that he sounded like a wounded dog. He lifted his face to howl at the now-absent moon.

"Afraid that the harlot shall pox ye."

Annoyed for reasons that had little to do with either of their gloriously drunken arses, West careened into him, sending Grant staggering straight into his puddle of piss.

"What was that for?" Grant cried, shaking off his shoes.

"That is my family's bush you are pissing on."

"Well, then consider yourself fortunate I didn't crap on it instead." Grant grinned. "Although speaking of bushes . . ." He craned his neck down the street, squinting against the new sun. "What was that you were saying about a lady?"

West frowned. Usually, he found his friend's drunken antics and irreverently foul mouth amusing. A side effect, he supposed, of having survived their Harrow boarding school bullies and an ill-advised turn in the Royal British Navy together. One tended to bond over months spent on board a ship in the Crimea, commiserating about the bloody purpose of that terrible war. With a friend like Grant, you learned to enjoy your amusements where you could find them.

This, however, was not one of those times.

"She's not interested in either of us, you stupid sod." Whoever she was, West hoped she would learn from this little experience and make sure she was properly dressed for her next turn about the garden. He'd done her a favor, teasing her like that. Not every drunken soul she met on the street could be counted on to act the gentleman.

Grant took a reeling step backward, in the direction of Lord Ashington's house. "I reckon I could change her mind."

"Christ, haven't you had enough of women tonight?" West

squinted at his friend. "You've just spent six hours in one of the most exclusive brothels in London. You didn't come out of that last room for three hours. I should know, given that I was forced to wait for you."

Grant swept his top hat from his head, revealing tangled black hair in need of a barber's shears. "Ah, yes. The fair Vivian." He placed his hat across his chest and raised his eyes in a parody of prayer. "Lovely feet, she had."

West snorted. He might be a bit torched himself, but it wasn't a woman's feet that usually interested him. Perhaps Grant was drunker than he thought. "So surely you are sated by now." He took Grant's arm and pointed him toward home. "Off you go then. Time to sleep, my friend. Tomorrow's another day."

"You're a good chap, West." Grant nodded, as if coming to this conclusion for the first time—though in truth, it was an oft-repeated soliloquy, usually launched from the bottom of a bottle. "The very best. You deserve better than a friend like me."

"So you keep saying." West grinned in spite of his annoyance. "Friends forever, eh?"

"Friends forever." Grant pulled a rolled cigarette from his jacket pocket and waved it about. "But just in case forever ends too soon . . . before I go, do you think you could give me another light?"

West dutifully reached into his jacket pocket and produced the small silver case that contained his matches. He rarely smoked himself—not that anyone knew it, reeking of Grant's cigarettes as he so often did. His sisters were always haranguing him about the habit, one he and Grant had picked up in Crimea. But an occasional cigarette with Grant was a welcome source of camaraderie when his demons closed in. Grant was one of the few people who understood West. They knew each other's faults and tolerated each other's vices. Each owed the other his very life.

One couldn't ask for a better friend.

Unless, that was, it was a friend who remembered to carry his own matches.

Then again, he supposed he took enough swigs from the hip flask Grant always carried about to call it an even trade.

Grant lit his cigarette and took a long, enthusiastic pull, then tipped his head back, exhaling a gray stream of smoke. "Shall we meet up at White's later this evening?"

"Of course." West hesitated. "But we'll have to fit two nights of carousing into one. Tomorrow night I've promised my sister Clare . . . something." Something important, to do with the hospital charity she and her physician husband, Daniel, supported.

And as soon as he sobered up, he felt sure he would remember what it was, too.

"Seems to me we always fit two nights of carousing into one." Grant laughed like a maniac. "Then again, we've our fulsome reputations to maintain." He staggered on his merry way down the sidewalk, a fine trail of smoke lingering behind him.

West climbed the front steps of Cardwell House, weariness dragging him by the stones. He fumbled in his pocket for his house key, but before he could unlock the door, it swung open. Wilson, the Cardwell family butler, loomed in the doorway, an old-fashioned candlestick in one hand. "Wilson, old chap!" West leaned against the door frame. "You are up bloody early."

The butler frowned. "Pity we cannot say the same about you, Master Geoffrey."

"Well, aren't you full of piss and vinegar this morning?" West looked from right to left, then leaned closer. "Not me, though. I left all *my* piss on Ashington's roses."

"I see you've been out drinking with Mr. Grant again." Wilson lifted the flickering candle higher, as if he was assessing the state of what had shown up—again—on the doorstep. "No visible blood I can see. An improvement over last week, at least."

"Grant spent the evening bedding, not brawling." West fought off a yawn. "And as we've long discussed, I don't need you to wait up for me."

"Someone must." Wilson's frown deepened. "Otherwise you'll be sleeping on the steps again. The neighbors are still talking about that." Although he was close to seventy and starting to stoop, the butler shoved a shoulder beneath West's arm and began to steer them both toward the dark staircase, the guttering candle held out to light their way. "I'll just get you upstairs, then wake the scullery maid and have her bring you up a pot of coffee."

"*No*." West's boot fumbled on the first step. Not coffee. God, no. He was finally—*finally*—tired enough to contemplate sleep. "No need to wake anyone. I would prefer to just close my eyes for a few minutes, if you don't mind."

"Sleep away the day again, you mean?"

West gave Wilson a pitiful look as they began to climb the stairs. The old butler held West's furtive ability to sleep in one gnarled, aging hand. With one word, the man could have the drapes in West's bedroom drawn tight and order all household activity near his bedroom to cease. Or, he could direct an entire army of servants at Cardwell House to troop in.

Time to clean the chimney. Or beat the rug, as the man had ordered last week.

He held his pout until Wilson offered a long-suffering sigh. "As you wish. Shall I wake you later, Master Geoffrey?"

"Yes, please. Half past three, per usual, if you would." He fought off a yawn. "I'm to meet Grant at White's again tonight."

"Yes, Master Geoffrey."

West concentrated on placing one foot in front of the other. "You do realize you are the only one who calls me that."

"Master?"

"Geoffrey. Only my family still calls me by my given

name." Although Wilson surely qualified as family. He'd been butler to West's father, Viscount Cardwell, for as long as West could remember, and had faithfully served West's grandfather before that.

"I think I've earned the right to call you whatever I wish," the butler said, beginning to puff a bit as they neared the top of the staircase. "After all, I wiped your nose *and* your bum when you had your nursemaid too terrified to come near you with your pranks. And I'm the one who waits up worrying for you now. Your parents have long since given up."

"Wiped my bum?" West managed a laugh. "Wilson. I am a grown man. One day I shall be Viscount Cardwell." He managed to lift a drunken brow. "You ought to treat me with a little more respect."

"Yes, well, if you would act like a future viscount, I feel sure I might find it easier to remember you *are* a future viscount," Wilson replied in his dry, judging manner.

That stung a bit, however well deserved. And so, as they neared the top of the long flight of stairs, West set his foot on the exact right spot on the third step from the top, pressing the heel of his shoe down hard. A long, unmistakable flatulence echoed through the otherwise silent house.

The butler jerked still.

"Wilson," West chortled. "You might need to see a doctor about that."

The butler heaved a sigh and began to move them upward again. "That one was fairly juvenile," Wilson said, "even for you."

"Oh, it's just a bit of fun." That West had painstakingly inserted the inflated bladder beneath the boards yesterday and then waited for the perfect opportunity to unleash its brilliance was something he was somewhat proud of at the moment.

Wilson, however, appeared unimpressed. Per usual.

They reached the top of the staircase and turned left

down the dark and silent hallway. "If I might speak plainly," Wilson huffed, "you need to find something useful to do with your waking hours. When I think of the time you waste planning and executing these ridiculous pranks . . . cavorting about all night with your friends, stumbling home reeking of smoke and perfume . . ." He made a disgusted sound. "Just imagine the good you could be doing instead."

"Good?" West snorted. "Now there's a word one doesn't often hear attached to my name." He stumbled a bit, leaning heavily on Wilson's stooped frame, then laughed. "Unless it is used in association with certain . . . nocturnal activities."

As they staggered toward his bedroom door, relief swept through him at the thought of his mattress. He half-aimed, half-fell in the door's direction, then he threw himself toward his bed, falling facedown into the feathered softness with a muffled "ooooomph". It was tempting to just lie there and let the mattress have its way with him, but he rolled over with a groan and hopefully lifted his boot.

Wilson stood, immobile at the foot of the bed, staring down at him.

"Why are you still glowering?" West protested. "I made it home." He tapped the eye he knew was still faintly blackened from last week's pub brawl. "Safely, this time." He waved his foot around but the servant made no move to help him, and the boot remained firmly in place, fitting West's calves as tightly as any glove. "Perhaps, if you are refusing to offer a hand with my boots, you could summon my valet?"

"And wake the poor man from a sound sleep?" Wilson snorted. "I think not." He placed the candlestick down on top of the bureau. "You terrorize him enough with your laundry, slinking about the gutters and burning holes in everything with those filthy cigarettes." The older man lifted something up from the top of the bureau, fisted in one hand. "I want to speak plainly, for a moment."

After a moment of squinting in the servant's direction, West could see that Wilson was holding up the damned Victoria Cross he had been awarded by the queen last June for nothing more than stupidity and honest-to-God luck.

Grant had nearly wet himself laughing when West had received it, and West was inclined to agree with the sentiment. He needed to stop leaving that bit of frippery out on the bureau top.

Made people think he cared about it.

"What do you want with me, Wilson?" he groaned.

"You've been home from Crimea for nearly two years now." Wilson waved the bronze cross about. "Returned a proper hero, the world at your feet, but it seems as if you have become one of your own jokes. Don't you care what your family thinks of you? What the world thinks of you? What happened to the boy I knew, the interest you once showed in architectural design, when you were at university? You could do, you could *be*, anything you wanted."

West closed his eyes and let his head sink back onto his pillow. "All I want is sleep," he moaned. And if Wilson refused to help, he would sleep with his boots on, thank you very much.

It wouldn't be the first time, and likely not the last.

"Master Geoffrey." The voice was stern and disapproving.

But West refused to open his eyes. He was a grown man in charge of his own actions, and Wilson was *supposed* to be his servant. And what was this nonsense about Crimea? His year of service in the Royal Navy was scarcely more than a prank, a glorious, ill-conceived frolic he and Grant had undertaken to impress past and future lovers.

Not that he had ever spoken of it to any of them.

And he didn't want to talk about it now.

"What, exactly, is your point, Wilson?" he muttered, wanting only to forget. It was difficult enough to sleep most days without being reminded of the war.

"You've not resumed your studies since you came back. Mr. Hardwick has sent his assistant around, asking when you might return to your apprenticeship. I had thought you might wish to send him a reply."

West rolled his eyes beneath his closed lids. The mention of Phillip Hardwick, one of the city's most prominent architects, reminded him too much of his present uselessness. He'd once imagined he might create beauty from chaos, build the sort of soaring ceilings and useful structures that Hardwick designed with such ease. But Crimea had changed all that.

West didn't see beauty in such things anymore.

And destruction was easier to embrace.

"There is no need," he mumbled. But his words sounded slurred and pathetic, even to his own ears. "I'm going to be a viscount, not an architect."

"Then you might act like it, on occasion. You've responsibilities, Master Geoffrey. Your father is no longer a young man, and if you aren't going to resume your education or your apprenticeship, he could use some assistance managing his affairs. You could be learning how to be this 'viscount' you speak of. Instead, you're out carousing every night."

"Right. Making myself *useful*."

"Useful to whom, exactly?"

West cracked open one eye and offered the servant a cheeky grin. "Why, to the female species, of course. And I'm a heroic friend to barkeeps and brothel-goers everywhere. Now, be a good man and close those drapes. It's getting bloody bright in here."

How am I to survive these two miserable months?

My hope to occasionally escape to the garden and read my books in peace has been sorely dashed. I can't even open my bedroom window now. Every time I smell flowers I can't help but think of the man from the garden. There is no doubt in my mind I have met a real-life villain. He probably steals from the tithing tray at church. Kicks at innocent chickens, and eats small children for breakfast. Well, if I have learned nothing else from books, it is that villains— particularly the handsome ones—must be avoided at all costs. A heroine must be true to herself.

Unless her true self can't stop thinking about handsome villains.

Then she must lock herself inside and pull the drapes.

Chapter 2

"Must we read another chapter?" Mary sighed.

Normally, she would rather bite off her own tongue than say such a blasphemous thing. The book she was reading aloud to her sister—*Villette*, by Charlotte Brontë—was interesting enough, but it was difficult not to pray for an end to the current torture. Because three feet away on a bedside table, a vase of fresh-cut flowers sneered at her.

Every time she took a breath, her nose filled with the scent of roses.

Eleanor struggled to find a comfortable sitting position on her bed. "Not if you do not wish it." She lowered her bare feet from the pillow—a necessary concession, given that her house slippers had purportedly ceased to fit sometime last week. "I confess, I have already read it. Ashington bought me the book before he left." She smiled dreamily. "He thought it would help me pass the time until his return, the sweet dear. He really is the most thoughtful husband."

Mary schooled herself not to react to the sound of her brother-in-law's name. It had been this way for two exasperating days. *Ashington, this. Ashington, that.* Good heavens, the way her sister nattered on about her absent husband, one would think Lord Ashington hung the moon each night and single-handedly paved streets of gold.

Mary herself was less than impressed. She couldn't help but think that a properly thoughtful husband might have timed his business trip to avoid his new wife's final days of pregnancy.

Irritated by her own irritation, she looked down at her ink-stained fingers, rubbing at a particularly persistent spot on her thumb. She'd spent more time than usual writing in her journal since her arrival, and her fingers bore witness to her boredom, but writing in her journal was preferable to sitting here breathing in rose-scented air. "If you have already read it, you should have told me." She felt more than a little cross. "We might have chosen to do something different."

"But I thought you would enjoy it. It is by one of your favorite authoresses—"

"Eleanor," Mary interrupted, her voice coming out sharper than she intended. How long had she been here in London? Two days? It felt like a year. Since her brief, ill-advised foray into the garden yesterday morning, she'd stayed safely—and miserably—inside the town house. She spent most of her time with her sister, who spent most of *her* time in bed. And Eleanor's bedroom was beginning to feel as though there ought to be bars on the windows.

She looked up, not even sure why she felt so out of sorts. "I appreciate your thoughtfulness, Eleanor, but you shouldn't be worrying about me. It is *my* job to worry about you. I am supposed to be your companion during this confinement."

But she wasn't proving very good at it, snapping over kind gestures, unwilling to read a perfectly pleasant book. An apology was needed, of that she was sure. But before she could find the words to beg forgiveness for her churlish behavior, her sister gave a low moan from the bed.

Mary jumped from her chair, the book and the flowers and her irritation forgotten. "Is everything all right?" She placed a hand against Eleanor's forehead, her mind racing with all the things that could be wrong.

Ruptured spleen. Cholera.

Poisoned by the beef served at luncheon.

But one possibility needed no imaginative embellishment to send her stomach twisting: it was at least two months too early for the baby to come.

"Should I ring for a maid?" she asked, worried. "Call the doctor?"

"No, the doctor is due to stop by this afternoon anyway, and I—*oomph*." Eleanor breathed out through her nose, then took up Mary's hand and pressed it against her abdomen. "I think the baby is just feeling a bit vigorous today."

Mary felt a violent kick beneath her palm, and gasped at the force of it.

Eleanor offered a thin smile. "He is going to be as strapping as Ashington, I fear."

Mary hovered, afraid to keep her hand in place, afraid to pull it way. The thump came again, hard enough to startle her, even though she was anticipating it now. Good heavens, how was her sister surviving such an internal assault? It suddenly occurred to her that a ruptured spleen might not be such a far-fetched notion, after all.

She looked up at her sister, studying her face. Eleanor tried to hide her exhaustion behind a veil of happy smiles and rice powder, but the powder couldn't hide the dark smudges beneath her eyes, or the way her shoulders hunched forward. Mary was reminded, in that moment, of how much she didn't know. How much she would *never* know. She was twenty-six years old, unmarried, and only permitted this terrifying glimpse into impending motherhood because her sister had sought to share it with her.

She pulled her hand away from her sister's stomach as the

maid came in to announce the doctor's perfectly timed arrival. She still felt shaken by the strength in that kick. She'd read enough about heroines who died in childbirth to know what was at stake here.

As they waited for the doctor to be shown up, Eleanor pursed her lips, seeming to sense the shift in her mood. "What is the matter?"

Mary shook her head. Eleanor always teased her about her vivid imagination, and she'd learned long ago to keep such thoughts to herself. "It is nothing."

"Don't lie to me, Mary." Eleanor wagged a finger at her. "I've always been able to sense when something is bothering you."

"That's because *you* were usually the one doing the bothering."

"Tell me." Eleanor wiggled her fingers. "Or I shall have to tickle it out of you as I did when we were children."

"As if you could catch me in your condition," Mary scoffed, softening her sarcasm with a smile. "It is just . . . aren't you worried? About the coming birth?"

"Goodness, what a question." Eleanor shook her head hard enough to set her diamond earbobs swinging—another gift from dear Ashington, no doubt. "Why should I be worried?"

Mary swallowed her immediate response. Not to put too fine a point on it, but why *shouldn't* her sister be worried? Books were full of morbid examples of women dying, in the most terrible, gruesome ways. Childbirth was but one of the ways a heroine could meet her end. There was also gunshot, consumption, carriage accidents, summer colds . . .

Not to mention the ever-popular pox.

But those were not the sort of things one said out loud, especially not to a woman in the final stages of her confinement. "You could have twins," Mary improvised, trying to steer her own mind away from the worst possible outcome. "Or triplets." She leaned forward. "I recently read an article in the newspaper where a woman had four babies at once."

Eleanor gaped up at her. "Honestly, Mary, four babies? At *once*? I am not a dog delivering puppies, you know. Your imagination is given too much free rein." She rolled her eyes. "Too many books, I should say."

"It isn't *that* imaginative of an idea." Mary flushed. "Multiples are not uncommon. *We* are twins, after all." She hesitated, wanting to say more. She couldn't tell Eleanor the full direction of her thoughts, not when her imagination—always active, thanks to reading so many gothic tales—was insisting on conjuring the specter of a future without her sister.

But she couldn't quite leave it alone, either. She picked up her sister's hand and squeezed it gently. "In all seriousness, aren't you afraid of . . . complications?"

"Why must there be complications?" Eleanor looked pained by the notion. "Childbirth is a very natural process. Nothing to fear. I am young and healthy and, most importantly, determined to deliver this child with all due haste." She looked up at the sound of the door opening, a genuine smile replacing her frown. "Isn't that right, Dr. Merial?"

Mary turned her head to see a handsome man stepping into the room, a light dusting of gray hair peppering the dark hair at his temples. Surprise and dusty memories swept through her. Dr. Merial had been her family's doctor when she was younger, but he'd moved his practice to London over a decade ago. She hadn't seen him in an age.

"Dr. Merial!" she gasped.

The physician set a leather bag down on the bedside table as he smiled at Mary. "Miss Channing, what a pleasant surprise to see you again. I trust Lord and Lady Haversham are doing well?"

The mention of her brother and sister-in-law untangled Mary's tongue and reminded her that this man was a close family friend, no matter that it had been some time since she had seen him. "Er . . . yes, Patrick and Julianne are doing very well, thank you." She shot her sister an accusing glance. "It is just . . . that is . . . Eleanor didn't tell me you were her doctor."

"If you ever came to London, you would have already known it without me telling you," Eleanor answered dryly.

"I see many patients in Mayfair," Dr. Merial explained. "My wife's family lives just down the street, so it is convenient to check in on Lady Ashington regularly." He turned to Eleanor and picked up her wrist, measuring her pulse. "It is good to see you are properly following my orders for bedrest, Lady Ashington, especially after that fainting business last month."

Eleanor shrugged meekly. "Ashington told me I must follow my doctor's orders. And I *always* do what Ashington tells me."

Mary frowned, and not because of the mention of Lord Ashington's name again. Eleanor had fainted last month? And was under orders for bedrest? *Good gracious.* That was the sort of information one really ought to share with one's companion.

"Dr. Merial," she blurted out, as if she and Eleanor were ten years old again and telling on each other for every imagined transgression. "You should know she greeted me at the front door when I arrived and climbed the stairs to personally show me to my room. And she takes breakfast downstairs every morning."

From the bed, Eleanor rolled her eyes. "Need I remind you, dear sister, that you are here as my companion, not my jailor?"

"Still arguing, I see." Dr. Merial chuckled as he loosened his hold on Eleanor's wrist. "Never did see a pair of twins less alike. Well, I suppose an occasional turn about the upper floors won't do you any harm, Lady Ashington." He looked sternly down at his patient. "I would not recommend you attempt the stairs without a sturdy footman to support you, however. It's easy enough to take your breakfast abed, and given your recent fainting spells, you risk a fall too easily." He moved on to place a hand on Eleanor's swollen middle, pressing gently. "As we have discussed at length, you need to avoid undue excitement and surprises, at least until after the baby is born."

"Yes, Dr. Merial," Eleanor said meekly.

Too meekly.

Mary's eyes narrowed. Eleanor had never been one to accept her lot in life without argument. And that meant Mary was going to need to watch her sister more closely.

Dr. Merial completed his examination and took a step back, relief evident on his face. "Well, the good news is the baby has started to turn. I don't think you will need to worry about the possibility of a breech birth." He picked up his bag. "In fact, I think you might need to be prepared for the possibility you may deliver early. Perhaps as early as July."

Eleanor blushed, prompting a faint suspicion to take root. Mary began to count in her head. It had been seven months since Eleanor's whirlwind October wedding, so hastily arranged no family from Yorkshire had even been able to attend.

An eight-month baby was not unheard of. But then . . . shouldn't such a baby be small? It felt as if there was a cricket player batting about inside her sister's stomach. Perhaps dear Ashington wasn't nearly the saint her sister had painted him to be. It was a notion that nearly made her smile.

As Dr. Merial turned in the direction of the door, his gaze drifted toward the discarded book that still lay on the chair beside the bed. "Still reading, I see." His eyes met Mary's. "I recall you always had your nose in a book as a child, but it seems you have moved on from fairy tales. Are you enjoying Miss Brontë's novel?"

"Yes. She is quite a gifted authoress." Mary hesitated, given that thinking of Miss Brontë's eventual dismal fate in childbirth made fresh worry crawl beneath her skin. "But I prefer Mrs. Gaskell as an authoress, truth be told," she added, thinking of the novel *Ruth*, which she had read just last month and which was waiting abovestairs to be read again.

Of course, the heroine of that particular story had been pregnant as well, led astray by a handsome, dastardly villain. Goodness, why couldn't a book's heroine lead a staid, bookish life once in a while? Probably because no one would ever want to read about a character like that.

For example, she doubted anyone would ever write a biography about *her*.

Not unless they meant it to be an aid for insomnia.

"Mrs. Gaskell is an acquaintance of my wife's. Mr. Dickens, as well." Dr. Merial's eyes met hers. "Would you like to meet them?"

The question made Mary squirm. "M-meet them?" she stammered. An image flashed through her head, of Mrs. Gaskell personally signing her cherished copy of *Ruth*. Or Mr. Dickens, signing her well-worn copy of *Bleak House*. But in spite of those exhilarating notions, other possibilities stirred in her mind. She might also collapse in a heap at Mr. Dickens's feet, so overcome with excitement as to forget to breathe. Or she might trip over the hem of her gown and careen into Mrs. Gaskell, making *her* collapse in a heap at Mr. Dickens's feet.

She suddenly realized both Eleanor and Dr. Merial were staring at her expectantly, waiting for her to say something. "I . . . ah . . . that is . . ." She flushed. *Oh, good heavens.*

Perhaps she might collapse in a heap right now.

"You must excuse my sister's reaction, Dr. Merial." Eleanor finally laughed from the bed. "You see, she quite worships books and their authors."

Dr. Merial smiled kindly. "My wife is hosting a salon tonight, a charity event at St. Bartholomew's Teaching Hospital. To benefit injured soldiers and see to their long-term care. A good many have settled in London since the war, and so many of them are damaged, some in ways you can't even see. I understand Mrs. Gaskell will be reading from her latest work, and Mr. Dickens will be there as well. If you enjoy reading even half as much as I remember you did as a child, you should go."

"Go?" Mary echoed weakly. No matter how exciting the notion of meeting someone like Mrs. Gaskell, the idea that she might well make a fool of herself made her shake her head instead. "I am afraid . . . I couldn't."

"Of course you could. You will," Eleanor interjected. "You *must*."

Mary shot her sister a glare that—properly interpreted—meant they would talk about this later. "I'm afraid it isn't possible. I am here in London as your companion, and I need to be here to make sure you follow Dr. Merial's orders. What if you faint again?"

"I don't need you to hover over me." Eleanor gave her head an impatient shake, setting those diamond earbobs flashing. "I've plenty of servants to see to my every need, and besides, I am usually asleep with the sunset these days. And stop trying to change the subject. We are talking about you, at the moment, not me. You *must* go. I quite insist."

Mary spread her hands. "But I am unmarried," she protested, knowing enough about rules and etiquette to at least understand the impossibility of it. "I don't have a proper chaperone."

"And whose fault is it that you are still unmarried, given that you refused to have a Season?" Eleanor shot back, her cheeks growing pink with agitation.

Dr. Merial stepped in between them, his hands raised in a conciliatory fashion. "Now, ladies, surely there is no need to argue about this. My wife would be happy to serve as chaperone, as well as provide a personal introduction to Mrs. Gaskell and Mr. Dickens. And Lady Ashington, I am sure, will promise to stay abed tonight." He looked between them, as if the matter was decided. "Shall I send the carriage around at seven?"

"She is pleased to accept," Eleanor answered firmly.

Dr. Merial turned back toward the door, then seemed to think of one more thing. "Oh, and Lady Ashington?" he called over one shoulder.

"Yes?"

"It is all well and good to always listen to your husband, though I have yet to meet a female who actually does, but do try to do everything *I* tell you as well. No more arguing with your sister." He winked in Mary's direction. "It isn't good for the baby."

Eleanor nodded meekly from her bed. "Of course." But as soon as Dr. Merial pulled the door shut behind him, she swung her legs over the side of the mattress, her eyes rounded with excitement. "Now, first things first. We need to find you a proper dress." She began to waddle toward the wardrobe, one hand pressed against the small of her back.

Mary trailed behind, her hands fluttering in objection. "Should you . . . ah . . . that is, shouldn't you be in bed?"

"That brown serge you are wearing is hideous," Eleanor said, flinging open the doors to the wardrobe, "even by Yorkshire standards. My good blue silk should do for you, I think." She pulled a cerulean swath of fabric from the depths of the overflowing closet, regarding it with pursed lips. "Thank goodness at least *one* of us will still fit into it."

Mary wrung her hands, desperately wanting her sister safely back in bed. "I *can't* go, Eleanor," she countered. It wasn't that she couldn't imagine it. Her imagination was nothing if not vivid. She might go and have a lovely time. Meet a dozen authors and confess her secret desire to write her own stories. But none of that was going to happen. Nothing exciting *ever* happened, not to her. Exciting adventures were for fictional characters, not real life.

And that was why she was going to decline Dr. Merial's kind invitation and fall asleep reading a book tonight, thank you very much.

Her sister turned, her hands full of blue silk. "Oh, and I suppose you think it would be more fun to stay home tonight and *read* about your favorite authors?"

Mary cringed. Drat it all, Eleanor had always been able to see into her mind.

Her sister's brow rose high. "Or perhaps you think it would be more fun to write in your journal about all the things you *aren't* doing?"

Mary gasped. "How did you know I write in a journal?"

"For heaven's sake, your hands are always covered in ink!" Eleanor sighed in exasperation. "Honestly, Mary, can't you see why this is important? You can't spend the rest of your life hiding behind other people's stories."

"I'm not hiding. I am just . . . shy."

"*Shy?*" Eleanor snorted. "I should say spineless." She held the dress up like a threat. "You didn't used to be this way, you know. You used to be eager for a fun adventure. Do you remember when we were nine years old and I fell in the duck pond? You told me there were fairies imprisoned at the bottom, and said they needed to be rescued. And when I tried to save them and lost my footing, you waded in and hauled me out?" She narrowed her eyes at Mary. "*That* girl would be brave enough to go to a literary salon."

"I . . . that is . . ." Mary hesitated. What was she supposed to say to that? She well remembered the day Eleanor was describing, but she remembered it a bit differently. "That wasn't a fun adventure," she protested. "You nearly drowned."

"That is neither here nor there. The point is that it was your idea to save the fairies. You always had good ideas, endless lists of things we might do, adventures we might find. But something changed after Eric and Father died." Eleanor's face grew pinched. "You lost the spark that used to define you. The spark I *know* is still hiding in there, somewhere."

Mary winced, as much at the reminder of that dark time in her life as the criticism in her sister's voice. *Eric and Father.* It was too much, to hear Eleanor say their names, especially so soon on the heels of seeing Dr. Merial again. She could still remember the day Dr. Merial had sat them both down, his face ashen, to tell them of Eric's death. And then, not even a year later, he'd had to do it again, telling them of their father's sudden, unfortunate passing.

"Don't you want to meet a nice gentleman someday?" Eleanor went on, apparently oblivious to the dusty memories she was stirring. "Fall in love, have children? It is what Father and Eric would have wanted, you know."

"I . . . that is . . ." But the thought wouldn't form. Mary's head was spinning in reverse now. Their brother, Eric, had been killed when the girls were nine, not even two months after their "adventure" in the duck pond. He'd been shot in cold blood, and for a time everyone had believed his killer was their other brother, Patrick. Then their father, the Earl of Haversham, had been poisoned to pave the way for a cousin to inherit the title. If they had been ordinary deaths—influenza, or consumption, for example—they might have been easier to understand.

To accept.

But they had been violent deaths, the stuff of nightmares, and to Mary, the world had been painted in perfect, stark relief by those experiences. Books had become her refuge, a far safer way to learn about the world.

But it was clear Eleanor thought they had become her crutch, instead.

"The point is," Eleanor went on, "life is something you have to live, and husbands are something you have to seek. Neither falls willy-nilly into your lap. And you can't do either of those things if you keep reading those unrealistic novels!"

"My books aren't *that* unrealistic," Mary protested weakly. "And I do intend to eventually marry." At Eleanor's dubious frown, she trotted out the same tired argument she always gave when her feet hesitated to follow her imagination. "I *do*. I just need more time."

Time to rediscover that mysterious spark her sister was nattering on about. Time to find a husband who might have a hope of measuring up to the heroes in her books.

"More time?" Eleanor snorted. "For heaven's sake, you're nearly on the shelf! It's been over fifteen years since Father and Eric died, but you still act and dress as if you are in mourning. Life isn't a fairy tale, and you don't need more time, Mary. You need more opportunities, and I intend to see that you take them." She draped the dress she was holding across the wardrobe door, then placed her hand on the rounded shelf of her abdomen. "Don't you realize this is why I asked you to come to London?"

"I am here because you need me," Mary said slowly. *Stupidly.* "Your husband was called away on business, and you required a companion during your confinement."

"Not only that." Eleanor frowned. "I have plotted this for months, with Julianne and Patrick's help. We knew you wouldn't come to London for yourself, given that you refused to even have a Season."

Mary blinked, her imagination helpfully filling in the blanks. "Julianne and Patrick helped you plan this?" she whispered. She could well imagine Eleanor meddling in the tedious chapters of her life, but it hurt more, somehow, to know that her sister-in-law and brother were tied up in all of this, too. Embarrassment bloomed as she considered what it all meant. Her family pitied her. Pitied her boring, bookish days and her looming, lonely life.

And God help her, she was beginning to see why.

"Yes." Eleanor at least had the good grace to look uncomfortable about her confession. "We knew my confinement was our only chance to get you away from home, to help you see something of the world. You are generous to a fault, Mary. I knew you would not refuse my request, not if you thought I really needed you. But I did not ask you here to be at my beck and call. I want you to *enjoy* these two months with me. And this is the perfect occasion. You may never get another chance to meet Mrs. Gaskell and Mr. Dickens. You will regret it if you do not take this opportunity."

"I know," Mary breathed. And in spite of her irritation with the notion that her family was plotting against her, she found herself leaning toward the idea of going.

Perhaps it was her sister's harsh words, or perhaps it was an acknowledgment of her own failings, but she felt a restless shifting inside her. No matter what Eleanor thought of her, she *did* want to imagine her future held something brighter than books. That she might one day be something more than a timid spinster, reading about someone else's adventures.

"But it is my choice whether or not to go, not yours." Mary crossed her arms about her middle. "I will agree to think on it."

Eleanor, though, played her final, winning card. "No." She pressed her hand against her stomach, wincing. "You will *do* it, no thinking allowed. Arguing about it only threatens to push me closer to a premature labor, and you heard what Dr. Merial said about that. So you are going, dear sister." She picked up the blue silk gown again and thrust it toward Mary like a weapon. "And I won't hear another word against it."

It is nearly seven o'clock, and although I can scarcely believe it, I am dressed in Eleanor's good blue silk and waiting for the carriage to arrive.

In spite of my earlier agreement, I am a bundle of nerves. I want to be brave, but I am having second thoughts. How could Eleanor demand this of me? Didn't we read the same books growing up, educational tales where the moral lesson was always the same? I can see my demise clearly, too. The moment I leave this house, I'll be trampled by a runaway carriage on the streets of London. Or else I'll fall into one of the sewers and be washed away into the Thames.

Honestly, what was Eleanor thinking?

She knows as well as I do the best heroines always meet a tragic end.

Chapter 3

The foyer of St. Bartholomew's Teaching Hospital smelled faintly of chloroform and carbolic acid, no doubt from the countless medical students such scents usually clung to.

But tonight it also smelled of perspiration and perfume, and the odd combination of scents made Mary wish for the comforting smell of a library instead, with its books and leather covers and aging paper. Good heavens, even a flower garden and the scent of peed-upon roses would be better than this. Her feet hesitated. Twitched to turn around.

But she couldn't embarrass herself or Mrs. Merial by bolting for the carriage so soon, not when they'd scarcely gone ten steps inside the hospital.

"Are you excited about this evening, Miss Channing?" her chaperone asked over one shoulder. Mrs. Merial began to thread her way through the crowd, beckoning for Mary to follow. "It seems to be quite a crush. It is quite exciting to see so many people turn out for a benefit for St. Bartholomew's."

"Er . . . yes." Mary swallowed. "Quite exciting." At least,

she *hoped* the skittering of her stomach was excitement over the thought of hearing her favorite authors speak.

It could also be dyspepsia. Or the fact that Eleanor's blue gown and tightly laced corset made her feel dreadfully exposed.

She glanced down at the swell of her breasts, pushing rudely up above the neckline of Eleanor's gown. Her mind promptly began to catalog all the ways she might embarrass herself tonight. She could trip and fall on her face. She could bend too far to the right and give someone a peek down this disastrously low-cut bodice. She could . . .

She could die.

All right, perhaps that was less her overactive imagination and more wishful thinking. But she could faint . . . and in a crowd such as this, that was very nearly the same thing as dying. In fact, the dreadful pinch of her sister's whalebone corset made fainting seem like one of the more pleasurable prospects for the evening.

She wished for the tenth time since leaving Eleanor's house to be wearing her own serge day dress and her ordinary, front-lacing stays. But there was no help for it now, so she drew as deep a breath as she could manage and forced her feet to follow Mrs. Merial down the teeming hallway. As they stepped into the lecture hall, she cringed to see the number of people already there. Still more poured in behind them, pushing them forward.

A crush, Mrs. Merial had called it. How appropriate. She'd never before seen anything grander than a Yorkshire house party, and the knowledge of just how many people surrounded her here tonight made something akin to panic bloom, bright red, in her chest. Smells pushed in, silks heated by warm bodies, a dozen different perfumes, applied by too-liberal hands.

She closed her eyes. She'd never faced such a mob before. Couldn't imagine surviving it. And yet, she *must*. Eleanor and Julianne and Patrick pitied her. Worse, she was beginning to think she ought to pity herself. And that meant tonight, she needed to prove she was capable of a fun adventure or two.

Even if her dinner ended up splattered across her borrowed silk slippers.

"Miss Channing?"

Mary opened her eyes, startled, as Mrs. Merial placed a steadying hand on her arm.

"You look a bit pale." The kindly woman cocked her head. "Are you all right?"

"Yes." Mary tried to find a smile. "Just excited, as you said."

And suffocating in this corset.

Mrs. Merial studied her, a concerned pinch to her brow. "Perhaps you should sit down now. Catch your breath." She motioned to a nearby seat. "I'll need to leave you here, I'm afraid. My duties as hostess require me to introduce the authors tonight, which means I must be down at the front, by the lectern."

Mary swallowed. She was to be left . . . alone? A protest hovered on her lips. She wanted to follow Mrs. Merial down to the front, or else ask her to stay up here, where the crowd was thinner and the air was likely less toxic. But even as those thoughts swirled, she felt ashamed. For heaven's sake, she was twenty-six years old, a grown woman. Mrs. Merial was the hostess of the event tonight, a role that came with a good deal of responsibility and *she* didn't look the least bit nervous. The least Mary could do was muddle her way through without complaint, no matter how her palms were starting to perspire beneath her gloves.

"Yes, please go on," she blurted out. "I will be fine." She jumped as someone bumped into her from behind. "Crowds just make me a little nervous."

Mrs. Merial's eyes softened. "It should settle down in a

moment, once the authors take the stage. But if you find you need a quiet moment, the hospital library is just down the hallway, to the left. It is one of my favorite spots at St. Bartholomew's, full of the most amazing old books." She hesitated. "And it should be safe enough for you to be there, as long as you keep the door open."

Mary nodded. The knowledge that there was a book-filled room somewhere, to which she might retreat—or hide, if need be—made her feel a little better.

But as Mrs. Merial headed toward the front of the room, the skittering of her stomach intensified. Because, in the space of that brief conversation, the empty chair Mrs. Merial had pointed out was now taken. Mary turned in a circle, looking for a seat that wasn't already occupied, seeing none nearby.

And then it was too late. Mrs. Merial was addressing the crowd, offering a warm welcome. A gentleman who could only be Mr. Dickens stood just behind her, his beard full and bushy, his curly hair in wild disarray. People who had yet to find a seat began to fight their way down to the front.

Mary felt an elbow in her back, vicious and sharp. A stranger's hand flailed too close, ripping a patch of lace off the sleeve of her borrowed dress. Suddenly, it was all too much. She may have come here tonight to see her favorite authors and to prove to Eleanor that some spark still flickered inside her, but the thought of what she must endure first was overwhelming.

She needed to breathe.

She needed to leave.

And as it had nearly her entire life, the library posed her only chance for sanity.

WEST ARRIVED LATE—NOT an unusual feat, given his propensity to sleep the day away, but a fact for which his sister, Clare, would likely have his hide.

But instead of taking his seat, which would seal his fate, he stood morosely at the edge of the crowd, wishing for something more interesting in his immediate future than the gaggle of authors down front and the misguided fools who had come to adore them. God's teeth, but it was crowded here tonight. The room was packed elbow-to-elbow, giving him no hope of recognizing anyone, even should he know them intimately.

If Grant were here, he was sure his friend would have ideas for how to liven the place up. Pass about a flask. Flirt with an aging dowager and tweak her on the bum. Catcall a pompous author or two. But West wasn't going to embarrass his sister like that.

Not in public, at any rate.

Grinning to himself, he scanned the swollen crowd. Tripped over an isolated whisper of rich blue silk. Swung back for a second look.

Well now, this was more interesting. One woman stood apart from it all. He had no idea who she was, but he hoped to remedy that in due course. She was standing about thirty feet away, too far to make out her features, but he could see shining brown hair and a gentle curve of hip flaring out from a slim waist, all things that quite begged for a man's undivided attention. There was no gentleman on her arm, no scowling chaperone hovering close by.

Which meant she was a widow, perhaps. Safe for proper pursuit.

Grant would have already been heading toward the woman in blue, sniffing out her availability, turning on the rakish charm. But in spite of his own marked interest in furthering an acquaintance, West hesitated. He had come here tonight because his sister had asked this favor of him. There was also the small matter of guilt. A good many former sailors and soldiers sought much-needed care at St. Bartholomew's charity wards. By being here tonight, by purchasing his ticket and showing his support, he was doing what he could to ease his conscience. He certainly hadn't come to indulge some nonexistent appreciation for the fine arts, or to chase a pretty set of skirts. Bolstering the coffers of the hospital was the real point in his participation tonight, not actually listening to the authors.

But now that he'd seen the woman in blue, he was torn between very different loyalties.

Like a moth drawn to a gaslight, he moved toward her, even as the author readings began in earnest down at the front of the room. He might go to hell for this singular distraction, and would likely earn his sister's ire and a cuff on the ear.

But he was willing to risk it if it eventually earned him a spot in the mysterious woman's bed.

Although . . . if the woman was here, it stood to reason she liked books as much as his sister did. Well, he'd pretend to have read some of Mr. Dickens's blathering books, if he needed to. Recite a line of terrible poetry or two, and pretend they weren't actually drinking songs he'd learned from Grant.

As he drew closer, however, the woman turned and hurried out of the lecture hall. Perplexed, West followed, his top hat tucked beneath one arm. A sense of unease settled over him as he stepped out of the doorway. The hall was devoid of a single other soul, save the woman in blue, and she was drifting away from him, deeper into the bowels of the dark building.

West frowned. A woman alone could not be too careful. Someone who understood the ways of the world would not drift toward the hall's shadowed edges, oblivious to her surroundings. And now that he was closer, her shape looked . . . familiar.

Odd, that.

She turned into an open doorway, just to her left. West

was confused—and intrigued—enough to follow. As he stepped through the door, his nose caught the distinctive smell of aging paper and leather bindings. The open curtains of the room draped the space in late evening shadows, and illuminated shelf after shelf of books, but he scarcely needed more light to realize their location. They were in the medical library.

A sense of anticipation returned. Perhaps she knew what she was about.

He *did* love a tryst in a library.

And it could fit, he supposed, with the theme of the evening. If this was a woman whose romantic yearnings were stirred by Charles Dickens, perhaps she might wish to be pleasured against a shelf of books?

She was facing away from him, staring up at one of the thick shelves of books, running a finger across their bindings. He moved closer, until he could see the long curve of her neck, the delicate knob of each small bone marching down to disappear into that temptation of a dress.

He cleared his throat.

She whirled around, a book clutched in her hands. Her eyes widened as she caught sight of him, and she jerked backward. Bumped into the bookshelf.

Jumped forward two feet and dropped the book in her haste.

West fought back a sympathetic chuckle as she scrambled to find both her balance and a proper distance from him. But he felt no guilt in the matter. Her surprise could be laid at her own feet. She really ought to pay more attention to her surroundings. He hadn't exactly been silent as he'd followed her down the hallway.

The sense that he knew her sunk its claws in more deeply. He let his eyes trail across her curves, probing the delicate swell of her décolletage. Grant might catalog memories of women's feet, but West nearly *always* remembered a woman's breasts. All signs pointed to this one's bosom being of the ordinary variety, and the gentle rise of flesh sparked little by way of memory. Yet, the sense that he knew her had hold of him now.

Had he already had her, on another night? In another life? It pained him that he couldn't remember.

Perhaps he and Grant had been on a few too many binges of late. What good was drunken revelry if one didn't remember the good parts?

"Do . . . I know you?" he asked, genuinely curious. He took a step toward her, and then another, and then followed her as she edged away from him toward the window. It was getting dark enough he'd have liked to light one of the lamps on the reading tables, but then, the evening shadows seemed to suit her.

"No," she choked out.

"Would you like to know *me*?" he teased.

That seemed to pluck a string inside her. "That is quite close enough, sir," she said, her voice terse and angry. "Have you come to urinate on the books, too?"

Awareness flared. *God's teeth*. He remembered now. How the white linen of her nightclothes had draped against her body. How he had teased her, and how she had squeaked in protest. It was the woman from Ashington's garden. And whoever she was, she was no one's maid. A servant would have said "piss" or "piddle", not "urinate". This one's words were too polished to belong to a servant.

And her tongue seemed intent on lashing him with insults instead of kisses.

"You are the girl," he said stupidly. "From the garden."

"Scarcely a girl. Older than you, I'd wager."

West took a step away from her, intending to give her space. Even angry, her voice was close to trembling—it was obvious he made her uncomfortable. He probably ought to leave her alone. Only, some devil made him stop short of actually leaving. His hand reached for the library door. He glanced back at her speculatively. Something about the set of her lips made him want to soften them. To do *that* properly, he needed a bit of privacy.

The door swung shut with a flick of his wrist.

Her gasp echoed in his ears. The color had fled her cheeks, but her eyes . . . ah, those were a reckoning, narrowed in his direction and spitting fire. "You, sir," she said, her voice gaining in strength and confidence, "are no gentleman."

"Strong words, coming from the lady who just led me on a merry chase down a deserted hallway." He waited a beat, then let his smile spread across his face. "And who even now waits for me behind a closed door."

"I did not—" She stopped abruptly, clenching her fists. "I *am* not—" She drew a breath, and then lifted her sharp chin. "I did not lead you anywhere, and you well know it. And do not suggest that you are doing this to teach me a lesson, as you did yesterday morning in the garden. I did not ask you to close the door. Open it, please." Her chin poked higher. "Or someone might form a misimpression of our association."

The understanding that she didn't want him did little to assuage the fact that West wanted her. Worse, it was hard to countenance the impulse. Up close, she was hardly a great beauty. Pretty enough, in a plain sort of way, but then, London was full of plainly pretty girls who hardly turned his head. He usually preferred women who were a bit more generous in their curves and less pointed with their barbs. But she was interesting, he'd give her that.

More interesting than Dickens, certainly.

Bugger it all, what was he doing? He had followed a plain and innocent mouse into the library, and then shut the door on the world outside.

And in spite of the idiocy of such an action, he wasn't quite ready to open it yet.

Chapter 4

"**D**id you hear me, sir?" Mary demanded, her chest tight with what she assumed was fear.

It *had* to be fear making her heart tear about in her chest like a frightened rabbit.

Anything else was unconscionable.

Although, perhaps he wasn't a mere "sir". Unlike his disheveled appearance outside the garden fence yesterday morning, tonight his cravat was perfectly tied, not a wrinkle to be seen anywhere on his clothing. But it scarcely mattered if she noticed the way his tailored evening jacket clung to his lean body, or if he carried a title about on those handsome shoulders.

He was a bona fide, dyed-in-the-wool villain.

He appeared young—two, perhaps three years younger than herself. Old enough to be a proper man, though, and larger than her by far. He stared back at her, silent, a wave of longish-blond hair falling into his eyes. She began to form an impression from his silence that he might be stupid. *Thank goodness*. Stupid villains tended to fare poorly.

It was the smart villains one needed to avoid.

"Are you deaf, as well as incorrigible?" she asked, growing bolder now. She tried to call to mind her favorite heroines, and how they stood their ground when finally facing their villains. But while such examples gave her courage, she needed to remember that while he might be young and stupid, he was also still dangerous. "I asked you to open the door," she said, repeating her demand.

But he didn't open the door. He stepped away from her—which made her breathe a bit easier—and set down his top hat on a table—which made her throat close tight. He pulled a book down from the nearest shelf and hefted it in one hand, as if testing its weight.

Mary stared, frozen by the sight of that book in his hand. Her imagination took hold of her thoughts. A book could be an effective weapon, if wielded with enough force.

She recalled a novel she had once read where the villain had merely threatened to use force, and the heroine had capitulated her very innocence. She'd marked the passage and returned to it, over and over again, each night for a month. She was horrified by the tale, to be sure, but there was also something of curiosity lying below the surface of that terror. The heroine—a silly girl, to be sure—had strangely *enjoyed* the things she had done, though she'd suffered for her sins and died of the pox by the end.

As all proper heroines must.

"Do you mean to threaten me with that?" she asked warily.

"With a *book*?" He turned it over, as if examining it. "You think I intend it to be a weapon?" His gaze lifted and held hers. "I assure you, I have never in my life threatened a woman. I do not have to, you see." He smirked. "They all beg me for a kiss."

Mary flushed. Good heavens. The man was insufferable . . . in a curious, heart-pounding sort of way. "Then what are you doing with it?"

"Perhaps I am reading." He opened the cover and offered

her a flash of teeth against the growing dimness of the room. "It is, after all, what one does in a library." He waited a beat, then closed the cover. "Unless you have something *else* in mind?"

She was reminded, in that moment, that he might be stupid but he was also very handsome. In too many books, the handsome ones could be stupid and still cause a good deal of trouble. "Stop lying to me," she snapped, feeling flushed for reasons that unfortunately had little to do with panic or timidity. "Why did you follow me into the library?"

"I enjoy a good novel."

"Then you should try *Bleak House*. Or *Wuthering Heights*." She strained her eyes in the direction of the book he was holding, trying to read the gold embossed lettering along the spine. "Not *The Prescriber's Pharmacopeia*."

His laugh caught her off guard and Mary felt a blooming of heat in her abdomen at the sound. She should not be here, listening to this man's laughter. *They* should not be here, together in such an indelicate situation. He should have opened the door when she'd demanded it.

But she was capable of opening the door herself, wasn't she?

He put the book down on the table beside his hat, freeing his hands for other more dangerous pursuits. His gaze met hers. Warm. Questing. She felt an answering heat spreading through her stomach.

That was all the cue she needed to end this *now*. Mary took a step around him, heading toward the door to the hallway, seeking solace from her own apparent propensity for folly. She reached a hand toward the door, but froze as she caught the faint sound of voices outside, hushed and furtive.

Her mouth went dry. Oh, but could this night get any worse?

A scratch came at the door. She opened her mouth, but without warning, the scoundrel's hand—*good heavens*, was it possible she still didn't know his name?—closed over her upper arm and pulled her behind the nearby drapes, yanking them closed, dust motes stirring. Before she could so much as gasp in outrage, he'd pulled her flush against his very solid chest, her back pressing against his front, one large, capable hand clapped over her mouth. That was when she realized he might be young and stupid, but he was also very strong.

And this night could *definitely* get worse.

GOOD GOD, THE woman was going to get them discovered.

Was she really so naive as to think that calling out, identifying their unchaperoned presence behind a closed library door, was a *good* thing?

Bloody hell, this was why West never dealt with innocents.

They were so damnably . . . *innocent*.

She might know her way around a library and be able to rattle off an impressive-sounding list of books, but it was clear she knew nothing of how the world—or, more terrifyingly, London society—worked. If they were seen together like this, there would be hell itself to pay.

The scratch on the door came again. West well recognized it, given that he and Grant had used such signals on more occasions than he could count. Another couple wanted to use the library for a clandestine tryst but didn't want to risk their own discovery. Whoever they were, they were growing bolder for the lack of an answer. A faint knock came next, followed by a man's low voice, murmuring to someone in the hallway.

In spite of their sticky predicament, West grinned. This could be . . . interesting. Was his poor mouse from the garden going to be forced to listen to another pair coupling? That, surely, would be an even greater horror to her sensibilities than witnessing the harmless desecration of a rosebush, which had probably benefited from his generous fertilization. He drew his hand away from her mouth, letting a finger rest against her lips, the warning clear. *Not a sound.*

She twisted around to face him. She smelled like . . . lemons. He sniffed, the scent tickling at his nostrils. Perhaps she used a scented soap. Or perhaps she sucked on them, to give her mouth that decidedly prudish pucker.

A knock came again, and a rattle of the door latch. He pulled the drapes more tightly around them, then tightened one hand about her waist, giving her both a warning to stay quiet and a salacious sort of squeeze. "Be still," he warned in a soft whisper.

"Don't touch me like that," she choked out. "I will scream!"

He permitted himself a chuckle. "Oh, luv." He lifted the offending hand to trail a finger against the curve of her cheek. "I confess I'd *like* to make you scream." He paused, one finger lingering at the point of her chin, then gently tipped her head back until she was staring up at him, her brown eyes wide with something other than fear. "But I promise," he added, "you would do so in pleasure, not fear."

Her slowly indrawn breath pleased him, teased him with other possibilities. Perhaps she wasn't as much of a prude as he'd imagined.

But he could scarcely tell her the direction of his thoughts. He couldn't say another word. Because the door was opening, and someone—several someones, in fact—were moving into the room, multiple voices melding into a low hum of whispers. His grin returned as he caught the timbre of two male voices, and two lighter female tones.

Ah. Four of them, was it?

That was an even more delicious outrage to a mousy virgin than listening to a single pair tup themselves senseless against her precious bookshelves.

The woman in his arms seemed to think so, too. Her chest rose in indignation, and that tempting mouth opened in panic. It was clear she was about to do something imprudent.

He didn't have time to think, only to act. He needed to silence her, *immediately*.

The danger of discovery was far more real now that the room had been claimed by others, and now that she'd turned to face him, he was no longer positioned to clap a warning hand over her mouth again. And so he kissed her, muffling her squeak of outrage with a generous sweep of his tongue. She began to struggle against him, her protest muffled against his lips.

"What was that?" came one of the male voices.

She quieted, her mouth going still beneath his, submitting to the invasion with surprising rapidity. She went almost limp in his arms, letting him do what he would.

Smart woman, to finally recognize the danger.

But was it too late?

Footsteps echoed, too close for comfort. West kept his mouth pressed to hers, not even daring to exhale. He could feel the tension in her body coil tighter, until it seemed as though she might shatter beneath his lips. But she didn't pull away. She didn't so much as twitch.

"Is someone there?" a female voice whispered, inches from where they breathed.

"There's no one." The second woman's faint laugh echoed. "Just a mouse, I think."

The footsteps retreated toward the center of the room. The voices shifted, low murmurs and an occasional husky female laugh. Despite the surge of relief he felt to have escaped discovery, West didn't relinquish his control of her lips. Yes, it was a mouse.

A very *tempting* mouse, frozen in his arms.

She surprised him. He'd thought, perhaps, that she'd have some bite to her kiss, given the way she'd sniped at him, but this was a sweet surrender.

He slowly lifted his mouth, thinking perhaps she might need to breathe. Her eyes seemed huge in the gathering darkness, her lips swollen from their recent good use. She lifted a finger to her mouth, running a fingertip along her lower lip.

And then with a small hitch of breath, her arms snaked up around his neck, and West found himself pulled back into another kiss, this one far more real than the first.

Chapter 5

What, oh *what*, was she doing?

The buzz of impending danger hummed in Mary's head, but it couldn't drown out the rush of her pulse, or the low, building heat in her womb. No matter how or why it was happening, this was her first real kiss not experienced between the pages of a book.

And she wasn't yet ready for it to end.

Later, she would burn in humiliation to think her first kiss had been delivered at the hands of an utter scoundrel, a man who had not even told her his name. A man whose hand had gripped her bum and pulled her too tightly against him, letting her feel his hard, unforgiving body. A man whose tongue had done wild, wicked things in her mouth and tangled her already vivid imagination into a great, hopeless knot.

But at present, she wasn't thinking of how she would feel later. She was thinking only of how she felt now. She had no experience with such things, but something told her he was a *very* good kisser. She opened her lips, wanting to feel the sweep of his tongue inside her mouth again, and he obliged as if he could read her mind.

It felt *so* deliciously depraved to kiss in such a manner. Had any of the books she'd read through the years gotten it right? She didn't recall reading anything about kisses beyond lips fervently—and quickly—pressed together. But this was a different experience entirely, warm and wet and *wicked*, an invasion of her very soul.

Her fingers wrapped tightly about his neck, pulling him closer. He tasted of whisky and salt and utter sin, and in a startled burst of awareness, she realized she felt his hand, warm and sure against her breast. He paused there, his mouth still doing head-spinning things to hers, but his hand asking permission for something she didn't even understand. She only knew that she liked the feel of his palm there, and so when his hand dipped into the top of her bodice and she felt the shocking warmth of his skin against hers, she didn't—couldn't—push him away.

His fingers dipped lower, questing, promising, but then his hand stilled, going no lower, a wish only half-fulfilled.

The voices outside the curtains remained muffled by the pounding of her pulse in her ears, but she caught a few distinct phrases.

"Did anyone see you?"

"No, I came in after everyone took their seats."

Through the haze of pleasure, she understood that the man with his mouth currently fastened over hers was no longer focused on their kiss. Instead, he was listening intently to the conversation taking place outside the heavy drapery. She tried to listen as well.

"Constitution . . ."

An odd thing to hear whispered, certainly. Then again, what did she know of love words? Nothing beyond what was offered in books, unfortunately. She caught another word, this one whispered loud enough to set her heart pounding in a different direction.

"Assassinate."

She tore her mouth away to suck in a silent, startled breath of air. Whatever else she'd imagined was happening outside their curtains, this was not it.

Her scoundrel had frozen, too, his body stiff beneath her palms. She wanted to ask if he'd heard that terrible, unmistakable word as well, but she gulped down the question as he set her away from him. He lifted a finger to his lips, warning her to stay silent, then turned and separated a sliver of drapes with one finger.

" 'Ere, I think," Mary heard one of the men say, his whispered dialect identifying him as a commoner. There was a rustling of paper. "That's the location to do it, right enough. But when?"

"The date has not been set yet," a second male voice answered, his crisper diction and more authoritative whisper suggesting a more aristocratic upbringing. "As soon as the end of June, perhaps."

Mary craned her neck, trying in vain to see over her scoundrel's shoulder into the darkness beyond the safety of their curtains.

"Given the uncertainty with dates, you must deliver the funds as soon as possible," she heard the second man say. "These men are not so committed to their grand cause they will not abandon the plan for lack of payment."

"Must it be me that delivers the money, Your Grace?" came one of the women's voices, a faint fog of worry threading her words.

"We've been over this a dozen times, at least." A second woman spoke up, her voice more impatient. "No one will question your association, but ours would raise too much concern. And never forget, you are being paid well for your trouble."

"When it's all over, we'll have a handy scapegoat to pin it upon, and we shall all be free from scrutiny," came the strong male voice again. "I shall see the money is delivered to St. Paul's Cathedral, on Sunday, but then you must see it on."

"I will," said the first woman, though she sounded none too happy for it.

There was a rustling, as if papers were being rolled up, shoes shuffling toward the door. Mary bit her lip, praying for their departure, bursting with questions and no small degree of fear.

But then the first woman's voice came, faint and suspicious. "Are you forgetting your topper?"

There was a moment's pause, where Mary was quite sure the room's occupants must be able to hear her heartbeat. *Oh, no.* She could see in her mind, all too clearly, her scoundrel setting his top hat down on the table, as if coming to a decision to stay and torment her further. He seemed to remember it, too, his body strung tight as a bow beside her, quivering with barely suppressed energy.

"Just a 'at that belongs to one of the 'ospital's physicians, surely," came the first male voice, so low as to be nearly inaudible.

There was a pause, as if they were all considering what to do with it.

The second man spoke. "Although, I would imagine whoever owns it could come back at any moment to claim it."

A muffled curse came next, an expletive that made Mary's ears burn.

"We shouldn't be seen together," said the second woman. "There is too much at stake. We need to be more careful." The rustling in the room intensified, footfalls heading toward the door. The door latch clicked again. Silence filled her ears.

And then her scoundrel—whoever he was—was pulling her out of the tangled velvet drapery and into the very room where she had just overheard the murky details of an assassination plot.

THOUGH HIS ERECTION was still one for the record books, West had never felt more impotent.

Stumbling out into the dark room, he bumped into a chair. Cursing beneath his breath, he pulled a match from the case in his jacket pocket and lit a lamp on a reading table. With more light to guide the path for his agitation, he began to pace, trying to sort out what to do next.

Assassinate. Constitution.

They were damning words, but what on earth was he supposed to *do* with this information? The second man's voice had sounded vaguely familiar, no matter that it had been delivered in nothing more distinct than a hoarse whisper. But despite that niggling sense of familiarity, he had no idea who the traitors were.

Or who their intended target might be.

He couldn't even say what they looked like: the room had been dark as pitch with the drapes closed. He had a sickening suspicion, though. One of the women had clearly said "Your Grace". It was a terrible suspicion to hold of a duke, but if West's interpretation of the conversation was anything close to accurate, someone very high within London society was plotting an assassination.

"What are we going to do?" came a trembling voice.

West jerked around and stared at the woman who had asked the question. She was still here. And unfortunately, she was the smaller of his two problems.

He felt jerked back in time, to that day on board ship when it had all gone to shite and the decisions he made—good or bad—became irrevocable stamps of fate.

He would not be responsible for more deaths.

Not if he had anything to say about it.

"*We* aren't going to do anything." He pointed to the door. "You are going to leave and return to the pleasantries of Mr. Dickens." But even as he issued the order, his gaze insisted on lingering on her swollen lips. Damn it, he shouldn't have kissed her, and he certainly shouldn't have kissed her like *that*. She was a mature woman, old enough to know her own mind and take her own risks. Yet, in spite of the fact that she was a few years older than he was, he'd tasted the inexperience on her lips, felt the quickening beneath her skin.

This was why he didn't dabble with innocents. He'd kissed her, and now she looked close to crying. But he couldn't deal with affronted feelings right now, the trembling lips, the claims of bruised feelings. For God's sake, there was treason afoot.

"We need to tell someone." Her small voice made him want to snarl. She even *sounded* innocent. "Did you not hear what they said?"

"I heard them." He needed to think, to form a plan. Who had they been? Who were they targeting? And what could he do about it, given that he had no proof in hand beyond what he had heard? All pertinent questions.

None of which could be properly answered with her looking up at him with other unanswered questions shimmering in her eyes.

"Out you go now." He took her by one elbow, intending to escort her outside himself.

She jerked away, surprising him. "If you heard them, then you must realize the gravity of the situation," she said, sounding decidedly less innocent of a sudden. "What are we going to do?"

It occurred to West that her voice might be small, but her spine held a bit of starch. He looked down at the image she presented, her hair mussed up by their adventure behind the drapes, a delectable slice of nipple peeking out above the rucked blue bodice.

Had he thought the shadows suited her?

It turned out Miss Mouse looked equally well in lamplight.

"I am not going to do anything," he told her. At least, he

wasn't going to do anything more where this girl was concerned. The odd attraction he felt toward her was disconcerting. The sooner she left, the better. "Please, just go now,
before you make it any worse."

"Please don't tell me you are a coward as well as a scoundrel." Her eyes looked huge, mooning up at him against her
pale cheeks. "Because I don't think I could bear to know I
just kissed a man who was both."

That gave him a start. He'd long been called a scoundrel,
but she was calling him a coward now, too? West raised
a brow. "Then perhaps you ought to be a bit more careful
about who you kiss."

She gasped, but the sound died on her lips as the latch on
the library door rattled, jerking both of their attentions to
the door.

"Miss Channing? Are you in here?" A woman's worried
voice called out from the hallway.

"Don't—" he began, only to be summarily cut off.

"Yes, I am in here!" she cried out, shooting him an irritated glare.

West clenched his fists. After all he'd gone through to protect her, she had just instantly, injudiciously thrown her car-
cass to the wolves? *Good Christ.* He felt like throwing up his
hands. He was reminded, again, that she was an innocent,
apparently unaware of the danger this situation posed to her
reputation. Unfortunately, he himself was all too aware.

After all, he flirted with the brink of propriety on a regu-
lar enough basis to recognize that razor's edge, the need to
protect oneself from the fall.

But no matter her idiocy, perhaps it wasn't a fatal mistake.
Because he recognized the voice on the other side of the
door. It belonged to West's oldest sister, Clare, though how
she knew the woman he'd just kissed was anyone's guess.

He had a name to identify his mystery woman now. No
longer Miss Mouse.

Miss Channing. It suited her, he supposed.

Had a bland, mouse-like ring to it.

He stood fast as the door swung open, hoping for the best. Surely his sister would not make a fuss, would recognize the danger, the need to protect Miss Channing. At least, he *hoped* she wouldn't make a fuss. In spite of having scandalously wed a mere doctor, Clare could be rigid about some aspects of propriety. But as the doorway opened, he realized the situation might not be in Clare's control. His sister had not come alone.

"*Geoffrey*," Clare hissed, her eyes wide with horror. Her gaze darted between Miss Channing and himself, while behind her, an eager group of authors crowded in, Mr. Dickens himself at the forefront of the gathering crowd. "What on earth is going on here?"

Beside him, Miss Channing gave a small, desperate squeak.

"I . . . that is, we . . ." His explanation trailed off. Because what was he supposed to say? Miss Channing was well and truly ruined.

And the truth was, he hadn't even touched her properly.

"Miss Channing," Clare said in a desperate tone. She motioned in the area of her own properly buttoned bodice. "You might want to . . . ah . . . cover yourself."

Miss Channing looked down at the hint of a coral nipple peeking out above her bodice. Her squeak evolved into more of a squawk. She began to pant, tugging at her neckline to cover the offending bit of flesh. But then her attentions shifted elsewhere. Her face turned white and she clawed at her sides before going limp, sliding against West in a dead faint.

He caught her, one-armed, and then lowered her carefully to the floor, cradling her head in his hand. He crouched beside her and stared down at her pale face, smoothing strands of dark hair from her forehead. Miss Channing was the fainting type?

It figured. Went with her mouse-like demeanor.

Although . . . she certainly hadn't fainted when he'd kissed her . . .

"Somebody call a doctor!" one of the authors cried out.

"No need." West reached into his jacket pocket, pulling out a vial of smelling salts. He uncorked it and waved it beneath Miss Channing's nose. After a moment, she began to sputter, her head thrashing from side to side.

Clare pushed him aside, falling to her knees beside the girl. "For God's sake, Geoffrey," she snapped, putting a hand beneath Miss Channing's head and helping her to a sitting position. Her eyes narrowed suspiciously in his direction. "Why are you carrying smelling salts around in your jacket, anyway?"

"Haven't you heard? Women are always pitching over in dead faints around me." He shrugged. "I find it better to be prepared." He eyed the milling group of authors, the whispers behind cupped hands. He tried on an apologetic grin, hoping he looked charming instead of rakish. "Must be the Westmore charm."

Clare helped Miss Channing gain her feet. The poor girl was swaying, almost as if she had too much drink, and Clare led her toward two uncomfortable-looking chairs that several of the authors had hastily pushed together to make a sort of bed. Seeing that she was being cared for, West let his thoughts pull to the dilemma even more concerning than what to do with her.

In spite of the drama unfolding in front of him, he could not forget the conversation he'd just overheard in this room. *Assassinate. Constitution.* Those were not words used in jest.

He ought to know.

He'd done enough jesting in his life.

As soon as he could, he pulled Clare to one side, leaving the others to tend to the situation. "Listen, Clare, I think you ought to know . . . this business with Miss Channing . . . put it aside for a minute. We have just overheard an assassination plot."

There was a moment of silence, clearly laced with disbelief. "An assassination plot?" Clare raised a dubious brow. "Involving whom?"

"I don't know. Not yet."

"Oh, for heaven's sake!" Clare smacked him, hard against the ear. "Stop trying to distract me with your incessant games," she fumed, letting her anger wind up the way she used to, when they were children and he'd done something terrible to vex her. "I've never heard of such a ridiculous thing—an assassination plot. Anyone with eyes in their head can see what you've been doing with Miss Channing behind closed doors!" She lowered her voice. "Her *breast* was exposed. What were you *thinking,* Geoffrey?"

"This isn't a game." West rubbed his ear. "And don't call me Geoffrey, as if I'm still a child."

"It is *always* a game with you. And if you don't want to be called a child's name, stop acting like a child."

Guilt swirled, hot and thick, but so did resentment. But just as quickly as the anger rose up, his shoulders wanted to slump. Clare was right. Miss Channing wasn't exactly a problem he could ignore. But perchance she was a problem he could pass off, at least until he could collect his thoughts. "Look." He flashed his sister a hopeful smile. "This is all just a misunderstanding, and things will look better tomorrow. But . . . could you . . . ah . . . help her home?"

"Can't you see?" Clare hissed, eyeing the group of authors who were all clucking over Miss Channing like a brood of agitated chickens. "I *have* to see her home. I am her chaperone!"

West blinked. "You are Miss Channing's chaperone?" At his sister's terse nod, he groaned. Miss Mouse was a woman whose pristine reputation required a chaperone?

Christ above. There was definitely going to be a fuss.

Clare's eyes narrowed back at him. "You've been side-stepping your responsibilities ever since you returned from Crimea, acting more like the thirteen year old you once were than the grown man you ought to have become." She crossed her arms. "I am sick of it all. And if I find out you forced yourself on her, so help me God . . . "

Shame coursed through West. He wasn't a man who co-erced unwilling women.

But she hadn't been unwilling, precisely.

She *had* kissed him back.

In the wake of his silence, Clare glanced toward the gaggle of authors, who were bent over Miss Channing's form, murmuring false sympathies. She frowned in that big-sisterly way that had always set him on edge when they were children. "It's not only about Miss Channing, though that ought to be enough to bring you around to the right deci-sion," she warned. "If you do not fix this, you will harm my and Daniel's reputation as well."

West flinched. His brother-in-law, Dr. Daniel Merial, was a good man, someone who had always believed in West's potential and encouraged him against poor behavior. If there had ever been anything good in West, it was only there be-cause it had been noticed and encouraged by Daniel. The thought of disappointing his brother-in-law was definitely enough to make him cringe. "I would not purposefully do anything to harm either of you—" he began.

"Purposeful or not, you *know* we depend on the good will of those influential in society to keep St. Bartholomew's in enough funds to operate the charity ward here. It's been a lean year, which is why we held tonight's salon to raise more funds. If we are forced to close the charity ward because of this, you'll be directly responsible for people's *deaths*, Geof-frey."

West remained silent.

Better that, than to confess to his sister they wouldn't be the first.

She drew a deep breath. "You've really stepped in it this time, and you can't brush this away the way you do your other indiscretions. This isn't some willing widow, or a doxy who understands the rules of the game. This is the sister of the Earl of Haversham, one of Daniel's dearest friends."

"*What?*"

"And she is the sister of Lord Ashington's new wife, as well."

West reared back, feeling nearly as if his sister had struck him again. Ten feet away, a group of very famous authors were hovering over one very fragile girl, no doubt spinning stories in their mind, even as they pretended to care. A girl with apparently *excellent* connections, one who ostensibly moved in circles more lofty than his own.

"Bugger me blue," he groaned.

Clare rolled her eyes. "*That* particular sin might not have gotten you in as much trouble."

From the Diary of Miss Mary Channing
June 2, 1858

So this is how it feels to be ruined.

It is almost a relief to turn myself over to it. All those years of imagining it, reading about it . . . and now it has happened. I am ruined, and nothing worse can happen to me.

Eleanor, of course, was horrified, and spent all morning begging my forgiveness for forcing me to attend last night's salon. My scoundrel's name is Mr. Geoffrey Westmore, apparently. The future Viscount Cardwell. Mrs. Merial said she will ensure her brother does "the right thing", whatever that may be.

Well, I must do "the right thing" as well. I am humiliated, of course, but I am far less frightened of my newly blemished reputation than by what I overheard in the library last night. I've read enough books to recognize a nefarious plot when I hear one. If Mr. Westmore doesn't plan to do something about it, I fear I will be forced to take matters into my own hands.

If only I was brave enough to step outside . . .

Chapter 6

West sat at the Cardwell breakfast table, his head cradled in his hands, though he'd not had a drop to drink. In fact, after the debacle in the library, he'd come straight home—an uncharacteristic diversion from his usual nocturnal patterns. He'd paced his carpet into the wee hours of the morning, studying both of his dilemmas from every possible angle.

And finally, he'd reached an unpalatable decision.

Nearly as unpalatable as his breakfast. After such a long night, he ought to be ravenous, but the sight of eggs and toast this morning made his stomach turn. The only good thing he could imagine doing with his fork this morning was sticking it in his eye.

"You are up early today, Geoffrey," his father observed from across the table, rattling his morning paper.

"Yes, it is good to see you up for a change, and on a Wednesday, no less," Mother chimed in as if the day of the week made a difference. She lifted a cup of chocolate to her lips. "Though, you've shadows beneath your eyes. Are you getting enough sleep, dear?"

"Mmmph," West replied, capable of little else. His parents might think his appearance this morning at the breakfast table was a good sign, but they didn't know the truth: he was only here because he'd been unable to sleep.

And because he had a sour bit of business to tend to this morning.

He stared down at the eggs on his plate, contemplating whether he could choke them down. Relief from that decision came in the sound of shoes clicking against the floorboards. His gaze pulled toward the dining room door to see Wilson appear, a smile replacing the servant's usual scowl. "You've a visitor, Lord Cardwell," he announced, sounding happy for once.

"A visitor?" Father nudged his spectacles farther up the bridge of his nose. "It is scarcely nine o'clock in the morning." He looked down at his plate. "And we already finished all the eggs, thanks to Geoffrey's unexpected appearance at breakfast."

Clare appeared at Wilson's side. "Fortunately, it is a visitor who doesn't expect to be fed," she announced, looking crisp and polished as she sailed into the room. She slid seamlessly into the chair where she'd always sat growing up, and beamed up at the butler. "Thank you for announcing me so formally, Wilson. My life is so different now—sometimes I forget what it is like to have a lovely friend of a butler greet you at the door." Clare's smile shifted to their parents. "Mother, Father, it is good to see you all."

"Well, I must say, this is a *lovely* surprise," Mother exclaimed. "Just like old times, when we'd gather every morning for a family breakfast." She sighed, almost wistfully. "If only Lucy and Lydia were here too. Though there are times I enjoy the quiet, I miss having my children in the house again. Geoffrey is hardly ever up in time for breakfast anymore."

"Oh, I don't think we want Lucy and Lydia to hear what

I've come to discuss just yet." Clare's smile faltered, and she pulled a folded up bit of newsprint from her reticule and placed it in front of her. "It's a bit delicate, actually."

His mother put down her cup of chocolate. "Has something happened to you or Daniel?" Her hand fluttered near her throat. "Or one of the children?"

"No, no, the children are fine, and already at their lessons for the day. As for whether something has happened to me or Daniel, I think that depends on Geoffrey's decisions this morning. We'll be fine, I think, if he comes up to scratch." His sister looked at him, her hazel eyes narrowing. "Has he told you about what happened last night?"

"Clare—" West warned. Surely this was the sort of conversation best had in private.

"What has he done now?" Mother asked, sounding resigned. "Is it worse than last year, when he took out an advertisement in the *London Times* and advertised Cardwell House for sale?"

West winced. That had been blown entirely out of proportion, a bit of fun intended to make his father sweat after threatening to cut off his monthly allowance for some small transgression. The advertisement had offered the house and its furnishings—including several Ming dynasty vases and the gold-plated china—for two hundred pounds. There'd been a line of agitated buyers a half mile long wrapping around Grosvenor Square, all desperate to purchase such a valuable property for such a paltry price. His father had certainly been surprised.

So had West when the authorities had knocked on the door and accused him of fraudulent advertising.

Clare shook her head. "Worse."

"Is it worse than that time he let the rats loose in the room of that bully at Harrow?" Wilson chuckled.

The pounding in West's head got worse. However well-intentioned, that had been an adolescent prank that had miscarried. Although the rats were intended to terrorize Peter Wetford—the son of the Duke of Southingham, a brutish young man who liked to pummel those with lesser titles and who, thanks to room assignments based on alphabetic order, occupied the room next door to him at Harrow—the rats showed no allegiance to worthy causes. They had chewed beneath the walls and found their way back to West's room.

He still woke up sometimes at night, drenched in sweat, the sensation of rats climbing over him all too real, and in all too delicate of places.

"It is worse than Harrow," Clare said firmly.

The serving maid giggled. "Surely it isn't worse than the time he snuck into the Duke of Southingham's house?" The girl's cheeks pinked up. "My friend told me about that one. She told me the entire household was in an uproar when he was caught with the duchess's maid."

West slumped in his chair. *Bloody wonderful.* Now, now even the downstairs crowd was spreading tales of his exploits, and ones scarcely suitable for his mother's ears.

"I feel quite sure it must be worse than his inflated-bladder-on-the-stairwell routine," his father interjected. "Stepped on that one this morning. Nearly scared the living daylights out of me." He looked sternly over the top of his spectacles. "Honestly, Geoffrey, you need to find another place to put it. Frightening people on the stairs could have dire consequences. You wouldn't want someone to fall."

"It is worse than any of it, I promise you." Clare leveled a look at him, a look he knew all too well from growing up with a shrew for a sister. "I suppose he'll claim it's all a misunderstanding, as he only did it to thwart an assassination plot," she said, bringing a round of laughter from family and servants alike.

West looked down at his eggs again, his gaze lingering on the glistening mess. Thanks to Clare, they'd never believe him if he told them what he'd heard now, would presume it was just another one of his infamous tricks.

Come to think of it, the authorities probably would think it another one of his practical jokes as well. He knew all too well there was a two-inch-thick file with his name on it in the local constable's office, overlooked only because of his father's generous contribution to the Fund for Constabulary Widows and Orphans.

How was he to convince someone to take his worries seriously if they all refused to believe he was capable of anything more than an elaborately planned hoax?

Clare slid the folded bit of newsprint across the table to their mother. "His newest sin is ruining Miss Mary Channing, the Earl of Haversham's sister. It happened last night, and the gossip columns have all covered it quite thoroughly this morning, even going so far as to identify the poor woman by name." She leaned back in her chair, not needing to say the rest of it.

And I've come this morning to ensure he makes amends.

West's mother unfolded the gossip column, her lips moving silently as she read. West waited in stiff silence. It was usually considered quite a badge of honor to hold a featured spot in the daily rags, but this morning it felt far less a badge than a noose.

"Geoffrey," his mother gasped, looking up through rounded eyes. "Is this horrible bit of gossip *true*?"

"Yes." He met and held his parents' shocked gazes. They might not believe an excuse of a treasonous plot, but his past romantic adventures and rumors of his exploits about town ensured they would believe *this* about him. "I simply hadn't had a chance to say anything yet. I had planned to tell you both."

And he had. This was no simple rig, to be swept under a rug. He wasn't at school, where expulsion was the worst he could expect, or on board a ship, where a half-dozen lashes with a cat of nines would set things straight. He could feel the weight of his sister's disappointment and the desperation that had brought her here, running below the surface of this conversation. He couldn't ruin his family. Clare's and Daniel's hard work was the only thing holding the hospital together.

And he couldn't leave Miss Channing to face the gossip alone, either. He'd picked the worst woman possible to follow into the library. No matter the wild nature of his randy exploits, he'd never before—not even once—been linked to the ruin of an innocent. This was all new territory, and he felt as if he was floundering, coming up for air only to find he was destined for a life below water.

He glared at Clare, irritated she'd not had enough faith in him to let him do the right thing without coercion, for telling their parents before he'd found a chance to do it himself. He wasn't skirting his duties. He'd known his path from the moment that library door had opened last night and he'd discovered a crowd of gaping eyes, instead of just his sister. Even if news of this misadventure hadn't gotten printed in the gossip columns, he would have still done it.

"Father," he said, looking up with a grimace. "I must ask you to put in a good word for me with the Archbishop this morning."

"The Archbishop?" Lord Cardwell asked in confusion. "But . . . why?"

"Isn't it obvious?" West pushed his untouched plate away, nearly, in that moment, hating his life. "Mother was just wishing for children at the breakfast table again. Well, it seems she shall have her wish, because I'm bringing home a bride."

"Look on the bright side," Mary suggested. "It's done, and I can't be ruined twice." She glanced down at her lap, at the small but disastrous column that was printed in the morning's gossip rag. She traced a finger over the caricature someone had drawn of her, her nipple bared to the room, a sea of shocked faces peering in from all sides.

It wasn't even a good likeness of Mr. Westmore.

He hadn't had *quite* such a leering expression on his face last night.

"Though I am a bit affronted my downfall has been chronicled in a gossip rag, instead of a good book," she added, trying to lighten the mood. Why would her sister even subscribe to a scandal sheet like this? There were so many more interesting things one could read.

"How can you joke about this?" Eleanor moaned, rubbing her eyes. The circles under her eyes had grown darker since yesterday, and as Mary remembered Dr. Merial's warning, she eyed her sister with unease. "Patrick and Julianne are going to have my very skin," Eleanor added, sounding distraught. "I promised them I would keep you safe on this trip to London, and instead I have orchestrated your ruin."

Mary sighed. "Could we not talk about something else?" Yes, she was ruined. Humiliated, mortified, shamed, disgraced . . . any word would do. Eleanor and the gossip rag seemed to have used all of them, *ad nauseam*. But as Mary had never had any actual prospects to disappoint, surely this definition of "ruin" was a matter of semantics.

And now that it was done, she was having trouble understanding why everyone was so upset, why it was portrayed as such a tragedy in the books she had read. As altered as she was supposed to be, on the inside she felt much the same person she had been yesterday.

Albeit, now with a heated memory of a kiss that kept returning at the oddest moments.

She was really rather impressed with her fortitude. Perhaps she *was* more suited for adventure than her family believed. And besides, there was a far bigger matter at stake than what to do about her reputation.

Someone was plotting an assassination.

It had been a devastating thing to overhear last night.

Worse still, to contemplate this morning. The urge to tell Eleanor itched beneath her skin.

"About last night." Mary tossed the gossip rag to one side and leaned forward. "I overheard something important, when I was in the library."

"Was it the sound of your reputation shattering?" Eleanor asked sharply. "Because I am surprised I didn't hear it in my sleep."

Mary flinched to hear her sister's harsh words. "No. It was a plot."

"A plot?" Eleanor clutched a hand to her swollen abdomen. "A *plot*?" She breathed in through her nose. "Mary, you need to stop it."

"Yes, exactly, that is what I am trying to do—"

"*No*," Eleanor snapped, the smudges beneath her eyes looking more like bruises now. "Stop inventing excuses, stop imagining things . . . just *stop*!"

Mary gaped at her sister. "You don't understand. At the end—"

"The *end*?" Eleanor was nearly shouting now, her words raw and trembling. "The only ending you ought to be worried about is your own! How can you sit there, nattering on about an imaginary plot? This isn't one of your novels, Mary. This time it's real. Do you realize your life is now *ruined*? Any hope you might have held for meeting a nice gentleman during your time here in London, of finding the husband that just yesterday you confessed you wanted, is now moot!"

Mary cringed. Not because it was all true, but because she could see, then, her sister didn't believe her about the assassination plot she had overheard.

Or rather, *wouldn't* believe her.

And perhaps that was a good thing. Eleanor was growing more agitated by the second. Piling additional horrors like assassination plots on top of her scandal might well force her sister into an early delivery. Dr. Merial had issued a stern warning for her sister to avoid any and all excitement, and as her companion during this confinement, it was supposed to be Mary's responsibility to ensure it. Instead, she'd invited dark circles and drama into her sister's life.

What had she been thinking, trying to talk to Eleanor?

She couldn't talk to *anyone* about this.

Anyone, that was, except her villain.

The thought of him made Mary's cheeks heat in a most unfortunate fashion. *Mr. Westmore*. Not that she needed to say his name to think of him: every time she closed her eyes, she saw the face of a perfect scoundrel.

"On the matter of suitors . . ." she said weakly, deciding that perhaps a change of subject was in order. "Perhaps hope isn't entirely lost. Mr. Westmore could still call on me, you know."

"Mr. *Westmore*?" Eleanor retorted, rolling her eyes. "You should not admit him if he did!" She shook her finger at Mary. "I want you to stay far, far away from that man."

Mary recoiled from the venom in her sister's tone. Clearly, she ought to have chosen her new topic with greater care. "I should think keeping far, far away is going to be a bit difficult, given that he is one of your neighbors," she said cautiously. "What have you heard about him? That is, beyond what was printed in the scandal sheet this morning?"

"What *haven't* I heard about him? He's not to be trusted. He's a . . . a . . ."

"Scoundrel?" A delicious shiver ran up Mary's spine to finally say it out loud.

"Degenerate!" Eleanor declared. "This isn't the first time he's been in the gossip rags, and it won't be the last. His antics are legendary. He and his friend Mr. Grant are no better than drunkards, and he always seems to be in the thick of any controversy."

"So, he is high-spirited?" Mary thought back on her vari-

ous interactions with the man. Though he'd certainly confirmed her sister's claims that morning in the garden, he
hadn't seemed drunk last night—not even close. His lips had
closed over hers with straight assurance.

Surely a drunk man would have slobbered?

"High-spirited? For heaven's sake, he's not a horse," Eleanor snapped. "Though, judging by the rumors he's as randy
as a stallion, chasing after women twice his own age." She sat
up straighter, then looked from right to left, as if searching
for servants who might overhear what she was about to say.
"They say he once had relations with his sister's governess."

Mary's imagination immediately conjured a vision of an
adolescent boy peeking under his gray-haired tutor's skirts.
Mr. Westmore seemed young, perhaps even a year or two
younger than herself. Although . . . perhaps he was an early
bloomer?

And who on earth was this "they" Eleanor was talking
about?

Surely her sister didn't believe everything she heard or
read. "Hearing a bit of gossip does not necessarily mean it is
true," Mary argued weakly, though she could scarcely countenance the urge she felt to defend the man. She gestured
to the discarded gossip rag, knowing that the details of last
night's shameful encounter had been grossly exaggerated.
For example, only *one* of her nipples had been exposed. The
cartoonist had gleefully drawn two. "I generally prefer to
believe things I see myself," she added, "not a rumor someone has overheard."

Eleanor flushed. "Well then, you should know *I* saw
him engage in entirely disreputable behavior with my own
eyes, just last month at the opening of the new Royal Opera
House."

"You *saw* him?"

"Everyone saw him. He was with his friend, Mr. Grant,
and a red-haired prostitute in the Cardwell opera box!"

Mary's cheeks burned. In fact, her whole body felt feverishly hot, and an odd fluttering had started up in her stomach. "What did you see?" Her ears burned in anticipation.

Eleanor finally had the grace to look less sure of herself. "Well, I kept my eyes focused on the stage, as any proper lady would. But from the corner of my eye I could see the woman's feet thrashing about. One of her slippers came off and went sailing over the balcony railing. She appeared to be *quite* enjoying herself."

"With two men?" Mary closed her mouth, which had somehow popped open in astonishment. *Good heavens.* How would that even work?

"Oh, it gets worse than that." Eleanor leaned forward. "Ashington told me that he heard Westmore once had four women at one time. And two of them were sisters!"

Mary squeaked. Four women at once? She'd never heard of such a twisted, unnatural thing. She wished suddenly she could go back to Mr. Westmore's transgressions only being about an aging governess. At least there had only been *one* of her.

"Well, as long as they weren't *married* women," she laughed weakly, striving for a joke.

"Oh, I am quite sure he considers married women fair game as well, and most of the matrons in town seem all too indulgent of his carnal appetites. He's already caused one duel, thanks to his philandering nature."

"But, I thought duels were no longer strictly legal," Mary protested.

"Well, I don't think legalities mean much to a man like Mr. Westmore, because there are also rumors he once had intimate relations with a corpse," Eleanor said tartly.

Mary gasped, forgetting, for the moment, about the rumored duel. "A *corpse*?" Her cheeks were now so hot they ought to blister. It was worse—far worse—than anything she'd ever read in the pages of a novel. She'd been kissed by a man who'd done unspeakable things to a dead body?

And then—and really, this was the most mortifying piece of it—she'd kissed him back?

"Not that it's hampered his appeal in any way, mind you," Eleanor said, sounding disgusted. "The society cows are all aflutter whenever he walks by. Why, women practically knock themselves over in the stampede to earn a chance in his bed. And he cavorts about, basking in their adoration. Can you imagine?" she demanded, her voice going shrill. "The utter egotism of the man?"

Mary could believe it, too well. She recalled Mr. Westmore's words from last night. How he'd claimed that most women "begged him for a kiss."

He certainly had a unique . . . *confidence* in his abilities.

Mary looked down at her ink-stained hands. She was beginning to imagine something else, as well, something beyond a belief in Mr. Westmore's arrogance and willingness to consort with corpses. Could he really be that . . . *exemplary*? So skilled, as a lover, that women might truly elbow their way to the front of a line for a chance in his bed? That was an entirely different notion of ruin than the one she was facing at present.

And in spite of it all, it hardly seemed fair to get the short end of that stick.

Chapter 7

West was shown to Lord Ashington's drawing room, with an apology from the butler that Lady Ashington regretted being indisposed due to her condition and was therefore unable to "rip into him herself." Not that he didn't deserve the sentiment, given what had occurred with the woman's sister, but still . . .

Perhaps a lack of decorum ran in her family?

Bloody wonderful. Any children resulting from this terrible plan would almost certainly be laughingstocks, given that a lack of decorum most definitely ran in his own.

He shifted from foot to foot as he waited to see if he would be received, as if such a mindless movement could redistribute the embarrassment of his morning and the weight of the special license sitting in his pocket. He caught sight of the clock on the mantel. Realized it was already half past three. Normally, he would be just shaking himself from bed about now. Heading to White's to meet Grant for a glass or five, throwing himself into a ripping good game of billiards, plotting his next rig.

Instead, he'd been up since dawn, and had spent a useless

few hours at Scotland Yard, where he'd first tried to lodge his complaint. The uniformed officer pretending to take his statement had sniggered, especially when West couldn't give an actual name as to whom the plot might be directed against. The man had shooed him out, waving the gossip rag in his face, snorting about past jokes and the like.

A reputation with the ladies was all well and good, but it seemed West's legend in those areas was proving a poor inducement for constabulary action.

Miss Channing appeared in the drawing room doorway so quietly his initial misnomer was brought to mind. *Miss Mouse.* She looked it today, too, clad in a hideous, mud-colored dress, her dark hair pulled back into a braid wound about her head, her nose lacking only whiskers for the full, mousy effect. He thought back to their first meeting, when he'd teased her over the sodden rosebush. That, he suspected, was the *real* Miss Channing, not the kiss-seeking siren who had given him a cockstand in St. Bartholomew's medical library last night.

Today there was no tempting nipple in sight, nor hint of rounded bosom either. She must be wearing one of those utilitarian corsets beneath all that wool, the ugly sort women wore when they weren't trying to tempt a man. That was the first request he'd make as her husband.

Miss Channing should wear only French lingerie.

Something scandalous underneath to brighten up the bland exterior of their future lives.

A gray-haired housekeeper hovered a few steps behind, no doubt intended to serve as chaperone. Perhaps Miss Channing was suffering an ill-timed return to respectable behavior.

Unfortunately, it was a little too late for that.

She stepped into the drawing room, her hands laced in front of her plain wool skirts. He cleared his throat, suddenly nervous, though he'd known what his path must be from the moment Clare had revealed who, exactly, this woman was.

"Miss Channing," he began, before his nerves utterly failed him. "I have come to make amends."

She said nothing in response, merely raised a brow.

He summoned the words he'd practiced no less than a dozen times on the way here. "Given the unfortunate events of last evening, I am prepared to marry you with all due haste."

Plain brown eyes assessed him, as unexceptional as her hair. She wasn't his usual sort at all—which was to say she was neither overtly attractive nor skilled in ways that mattered.

And good God, was that *ink* he spied staining her hands?

He was doing her a favor, coming up to scratch like this. He could have any woman he wanted in London—and frequently did. She ought to be very glad he was a man who owned up to his mistakes.

She lifted her chin. And then she said . . . "No."

And not a whisper of a word either, but an emphatically delivered syllable that bounced about in his skull before falling into a final state of understanding.

Was she deranged? Deluded? "But . . . you *have* to," he protested. "Your reputation—"

"My reputation is hardly the concern of a man who hasn't a care for his own."

West stopped. *Good God.* She had him there. His only concern for his own hide at present was that he feared it was about to be shackled to her. "Nonetheless, I must beg you—"

"Begging does not suit you, Mr. Westmore. You will not change my mind. I will not marry you. Honestly, I do not even *like* you."

West gaped at her, still trying to wrap his head around the fact that she had refused him. For God's sake, did the woman not understand her starring role in the morning's gossip rags? "I am not sure liking me has much to do with marriage," he muttered. His vision felt blurred at the absurdity of this conversation. She had refused *him*?

His ego was positively twitching.

Usually, women knocked themselves silly for a chance in his bed, emboldened by the rumors of his exploits, wanting to count him among their conquests. He'd never had a woman refuse him before. At least, not since that trip to Florence, when he and Grant had been nineteen and utterly full of themselves. That trip had inspired his early academic interest in architecture, but it had also inspired some memorable misbehavior. Grant had dared him to proposition a pretty—but devout—nun for a kiss in the vestibule of the *Cattedrale di Santa Maria del Fiore*. Never one to back out on a dare, West had turned on the charm.

The nun had said "no", too, in much the same tone.

West had regrouped. Dusted off his self-esteem.

And chosen his targets more carefully in the future.

But Miss Channing didn't seem interested in being his latest target. In fact, she was pinching her lips into a straight line that bespoke a great irritation, rather than any great attraction. She cut a pointed look toward the housekeeper. "Would you please give us a moment alone, Mrs. Greaves? It seems Mr. Westmore needs a bit more convincing of my feelings on this matter. I would spare him the humiliation of another public refusal."

The housekeeper did as she was told, and Miss Channing closed the door firmly behind the woman. As she turned back to face him, West glanced uneasily at the closed door.

What in the devil? "I . . . that is . . . shouldn't we leave the door open?"

She lifted her chin. "No."

He was beginning to hate the word, no matter that this morning he'd felt like shouting it himself as he'd considered his limited options to fix this mess. The single syllable flowed off her lips like melted butter, but it scalded like molten lead on impact. "Isn't this a little too close to the situation that got us into this trouble last night?" he pointed out.

Her brows rose, mocking him. "*I* shut the door this time, which means it was my decision, not yours." She moved toward him, her mouth losing some of its pinched shape. "And there is the small matter that no one in this room is plotting an assassination."

Good Christ. "You don't mince words, do you, Miss Channing?"

"On the contrary, I just minced them for Mrs. Greaves." She advanced on him. "But I didn't want an audience for this discussion, not until we have a proper plan in place. I don't know who to trust, and the servants are prone to gossip."

"Well, trusting *me* is a poor idea." God knew he didn't trust himself, especially not around her.

"Do you know, that is just what my sister said?" She took another step toward him, sparking a feeling in his gut the very opposite of unpleasant. "But I have to, you see. There is no one else. I tried talking to my sister, but she didn't believe me, and I . . . well . . . she is expecting." She winced. "Such unpleasantness could be harmful for her and the baby."

She came to a stop within touching distance—but not, he noticed, within kissing distance. As he had last night, he caught the lovely, titillating scent of sugared lemons, floating off her skin. Did she bathe in the stuff?

Perhaps she intended to ward off suitors and vampires?

"So tell me, Mr. Westmore." Her chin lifted. "What are we going to do about what we heard in the library?"

"As I said last night, Miss Channing," he ground out, "*we* aren't going to do anything. This isn't a matter you should concern yourself with." Though, maddeningly, it wasn't a matter anyone else seemed willing to concern themselves with either. The peelers at Scotland Yard ought to have at least written his statement down. Looked into things.

Humored him.

"Well, I *am* concerned. Someone is plotting to kill someone important by the sounds of things, and if I may be frank, this business of trying to swoop in like a white knight to save my reputation with a marriage proposal is a distraction we don't need right now. We have to *do* something. Given that my sister doesn't believe me, it falls to you." She hesitated. "Have you told anyone?"

West's jaw grew tighter. She might have a mousy exterior, but she seemed to know just how to poke at him, stir his agitation. He was well-tested in battle, but the voices from the library belonged to a nameless, faceless sort of enemy. And no matter Miss Channing's enthusiasm for the topic, he was the wrong man for the job.

"I tried to talk to my sister about it," he admitted. "She doesn't believe me. No one in my family will. They all believe it is a joke of some kind. I am afraid I have a bit of a reputation for such things."

"Yes, I've received quite an earful this morning about your *reputation*."

In spite of the gravity of the situation, West's lips twitched. So, Miss Channing had heard something of his reputation, had she? And she was still standing in front of him, close enough to touch? That was . . . interesting.

She tapped a finger against her lips. "Then I suppose we must go to Scotland Yard. They will know what to do."

"I've already tried this morning," West confessed. "I am afraid they didn't believe me either."

Her eyes narrowed. "Why ever not?"

"I am on a list."

"What sort of a list?"

He shifted uncomfortably. This morning's experience with the police had been illuminating. It was going to be an impossible task, getting someone to listen. Thanks to the gossip rag confirming their little adventure last night and his own less-than-stellar history, no one in a position of authority would believe either of them. They could tell the unvarnished, God's honest truth, and everyone would presume it was a distraction they had invented to divert attention from their own scandal.

Worse, facing Miss Channing's question reminded him how he'd dug this hole for himself since his return from Crimea. He might have a goddamned Victoria Cross gathering dust on top of his bureau, but he wasn't a man people should trust, and for arguably good reason.

"Apparently, I've caused them to waste too much time of late," he admitted.

Her mouth rounded in surprise. "Scotland Yard has you on a *watch list*?"

"Yes, they tend to do that after you play a joke on the bride of a duke."

She gaped at him, her mouth open in a perfect "O" of surprise.

West shrugged. "It was harmless, really. Just a bit of fun." *And perhaps a bit of revenge.*

When West had returned from Crimea, he and Grant sought distractions at every turn, be they bottles, barmaids, or bullies. When he'd heard Peter Wetford had come into his title as the new Duke of Southingham, he and Grant had hatched a proper prank, one for the record books. Stealing a kiss from the duke's new bride seemed the perfect lark, sure to needle the man into an attack of apoplexy, and in truth, Grant hated Southingham every bit as much as West did.

"My friend Grant and I dressed as chamber maids and tried to sneak into the Duke of Southingham's house, on the night of his wedding. Our goal was to reach the bedchamber of his new bride before Southingham did and steal a kiss or three," he admitted. "But my ruse was found out too soon."

Her eyes widened. "What gave you away?"

He swiped a hand across his chin. "Apparently, it isn't acceptable for a chamber maid to have beard stubble." He grinned. "Or for that matter, a proper pair of stones."

MARY'S CHEEKS FLAMED with heat. Surely he just hadn't said that word, a word so embarrassing, so crude she couldn't even repeat it.

"But . . . how would they know you had a pair of . . . well, how would they know that?" she asked, her throat tight. "Weren't you wearing skirts? Honestly, what sort of practical jokester doesn't even know to do that?"

"I was wearing skirts at the start of the adventure," he admitted sheepishly. "But I was distracted by the duchess's uncommonly pretty maid. And then one thing led to another . . ." He chuckled. "Suffice it to say we were discovered *in flagrante delicto.* And I never was able to steal that kiss I was after."

Mary couldn't help it. She rolled her eyes. Eleanor had given her a dozen good reasons to vigorously distrust Mr. Westmore. She had her own reasons after the disastrous kiss behind the curtain last night. And now he was openly admitting he'd seduced a maid while dressed as a woman and plotting to kiss someone's brand-new bride? She tried to summon the appropriate degree of disgust, but it was difficult to sort out the proper degree of outrage she ought to feel when he delivered the story with such a saucy grin.

He didn't *look* like a man who might enjoy relations with four women. Or a governess.

Or a corpse.

No, drat it all, he looked like a hero from the pages of one of her books: earnest and faithful and unerringly handsome. But that was neither here nor there. His bedroom habits and his penchant for saying and doing scandalous things were not her primary concern. Someone was plotting an assassination attempt, and her imagination was insisting the target must be terribly influential to require four people, a clandestine meeting, and the future exchange of a large sum of money.

Britain's reach was vast—India, the Orient. She imagined the world thrown into chaos, wars potentially lost. Beyond the political cost, though, lay something sharper. A fierce understanding that if not her, if not *them*, then who would act? If Scotland Yard would not help, if neither of them were to be believed by skeptical family members, then that meant they were the only ones who possessed the ability to *do* something here.

Ever since she'd heard those dreadful words from behind the library curtain, she'd felt jerked back in time, unpleasant memories crowding out the embarrassment of her ruin. So many years ago, when her brother and father had been killed, she'd been a helpless child, reeling in the face of that unimaginable loss. On more occasions than she could count, she'd wished for the ability to go back in time, to do something that might change the new, terrifying course of her life. Well, here she was. On the cusp of another tragedy.

Only this time she was a woman grown. She was here, in London, supposedly tasked with "rediscovering her spark." She had been miraculously unsheathed from her usual timidity, thanks to a gossip rag and a bit of embarrassment.

And this time, she was not going to shrink into herself and let this terrible thing happen without at least trying to do *something* to stop it.

"Well, if Scotland Yard will not help, we must track them down ourselves," she said, determined to be brave. She extracted the list she'd made earlier from her sleeve, and opened it with a flourish. "I took the liberty of compiling a list of likely targets, so we might organize our thoughts." She smoothed a finger over the three names she had written down. "Number one: The prime minister."

She received only a pointed silence in response.

She looked up, wondering if perhaps he had become distracted by something shiny. But no, he was gaping at her. She lifted a hand to her temple, wondering if perhaps he was staring because her hair was coming down. It was still anchored firmly in its braid.

"Mr. Westmore," she said sharply, "I need you to focus." She handed him the list to read himself, then began to pace the length of the drawing room, avoiding the freshly cut flowers sitting in a vase on the mantel. The smell reminded her, too much, that Mr. Westmore was a scoundrel in whom she was being forced to place some measure of trust. "Read on, if you please."

"Number two," he said weakly, looking down at the piece of paper she'd thrust into his hands. "A foreign diplomat or spy." He rubbed his forehead. "Actually, that suggestion makes a good deal of sense."

"Of course." She rolled her eyes. "What do you think of Number Three?"

There was a moment's hesitation as he glanced down once more. "The queen?" he said, his voice tightening.

"I put her as Number Three because I was trying to give the other ideas due merit, but I really think she is the most likely target, don't you? After all, there have been several past assassination attempts."

He folded the paper, his face unreadable. "None of which were successful. Just the rambling efforts of madmen."

"A good point," she conceded. "We should probably consult with the staff at Bedlam. We could see if anyone has been released recently, someone who might harbor political ill will toward the Crown."

His gaze lifted, and she felt the impact of his doubt like a sharp pinch to her arm. "I hardly think a visit to Bedlam will help, Miss Channing."

"Why not?" she asked, growing irritated by his lack of enthusiasm.

"Because those who are admitted to Bedlam rarely come out, particularly not if they've been spouting nonsense about killing the queen. Suffice it to say I feel sure Scotland Yard would take their word far more seriously than they seem inclined to take my own."

She glared at him. "But perhaps someone on staff there might offer us guidance as to the sort of person we ought to be looking for, the kind of man who might do such a thing. Presumably they have a good deal of experience with madmen."

He inclined his head, studying her as though she had two heads. Which she didn't. She only had one. But it was quite a *useful* head, thank you very much. And she wasn't inclined to pretend it wasn't, just because his proximity made her squirm like a fish on a hook.

"It seems you have given this matter a good deal of serious thought." He shoved the folded list into his pocket, and his lips twitched upward. "Tell me, Miss Channing." He spread his hands in front of his body. "Did you lie awake in bed last night, thinking of . . . all of *this*?"

The suggestion in his voice was unmistakable.

It was not at all proper for a gentleman to say such things to an unmarried woman. And worse, his words were too close to the truth for comfort.

"Well, I certainly didn't lie awake last night thinking of *you*," she retorted, hoping he couldn't see through her bravado to the lie lurking beneath. In truth, she'd taken it upon herself to make the list last night because she had required a noble distraction: she couldn't otherwise stop thinking about him. Even now, her thoughts kept drifting insistently toward the kiss they had shared. The way his hand had felt, pressed against her breast.

The way she had felt, kissing him back.

Her face heated, and she pressed a hand against the side of her cheek. Drat it all, now she was most *definitely* thinking about him. And she couldn't distract herself with lists at the present moment, not when the list that wanted to materialize in her mind started with:

Number One. Close the distance between them.

Number Two. Press her lips against his, one more time.

"Are you ill, Miss Channing?" He smirked at her, and in that moment she could have sworn he could see through her thoughts and her dress to what lay beneath.

She shook her head impatiently. "No." He might be smirking, but at least he wasn't laughing at her yet. Then again, he wasn't yet aware of her very active imagination and the long history of teasing from family and friends that came with that. "Just impatient. You've not commented on the likelihood of anyone on my list beyond the queen."

"Very well then." His smirk fell away, and he sounded nearly pained by her insistence on a proper analysis. "Why the prime minister? Lord Derby is newly appointed. Surely it is too soon for him to have developed such motivated political enemies."

"The men in the library mentioned the word 'constitution'," she said, taking a cautious step toward him. "That seems to imply some connection to a government, and Lord Derby is presently the most powerful political figure in Britain."

"Except you are forgetting the fact that Britain doesn't *have* a proper constitution." He shrugged. "Although, I suppose it could be the Americans. They are always going on and on about theirs, as if it is necessary to have a piece of paper and a handful of signatures to establish a nation's civility."

Another idea took hold. "Could they mean Constitution Hill?" She thought of the popular, open road that led from Buckingham Palace to Hyde Park. Important figures travelled the route with predictable regularity. "Weren't shots fired from there during one of the queen's previous assassination attempts?"

He lifted a brow. "You know your history, Miss Channing."

"I *do* possess the ability to read. It was in all the papers."

"Ah. Yes. Reading." His lips quirked. "Not surprising you

might enjoy such a pedestrian activity. We did, after all, first meet in a library."

Drat the man, for reminding her of that, when she was trying so hard to forget. Though, to hear him denigrate the one activity at which she actually excelled made it a bit easier to hate him in this moment. "Actually, I believe we first met in a garden," she pointed out. "You were urinating on a rosebush."

"The problem," he said, not seeming the least bit bothered by the reminder of what should have been a shameful encounter, "is that the word 'constitution' could refer to so many things. They might have been referring to the charter of some organization, or they could have simply been describing their chosen assassin's specific constitution for drawing blood." He shrugged. "It is better not to speculate, lest it lead us down a wrong path."

Mary looked at him. Her gaze wanted to linger a little too long on the angular planes of his face—not an impulse one wanted to suffer with a man one didn't intend to marry. Irritated with herself for such weakness—and angry with Mr. Westmore for posing such a singular distraction—she straightened her shoulders. "We *must* speculate as to the meaning. The word 'constitution' is one of our only clues, and we need to follow it."

He snorted. "It is to be 'we', is it?"

Mary hesitated. She would be the first to admit she wasn't exactly a good choice for this adventure. She still hadn't conjured enough bravery to venture back out into the flower garden, and Eleanor needed her here, in case the baby came early.

Still, that burning desire to act, to *do* something, would not leave her be. "I only meant—" she started, but stopped when she saw his upraised hands.

"You are forgetting," he said, "that I have other clues."

She resented, a bit, how easily he'd substituted the word "I". "Such as?"

"One of the women in the library called one of the plotters 'Your Grace.' There are only a few dozen men who can claim a ducal title in Britain."

Excitement began to buzz in her head. It was very close to the way Mary felt when she was reading a delicious new book and the hero managed to surprise her. Why hadn't she thought of that? Probably because she spent very little time in the company of dukes.

Or, for that matter, future viscounts.

"And they made plans to meet this Sunday, at St. Paul's Cathedral," she exclaimed, her enthusiasm drumming louder now. She took a step closer, forgetting, for the moment, that Mr. Westmore was supposed to be dangerous. And that she was supposed to find him abhorrent. He was now close enough to touch, and her fingers nearly twitched with the temptation of that thought. "So, we must go to service at St. Paul's this Sunday," she said, "and see which dukes are in attendance!"

Westmore's hand came up to chuck her under the chin, even as he flashed her another smirk. "To quote a woman of my very recent acquaintance," he drawled, "*no.*" He turned away and headed toward the drawing room door, his voice trailing over his shoulder. "*I* will provide the legs for this investigation. You will stay out of this and leave the matter to those who can handle a bit of danger without fainting dead away."

"But . . . I *want* to come," she protested, resenting the way his hand was already reaching for the door. As odd as the sentiment was, given that she'd practically had to be dragged to last night's literary salon, she found that in this moment, she wanted to be involved.

And in truth, she'd only fainted last night because of the unnatural, vise-like grip of Eleanor's borrowed corset. She'd found it impossible to breathe when she'd most needed to.

But wearing her own front-lacing corset, surely she'd be able to—

He glared at her over his shoulder, severing that line of thought. "This is far too dangerous a mission for you, and I'll be damned if I will be held responsible for your ruin *and* your death, Miss Channing. I will attend services myself on Sunday. Identify and stop the traitors, if I can."

"And if you are unsuccessful in that endeavor?" she retorted. She ought to be glad he seemed poised to do something, but instead she felt hurt. He was planning to exclude her, when it had been her own idea to attend Sunday services to look for them. How *could* he? She was every bit as much a part of this as he was.

More so, in fact. She had sacrificed her reputation— furtive, fledgling thing that it had been—to uncover this plot. He'd done nothing more noteworthy than kiss her behind some curtains and then give her a fumbled proposal of marriage.

His face turned grim. "Then at least I will have more information on which to make an informed decision. And you shall be safely at home, where you belong."

When did my life become so reminiscent of the plot of a torrid novel? Even my situation with the gossip rag has a ring of gothic tragedy to it, tinged with a touch of comedy. Perhaps it is an unfortunate side effect of being "ruined", but it seems as if I no longer have anything to lose. I ought to be terrified, hiding in my room, reading my precious books.

But instead, I am angry that Mr. Westmore has dismissed me from his plans.

Eleanor congratulated me on turning Mr. Westmore down in his offer of marriage, and assured me I have made the correct choice. But a betrothal would have forced Mr. Westmore to take me seriously. At the very least, he would have had to take me along with him this coming Sunday. Which means, I am sorry to say, I am no longer sure I did the right thing.

Chapter 8

West woke up in sweat-soaked sheets, his arms thrashing, lungs working like a bellows.

Damn it all, the nightmares were back.

He'd begun to imagine he'd outrun them. In the months after his return from Crimea, they'd come close to consuming him. Their determination to creep into his nocturnal thoughts was part of the reason he preferred late nights in strangers' beds. A dreamless sleep was a hard-fought luxury in his world, most commonly achieved with a potent combination of strong spirits and the distraction of sweet, feminine flesh.

But in the past few days, those nightmares had returned with a vengeance.

And strong spirits and sweet, feminine flesh had been sorely lacking in his world.

He scrubbed his forehead, slick with sweat. Miss Channing had been in this dream, which was a terrifying departure from the usual script. He ought to be relieved she'd refused his offer of marriage so neatly, releasing him from any obligation of propriety. Ought to be forgetting all about her, instead of dreaming about her at importune times.

And what cause had a mouse-like virgin to be gallivanting about his battle scenes? In this nightmare, she'd been in grave danger, held at the point of a traitor's gun.

No doubt that was why he felt strung as tightly as a bow.

He was convinced now, more than ever, of his rightness in dismissing her earnest attempts to help track down the traitors. She might be a bookish miss with a few good ideas, but Miss Channing was also an innocent. He couldn't apply his mind to the problem at hand if he was constantly worrying about her safety.

And if nothing else, this morning's dream was a vivid enough reminder of why she shouldn't be involved in this.

He forced his body to unclench, though he still felt the thump of readiness in his veins. Thoughts of danger and mousy virgins receded to their proper shadows, and he turned an ear to the house outside his door. Had he awakened the house with his shouts this time? He didn't hear anyone stirring about—but then, when he'd come back from Crimea, he'd asked for a room on the little-used west wing of the house because he'd known his nightmares would cause worry if others heard him. If Wilson had any idea that he sometimes still slept poorly, or that his nocturnal demons had returned, the servant would probably launch into yet another ill-timed lecture.

The nightmares were almost preferable.

He dragged a hand through his sweat-dampened hair. Outside his window, the light was just warming. He well knew this time of day. Usually, he'd just be stumbling home from his evening's exploits. It was too bloody early to be getting out of bed.

Perhaps that was the trouble here. Since the business with the assassination plot, he'd been . . . distracted. His parents had been nearly relieved when he'd told them Miss Channing had very sensibly refused his honorable offer, but he'd felt a lingering sense of unease.

Not because he wanted to marry her.

He *didn't*.

But something about the notion that she didn't want to marry him sat poorly in his gut.

He'd spent the past few days pursuing the leads on Miss Channing's rather well-thought-out list. In spite of his claims to the contrary, he'd even made inquiries at Bedlam, not knowing what else to do. Unfortunately, the officials there had taken his inquiries about as seriously as the authorities at Scotland Yard, and he'd come to the conclusion that escape—and lucid plotting—were probably beyond the capabilities of anyone fortunate enough to survive a stay there.

So he'd returned to Scotland Yard, trying to argue his case again. This time, he'd come close to smashing the nose of the sniveling constable who—once again—refused to take his statement. Since that memorable failure, he'd been waiting for Sunday, restless and relentless. He'd come to the irrevocable conclusion he needed to find the traitors himself, if only so he could descend back into a welcome oblivion.

And while his quarry may have eluded him so far, he was determined to end it today.

Which was why ten o'clock that Sunday morning saw the birth of a proper miracle: West, up, properly dressed, and stepping through the doors of St. Paul's Cathedral.

In a past life, he would have come here with his family on a Sunday just to ogle the gorgeous, swooping lines of the high, arched ceiling. But his taste for unique architecture had dulled since his return from Crimea, and today he pushed inside without looking up. God, how long had it been since he'd attended church? For one, these days he was rarely up early enough on Sunday mornings to drag his still-inebriated arse to a pew. And for another, he found it difficult to truly regret the various lust-fueled sins he was expected to repent.

He half-wished Wilson could see him now. Then again, he'd probably just earn a lecture from the old servant for having missed so many Sundays in the past.

The day was hot, and bound to get hotter. The crowd seemed lighter than usual, no doubt thanks to the smell rolling in through the open doors at the rear of the cathedral. The overheated Thames had blanketed the city with its stench for nigh on a week now and seemed to only be getting worse. Many families who usually stayed through the end of the Season had already packed their things and retreated to the cooler countryside. There was even talk of ending the current parliamentary session early, and it looked as though many of the pews were empty today.

West was glad to see it. Fewer dukes to sort out.

Those who had braved the stench were just settling into their seats. As he lurked near the center of the outer vestibule, studying those in attendance, he considered again whether the traitor he sought might be someone he knew. Though the voice he remembered from the library had seemed vaguely familiar, he couldn't quite put his finger on where he'd heard it before.

And unfortunately, West knew an awful lot of dukes.

To his right, he could see the Duke of Rothesay, his bulk spreading across the bench. West discounted the man almost immediately: that night in the library, his view had been hampered by darkness, but he'd at least gotten a glimpse of the men's profiles. Rothesay's girth was too large to match either of the men from the library.

The Duke of Strathearn shuffled past, and West considered whether the stooped old man might be a viable candidate for treason. But the voice he'd overheard in the library, while delivered as a terse whisper, had struck him as belonging to someone younger.

Strathearn was seventy, if he was a day.

Unfortunately, discounting two dukes didn't even scratch

the surface of the possibilities. He stared out across the rows of benches, discarding some ideas, turning over others. He didn't particularly like dukes, although he could allow there were a few out there that weren't so dodgy. The thought of bringing at least one of them down a peg or two gave him a devilish sort of pleasure. He thought back to his experience at Harrow and the endless torture he and Grant had endured at the hands of Peter Wetford, the eldest son of the Duke of Southingham. The boy had used his superior standing as a formidable shield against retaliation. The one time West had even *tried* to physically defend himself, he'd found himself dragged before the headmaster, threatened with expulsion. It had been a lesson he'd long remembered.

One didn't go about striking peers of a superior rank, no matter what they did to you.

Truly, the rats had been his only option for teaching the arrogant sod a lesson.

West was startled from those unwelcome memories by the sudden scent of lemons, nicely pushing out the *eau de Thames*. The realization of what that meant made his hands curl to fists.

He turned his head and caught Miss Channing's slender profile marching by.

Bloody hell, it was the woman who'd refused to marry him. He stared at her as she passed by, his mouth open in surprise. Had she come to church because she'd changed her mind on that front? Perhaps she wished to accept his offer after all? For some bizarre reason, the idea didn't seem to carry quite the same degree of dread today as it had only a few days ago.

And the sight of her felt like a punch to the gut.

She was wearing brown wool again, and she was walking beside the same stern-looking housekeeper who had served as a chaperone during their drawing room conversation. She did not glance toward him, or give any sign that she recognized him. In fact, they sailed right by him, as if he was beneath their notice. But then Miss Channing suddenly stopped. Reached into her reticule. Pulled out a handkerchief and clutched it to her nose.

"Oh, Mrs. Greaves," he heard her gasp. "What is that terrible *smell*?"

"'Tis the Thames, miss." The older woman frowned. "They've got the doors open on account of the heat. Is it bothering you too much to stay?"

"No, we can't leave when we've come all this way. I . . . I think I'll be all right." Miss Channing waved the older woman on. "Do go claim our seat down at the front. I just need to stand here a moment and adjust before I sit down."

"Are you sure?" the housekeeper asked dubiously.

"Yes, quickly now. Before someone takes our row." But as soon as the older woman headed down the aisle and settled her bum onto a pew, Miss Channing rounded on him, her brown eyes close to sparkling. She grabbed him by the arm and dragged him behind a large marble column, until they were hidden from the view of her somewhat useless chaperone. "All right, Westmore, what is our plan?"

And that was when it hit him. He was not entirely beneath her notice.

She had plotted this. Come to church to vex him.

And while irritation twitched through him, so, too, did admiration. Worse, it occurred to him that in spite of the worry that spiked through him, he was not averse to seeing her again.

"Damn it, Miss Channing," he growled. "What are you doing here?"

"I should think it would be obvious." She shrugged. "I am attending church."

"But *why*?"

Coy brown eyes met his own. "To pray for your depraved soul, of course."

"It seems you could pray for me just as well from the safety of your home."

"It is a public service here, is it not? I should think my attendance would be expected. Mandatory, even, considering the tatters of my reputation." Her lips quirked upward. "I've amends to make with God." She waited a beat, and then added, "Not to mention Mr. Dickens."

West choked on the laugh that wanted to escape him. He'd imagined her many times this week, wondering if she was regretting her refusal of his offer of marriage. In spite of what ought to have been his sense of relief, he remained worried for her, what their scandal might mean to her future. He'd imagined her sad. Worried. But he hadn't imagined her . . .

Smiling. She quite caught him by surprise.

"You should be home," he warned, shaking his head, "where you are safe."

She rolled her eyes. "I am not convinced I am any safer at home, Mr. Westmore. There are villains, you see, just outside the flower garden. Perhaps you've seen them? Heaven knows *I* have, though it's an image I've tried to scrub from my mind."

This time, he couldn't contain the bark of laughter that shot out of him, echoing against the high, arched ceiling. A few people in the pews across the way turned around to glare at them, but he ignored them. So she wanted to spar, did she? Well, she'd picked the wrong gentleman for that. He'd honed his debate skills with his sisters, each of whom could reduce grown men to tears with their verbal fortitude. She didn't stand a chance.

"I'll tell you what I've *seen*, Miss Channing," he said, lowering his voice. "I've seen you faint dead away, and over something as small as a bit of flesh inadvertently exposed to the literary world. Infants have more courage, resisting their afternoon naps. Drunken goldfish could navigate these waters better than you." His gaze drifted over the pretty pink curve of her lips, and in spite of himself, he had to admit her plain brown gown nicely offset the hue. "Admit it," he said, more softly now. "You don't have the fortitude for this."

She lifted a hand to the rows of benches leading to the front of the cathedral. "For church?" she scoffed. "I hardly think the service will be *that* extraordinary."

In spite of himself, West chuckled. He couldn't help but approve of her grit. And damn it all, her eyes were *definitely* sparkling. This was a side of her he'd not seen before. "I think you've had ample time to adjust to the smell of the Thames now." He gestured to the front of the church, where most people had taken their seats. "Your pew and your entirely too obedient chaperone are waiting."

"Not just yet." She bit her lip. "Have you . . . ah . . . looked for the traitors this week?"

West opened his mouth. Shut it again. *Good Lord.* The woman was trouble in a brown dress. And she *really* needed to lower her voice. He demonstrated the way forward, shifting his voice to more of guttural growl. "I'm considering a few possibilities."

"Who are you considering?"

"Those who might have cause to target one of the people from your list."

She gifted him with a full-blown smile, the first he had seen from her. He sucked in a breath as the force of that smile hit him like a runaway carriage. It transformed her face from something mouse-like to some something that had a hope of stirring his fantasies.

Bugger it all.

If she wore a smile—and nothing else—he could see how she might be beautiful.

"Then tell me, Mr. Westmore." She stepped closer, until her skirts brushed indecently against his trousers. "Who are your primary suspects?"

"I really don't think—"

She looped her arm through his and pulled him deeper into the vestibule, even farther out of sight of her gullible chaperone. "Stop dismissing me, Mr. Westmore. I am here now, and you are not doing this without me. Now, I've read a few mystery novels, and I know how this needs to be done." She peered around a marble column, looked to the left, then to the right. "We should split up," she told him, loosening her hold on his arm. "Cover more ground. Ask people questions regarding their whereabouts on the evening of June 1st."

West gaped at her. Was this even the same woman who had fainted in the library? "Good God, woman, you can't believe that reading a mystery novel in any way prepares you to deal with tracking a real-life traitor." The woman was going to get herself injured—or worse. *This* was why he'd pushed her away, why he'd insisted on doing this alone.

Did she really think you could just walk up to a duke and ask if he was plotting murder?

"And there is no way in hell we are splitting up," he added. Now that she was here, she almost *had* to be a bona fide thorn in his side. He couldn't risk letting her go off half-cocked today. Any hint of their knowledge and the man might bolt, go underground, and then they would have lost the opportunity.

She put her hands on her hips. "Well, if you don't like my plan, Mr. Westmore," she huffed, "perhaps you might be so good as to share *yours*?"

Worse than a drunken goldfish, was she?

It seemed like she wasn't the only one with a vivid imagination.

But as she waited for his answer, his colorful observation gave her pause. He wasn't that far off the mark—at least, not that far off her usual mark. Mary couldn't help but wonder a little herself at her seeming lack of unease. Usually, she'd be hugging the walls in a place like this, avoiding eye contact, keeping her head down. But her usual reaction to strange situations seemed held at bay. Was it because she had spent days plotting this foray, stewing in her stuffy room?

Or was it because now that she was ruined, she no longer had anything to lose?

Whatever the reason, she couldn't bring herself to second-guess her behavior. She was finally doing something, not sitting back letting life slide by, living vicariously through the pages of a book. She was going to turn her *own* page, for once.

"Well?" she said, growing impatient with his silence.

"If you must know, I was planning to stand here and listen for the voices we heard the other night."

"That isn't a plan." Mary felt a bit annoyed that he'd put so little thought into it, when he'd all but promised her he would take care of the problem. She herself had lain awake for hours, turning over matters in her mind, scribbling thoughts down on paper. "Especially given the fact that we only heard the men speak in whispers that night. Relying on your memory to identify them is relying on little more than chance."

"And yet, sometimes chance has a way of working out. Take our first meeting, for example." His voice deepened. "If I hadn't *chanced* to piss on Ashington's rosebushes that morning, we wouldn't be here now."

In spite of her twitching irritation, Mary smothered the laugh that tried to bolt out of her at that. "I suspect, sir, your propensity for drink and boorish behavior means there was more than a mere chance that poor, pathetic rosebush would be your target that unfortunate morning." Her gaze really shouldn't be lingering on the smooth swoop of nose, the way his forehead wrinkled when he laughed. She needed to re-member she was here for a serious reason.

But somehow, the shape of his lips quite scattered her wits. She felt out of her depth, but not on account of her usual shyness. No, she felt out of her depth here today because she was coming to feel *at ease* in his presence. She didn't know quite what to make of it.

"But very well then," she finally conceded, cocking an ear toward the rustling pews. "Let's pretend for a moment that yours is a good idea." She stood, listening. "There are an awful lot of voices to sort through." She gestured toward the half-filled pews. "Wouldn't it be better to sit down to listen?"

"I doubt an exchange of money this important will occur out in the open like that. More likely it will occur somewhere back here. That is why I chose this particular location, Miss Channing."

"Oh." That really made quite a lot of sense. In fact, she should have thought of it herself. She reached into her reticule and pulled out a folded sheet of paper. "While we listen, have a look at this."

He took up the paper. "What is this, Miss Channing?" he teased, his grin returning. "Have you written me a love letter?"

"Hardly." She snorted. Honestly, did his ego know no bounds? "In case our pursuit of this duke comes to naught, I have compiled a list of potential villains I think we should investigate."

"Another list?" The smile slid from his lips. "You have been busy these past few days."

She shrugged. "A woman without prospects tends to have free time on her hands."

He had the good grace to look chagrined. "I did offer you marriage."

"And I refused, with good reason. Marrying you would be a nightmare."

There was a moment's pause. "Take it from someone who suffers nightmares, Miss Channing. You misuse the word. Either that or you sorely misunderstand the pleasures to be found in my bed."

Her cheeks heated. Good gracious, the man appeared to just say whatever he wanted, whenever he wanted. Had he never had a moment's discretion? "The list, Mr. Westmore." She gestured to it, annoyed with herself for reacting to his bold taunts. "I did not compile it merely for my health."

He looked down at the paper and unfolded it. "Number One: The Orsinians." His eyes narrowed. "That is actually an excellent suspicion."

"I thought it was important to consider the possibility, after that recent assassination business in Paris this past January."

He cocked his head. "You know something of international politics?"

"I read the newspapers, of course. And we sometimes discuss politics over the dinner table, at my brother's home." Though oddly, she had been thinking about that home in Yorkshire less and less, thanks to the distraction she'd been tossed into here in London. "The Orsinians involved in the Paris plot this year were British citizens, so it could fit. And by my understanding, the business with Italian unification and the extremists is nowhere close to finished."

Westmore nodded. "It is a good thought. We—" He stopped himself. Started again. "That is, *I*—could make some subtle inquiries. See if anyone has heard rumblings of further discord on that front." He looked down at the list again. "Number Two: The Fenians." His mouth quirked upward on one side. "Honestly, Miss Channing, the *Irish*?"

"They have a reputation for ruthlessness," Mary argued, knowing this one was a bit far-fetched. "And they are gaining ground in their demands for independence."

"Nonetheless, the Irish nationalists are poorly organized at present, and none of the people we overheard had any hint of an Irish brogue. More likely for it to be a British aristocrat who wants to pin it on the Fenians."

"Exactly." She nodded, glad to hear him thinking. "Which brings us to Number Three."

He looked down again. She could hear the paper crinkling beneath the grip of his fingers. "The prime minister?" he asked, followed by a slightly dismissive laugh. "Come, now, Miss Channing. I thought he was on your list of possible targets."

"I mean the *former* prime minister. Lord Palmerston."

He made a strangled sound. For a moment, she was tempted to whump him on the back. Dislodge whatever was making his face turn pale like that. But no . . . whumping would involve touching him, and touching him seemed too . . . *tempting*.

Best to keep her whumps to herself.

"That is a very serious charge, Miss Channing," he finally choked out. "One that could get us both in a good deal of trouble."

"Lord Palmerston's resignation was forced in the wake of the Orsini affair, so it seems he has every reason to hate those in power." She plowed on, having been over this a dozen times in her head. "And inventing an enemy in the Irish could help him regain favor. And then, of course, there's Number Four."

He pinched the bridge of his nose. Looked down warily. "The Russians?" he asked. "Truly? Haven't we reached a proper accord with them by now?"

"I know this one may seem less likely, given that the war has been over for some time. But it stands to reason there are some people who might still harbor ill will over the embarrassment of Crimea."

"An embarrassment, is it?" Blue eyes lifted to meet her own. "Is that what you think of that business in Crimea, Miss Channing?"

She hesitated. She'd read of the terrible accounts from the field, the detailed coverage in the papers, the unconscionable deaths of good men due to illness and injuries, simply due to a lack of medical supplies and trained doctors. "I think the men who fought were very brave," she said slowly, "but I think the men who sent our young men to that war did not always give the consequences due consideration."

Westmore stood, still as stone, the rigid slant of his shoulders telling her very little about his mindset other than the fact that he, too, had an opinion about such things. And then he folded up the paper and shoved it in his trouser pocket. She stared at the small motion, irritation twitching through her. Did he not agree with her reasoning? She'd put a good deal of thought into that list. They were *good* ideas.

She felt it in her bones.

And then she felt something else in her bones, a prickle of awareness.

Up front, the service had started, the organ music going silent, which only made the noises around her seem more acute. She caught an urgent whisper, a rustle of silk.

"Westmore—" she began.

"I hear them," he said tersely.

She clutched at his arm, and was relieved to feel his hand cover her own. A light squeeze, warning her to stay silent, but she didn't need the reminder.

Together, they stepped around the column, eyes and ears straining toward the farthest edge of the vestibule. Mary could see a woman dressed in yellow silk, her hair tucked under a straw bonnet. She was speaking to a man who was too deep in the shadows to discern. The thought that it could be their duke made her pulse bound in her ears.

They inched closer, until gradually, the whispers became more distinct. "Why did he not come himself?" the woman asked, sounding almost angry. Mary gasped to recognize that the voice sounded the same as one of the women's from the library.

" 'E sent me instead." It was one of the men's voices from the library, the one with the harsher accent. Mary leaned forward, trying to hear.

"That wasn't part of the plan."

"Plans change, and you're to change with them. 'E says for you to deliver the money promptly, and then wait for his word."

"Oh he does, does he?" The woman sounded irritated. "Well, we must do as he says, mustn't we? Deliver the money, kill the queen?"

A chill rippled down Mary's spine. Oh, God. It wasn't the prime minister, it was the *queen*. For the first time in her life, her wild imaginings had come true.

But being right had never felt so horribly wrong.

If the traitors succeeded in killing Queen Victoria, there would be political hell to pay. Alliances would be shattered. Fragile holds on peace dissolved. Worse, there were children involved—princes and princesses—who would be left without a mother. And Mary rather *liked* the queen, who proved, by her very rule, that women should not be discounted in this world of suffering male politics.

A basket was passed, the sort that might rest on the arm of any woman on market day. The woman in yellow turned. Moved. Head down, she hurried past them toward the open doors of the cathedral, the basket full of money looped over her arm.

"Stay here," Westmore snarled. From his pocket, he pulled out a pistol.

Mary gasped, her heart thudding against her chest. The sight of that pistol was every bit as terrifying as the transaction they had just witnessed. "Westmore! You can't shoot a woman!"

"I am not going after her. I am going after the man, given that our duke was too much of a coward to show up himself." He glared down at her. "Stay right here and do not move a bloody inch, not even if the queen herself shows up, screaming at the door."

Mary cast a wild glance toward the woman, who was just

disappearing through the cathedral doors. The sight of the pistol in West's hand made her stomach swirl, but so, too, did the thought of losing the woman who was such a significant clue. "But—"

"Your promise, Miss Channing." But instead of waiting for an answer, he pressed a shocking, sudden kiss against her lips. And then he was off, sprinting toward the edge of the vestibule. She could do nothing but watch, her heart clawing its way up into her throat. She waited, every nerve stinging, terrified by the possibility of hearing a shot ring out, seeing him slump to the ground, blood spreading out around him.

But miraculously, no such sound reached her ears.

The sermon droned on, punctuated by the occasional, rattling snore from the congregation. The smell from the Thames outside swirled around her, just the same as before. And eventually Westmore returned, more slowly this time, his revolver close to his leg and pointing down toward the marble tile.

"Did you recognize him?" she demanded, trying not to look at his gun as he drew closer. But her eyes kept pulling toward it, fear skittering through her chest.

She decided that for once it was safer to stare at his sinfully shaped mouth.

"No." Westmore didn't even sound winded, though the pace he'd set in pursuit was impressive. "But I got a good look before he escaped. Dark hair, scar on his face. I would know him again if I saw him, but whoever he is, he's gone."

In spite of her resolve, Mary's eyes drifted back down to follow the glint of steel sliding back into his pocket. Somehow, knowing Westmore came to St. Paul's Cathedral armed made the situation seem more frightening, not less. Guns had never meant good things in her life.

"Was that in your trousers the entire time?" she asked weakly.

"Yes." Bemusement eased the tension in his jaw. "If you

continue to make a habit of consorting with me, you will find that I am *always* prepared."

"Do you even know how to use it?" Though, he had very much looked as though he did.

"Miss Channing." He leaned one shoulder against a marble column, almost casually, drat the man. "I'll have you know I know how to use *everything* in my trousers."

Her cheeks heated, as he must have known they would. She was beginning to have the sense that he said these things just to garner some reaction from her, some outward sign of discomfit. But now was not the time to ponder his purpose, and so she pushed those thoughts aside to deal with the notion at hand, which was more intriguing—and frightening—than what Mr. Westmore may or may not be hiding in his trousers.

"Did you hear what they said?" she whispered.

The corners of his mouth slid south. "I heard. You were correct, it seems. It's the queen." He dragged a hand through his hair. "Not that having a target in mind is going to help anyone believe us, mind you. I need proof I can take before Scotland Yard. A piece of paper, a witness who can be trusted. Either that or someone in our custody, offering a confession."

She glanced toward the edge of the vestibule, where the man had disappeared. Westmore might have had a very good chance of catching the suspect if he hadn't been distracted by making sure she was safe. "I am sorry if I slowed you down."

"Slow me down? What on earth are you talking about?"

"If you hadn't paused to . . . er . . . argue with me, you might have been able to catch him. Now we have lost them both."

He reached out a hand. "I didn't pause to argue with you, Miss Channing." He dragged a gloved finger across her lower lip, making something other than fear bloom inside her. "I paused to kiss you. Two very different things. So if we have lost him, the fault is mine."

"Oh," she breathed.

He stared down at her, as if working through a mathematical formula. "Besides, we may have lost our clue to our duke, but we have gained another. I recognized the woman."

Surprise slid through her. "You did?"

"Her name is Vivian. She works at a nearby brothel."

Mary's ears burned with something that might have been envy. If anyone would recognize such a woman, she supposed, of *course* it would be Westmore. She ought to be glad he possessed such knowledge, if it helped them track a traitor.

And she was. She *was*.

However he'd acquired this knowledge, he was using it for the Crown.

"If we find this woman," Mary said, "we might be able to halt the flow of money and extract the confession we need."

"Precisely." He offered her a grudging smile. "The only question is, are you going to follow me there, too?"

Chapter 9

Madame Xavier's looked different enough in the daylight that West's feet hesitated on the front steps. With its red shutters and crimson brick walls, the three-story building seemed less like a brothel and more like a respectable home.

He'd been here on enough occasions to be well-acquainted with the establishment, but always at night, always with Grant, and always deep into his cups.

But daylight revealed surprising new distractions. The building boasted a Palladian architecture, its pediments and symmetry on clear display should one have the wherewithal to look. West ran a finger along one column, remembering that old, dusty piece of his life, a time when he'd been eager to attend classes at university, when he imagined a future creating things more memorable than a good prank.

Perhaps therein lay the problem. Had he ever really looked at this house? Or the women who worked here? He generally spent his time here sitting in the receiving room while Grant busied himself abovestairs. He belted out bawdy tunes on the pianoforte and teased the scantily clad women until they blushed like schoolgirls, but he'd never lingered on the front steps with enough sobriety and presence of mind to pay attention to the shape of the columns.

Perhaps he ought to have, especially given that he wasn't particularly interested in the more carnal offerings on the menu.

Scarlet, the one woman at Madame Xavier's with whom he could claim a prior acquaintance, had sought *him* out, not the other way around. He'd treated her like a proper gentleman, even taking her to the opera, but the distraction she offered had ended weeks ago.

Not that Scarlet seemed to understand it was over.

With his hand against Miss Channing's elbow, they stepped through the front door. No matter the Palladian exterior, upon stepping inside, Westmore was reminded that he was taking Miss Channing to a place that was anything but respectable. The house's red color scheme had been extended inside to include the floor covers and the drapery. The rich proliferation of red somehow seemed more obscene in sunlight, pink shadows spinning across the floor.

Miss Channing's eyes were as wide as saucers, her head swiveling to take it all in. "I can't believe I've come from St. Paul's Cathedral to a brothel, all in the space of an hour," she breathed. "It's like falling straight from heaven to hell."

West chuckled. "Some might say it's the other way around."

He'd have liked to say more, to explain that Madame Xavier's brothel was legendary. That some of the girls were cultured, even educated, and more than one of them could spend an evening engaging a gentleman in political discourse as easily as bed sport. But explaining any of this to Miss Channing, who had clearly already formed a strong opinion of his character and this place based on the oppressive line of her lips, seemed like a waste of breath.

Bald truths would be unlikely to win him any favor where

she was concerned. Better to keep his knowledge of the place under wraps.

And besides, standing here in daylight, he was no longer sure he'd properly considered all the reasons a woman might choose to work in this place. The notion that someone like Vivian might lead a double life—what other secrets were hidden here?

"Please don't say anything of that nature to the women who work here," he told her as he pulled a red velvet rope. The sound of a tinkling bell rang out, alerting the house to their arrival. "Let me handle the conversation."

"As long as conversation is *all* you are planning to handle." She glowered at him, crossing her arms over her buttoned-up chest.

Within a minute, Madame Xavier herself glided into the parlor clad in a tea dress that left little to the imagination. He thought perhaps it was meant to have a gown beneath it, but the brothel owner wore only the outer robe portion of the ensemble, and you could see all the way through the sheer fabric. Miss Channing gawked at the woman, and then promptly attached herself to his arm with what felt like talons.

"Westmore!" Madame Xavier purred as she drew to a stop in front of him, her painted lips curving into a feline smile. "It is *so* good to see you again." Her gaze shifted to Miss Channing and her eyes flickered with undisguised interest. "You know we don't usually open for business until evening, though for such an old friend, I feel sure we can make an exception. Is your friend Mr. Grant not accompanying you today?"

"Er . . . no." West hesitated, not yet sure how much to reveal. What if Madame Xavier knew of Vivian's treachery? Perhaps she was even involved in the plot . . . after all, there had been *two* women in the library, and he only knew the identity of one of them at present.

Discretion was needed until they knew more.

Inspiration came in the form of Miss Channing's finger-nails, digging through his jacket hard enough to draw blood. "My . . . ah . . . companion and I were hoping to see one of your girls."

Madame Xavier's gaze drifted across Miss Channing's face. Her finger reached out to touch Miss Channing's chin, and tilted it up, as if considering her like a horse at auction. Then, without warning, the brothel owner dipped her head and pressed those painted red lips against Miss Channing's flattened pink ones.

It was mercifully quick, just a peck, but the squeak that escaped Miss Channing was priceless. As the brothel owner stepped back, West burst out laughing at the expression of confusion on Miss Channing's face, the smear of red paint now trailing across her lips.

Madame Xavier turned to West with a low, seductive laugh of her own. "Now that I've had a taste of her, if you've come for a threesome, I think you'll need to add someone to the mix who can balance out this one's innocence. Who were you thinking? Perhaps Scarlet? The girl still talks about that night you took her to the opera like a proper gentleman."

Beside him, Miss Channing squeaked again, and then wiped a sleeve across her mouth, which unfortunately just smeared the paint across her chin. The prudish Miss Mouse was back in force, it seemed. He liked the juxtaposition of innocence draped in shifting pink shadows, her mouth baring the remnants of another woman's kiss.

Whether or not they left here with a traitor, Miss Channing would leave with an education, of that he had no doubt.

"No," he told Madame Xavier, "not Scarlet. We are interested in one of your other girls today. The blond woman called Vivian."

Madame Xavier inclined her head, her eyes widening in surprise. "I thought it was your friend Mr. Grant who enjoyed Vivian's company."

West felt guilty, remembering how Grant had waxed poetic on the woman's various assets. But he was here to track a traitor, not poach on his friend's public territory. "What Mr. Grant doesn't know won't hurt him." He gave the brothel owner a winning smile, the sort that usually had women tripping over themselves to please him. "May I count on your discretion?"

"As you know, our establishment is built upon tightly closed lips." Madame Xavier laughed softly. "Unless, that is, the gentleman prefers our lips open." She raised a groomed brow. "And of course, it all depends on whether Vivian is interested in *you*."

West pulled a five-pound bank note from his pocket. "Well, surely there is no harm in us simply asking her."

Madame Xavier plucked the bank note from his fingers and tucked it between the generous swell of her breasts. "Vivian's door is just upstairs, fourth door on the left." Her eyes drifted back toward Miss Channing, and lingered overlong. "I'll admit, though I really don't do such things anymore, I would consider giving you both a go myself. Show this little one here how to have a little fun. She's really quite delightful." Her soft laughter trailed them as they headed for the stairs. "But she seems a little stiff. Remember, West, that's supposed to be *your* role. And judging by what Scarlet has told me, you do it exceedingly well."

As she set her silk slipper on the red carpet runner leading up the stairs, Mary's ears rang with embarrassment. She'd just survived her *second* kiss of the day.

And in spite of her vivid imagination, in spite of the very many books she'd read on all matter of topics, good and bad, no heroine of her memory had ever experienced anything quite like it.

"Are you coming along?" Westmore asked, the rumble of

his voice tangling with her distracted thoughts. She looked to realize he was waiting for her.

She placed her gloved hand in his, and then up the stairs they went, her palm growing more damp with each step. Not because of where they were, or where they were going, or who they were here to meet, but because she was holding Westmore's hand, and even through her gloves, his palm felt warm and solid against her own. It quite stretched the limits of her imagination.

And she had a *very* good imagination.

"Did you know I can feel you sweating through your gloves?" he observed as they reached the top of the stairs.

"It isn't polite for a gentleman to notice such things." Her fingers curled against his, slick with perspiration beneath the thin leather. "I . . . I am just nervous about what we may find inside the fourth door on the left."

"Pity." He glanced back at her, one wicked brow shifting upward. "I was thinking, perhaps, that it might be because you are here with me."

She shook her head. "No."

He turned to face her as they reached the upper landing. "That word again, Miss Channing. I do believe it is your favorite word, in all of the English language."

"No. It isn't." She flushed, realizing that in spite of her protest, she had said it again. She was beginning to suspect she had another favorite word, and that word was *perhaps*. Because that was what she felt when he looked at her this way. Not "no" and not "yes", but "perhaps".

Perhaps there was something more to him than the gossip. And perhaps there was something more to *them* than this business of causing a scandal or hunting a traitor.

"Miss Channing." His smile tipped upward. "You've said it again. Are you teasing me?"

"No." Her cheeks warmed as he laughed out loud, and

she willed herself to say anything but "no". "I . . . ah . . . think, given our partnership, it might be appropriate to call me Mary," she improvised, though she'd never once in her life had an opportunity to invite a gentleman to do so. It was a day of several firsts, it seemed. "Miss Channing sounds so—"

"Formal?"

"Spinsterish." And in this moment, in this garish hallway that smelled of perfume and smoke and things she couldn't even contemplate, she didn't want to feel like a spinster anymore. Not with him.

His hand gripped hers and she found herself pulled closer to him. A delicious shiver claimed her spine as her front met his chest and his mouth dipped toward her ear. "Mary, then." At her indrawn breath, he chuckled again. "Are you *sure* I don't make you nervous?"

She shook her head.

"But you *should* be nervous." His lips brushed against one of her ears, leaving behind a searing sort of pleasure that sent wisps of want curling through her abdomen. "You should be very, very nervous." His finger came up to brush against her lower lip, once, twice, lingering. "Because being here with you and seeing that appalling red paint on your innocent little mouth makes me want to pull you into one of these rooms and do unspeakable things to you."

Mary gasped. Had she just heard him correctly? A declaration of desire, from the man who had given her a proposal of marriage with the sort of muted enthusiasm one expected of a man facing a firing squad? He claimed he wanted to do unspeakable things to her.

That night at the literary salon, he *had* done unspeakable things to her, though her conscience insisted on reminding her she'd been every bit as much a party to that kiss as he had, at least in the end. And now they were standing, drunk on the cusp of another ill-advised kiss, his fingers humming against her skin.

She pursed her lips—oh, good heavens, did she *really* have red lip paint there?—and tried to convince herself to retreat to a safer distance.

But she couldn't have escaped with a team of horses at the ready.

From the corner of her eye, she could see the long hallway before them, dangerous red doors marching in neat, even rows. She tried to imagine the things that went on behind those doors. The things that *he* had done behind those doors.

The things he wanted to do to *her* behind those doors.

And then one of those doors opened.

"Westmore?" A woman stepped out into the hallway.

Beside her, West pulled away, a low curse echoing beneath his breath. He straightened. Smiled. "Scarlet," he acknowledged.

Mary couldn't help but stare. So, *this* was Scarlet. Her mind pieced it all together, and she knew in that moment this was the prostitute her sister had described seeing at the opera. The woman had bright red hair and a gauzy red dressing gown knotted at her slim waist, and—judging by her generous décolletage—she wore little else beneath it.

"It's been a while, Westmore." Scarlet glided toward them.

"Yes, well. I'm afraid it will need to be a little longer." West cleared his throat. "We've come to see Vivian today."

"*Vivian?*" Scarlet's pretty face crumpled.

The seconds stretched by, and Mary gritted her teeth into the silence. *Oh, for heaven's sake.* They were here for a very important reason, and this hallway distraction was becoming a nuisance they couldn't afford. "You really must forgive him," she said, lifting her chin. "The request for Vivian is for me. You see, I have *very* singular tastes."

Scarlet's eyes narrowed in Mary's direction, assessing her.

Dismissing her. Then she brushed past them, swinging her hips in an unmistakable invitation. "Well, do come and see me when you are finished," she drawled over one creamy shoulder. "I'll help you forget all about both of them."

Mary rolled her eyes as she watched Scarlet's red head disappear down the stairs. "Honestly, that woman needs to wear more clothes," she muttered. She realized, then, that West was grinning down at her. "Why are you smiling at me like that?"

He shrugged. "It is only you have managed to surprise me again."

His praise made her skin tingle in anticipation, and that only served to irritate her more. Had they really just been standing in the hallway, about to kiss? Good heavens, she wasn't supposed to like him. She reminded herself of his reputation, his experience, his depravities.

And yet, the flush creeping down her neck would not be tamed.

She drew a deep breath. "Right then. Fourth door on the left. We ought to hurry, don't you think? I imagine Mrs. Greaves is starting to panic about my disappearance from St. Paul's Cathedral right about now. And if my sister goes to Scotland Yard to report my disappearance, I suspect they'll be more than willing to believe the worst of you in that regard."

He laughed again, but didn't disagree.

Together they approached the fourth door on the left. Mary placed her ear against the red-painted wood, straining to hear anything inside. She could hear nothing but her own pulse, pounding in her ears. "It's quiet," she whispered back at Westmore.

Too quiet. Her imagination helpfully supplied a few opinions on what might be waiting for them behind that door. A blond woman, prone on the bed, a scarf wrapped around her neck, her voice silenced forever. Or, a dead body, not even cold, blood seeping onto the floor from the knife wound in the chest.

Good heavens. She really needed to choose less macabre reading material.

And truly, a murder wouldn't make sense. The traitors needed Vivian to pass on the money, and one tended to need a live body for such things.

Westmore pulled the revolver from his pocket. Mary cringed. She'd imagined they would go in and *talk* to the prostitute, not threaten her. And this was the second time today she'd seen a gun. Truly, she'd rather suffer another one of Madame Xavier's kisses.

"West," she hissed. "You will frighten the girl to death."

If, that was, she wasn't already dead.

"This is a woman who is plotting to kill the queen," he whispered back. "I imagine she will be all too prepared to defend herself." He reached out a hand. Knocked once. "Vivian?" he called, purposefully slurring his words, as if he had been drinking. "It's Westmore. I'm a friend of Grant's. Madame Xavier sent me up," he called out, scratching a finger against the wood.

There was no answer.

Holding the revolver up with both hands, West motioned with his chin for Mary to turn the latch on the door. She obliged, her heart a hammer against her ribs. The door slowly swung open on creaking hinges to reveal . . .

An empty room.

Her breath whooshed out of her in a disappointed gasp. She stepped inside, hoping she was wrong, but the empty corners confirmed the worst. But the room hadn't been empty long. The yellow dress they'd seen this morning lay bunched on the floor. The window sash was open, the curtains fluttering in the foul breeze drifting in from the street. She imagined she could catch the faint edge of their quarry's perfume, lingering in the air.

West dashed to the window and leaned over, searching the street below. "God damn it!" He slammed a hand against the window frame. "There's a tree outside, she must have gone down it. We've missed her!"

Mary began to pull open the drawers of the bureau, searching for some sort of clue, but they were all tellingly empty. She stooped down, picked a lone silk stocking up from the floor. "Wherever she's gone, she left in a hurry."

West pulled a hand across his face, clearly frustrated. "I don't understand. She can't have known we were coming. We came straight here."

"Perhaps she was planning to leave all along," Mary mused. Though, the specifics of the prostitute's hurried disappearance hardly mattered. The woman was gone, the money as well.

Judging by the bare wardrobe, Mary had a notion she wasn't coming back.

And they hadn't any more clues to follow.

Chapter 10

West stomped down the stairs, Mary's hand gripped tightly in his, growing more frustrated with every footfall.

He was frustrated with Mary, for making him forget himself at critical moments. Frustrated with Scarlet, for costing them precious seconds in the hallway. Frustrated with the woman Vivian—if that was even her real name—for leaving in such a hurry, taking the trail along with her. And most of all, frustrated with himself, for being so foolish as to involve Miss Mary Channing in this business in the first place.

If they'd not dallied in the hallway, would the outcome have been different? It was time to face the facts. Mary was like a breath of fresh air in his sordid life, and he'd wanted to nurture the spark he'd seen growing in her eyes. Even the feeling of her gloved hand gripping his felt oddly right. He wasn't a man given to flights of fancy or archaic courtship rituals.

But here he was, holding this woman's *hand*. She was an undeniable distraction.

And he couldn't afford distractions now, not with so much at stake.

Before they could reach the front door, Scarlet stepped out of the first floor receiving room. "Westmore!" She positioned herself in the hallway, blocking their egress. "Finished so soon? That isn't like you at all."

"Vivian wasn't there," he said grimly. "And all her things are gone. It appears as though she has left for good. Do you know where she might have gone?"

Scarlet stepped closer. "No, as you know, the girls here are free to come and go, no questions asked. Perhaps she found a proper protector." Her lips shifted from a practiced smile to more of a pout. "You know, I had thought you might make me a similar offer."

"Well then, I am sorry to have disappointed you." Though, to his recollection he'd made Scarlet no promises on that front. Theirs had been little more than a two week fling and a single, forgettable trip to the opera. "If you'll excuse us now?"

She didn't move.

"Was there something you wanted?" he asked warily.

The prostitute stood up on her toes, her peaked nipples brushing against him beneath her red silk robe. "You know there is."

He gritted his teeth. "Now is not a good time."

He felt Scarlet's lips brush his cheek. "Later, then." Her breath rustled against his ear. "Tonight, after you've discarded your baggage."

West hesitated. Though Scarlet once held his attention quite effectively, today her charms seemed too . . . obvious. Was it because he had come to prefer a softer sort of voice, and a pair of sparkling brown eyes? Or was it because he was losing his mind?

He gave Scarlet a stiff nod, then stepped around her and pulled Mary toward the safety of the door. He had no intention of taking Scarlet up on her offer, but he knew from long experience she was not easily deflected. A nod would be the quickest way to get Mary to the door.

As he pulled Mary onto the street and raised his hand to summon a hack, he fought back a snarl of frustration. Damn it, they'd been so close.

But close was not enough to save the queen.

Their only real lead—St. Paul's Cathedral—had yielded no clue as to the identity of their duke. The prostitute, Vivian, had flown the coop, and there were at least a dozen young, arrogant dukes gadding about London, any one of whom could be the man identified as "Your Grace" from the library. Then there was the new list demanding his consideration. It would take weeks to investigate any one of the groups Mary had written down on that piece of paper.

Perhaps he should go back and try the detectives at Scotland Yard again. With a known target in the queen, perhaps they might take him more seriously this time. God knew, Her Majesty was a frequent enough target of assassination plots that *someone* there ought to take him seriously. But he knew it was impossible. Who in their right mind would ever believe he'd come to a brothel intent only on tracking down a traitor?

Or believe he'd brought with him the woman he'd so famously groped in St. Bartholomew's library, with no other purpose in mind but to kindle the excitement he'd seen sparkling in her eyes?

MARY SAT QUIETLY all the way back to Grosvenor Square.

She'd heard what the beautiful prostitute had whispered in West's ear. Would he really go back to Madame Xavier's? She stole a sideways glance at him as the hackney coach pulled onto the square, the steady clop of shod hooves slowing as they drew in front of her sister's town house. Of course he would.

He was "that damned Westmore", the man, the legend.

And he couldn't get her home fast enough.

He bustled her up the steps, his hand firm against her

elbow. But she pulled away from his touch as the front door loomed near.

"In you go then," he said, adopting a wide stance.

Something akin to envy flashed through her as she thought of why he was in such a hurry to be done with her. "Why don't you come in?" she asked irritably. "Have a cup of tea?" She exhaled. "We could plan our next steps."

He stared down at her, the set of his jaw hiding the direction of his thoughts. Did he think her silly? Tea, unfortunately, was all she could offer him. It was far less than Scarlet had whispered loudly in his ear, but Mary was loath to let him go without offering him *something*.

He reached out a hand and pressed his thumb to the corner of her mouth, rubbing gently, then turned it around to show her a smear of red lip paint. "Mouse," he told her, and her shoulders stiffened to hear the insult, though in truth, at times it seemed he said it like an endearment. "I don't know how I can say this more plainly. There are no next steps."

"But—"

"I think I've caused enough trouble with you today, and that was just going to church. Who knows what sort of disaster we would cause over tea?" He took a step away. "No, I think it is better if we plan to have you stay safely here at No. 29 Grosvenor Square from now on." He hesitated. "Be well, Miss Channing." A smirk claimed his handsome face. "And do try not to kiss any more prostitutes."

He shoved his hands in his pockets and tucked himself down the steps, heading down the street. Mary stood a moment, fuming. The man was even whistling, the merry tune trailing behind him. He seemed to not have a care in the world. And why would he? He'd taken her home, and now he was free to pursue other pleasures.

Drat the man and his . . . his *appetites*.

She turned back to her own door and put her irritation into a sharp rap on the door, then forced a smile at the housekeeper who opened it. "Oh, *there* you are, Mrs. Greaves," she exclaimed with false brightness. "I declare, I sat on that dusty pew for ages, waiting for you. I wonder, did you sit on the wrong one?"

Mrs. Greaves sagged against the door frame, one hand fluttering about her throat. "Oh my goodness, the wrong pew, did you say?" She shook her head. "I suppose I must have done."

"Don't worry," Mary said, patting the woman on the shoulder. "I will explain everything to my sister. It was my fault, not yours."

"Oh, miss, your sister . . . she's not well. I was out of my head with worry, losing you that way. Lady Ashington was nearly frantic when I told her I'd misplaced you, and then her pains started coming." Her hand lowered, fluttering about her heart. "The doctor's upstairs with her now."

Fear and worry collided in Mary's chest, making it hard to breathe. *Oh, no.* "Is she all right?" she gasped, looking up to see a grim-faced Dr. Merial coming down the stairs. She hadn't thought about the consequences of her actions today, just charged into everything, really. But she'd never be able to forgive herself if by her lack of foresight and planning she'd done something to harm her sister or the baby.

Dr. Merial drew to a halt in front of her. "As well as can be expected. False labor, I should say. Brought on by the excitement of the morning." He frowned, shaking his head. "I hope I don't need to remind you she is supposed to be resting quietly."

Mary placed a relieved hand over her heart.

Eleanor was all right . . . *for now.*

How could she have made such a mistake, forgotten her sister's delicate state, even for a moment? "I . . . that is, it was simply a small mix-up with the pews," she lied, "after I stepped out for a breath of fresh air. The Thames, you know . . . there was a terrible smell in the church." A small

lie, a falsehood that hurt no one. And the part about the
Thames was indisputable.

But how could she tell the entire truth, when it promised
to hurt someone she loved?

"Can I see her now?" she asked, feeling awful about causing her sister distress.

Dr. Merial nodded. "I am sure she will be glad to know
you are home."

Mary lifted her skirts and began to hurry up the stairs.

"Oh, and Miss Channing?" he called up after her.

She stopped and looked over her shoulder. "Yes?"

Dr. Merial's mouth twitched, as though he was trying to
hide a smile. He tapped a finger to his lips. "Do stop by your
washstand and mirror before popping in to see your sister.
You might want to remove that lip paint first."

WEST HEADED STRAIGHT for the only person he could think
of who might yield answers.

Though it was a Sunday afternoon—and early at that—
West found Grant slouched over their usual table in the back
of White's, staring into an empty glass.

Likely not the first of the day.

For the first time in memory, West wondered if perhaps
they both spent too much time here. White's was the most
exclusive gentleman's club in London, a cheerful male
domain without a flounce or ribbon or throw pillow in sight.
In the corners of these hallowed walls, wagers were placed
on the oddest of whims, and White's infamous betting book
was considered close to sacred among their set. When the
drinks were flowing freely, he and Grant would laugh and
smoke and avoid any semblance of a serious conversation—
usually because serious conversations tended to send Grant
into a foul mood.

But today the sound of billiard balls knocking about on
a Sunday afternoon and the thought of sliding into a table

with a glass of something in his hand seemed . . . unnatural. Particularly after a morning spent chasing criminals in the company of the effervescent Miss Mary Channing.

West slid into the seat opposite his friend. "Started early today, I see."

Grant's eyes lifted to assess him for a long, drawn out moment. West started to fidget in his seat. He was unused to such scrutiny from Grant. They'd been friends since Harrow, and knew each other inside and out. Undue scrutiny was not really a part of their friendship . . . unless one counted scrutiny of a good drop of whisky.

Preferably of the fine, smuggled variety, the sort that could burn holes through wooden tables and lurked in Grant's always ready flask.

Grant opened his mouth, finally breaking the stretched-out silence. "It's never too early, as you well know. Although, speaking of starting early . . ." He leaned back almost casually in his chair. "I stopped by Cardwell House today, thinking to collect your absent arse and see if we could get up to some fun, but your butler told me you'd gone to church." He snorted. "*Church?* You couldn't get me to church on a Sunday with a bloody team of horses. Was it devotion or curiosity that dragged you there this morning?"

West shifted uneasily in his seat. Grant was speaking too loudly, slurring his words, drawing attention from the other patrons. "It is . . . complicated."

"Ah. A woman, then. I should have guessed. To whom do we owe this sudden fit of pious devotion?" Grant's eyes narrowed. "The infamous Miss Channing, perhaps?"

West was startled. "How did you know about her?"

"For God's sake, the broadsheets have all gleefully chronicled your misadventures, and I haven't seen or heard a word from you since the night you dangled your prick in literary waters."

"Ah. That." West grimaced. "I've been . . . uh . . . 'busy.'"

"Well now, there's a good deal of interpretation that can be afforded a word like 'busy.'" Grant's voice sounded faintly accusing. "Did you at least shag her for all your trouble? Please tell me you didn't toss it all away for a kiss and a peek at her bubbies."

West fought back a snarl. "Have a care. Miss Channing is a proper lady."

"A proper lady?" Grant slumped in his chair. "It's worse than I thought, if you won't hear a word against her. So, have you succumbed to the demands for your head? Slapped a ring on her finger?" He lifted a fist above his head in a parody of a hanging. "Tied the old marital noose about your neck?"

West scowled at his friend. "No."

Though, he'd certainly tried.

"Well, there's a good bit of news." Grant straightened, looking suddenly more hopeful. "You didn't offer for the woman after all that? You've got bollocks, West, I'll hand you that. Ruined women are fearsome creatures, out for blood and whatever else you are hiding." He shuddered. "Of course, I hear she's a bit long in the tooth." He tapped a finger against his head. "Possibly addle-brained, hiding away in Yorkshire so long. Didn't even have a Season. You should count yourself lucky to have made your escape."

West clenched his fists. In his experience, Miss Channing was the opposite of addle-brained. It felt as if he could scarcely keep up with her endless lists and ideas. "You've got it all wrong," he said slowly. "I offered for her. But she wouldn't have me."

Grant burst out laughing. "Are you *sure* she isn't addle-brained? Rocked in the head? You've got half the women in London with their skirts in a twist, eager for a chance with you. If she doesn't want you, I say she's got coddled eggs for brains." He leaned forward. "Though . . . tell me. The rags don't always get it right, but the cartoonist drew her like this." He cupped two hands about his chest, roughly the size of oranges. "Which is all well and good, but did you happen to get a peek at her feet?"

West narrowly resisted the urge to smash a fist in his friend's face. Normally, Grant's raucous teasing made him laugh, but he didn't feel like laughing at the moment. He didn't like hearing Grant denigrate the woman he'd spent the morning with.

Not one bit.

"I didn't come here to talk about Miss Channing's feet." West lowered his voice, a warning should Grant only care to pull his head out of his arse long enough to take stock.

"Good." Grant lifted his empty glass to signal the wait staff to bring him another. "Because I was getting worried you'd succumbed to madness. But all's well that ends well. You've come to the right place to forget your troubles. Now, are you drinking whisky or brandy today?"

"Neither." West waved the aproned staff member away from his side of the table, then leaned forward. "I came to ask you something."

"As long as it isn't a request to stand up with you at your wedding, you've my undivided attention."

"Have you seen Vivian, the prostitute from Madame Xavier's, of late?"

"Why do you ask?" Grant looked suddenly uncomfortable. "Look, this isn't anything to do with that business with Scarlet and the opera, is it?"

"What?" West blinked, confused. What on earth was Grant blabbering on about?

Grant frowned. "I understand you might be miffed, but I would prefer to not share Vivian as penance."

West nearly choked on his tongue. *Good God.* Surely Grant didn't think he wanted Vivian for himself? "You've got it all wrong. I am not interested in her that way." West looked from left to right, then turned himself over to it.

"That night at St. Bartholomew's, I stumbled into a bit of trouble at the literary salon. Vivian was there."

"Vivian?" Grant's eyes narrowed in suspicion. "At a literary salon? What joke are you playing now? To my knowledge, she doesn't even know how to read."

West leaned in. It felt good to at last be relating this tale to someone who was bound by friendship to believe him. He probably should have told Grant about it days ago, but he'd not found time to come to White's, what with his madcap visits to Bedlam and church. Besides, finding a moment when they were both sober enough to have a logical discussion was a challenge he hadn't felt up to. Even now, the empty glass in Grant's hand told him his timing might be off, but there was no help for it.

"Miss Channing and I overheard someone plotting to assassinate the queen." West lowered his voice, hoping Grant was sober enough to understand what he was saying. "And your prostitute, Vivian, is tied up in it."

There was a moment of perforating silence. "Vivian?" Grant finally asked. "She of the lovely feet?"

"The very same."

"And Vivian is . . . the *only* one involved in this dastardly plot?"

"No." West frowned, remembering the other voices, both familiar and unfamiliar. "There is a duke as well. And two other people, but I don't know who any of them are yet."

For a moment Grant looked perplexed. Even pensive. But then he burst out laughing. "Oh, I see." He didn't just laugh, he whooped out loud, leaning so far back in his chair West was afraid he was going to tip it over. "Oh, but this is fekking *ingenious*!"

As his friend dissolved into convulsive laughter, irritation twitched through West. Judging by the redness of Grant's face, this wasn't going to go the way he had hoped.

Grant leaned forward suddenly, the front legs of his chair crashing down with a thump. "All right," he wheezed, "what's my role this time? Am I to be the duke? Do you want me to stand as lookout? Pretend to pull the trigger? Mayhap I could dress as a chamber maid and sneak into the *queen's* bedroom this time. Or do you mean for that role to belong to Vivian?"

West gritted his teeth. "I am not joking, Grant."

"Of course you are. You are always joking, and it's one of the things we all enjoy most about you." Grant tapped the side of his nose. "When do we sally forth? Mum's the word until then, just let me know when you are ready to go through with it. Vivian seems like a good sport. I suspect we would have to pay her, though."

"Grant." West placed both palms down on the table and leaned forward, enunciating clearly so there could be no mistake. "This is not a joke. Vivian is involved in a plot to kill the queen. She's disappeared from Madame Xavier's and taken all her things with her. Do you know where she might have gone?"

"Why would I know where she's gone? I hardly know her. She was just a lark. A lovely lark, to be sure."

"Well, as we speak, your 'lovely lark' is delivering funds to someone, funds that will be used to kill the queen," West told him. "And there isn't going to be anything pleasurable about it if I fail to stop it."

Grant sobered. Regarded him a long, unreadable moment. "Right then," he murmured. He staggered to his feet and turned, heading toward the back of the room.

"Where are you going?" West called out in exasperation. He shouldn't have told Grant—he could see that now. But even if it was fueled by drink, his friend's refusal to believe him stung. Grant, above everyone else, was supposed to be the one who understood him.

They'd been through brothels and benders together. Survived more bottles than he could remember, and one unfortunate battle he still struggled to forget.

Why couldn't Grant understand this? He wasn't joking. Not even close.

"I need to find the betting book!" Grant's laughter howled behind him. "Because I'm laying a wager you're losing your mind."

From the Diary of Miss Mary Channing
June 7, 1858

Westmore is up to something.

When he dropped me off, he did not head toward his house. No, drat the man, he headed south, toward heaven knows what.

Probably to take Scarlet up on her dreadful offer.

How can he be so unconcerned? Someone is plotting to kill the queen, and every day that slips through our hands is one the traitors gain for their cause. But regardless of where the scoundrel is passing his time, it finally struck me that in spite of the day's failures, I at least still have one clue worth considering.

If one of the parties we seek is a duke, I simply must go where dukes congregate.

Now, to find the perfect invitation . . .

Chapter 11

"While I am glad to hear you want to get out of the house," Eleanor said dubiously, "I am afraid a proper social event will be difficult to manage after your inauspicious debut in the scandal sheets."

Mary did not disagree. No, it would not be easy.

Yes, her life was an absolute muck.

But so were the potential consequences for England if she didn't find a way to get out of this house and begin questioning those who had cause to hate the queen.

The end of June, the traitors had said that night in the library. Time was marching by, and she felt the backward slide of each day acutely.

"All the more reason to look for a second chance to impress everyone." Mary forced a smile. "Surely there is something in the post. An invitation to a musicale, perhaps?"

"I really don't understand this sudden change in mood," Eleanor mused, shaking her head. "One would think after what happened, you'd not be so eager to go out and face the censure of Society. They will not be kind, Mary. Cruelty is the specialty of the ton." She cupped a hand absently around her abdomen. "You must trust me on this."

"I know," Mary said, more sure than ever that her sister's whirlwind October wedding had been an event born of necessity rather than marital enthusiasm. "And I know this request seems a bit out of character for me." She thought of her earlier fears for her trip to London, how she had written in her diary about being snubbed by the popular crowd or whispered about behind lace fans.

Those worries seemed almost amusing now.

Certainly nothing to fear.

"I want to do this, Eleanor," she said softly. "The worst has already happened to me, and I survived. And now I can go out and enjoy myself, because I no longer need to worry about what people may think."

"But . . . aren't you afraid?" Eleanor asked. "Of what they might say to you?"

Mary hesitated. How to explain to her sister that the events of the past week had been some of the most exhilarating of her life? That the thought of stepping out into a crowded room and speaking with strangers no longer made her want to curl into a ball? "No, I am not afraid. It is freeing, somehow, to have the veil of propriety ripped so cleanly away." She offered her sister a conciliatory smile. "And you *did* invite me here to London for this very purpose. To find that spark you claim has gone missing from my life."

"Yes, well, I must admit, you *do* seem more cheerful of late," Eleanor admitted grudgingly. "More like the old you." A sigh escaped her lips. "I suppose a small outing might not be the most terrible thing in the world." She glanced down at the silver tray lying beside her on the bed, her fingers sorting through the tangle of letters and correspondence. "Unfortunately, the invitations haven't exactly been flooding in." She looked up, her eyes assessing. "Although . . . perhaps you might consider a visit to the new opera house? Ashington purchased a box for me as a wedding present, you know. He really is the dearest man."

Mary shook her head, though in her opinion, the "dearest man" in question probably ought to be making his way back to London soon. "No, not the opera." Attending an opera would only make her think of *him*, drat his rogue's heart. Besides the question of what else she might be forced to watch beyond the performance on the stage, an outing like that required one to sit in the darkness and be silent, which wouldn't suit her needs at all.

"What about a dinner party?" Mary asked. Although, that idea didn't quite fit either. Dinner parties limited one's conversation to those seated in close proximity. She needed to be able to speak to dozens of people.

All of them dukes.

Eleanor eyed the tray again. "I am afraid it doesn't look promising."

Mary swallowed a groan of frustration. She had offered to help Eleanor answer her correspondence this afternoon—a task on which her sister was helplessly behind—with the intention of wielding an eye for prospects. The thought of what she was planning made her stomach twist in nervous knots, but those knots were neither so tight nor complicated she would be dissuaded from her course. Surely the perfect invitation was lurking somewhere in that pile of correspondence. "What about something with dancing?" she asked.

Eleanor looked up, her eyes wide with surprise. "*You?* Dancing? You can't be serious."

Mary shrugged. "You yourself pointed out that I never had a proper debut. And I thought . . . while I am here in London . . . I may as well . . . dance," she finished, a bit lamely.

"You never had a debut because you refused the Season Patrick and Julianne provided us," Eleanor pointed out. "On account of—let me see if I can recall the exact words you used at the time—*that horrid dancing*. You said you'd rather stay home and read a book."

Mary's cheeks heated. Yes, she could recall saying those very words, and how her family had wrung their hands over her refusal to do the usual thing. But thanks to their mother's passing and the requisite period of mourning, she and Eleanor had been older than was ideal by the time their come-out had been arranged. Old enough, in fact, that she had been of age by the time the opportunity arose. Which meant Mary had been able to refuse to participate, and there was nothing anyone could do about it.

"Well, perhaps I have had a change of heart, now that I've seen something of London," she murmured. It wasn't that she didn't know *how* to dance: they'd both been forced to learn a variety of dances through the years. But Eleanor was the only one who had actually used the skills they had practiced. To Mary, the idea of being held by a stranger on a dance floor made her feel . . . prickly. Being forced to speak to someone, the conversation stilted and false, everyone's eyes on you . . . she couldn't think of anything she'd rather do less.

Except nothing. She couldn't do nothing.

She leaned over the bed and plucked a letter from her sister's tray. This particular invitation, with its bold wax seal and beautiful looped penmanship, had definite possibilities. Even the weight of the paper screamed "duke". "What about this one?" She scanned the contents quickly and then handed the invitation to her sister. "It is for a ball this Saturday."

"The Duke of Harrington's engagement ball?" Eleanor asked, her voice going a few notes higher. "No, I don't think that is a good idea at all."

"Why not?" In fact, it was perfect. Where else would a duke be seen but at another duke's ball? Goodness, the traitor might even *be* the Duke of Harrington.

Excitement coursed through her.

"The duke will be announcing his engagement to the daughter of an Italian countess, and everyone will want to be there for their first glimpse of her." Eleanor sounded worried now. "It will be a frightful crush."

Mary nodded, hoping she looked convincing. "Yes. With *dancing.*" She smiled bravely, though in truth, the thought of dancing with strangers was a bit nauseating. But now was not the time to turn herself over to timidity. There was too much at stake here to let hesitancy dictate her actions, the way she had nearly her entire life. And her ears perked up, homing in on her sister's words. The duke was marrying the daughter of an *Italian* countess?

Thoughts of Orsinian plots swirled in her head.

Eleanor's forehead wrinkled with worry. "Mary, I don't think this is a good idea at all. Besides your disastrous visit to the literary salon and that one unfortunate outing to church, you've not even set foot outside the house while you've been here in London. You've not gone walking in Hyde Park once, nor asked to go shopping on Bond Street. For heaven's sake, I've never even seen you take a turn about the garden. And now you are proposing going to a *ball*?" Her voice turned tart. "Have you lost your mind?"

Mary worried her lower lip. Perhaps she *had* lost her mind. She considered, for a moment, trying once more to confess the real reason she was doing this, trying to explain to Eleanor the details of the conversation she had overheard in the library at the literary salon. But the words died on her tongue before they could be formed.

She remembered all too well how her sister had panicked the last time she'd tried to broach the topic of the plot, the complete and utter disbelief, the firm admonishment to stop letting her imagination run wild. Eleanor looked more exhausted with each passing day, and at the moment her forehead was puckered with worry.

And *that* was simply from the thought that Mary wanted to attend a ball.

Imagine how much strain Eleanor would feel if she discerned the real reason for her sister's sudden new interest in dancing? She couldn't tell her sister.

Not now, with so much at stake.

She plucked the invitation back from her sister's hands, then smiled, hoping it looked sincere. "You are right, of course. I don't know what I was thinking. The scandal sheets, you know. Probably best to let the gossip die down first."

"It is really for the best." Eleanor sounded relieved. "Maybe next month, things might be more settled, and you could venture out with less worry."

Mary brandished her pen. "Shall I pen a note expressing our regrets?"

Though, she was going to do nothing of the sort.

Eleanor nodded. "Yes. Of course." She glanced down at her tray, running a hand across the remaining letters. After a pensive moment, she looked back up. "On the matter of regrets . . . have you heard anything more from Mr. Westmore?"

Mary squirmed as she scribbled her acceptance. *Good heavens.* The mere mention of the man's name made her blush like an adolescent school girl, which was a remarkable feat, given that she was six and twenty and hardly besotted with him.

Or, was she? With nothing more than a rakish smile, he had made her feel as though she was the only person in an entire room. Or a brothel hallway.

She wanted to see him again with a desperation that shocked her. But the scoundrel was preoccupied with things that had nothing to do with her or the security of the country. She knew this to be true because she watched for him from her window, every dreadful night. He gathered himself up and set off down Grosvenor Square about ten o'clock every evening, just when the lights in Cardwell House were starting to go out.

And drat the man, he usually didn't return until morning.

"No," she answered, her fingers tightening miserably over the silver pen. "I haven't heard from him." And that, of course, was the crux of the whole problem.

THE DUKE OF Harrington's engagement ball was the sort of affair designed to bring out the hunting instinct in a man like West.

Everywhere he looked there were women. Wealthy widows and tittering debutantes, all sad to see the most eligible Duke of Harrington removed from the marriage mart, all seeking solace from their disappointment. Normally, he would be ready to relieve their suffering. Ready to offer a conciliatory kiss or more. But tonight West kept to the periphery of the action, hunting for a different sort of prey. And the women swirling in his line of sight—attractive and available though they may be—didn't interest him nearly as much as the mouse of a virgin he hoped was sitting safely in her bedroom, reading some obscure novel by lamplight.

Grant sauntered toward him, a glass of lemonade in each hand. He held one of the glasses out. "You look parched, my friend. I've brought you a peace offering, given that you seem to want to have nothing to do with me of late."

West's fingers closed gratefully about the glass. *Parched.* Yes, that was the perfect word to describe how he felt—at least where Miss Channing was concerned. He felt stripped of sensation, every nerve centered on something he could not have, and should not want. Worse, there was a blurriness to his thoughts and vision that did not bode well for the sort of singular concentration tonight's hunt required.

He'd not been sleeping well, and when he did find his bed, more often than not his sleep was plagued by nightmares. In between subtle inquiries about Fenian uprisings and Orsinian plots—delicate conversations to broach anywhere, but especially amidst drunken peers—he'd surreptitiously watched the courtyard garden three doors down from Cardwell House, hoping for some glimpse of her, a small sighting to ease the hopeless itch she'd conjured beneath his skin. He told himself his curiosity was because he wanted to make sure she was safely at home, instead of trying to stir up trouble.

But he suspected he was lying to himself.

West took a sip of the lemonade. Choked as it slid fitfully down his throat. "Good God," he wheezed. "What did you put in it?"

"Just a little something I had smuggled down from the north. Takes the skin off one's throat, doesn't it?" Grant grinned as he pulled his flask from his evening jacket and added more to his own glass. "You seemed a bit . . . distracted tonight. I thought some whisky might help."

West gritted his teeth, the taste of lemons and whisky lingering on his lips, sharp and head-spinning—a combination that reminded him too much of the potent Miss Channing. "I don't need your help." And he *certainly* didn't need more of Grant's smuggled whisky.

"Look, are you still miffed because of that business with the betting books?" Grant sighed. "I didn't actually place the wager you were losing your mind, you know." He poured another finger of light amber liquid into his glass, until it was more whisky than lemonade. "Although, speaking of wagers . . . you seem to be spending a good deal of time watching the crowd tonight. I would wager you are looking for someone in particular." His grin was sudden, and the opposite of infectious. "The infamous Miss Channing, perhaps?"

"Why does it matter?" West's shoulders tensed.

"I find myself curious." Grant shrugged. "You've not

been acting yourself of late. I would introduce myself to the woman who's knocked you off your perch and sent you off babbling about assassination plots and the like."

"She's not knocked me anywhere," West said, feeling cross. "And I am not babbling. Besides, she won't be here. She prefers libraries to ballrooms, and books over dance cards."

But even as he offered this factual statement, his eye pulled to a flash of blue silk. Recognition knifed through him, and his glass hit the floor, shattering to pieces.

Murmured speculations about his state of inebriation began to run around the room like a surge of electricity, but he could scarcely take the time to worry about it.

Because his mouse of a virgin wasn't at home reading some obscure novel by lamplight. No, she had just walked through the ballroom doors, lacking her biddable chaperone and all good sense. He glowered in her direction, watching as she gave her shawl to a footman and revealed the entire trajectory of her sinfully cut dress.

He wanted to skewer the men who turned to leer at her as she passed.

Wanted to protect her from the narrow-eyed women who bunched in her wake, whispering behind their poisonous fans.

For God's sake, what was Mary doing here? Didn't she realize that thanks to the gossip rags she was now a walking, talking scandal?

And where was her usual brown dress, the one that approximated the color of mud on a dull winter's day? For once, he would have preferred to see her in it. Because unfortunately, tonight she was wearing the blue gown again, the same one that had lured him like a siren that night of the literary salon. It clung to her scant curves as if applied by an artist's brush, highlighting her slender waist and long, elegant neck. And her hair—God in heaven—her hair was tumbling down the back of her neck like a lover's caress, the thick tresses shining beneath the gaslights of Harrington's ballroom.

Against the sea of coifed elegance, she alone looked ready for a tumble.

Or to put it another way, she looked close to having already *been* tumbled.

And that, of course, sent his thoughts straight there, to that carnal place he'd sworn to avoid where this woman was concerned. She was not for him. She was supposed to be untouchable. Innocence wrapped in steel. Off-limits, to apply a proper military term.

His limits, however, were stretching to the breaking point.

"Shall I fetch you another lemonade then?" Grant asked, swiping at the glass shards with his shoe. "Or would you rather just take my flask and bolt it down?"

"No, thank you." West was craning his neck now, trying to see what Mary was up to. He felt a frisson of alarm as he watched her approach the Duke of Salisbury and engage the man directly in conversation—a terrible faux paux for anyone, but for a woman so recently featured in the gossip rags, it was another unforgivable nail in her social coffin.

For Christ's sake, the woman needed a handler.

And the parts of her he'd like to personally handle were on too-ready display tonight.

The aging duke had noticed those lovely, tempting parts, too. His Grace couldn't quite seem to keep his eyes on Mary's face, and in spite of the duke's senility, in spite of Miss Channing's own incautious role in her downfall, West was afraid he was going to embarrass himself tonight defending her unraveling honor.

Grant's shoulder nudged into him. "Who is that woman you are ogling?"

West swore beneath his breath. He hadn't realized he was staring in such an obvious fashion. "No one of importance."

"No one of importance, hmm?" Grant offered him a roguish smile. "Then you won't mind if I introduce myself?"

Bugger it all. That was not happening—tonight or any other night, for that matter. There was no telling what Grant might say to her. Or worse, what she might say back.

"There is no need," West said tersely. "It is Miss Channing."

Grant squinted in her direction. Took a sip directly from his flask. "Oh, ho. I think I am beginning to understand the distraction."

"At least one of us does." Because to West's mind, understanding had just fled the ballroom. He was supposed to be here with one purpose in mind, but that purpose had disintegrated to little more than dust the moment Mary walked through the door.

A servant materialized to clean up the mess on the floor, and so West seized the opportunity to extract himself from Grant's ribbing. "Would you excuse me?" he said, shaking the clinging droplets and bits of glass from his shoe. "I've things to do."

"Interesting choice of words. Well, have fun with your *'things.'*" Grant waved him on with a grin. "But meet me later, at White's?"

West nodded, if only to put an end to his friend's badgering. As he moved through the crowd, he watched Mary from the corner of his eye. Though he was coming to know the exquisite detail of her face—the way her eyes sparkled when she was excited, the way she lifted her chin when making a point—she nonetheless remained something of an enigma to him. For example, he never would have predicted her showing up here tonight, not in a hundred years. It was becoming a problem, the way she kept him off-kilter. He couldn't get a proper read on her, and that was damned disconcerting to such a dedicated connoisseur of the female sex.

He took up residence in an offset hallway, where he could

watch her without fear of further harassment from Grant. He watched her approach a half dozen different gentlemen, and grew increasingly unsettled. In spite of the recent gossip—or perhaps, because of it?—the men all seemed eager enough to speak with her. He couldn't quite identify the emotion coursing through him as he watched her speak with so many of them. It wasn't only worry for her, the thought she might say the wrong thing to the wrong man.

He didn't like the way the men looked at her.

The things he imagined running through their minds.

Was he . . . jealous?

It was a startling notion. What cause had he to be jealous? She didn't belong to him. She had refused his offer of marriage. *Emphatically.* But tonight, the memory of that refusal stung for reasons that were far more complex than his wounded pride.

When at last she drifted close enough he could hear what she was saying—this time to the Duke of Rothesay—his blood ran hot with irritation instead of envy.

"Tell me, Your Grace," she said, smiling up at the duke, "did you perchance attend the literary salon at St. Bartholomew's on June 1st?"

West groaned beneath his breath. Was *that* what she was asking everyone and their brother? Good God, did the woman not understand the need for subtlety?

He emerged from his hiding spot to take her by the arm. A squeak escaped her lips, but he pulled her ruthlessly toward him. "Ah, Miss Channing, *there* you are." His words might be civil, but his tone held a curt warning. "Would you please excuse us, Your Grace? Miss Channing is an acquaintance of my sister's, and I have an urgent message for her about . . . er . . . books."

Without waiting for an answer, he spun her deeper into the hallway, grateful for the fact that the wall sconces here flickered with a less glaring light.

Once they were out of sight of the ballroom, he let his anger fly. "Well?" he demanded, loosening his hold on her arm. The chit was going to get them both killed, asking questions like that. But she wasn't asking questions now. In fact, she was almost mutinous in her silence. "You've been running your mouth all evening, to every peer within earshot," he ground out. "Do you have nothing to say to *me*?"

One gloved hand fluttered near her throat. "You . . . ah . . . you have startled me."

"Mouse, that's *nothing* compared to what you are doing to me." He glowered down at her. "Don't you know how dangerous it is to draw attention to yourself like that?"

That seemed to unpluck whatever was tangling her tongue. "Stop calling me that."

West bit back the impulse to tell her he called her that so he wouldn't think of her in more dangerous, desirous ways. "What are you doing here, questioning everyone and their uncle?"

"I think the more pertinent question is what *aren't* you doing?" She lifted her chin. "I'd imagined you as a hero, you know. Coming in, sword drawn, determined to save the day. Just like a hero from the pages of one of my books." She bit her lip, her gaze wavering. "And yet, you aren't doing any of the things a proper hero would."

He stiffened against the hurt accusation in her voice. She expected him to act like a hero in one of her bloody books? Good Christ, had this woman any notion of how the world actually worked? "Well now, there's your first mistake," he snarled, feeling her lack of faith like a sword to the chest, no matter that as her anti-hero, he lacked the damned sword itself. "The characters in those bloody books you are always blathering on about aren't real."

Her cheeks went pink. "I know they aren't real. I am not a simpleton. But while you seem perfectly able to ignore the things we heard that night, *I* cannot, not when the fate of the country hangs in the balance. So while you lurk in hallways like a bogeyman, I have been out asking the questions that might lead us to our traitors, something *you* don't seem to have the . . . the . . ." The delicate flush staining her cheeks intensified. "The *stones* to do."

West cocked his head. She'd called him a coward, and in this, at least, she very nearly had him pegged. But she was wrong about one thing. And so he leaned in, his hands splayed against the wall on either side of her, until she was pinned against the wall, her body trembling against his in a manner that brought nothing of fear to mind. "Let me be the first to assure you, Mouse, I've got stones enough to get the job done." He leaned in closer, until the very parts of his body in discussion pressed indelicately against her. His hips flexed, and a soft gasp escaped her lips. He bent his head, his lips brushing against her quivering earlobe. "Any job you wish."

Here, of course, was where a sensible woman should slap him. He was all but mounting her in the hallway outside of the Duke of Harrington's engagement ball.

Instead, she stilled.

And then . . . miracle of miracles, was she leaning back into him?

He pushed away from her and dragged a hand through his hair. Surely her capacity to surprise him should no longer come as such a . . . well . . . surprise. She ought to be shrieking. Slapping him silly. Fainting again. Instead, she was staring up at him with those wide brown eyes, her plump, pink lips almost begging for a kiss. This woman twisted him in knots, with her damning combination of innocence and determination. But the very traits that made the blood roar in his ears might actually get her killed.

"I beg of you, Mary, you must forget we ever heard anything in that library."

"You expect me to just forget what we heard? Let them

proceed without trying to stop them?" Her eyes narrowed. "Risk the life of our queen?"

West gritted his teeth. She was a distraction he couldn't afford, and he felt guilty as hell for involving her as much as he already had. "Better than risking our own lives," he lied, wanting her safely at home reading that obscure novel he'd imagined earlier. "Someone else can handle it."

"It *must* be us," she retorted. "There is no one else to do it, thanks to your reputation and my sister's delicate state!"

West wanted to shout at her. Or worse—kiss her, though that was arguably what had landed them in this trouble to start. "If we overheard them plotting," he ground out, choosing his words carefully, "it is likely someone else already has too, someone whom Scotland Yard will believe. No doubt the proper authorities are already on their trail and closing in."

Though, if the authorities had heard so much as a whiff of this plot, surely they would have taken his complaint more seriously. The memory of how the detective at the Scotland Yard desk had laughed at him still stung. It was the reason he was here tonight, and why he'd gone out every night this week, listening to conversations, cataloging voices, his thoughts centered on things less pleasurable than the usual distractions.

Not that *she* needed to know any of that.

He took a more prudent step away from her. "For Christ's sake, the Duke of Rothesay isn't the man responsible for this plot."

"Why would you say that?"

"The men I saw in the library were considerably less portly."

She pursed her lips. "Right then." She dipped her gloved hand into the low-cut bodice of her gown and pulled out a folded piece of paper. "I should probably cross him off my list."

"Oh, for God's sake." He snatched the folded piece of

paper from her. "Another list? No wonder your fingers were always stained with ink." As he scanned the very thorough list of names, dread pooled like a regrettable night, somewhere deep in his gut. "How did you even come up with a list like this?" he asked, though he shouldn't be surprised anymore where this woman and her surprising array of talents were concerned.

She'd even included some names here that he'd neglected to consider.

"*Debrett's Peerage*, of course. There is a copy in Lord Ashington's library." She waited a beat. "Books can be very instructional, you know."

He glared down at her. "Do you even realize how stupid it is to ask these sorts of questions?" he choked out. "To make a list such as this, and pull it out of your bosom and consult it in goddamned *public*?"

She frowned. "I only came to—"

"It seems to me you only came here tonight to yammer that pretty little mouth of yours," he interrupted, giving rein to his darkening mood. "Whoever this is, he is not an honorable man. Surprise was our only advantage in this game, and if you've spoken to the wrong man tonight, or said the wrong thing at the wrong time, you've just given it all away!"

Confusion colored her face. "You . . . that is, you think my mouth is pretty?"

He snorted. *Good God. That* was what she took from this conversation? "Don't let it go to your head." He was angry with her for making him feel weak, and angry with himself for making it so easy for her. He folded the list and shoved it inside the pocket of his evening jacket. "I just think there are better uses you could put those lips to. You need to go home, before you do something really stupid."

Like bite her lip again.

Because God help him, he couldn't be held responsible for the consequences.

Chapter 12

etter uses for her lips . . . ?

Good heavens, the man was a menace, saying the most outrageous things.

And no matter the way West was glowering down at her, no matter how many times he called her "Mouse", Mary didn't want to go home yet. Had he any notion of what it had taken for her to get here? She'd slipped from her sister's house under cover of darkness and walked two terrifying blocks to flag down a hack on Oxford Street. She'd braved brigands and bodily harm and more importantly, public ridicule. She knew everyone here was whispering about her. Knew what they thought of her. If she was brave enough to face the scandal that trailed in her wake, she was brave enough to face West's handsome, hovering frown.

And she wasn't leaving until she was ready.

"This conversation is growing as tiresome as that unimaginative nickname." She stepped around him, lifting her skirts in her hands and aiming for the hum of the crowd in the larger room beyond. "I came here tonight to speak with the men on that list," she said as a parting shot, "not to converse with a coward."

She nearly escaped, too. But just as she emerged into the brighter lights of the ballroom, she felt his touch on her arm. No doubt it was her imagination, giving life to things that weren't there, but she could almost believe there was a plea in that touch. She looked down at the shape of his gloves against the bare skin of her upper arm, her anger disintegrating.

"What do you want, West?" she sighed.

"I want you to dance with me," came his answer.

She hesitated. He was a rake and a boor and she ought to want nothing at all to do with him. More to the point, she hated dancing. But drat it all, she was already letting him pull her into his arms. Her slippers were on the dance floor.

It would be rude to pull away now.

As he began to swing her around in large circles, she waited for the prickle of awareness, the fear that too many people were watching. Those dreaded emotions didn't come. Instead, three years of dancing lessons, the preparation for her nonexistent come-out, proved useful now. The feel of his hand against the small of her back, guiding her with subtle pressure, made her want to follow wherever he might lead. Even if he led her to ruin.

The earlier flash of anger he'd shown seemed to have been shoved to a distant corner. Either that, or harnessed and held to a tighter rein. He was playing the perfect gentleman now, if a bit too quiet. Some devil in her made her want to test that restraint.

And so, as they began their second rotation around the dance floor, she peeked up at him through her lashes. "I've not yet had a chance to speak with the Duke of Harrington." She lowered her voice. "Perhaps you could introduce me when this dance is over?"

"I don't think so." Though his tone stayed pleasant, his jaw tightened.

She thought of the news of the duke's engagement, announced to an appreciative crowd not even a half hour ago. "He's on the top of my list, and he just announced his intentions to marry the daughter of an Italian countess," she countered, a little too loudly. She tempered her voice back to a whisper. "Who better to have sympathies for the Orsinian cause?"

West swung her with a bit more force. "The Duke of Harrington isn't our man."

"How would you know that, lurking in hallways as you have been?"

"I know," he told her, "because his Grace is connected to my family. He comes to dinner at Cardwell House at least once a month. He is an impressively honorable man."

"Oh." She bit her lip as the room spun by. Drat it all, West had already ruled out the Duke of Harrington as a suspect? She thought of how quickly he'd dismissed her suspicions of the Duke of Rothesay as well. And the list he'd kept, now tucked in the inside pocket of his evening jacket. She'd have to make another one, and the thought of it poked at her.

Couldn't he see? *This* was why they needed to do this together, why they ought to share their plans and suspicions with each other. She shouldn't have to waste her time considering leads that led nowhere. "Who else, then?" she pressed, trying to remember the other names written on the now-purloined list. "If you've already discounted Harrington and Rothesay, you must have an idea of who else we should be considering."

Instead of answering the question, he glowered down at her. "Tell me, Miss Channing. Why no chaperone this evening? Did Poor Mrs. Greaves die in a fit of apoplexy after your visit to the brothel? Or has your stubbornness gotten her sacked?"

Mary sighed in frustration. Why was he refusing to discuss this with her, avoiding the topic as if it might prove a deadly disease? She couldn't help but feel disappointed in his lack of enthusiasm for the chase. During that Sunday visit to the brothel, she'd imagined . . . well, she'd foolishly imagined him as a white knight, riding in on his charger to the save the day. But perhaps that was the problem with allowing her imagination free rein.

So often, heroes only existed on the pages of books.

"No, Mrs. Greaves is still alive and gainfully employed, if a bit more suspicious of me now," she replied, not wanting to talk about housekeepers. Or chaperones. *Or brothels.* "I claimed to have returned to the wrong pew, and she pretended to believe me rather than consider the less palatable alternative, I think. And why do you care whether or not I have a proper chaperone? I am already ruined." *He ought to know, given his starring role in her shame.* Although, she could perhaps look back on that night and admit that Westmore could not be held entirely responsible for that debacle.

Heaven knew she had played her own starring role in that bit of folly.

His head lowered toward her own, until his lips brushed her ear. "*Why* I care is scarcely the question, Mouse." This time, the sound of that nickname sent a shiver rippling down her spine—one he could no doubt feel through the indecent press of his hand, drat the man. With his breath warm against her ear, she could almost imagine it was meant as an endearment instead of an insult. "The fact is that I *do* care, whether I ought to or not."

His words made her head feel fizzy, shaken up inside. Surely it was just the unaccustomed nature of dancing, and not any real meaning behind such dangerously delicious words. He didn't care about her. He *couldn't* care. He was a man with a reputation, a man who sought only his own pleasure, and didn't give a fig about what others thought or wanted.

She needed to remember that, even as her pulse bounded beneath her skin.

His head dipped toward her ear again. "How did you even come to be here tonight, if you didn't bring a proper chaperone? Did you steal Ashington's coach?"

"If you must know, I slipped out of the house after my sister fell asleep and summoned a hackney cab."

His fingers tightened against the small of her back. "You took a cab here? By *yourself*?"

"I am afraid I lack a fairy godmother to conjure a more spectacular means of conveyance." She hesitated, wondering why his fingers were suddenly gripping her right hand with more ferocity. "And I also lacked the pumpkin." She met his gaze, feeling the edges of her mouth wanting to turn up, in spite of her continued annoyance with him. "Probably on account of the fact that people have a dreadful habit of urinating through the garden fence. Hardly a good location for growing vegetables."

WEST GLARED DOWN at her, his eyes lingering on the slight upward tilt of her entirely too-kissable lips. She was teasing him, clearly.

But had she any concept of what could happen to an innocent woman flitting about the streets of London? Riding alone in a hackney cab, traipsing darkened streets? Christ, even this dance floor was dangerous. He could feel the curious eyes on them, the appreciative glances she garnered from too many men. The way the women stared at her, jealousy sharpening their claws. He felt an overwhelming need to protect her.

He clenched his teeth. "It isn't safe to be out in the city after dark."

"*You* prowl the streets at night." She shrugged, the motion pulling against the grip he had on her. "I see you go out, nearly every night."

Her admission that she watched for him through her window made his feet stumble a bit. So, she spent her evenings peeking out her curtains, did she? It made him feel smug that she had sought a glimpse of him the past week, the same way he had looked for her.

But not so smug he could forget the danger.

Somewhere on this dance floor might very well be one of the men they sought. The thought that the traitors might be watching them now made his feet began to slow. The urge to whisk her away, ensure her safety, burned like an ember beneath his skin.

What was wrong with him, to be reacting in this manner?

"Speaking of finding one's bed . . ." he started, but then stopped as her lips parted with a soft gasp. He'd only meant to say perhaps it was time to find hers tonight, but he was loath to correct the misimpression, especially given that her gloved hand had just gone limp in his own.

Just to their right, he could see the open doors that led to the front foyer. He steered her toward them, and was relieved when she willingly followed him. Perhaps she thought he intended to walk with her outside? Steal a gentle kiss or three in Harrington's garden?

God, she really was a naive thing.

And trust was a matter best reserved for men willing to play the proper gentleman.

As they stepped out into the warm summer night, he raised a hand to a waiting footman. "Please bring the Cardwell coach around."

Surprise shaped her mouth into an "O". "Are you leaving already?"

"I am sending you home."

Her hand went tight again, the warmth in her eyes instantly shuttered. She twisted her hand out of his. "I will go home when I am ready, and not a moment before. You can't just send me home as if you own me."

West crossed his arms, blocking her way back inside. If she wouldn't have a care for herself, he had no choice but to play the role of chivalrous knight, however tarnished his armor. For a moment, he considered the image she presented, dark waves of hair swinging wildly over one temple, her cheeks the sort of pink a man would gladly die trying to bring out in a woman's skin. In spite of his resolve to stay far, far away, in spite of his determination to see her nowhere but home, lust speared him, sharp and unfortunate.

"If *I* owned you," he growled, giving himself over to the truth, "I'd be a damned sight less frustrated. And your cheeks would be flushed with pleasure instead of annoyance."

Chapter 13

*M*ary gaped up at him

Drat it all, but he always knew just what to say to disarm her. Every word that came out of his mouth was fashioned to send her body into spasms of want.

Though . . . what cause had *he* to be frustrated? He'd made his intentions toward her painfully clear. All week long he had avoided her. Or worse—ignored her. Tonight, though, for some reason, he seemed unable to leave her be. A silly hope, to have imagined he was escorting her outside for a kiss. She would not make the same mistake twice.

She forced her gaze beyond his shoulders, to the bright lights of the ball, waiting just beyond the front door. The music inside had shifted from the sweeping waltz they'd just shared into something lively. Her chance to dance with another partner and ask more questions was slipping from her hands. She considered barreling around him, returning to the fray.

But as if he could read her mind, those handsome lips shifted to a smirk. "I don't think so. Time for bed now."

Good heavens, he even managed to make *that* sound suggestive. Either that or her mind was flying there itself, urged on by his maddening words and easy smiles. He was a danger to the sanity and sanctity of women everywhere.

The Cardwell coach pulled up to the steps. With a small huff of irritation, she turned away from the hand he offered—as if he could play the gentleman now, ha!—and yanked open the coach door. Ignoring his offer of assistance, she climbed up in a profusion of skirts and silk. She imagined he would shut the door and instruct the driver to take her straight home. Instead, he surprised her by climbing in and settling on the seat across from her.

"You are coming, too?" she asked bitterly.

"I don't trust you to see yourself all the way home," came his infuriatingly mild reply. He rapped on the roof and then they were off, spinning through the evening, gaslights flashing by the glass windows in a muddied smear of light.

A moment of silence passed, a gasp of time during which Mary tried—in vain—to compose herself. How could she have been so foolish as to imagine he'd only wanted to dance with her? To walk with her in the moonlight and perhaps kiss her again? Those handsome blue eyes had knocked her sideways, destroyed her ability to think strategically. He had done it to distract her, and then waltzed her right off the dance floor before she knew which end was up.

She fixed her eyes on the ceiling of the coach, the door's fine-grained woodwork, gleaming in the occasional flash of light from the street.

Anywhere but him.

"You are trembling," he observed.

Mary's gaze jerked toward him, though it was dangerous to give her eyes such permission. He was brooding across the seat, one leg stretched out in front of him, brushing against her skirts. "I assure you," she retorted, "it is not from fear."

"Naive of you, I'd say, given the danger you stirred up tonight, asking questions of everyone in sight."

"I am not in danger," she snapped. "Good heavens, must you natter on about it so? I only asked a few questions of a few people. It isn't as if I stood drunkenly on the punch table and shouted, '*Does anyone here want to kill Queen Victoria?*'"

He stared at her for an undecipherable moment, then patted the seat next to him. "If you aren't afraid, you must be cold then. Come and sit next to me. I know how to keep you warm."

"I am not cold." In fact, she was incensed. She stripped off her gloves, hoping it might help cool the flush spreading beneath her skin. "I am trembling because I am angry, you dolt. With *you.*"

There was a moment of silence. She thought, perhaps, he was laughing at her. But in the sudden flash of an outside gaslight, she caught the tension in his jaw. He didn't look to be enjoying himself, precisely. "Why are you angry?" he asked, more softly now.

"You have no right to treat me this way."

There was a beat of hesitation, as if he was considering his answer. "Perhaps it isn't a God-given right," he said, "as much as concern that makes me take such an imprudent interest in your hide." His voice thickened. "But there is no denying I feel responsible for you."

Once again, his words spun circles in her ears. She didn't want to believe he felt anything for her but annoyance, but when he said things like that . . . and looked at her like this . . .

She could nearly believe he meant it. That she meant something to him, beyond a thorn in his side. But good heavens, could the man not decide his intentions? One moment he was cold toward her, the next he was too hot. Wasn't a changeable nature supposed to be a woman's purview? It was growing exhausting trying to guess his moods.

"Then you are fickle," she retorted, shaking her head clear of those dangerous thoughts and hopes, "as well as foolish."

"I am not the one taking foolish risks. And if you insist on cavorting about town without a chaperone, chasing all manner of ruffians, I will have no choice but to tell Lady Ashington about your adventures."

Mary gasped out loud. "You wouldn't."

"Wouldn't I?"

Fear kicked aside the potent combination of anger and attraction he'd kindled, the danger of such a threat all too real. "Have you forgotten about my sister's condition? She feels too responsible for my circumstances now, thanks to your insufferable behavior at the literary salon. She could not withstand the strain of such a surprise."

He spread his hands. "That would be on your head. Not mine."

Though it was the truth, his argument stung. She had done all she could to hide the circumstances of this newest adventure from Eleanor, but even as she let herself out of the silent, sleeping house, she had known there was some risk of discovery. She felt remorse in taking such a risk with her sister's health, but she didn't know what else to do. She was trying to help *everyone*, and lives were at stake on both sides of the equation. If only he showed some sign of taking the threats to the queen's life seriously, things might be different. But as long as he ignored the looming danger, how could she choose another path?

"She must not find out," Mary breathed. "Promise me, West. That you won't tell her."

"If it came down to a matter of ensuring your safety, I would have to." He pulled a hand through his hair, though he scarcely needed the help to look any more rakish. "Besides, have you considered that someone else might tell her of your evening's adventure?" he added. "That she might read about you once again in the gossip rags? *Everyone* saw us dancing. The gossip must even now be flying about the ballroom."

She looked down at her hands. Drat it all. He was right. She hadn't thought about that possibility when she'd permitted him to tug her on to the dance floor. The man made every sane thought in her head go straight to mush.

Good heavens, could this web of deceit get any thicker?

She looked up, anger splicing her shame. "You are insufferable," she shot across the few inches that separated them. Why, oh why, had she consented to a dance with him? He had probably known what he was doing from the start, plotting a public downfall, using it to press his advantage. "Incorrigible." Her mind flew to a simpler word, one that even someone as thick as he could understand. "*Selfish.*"

He shrugged. "I've been called worse."

"Indecent?" she retorted. "Irredeemable?"

"No, I believe 'cowardly' was the term used tonight."

She nodded. "Craven. Pusillanimous."

"I know how much you like to read, but I've had a few years at university myself. I studied architecture for a time, under Phillip Hardwick, so you should know that tossing around such large words isn't going to impress me."

His smirk plucked at her anger. So, too, did the reminder that he was not as stupid as she liked to imagine. Phillip Hardwick was one of London's most distinguished architects, and the thought that this man had once aspired to something more useful than to seduce scores of women sent anger coursing through her. "Well, large *stones* aren't going to impress me!"

"So you admit they are large."

Her eyes narrowed. Drat the man, he even managed to boast like a scoundrel. His ego was as enormous as his . . . well . . . his stones.

"You are the most egotistical man!" she panted. "Supercilious!"

"You forgot 'large'," he taunted.

She glared at him through the spinning shadows inside the coach. "Not so large." A lie, that. Because she had felt him well enough when he'd pressed his body against hers tonight. And heaven help her, she'd felt an answering curiosity, swirling inside her. "In fact, I think diminutive might be a better word choice. Miniscule. *Infinitesimal*."

"Have easy with such premature judgments." White teeth flashed in the darkness. "You can't really know how large they are until you hold them in your hands."

"I wouldn't . . . that is, a lady would *never* . . ." Her protest trailed off, and her cheeks flamed with unwelcome heat. Truly, she didn't know what a lady might or might not do. He'd no doubt had plenty in his bed through the years. "You, sir," she choked out, "are no gentleman."

"Haven't claimed to be, as far as I know," he said, even as the coach pulled to a stop, signaling their arrival at Grosvenor Square. "Most ladies prefer a bit of a rogue, truthfully." He glanced out the window, his brow furrowing. "Here you are. No. 29 Grosvenor Square. Safe and sound."

Mary hesitated. She might be safe, but she was hardly sound, given that part of her wanted to stay right here in the coach. Fuming at herself now as much as him, she shook herself from her scoundrel-induced stupor and reached a hand toward the door latch, only to find it suddenly trapped beneath his gloved hand.

Her pulse startled, like a bird flushed from heather. She glared at him. "Was there something else you wanted? Would you like to call me Miss Rat now, instead of Mouse?"

"*God* no," he choked. A curious shudder ran through him, and her hand absorbed it, though what it meant, she had no clue.

"Then perhaps you might like to come inside and start shouting in the stairwell? Hatch a plan to send my sister into early labor? I assure you, there is no need to pursue additional measures to ensure my compliance. I will not interfere again. The threats you've made are quite sufficient to muzzle any further nocturnal activities I might be considering."

"Nocturnal activities, hmmm?" He rose from his seat, nearly predatory over her, his hand still pinning hers to the door. "Where must that innocent mind be dwelling, to come up with such a specific phrase?"

"Must you always turn a simple conversation into innuendo?" she snapped, though she did not try to tug her hand free. "My mind is not dwelling on anything but irritation, I assure you. And the driver—"

"Will neither move nor speculate as to the cause of our delay."

She stiffened. "Because he is familiar with your reputation?"

"Because I supplement his salary, and he knows to be discreet." Gently, he tugged her hand away from the door latch. She let him. Settled back onto her seat. Watched—without protest—as he pulled down the shade over the little glass window. Confusion scattered her wits. Apparently West wasn't quite ready for her to go in yet either. The thought made her fingers curl over the silk gloves bunched in her hand.

He moved closer, his head bent down. She could smell the fresh soap and cinnamon scent of rum wafting off his skin, the faint, acrid scent of smoke, not at all unpleasant, clinging to his clothes. The melding fragrances were no less potent than the twisted promise in his words. She sank back against the velvet seat. "Why would you wish me to stay another moment? You've delivered your threats. Hastened me home, nearly trussed and bound. I can't imagine what else you feel we must discuss."

"Trussed and bound." He shook his handsome head. "Honestly, Miss Channing, you have a flair for carnal theatrics." He settled on his knees in front of her, his head now level with her own. "Can you not even admit you feel it?" He tugged the gloves out of her clutched fingers. Placed them on the seat beside her. "This odd alchemy between us?"

Mary's eyes drifted toward her discarded gloves, feeling the loss of that armor keenly of a sudden. Her heart was spinning on a broken axis. She had no experience in such things, possessed no standard against which to measure the depth of this folly. He described it as alchemy, but she suspected it came closer to sorcery. And as prettily as the words were delivered, as much as it made her skin flush warm, it was a claim she couldn't—mustn't—believe. "Hardly odd," she scoffed, lifting her eyes to meet his own, "from a man who's had half the eligible women in London."

"Surely no more than a quarter of them." His words might be infuriating, but something about the timbre of his voice was making her stomach turn in an endless loop of want. He chuckled. "Though, I've admittedly had some of the ineligible ones, too."

Drat it all, did he have to remind her? She understood she was sitting in a darkened coach with an insufferable rake. Understood, too, she was here by choice, not duress. She did not need the reminder of her foolishness. "Yes, I've heard of your substantial amount of experience in the field of alchemy," she said bitterly.

In response, he began to strip the glove from his right hand, loosening the fingers and then sliding it off in a smooth, practiced motion. Mary watched through the darkness, her breath trapped in her throat. Dear heavens, he even undressed like a scoundrel, every move destined to send women in paroxysms of want. She watched as the leather slid free and he dropped the fine kidskin onto the floor of the coach. "Perhaps," he said, almost lazily, "that substantial experience is how I know this chemistry between us is so odd."

The night thickened, the air in the coach stirring with small eddies of possibility. "I should think," she breathed, her eyes drifting to the tempting, bare gleam of his hand, "that 'odd' is too simple of a word." Especially given that her own emotions tilted more in the portentous direction.

He removed his other glove and then his hands were laid bare—though for what reason, she couldn't yet guess. Not for any safe, proper purpose, of that she was sure. She thought of how his hand had dipped into her bodice that night in the library. What if he meant to do that again?

What if she *wanted* him to do that again?

But no . . . his fingers were only shifting to dance over her silk-covered knee, the pressure and warmth of his touch shocking, even through all the layers.

"If not odd, perhaps you might choose another word then." His lips shifted into a particularly wicked smile. "Incongruous might be more pleasing to your vocabulary. Anomalous." His fingers swirled against her skirts, a silken, rhythmic promise. "No matter what else you may think of me, you must believe me when I say this sort of pull between two people, this rubbing along together . . ." He hesitated, as if sorting through the words to apply. "It does not happen every day."

She refused to believe it, even as she prayed he wouldn't stop. She'd read any number of novels, lost herself in the story on more occasions than she could count. She knew better than most that villains would say nearly anything to have their way with a heroine. "It feels more like we are rubbing in opposite directions a good deal of the time," she breathed, though she could not summon the good sense to pull away from his touch.

"Sometimes, the right friction creates the most delicious kind of pleasure." His other hand curled against her opposite calf, shifting her legs apart so he could lean closer, kneeling in front of her. Her skin prickled with awareness.

This. This was the proximity her body was craving.

His grin shifted to something wicked at her lack of protest, his handsome mouth hovering only inches from her own now. "And you must trust me when I say, Mary, that I know *exactly* where to rub."

The faint hint of whisky on his breath proved her undoing. She imagined if she pressed her tongue to the corner of his mouth, she would taste the spirit there. In the faint light drifting in from around the edges of the window shade, she stared at the sinful swoop of his upper lip, nearly flush with her own. The feelings he had so expertly evoked that night behind the library curtains welled up beneath her skin, nearly pushed her forward. "I . . . I should probably leave," she breathed.

"The coach door is not locked," he murmured softly. "You may leave whenever you wish." His touch against her knee lightened. "And you probably *ought* to leave, before you do something you will regret."

Mary swallowed. He made it sound as if the choice was hers.

As he crouched in front of her, his bare hands against her silk-draped skin, she realized that perhaps it *was* her choice. What would it cost, really? A moment in his arms? The entire city already believed her the worst sort of wanton. The entirety of Mayfair had seen the gossip rags, and moreover, had probably seen her leave tonight with the most infamous scoundrel in London tonight. What harm would come of kissing him again, when the world believed she'd done worse?

That knowledge, more than anything, propelled her to imprudence.

She leaned forward and pressed her lips against his, fumbling inexpertly at the mechanics of it, trying to remember the few pieces she had learned that night in the library and again during that fleeting moment in the cathedral. He *did* taste of whisky, and lemonade as well, and the flavors propelled her onward.

Pleasure spiraled in her abdomen, a centrifugal desire, centering low. His hands came up to cup the back of her head, loosening the few pins she'd ineptly placed there, and her hair gave up its narrow hold on propriety, tumbling down around her shoulders.

He offered a small groan of approval against her mouth. His fingers tightened against her scalp, shifting her head, changing the angle of how they met. And just like that, her initial blunder of a kiss shifted to something that nearly made the seat vibrate beneath her.

"*Oh,*" she breathed, her lips parting. An invitation. Naively offered, perhaps, but gladly taken by the rogue who currently held her in his expert hands.

His tongue began to move in lazy circles against her own, languorous sweeps inside her mouth. The feel of his thumbs cradling her face loosened a sigh of pleasure from somewhere deep inside her, a place she couldn't name or touch. His mouth played against her own, testing, the hot, warm sweep of his tongue melting inside her.

Her fingers fisted in his jacket, hauling him closer. Obligingly, his hands swept up and then down her bare arms, raising gooseflesh in their wake, and leaving behind a trail of trembling want. His fingers came down to twine into her own, and then he lifted her hands high above her head, pinning them lightly against the velvet backing of the seat, causing her breasts to rise high above her corset and brush against the wool of his evening jacket.

And then he was licking his way down her neck, branding each inch of skin with small pinches of teeth. Oh, but the man knew what he was doing. Her head lolled back against the soft seat back, the heat in her womb blooming into more of an explosion. Alchemy, he'd called it.

More like arson, a flame set to ready tinder.

She wished she could resent him for making her want this—want him—so very much, but that would require logic and reason, and those necessary pieces of thought had quite flown out of the coach window at the moment.

His touch became teasing. Though one hand kept her wrists lifted high, his other hand drifted down the swell of her breast to dip beneath her neckline. "Oh," she gasped as his hand found the magic of her nipple, rolling the needful skin between his fingers. "Yes, *there*."

His mouth came back to hers, diving in for a hot, wet, wicked kiss. Now her own hands moved, pulling from his slight grip, lowering about his neck, threading through the sinful softness of the hair at his nape. There was a familiarity here, a hint of memory. They'd done this before, behind the curtains that portentous night. It was nearly a relief to realize this was what she had been missing these heady, frustrating few weeks.

But there was newness, too. A rush of air tickled her silk stockings. She felt the slide of her skirts as he inched them upward toward her knees, the silk and crinolines fisted in one hand, even as the other hand played expertly against her breast.

His fingers danced—truly, there was no other word for it—against the quivering skin of her thighs, advancing, retreating, evoking a repartee of want and hope, promising more and yet warning her to wait. All the while he kissed her, wreaking havoc on every sense she had, and some she hadn't known she possessed.

WEST SLOWED HIS ascent, though every sense he possessed told him to reach his destination faster. Good Christ, what was he doing? He'd only intended to have a little taste of her lips.

Remind himself of her innocence, of all the reasons they shouldn't do this.

But the moment her lips had met his, his restraint went to shite.

Even now, as he gently broke away from their kiss, searching her face for clues as to how to apologize for such boorish behavior, his thoughts retained the blurred consistency of a fever dream. The taste of her lingered on the tongue like the sweetest of drugs, and in spite of his stern admonishment to make his mouth behave, he couldn't help but let his hands linger on the soft rise of her thigh resting beneath his fingers.

She didn't tell him "no".

He swallowed, almost wishing she would. If there was a reality to be found here, it was hazy, a muddied understanding that, however far she was willing to take this, he would not, *could* not, go as far as he wanted. But he couldn't quite resist sliding a finger along the ribbon that held up her garter, the knowledge of what the bit of frippery guarded making his fingers tremble. A world of temptation in that ribbon.

And a world of temptation in this woman.

"Odd", he'd called this thing stretching between them. He'd meant it. He could think of no other word that so adequately described the feelings she evoked in him, this sensation of wanting something so desperately, and yet not knowing where he was heading, or what he was doing. She'd called him fickle and foolish, and perhaps he *was* both those things.

But it was telling, perhaps, how steadfast he was in those sentiments.

No matter how hard he pushed her away, no matter how forcefully he drove himself in the opposite direction, he kept circling back to her.

He was an experienced rake. He'd welcomed women more worldly than this one into his bed, and made sure each one left happy. He was not supposed to tremble at the thought of untying a simple silk ribbon, or lowering a wisp of stocking. And yet, here he was, his fingers shaking as the ribbon slid free of its loops, a whisper of silk and sin. As he hooked his fingers about the top of her stocking, he met her gaze. She was staring down at him, eyes wide, her hair a dark curtain of rain about her shoulders and her sweet swell of chest rising and falling in encouragement.

Perhaps . . . perhaps there was *something* to be done here. Something beyond a mumbled, false apology. Something that would keep her innocence—and his sanity—intact, but still thrum the cords of pleasure he could feel vibrating beneath her skin.

He slowly began to inch the silk stocking down her leg, all the while watching her face for signs to guide this journey. A small puff of a sigh escaped her lips. Her eyes fluttered closed, and her hands curled against the velvet seat.

He hesitated as the stocking rounded her knee. What did that sigh mean? He felt out of his depth with uncertainty, wanting her with a ferocity that would have made those who thought they knew him fall down in spasms of laughter. How fast and hard the mighty fall.

If she told him "no" again—which was a word he knew well could fall so easily from those lips—he would stop. Leave them both wanting and unsatisfied, though he knew he had the power to bring at least *one* of them to completion this night.

But no . . . she was shifting against the velvet seat.

Slipping out of her shoes. Lifting her leg, ever so slightly.

Granting him an undreamed of permission.

A groan of approval slid out of him as he took the advantage she offered. He slid the silk lower, over the sweet, rounded curve of her calf, past a trim ankle. And then he turned his attention to the other side, repeating the process, moving by scant inches, until at last her legs were beautifully bared for him. He sank back on his heels, his heart a bloody hammer against his ribs. She had the *loveliest* legs, begging for the sort of attention he knew how to give.

He turned himself over to the pleasure of providing it. Pressed his mouth against the sweet curve of skin. Inhaled the lemon essence of her, sharply innocent and yet the most seductive fragrance possible. He kissed his way up the length of her leg, lingering on every curve, every hollow.

And all the while, his thoughts wrapped greedily around the sound of her pants and moans, filing them away for later dissection and enjoyment.

He nipped along the tender skin of her thighs, pushing the wire cage of her crinoline aside with a frustrated hand. Damned modern things, blocking a man's way to a woman's pleasure. His fingers slipped through the opening in her drawers. Brushed her damp curls, searching for her core. When he found it, relief and lust threatened to swamp him. She was slick with promise. At last, he could read her, though he doubted she realized she was now an open book. She wanted this. Wanted *him*.

His fingers found the place that made her hips lift, pleading, toward his hand. The very heart of a woman, the doorway to her desire. He slipped a finger inside her. Felt her quim tighten deliciously. Ah, God, but he wanted this woman. Wanted to see her undressed, flushed with pleasure beneath him, her eyes wide with the wonder he could show her. But all they had was this stolen moment, crinolines and coach seats and nighttime shadows. He would make it count, for her. He could do nothing else.

He took a moment to learn her. Focused on her small, breathy sighs, the way her body twisted toward his fingers. The sounds she made nearly made him spill in his trousers, but this was about *her* pleasure, not his, and so he forced his mind away from the demands of his own body. She helped him along, her gasps of pleasure like a symphony to his ears. She was twisting beneath him now, her hands roped through his hair, that telltale pressure against his scalp like a guidebook to her spiraling pleasure. He paid attention to that miraculous touch against his hair. Adjusted his approach. Added a second finger to her inner exploration, curling his fingers into the heart of her. *There*. He could tell by the way she drew in a sharp breath.

He'd found her, sorted her out.

Her breaths became pants, and her hands fisted to the point of near-pain against his scalp. He was relentless, driving her toward the cliff he knew awaited her, luring her over the point of hesitation, until he could feel her, trembling on the edge. He placed his thumb against her swollen nub. Pressed it there, insisting.

"Let go, Mary," he breathed, begging her to take the chance.

She slid over the abyss, her body rigid, the discovery of her own potential for pleasure a desperate cry on her lips. Her body convulsed about his needy fingers, the breath whooshing out of her. He'd never seen a more beautiful sight. And then she was settling back to earth, her eyes closed, her quim rippling about his fingers.

He tried to remember if he'd ever delivered a woman's pleasure with no expectation or possibility of finding his own. Couldn't think of a time.

The sight of her, tousled and languid, tempted him to dive back in and convince her of the need for another go. But instead, he slowly collected himself. Pulled her skirts back down. Smoothed a hand down her leg. He couldn't do much about the stockings.

Re-dressing a woman was a skill he'd never needed to learn.

He collected the filmy silk underthings from the floorboards, along with her gloves. Placed the items on her lap. Rocked back on his heels and waited for her to say something. *Anything.*

Her eyes fluttered open. "That was . . . ah . . . quite climactic."

He chuckled at her choice of word. "Are such things not discussed in those books you are always reading?" he teased. "You can do that endlessly. As many times and as often as you wish. Men, usually, need a bit of time between goes."

Though, he suspected that for him, that time would be

remarkably short, if she was the reward waiting at the end of his recovery.

He slipped her shoe back onto her bare feet, trying to sever the lustful nature of his thoughts. It didn't work. He was wound tighter than a clock tower, and relief was not to be found in this coach tonight. He dared to meet her eyes. Felt bowled over by the way she looked, her hair falling over her shoulders, her skin dewy in the meager light. He'd done that to her. He'd done that *with* her. And God help him, he wanted to do more.

Instead, he pushed away from where he was kneeling. She'd crawled under his skin, somehow. Made him lose his wits every time she walked into a room. Oh, but the things he could show her, if given half a chance. But no matter how delightful this interlude, no matter how passion flared so readily between them, she didn't want him as a husband. Had made it abundantly clear. So he stood up as well as he could in the body of the cramped coach. Straightened his jacket and turned the latch on the coach door.

Climbed outside into the streetlight and offered her his hand. She stared down at it, her mouth slightly open, her lips still swollen from his kiss.

"Come now, let's get you inside quickly now," he prompted. "Before your sister discovers you are gone."

That, finally, shook her out of her hesitation. She placed one bare hand in his, her gloves and stockings clutched in the other, and climbed out in a froth of wrinkled skirts and mussed hair.

They walked up the steps in silence. "Do you have a key?" he asked as they came to the front door.

"Yes. I lifted it from Mrs. Greaves's key ring during afternoon tea." She opened the front door, and her gaze met his over her shoulder. "I . . . well . . . that is . . ." She worried her lip in her teeth. "I suppose this is good night, then?"

He nodded stiffly. "Good night, Miss Channing. Sleep well."

As the door closed and he heard the sound of the key in the lock, he leaned his forehead against the door, trying to wrestle his emotions under control. He'd long imagined they would be a combustible mix when they finally found a way to do more than spar, and tonight had proven his suspicions true. What were they *doing*, pursuing this strange, dangerous folly?

She'd been correct when she'd pointed out that more often than not they rubbed in opposite directions. He felt like a foolish young man again, panting after that untouchable nun in the vestibule of the *Cattedrale di Santa Maria del Fiore*. Not even two weeks ago, this woman had refused his more honorable overtures. He could ask her to marry him again, but he suspected he would know her answer.

No. A thousand times, no.

Hell, she'd nearly refused his request tonight for a simple, uncomplicated dance. And could he blame her? She thought him a rake. He'd all but proven it tonight, kissing her in such a manner when he ought to be running in the complete opposite direction. He would be the first to admit he would make a terrible husband. And that meant this simmering thing stretching between them could go no further, could end nowhere but these front steps—for her own safety, as much as his own sanity.

There was no other choice.

He himself was as much a danger to her as the damned assassins.

From the Diary of Miss Mary Channing
June 12, 1858

After all that passed between us tonight, West delivered me to my front door with neither another kiss to say good-bye, nor a promise to meet me on the morrow. I had imagined, perhaps, that after sharing such an intimate moment, things had shifted between us.

That he considered me a partner.

Potentially something more.

It is embarrassing, really, to think of how easily I fell under his spell tonight. I should be angry with him, but instead I feel a mindless confusion. He isn't doing anything to find the assassins—at least, not that I can see. If Westmore would only give me some hint that he has the situation well in-hand, I would leave it to him. But he does nothing except drag me from ballrooms and distract me with heart-stopping kisses.

And now we have lost another day.

Chapter 14

*M*ary sat up in her bed, blinking in awareness. She could hear the echo of a clock somewhere down the hallway, outside of her locked door. She held her breath, counting. Five chimes.

Five o'clock then.

She glanced toward her locked window, the thick air already hinting at the warm day to come. Perhaps she should start sleeping with her window open. After all, she no longer had a need to be afraid of her villain from the garden. He'd delivered her to her front door with her virtue intact. As though he couldn't wait to be rid of her.

And then through the window, she had watched him saunter off toward the south of Mayfair, in the direction of Madame Xavier's. Which was really neither here nor there: where he spent his nights should not be her primary concern. But drat the man, last night he'd destroyed any chance they'd had to identify the traitors, with his possessive performance and his ready distractions.

He really was rather good at this business of ruining opportunities. And people.

Not that she was offering up much by way of a hazard to either enterprise.

Confused by her feelings, and irritated with herself for succumbing so easily to his charms, Mary reached over to turn up her low-burning lamp. In truth, she was as irritated with herself as she was at West. The debacle behind the library curtains might be debated as to cause and effect, but the responsibility for last night's misadventure could be laid at no feet but her own. But, *oh,* how he'd touched her. The sounds she had made, the things she had felt . . .

She supposed she would now be counted amongst the man's many conquests.

A number, a notch on his bedpost.

At least she'd accomplished *something* memorable during this trip to London.

She picked up her diary, intending to relieve some of her frustration in another journal entry, but before she could pick up her pen, something fell out into her lap. Reaching down, she lifted up a folded note with a plain, unmarked wax seal. Curious, she broke the seal and opened it.

The words swam menacingly toward her.

> *Have a care, Miss Channing.*
> *You are asking questions that will get you killed.*

For a moment, Mary sat frozen, one hand over her mouth, her heart tearing a hole through her chest. The words were printed in a hasty scrawl, the very loops of the letters as threatening as a noose. But the shape and meaning of the words themselves seemed almost irrelevant, compared to the inherent threat present in the appearance of the note itself.

Someone had placed it in her journal.

Someone had been in her *room*, rifling through her personal effects while she slept, intruding on her innermost thoughts.

Panic thickened inside her. She felt powerless. Violated. *Vulnerable*. It was as if she was once again that terrified, ten-year-old girl, helpless to protect herself against an unseen danger that seemed determined to snuff out the lives of those most dear to her.

But then, with a relieved gasp, she realized who must have left the note. Not just someone. The man ever-most present on her mind.

That damned Westmore.

Just who did he think he was, after everything that had passed between them last night, sneaking a note like that into her private journal? And *how* had he done it, given that her door—and her window—had been locked tight? Perhaps he had paid a maid with a key to slip it between the pages, though just what he would have paid the servant with, she didn't want to contemplate. Probably mind-drugging kisses.

It *had* to be him. She recalled his warnings of the previous evening, his specific choice of words. He claimed she was asking dangerous questions, and she hadn't believed him.

He'd decided that last night's threats weren't enough, and was resorting now to a childish prank to make his point.

She swung her legs over the side of the bed, snatching up her wrapper. Well, she wasn't going to sit here cowering in her room, or allow herself to be bullied. With the note crumpled in her hand, she flew down the stairs and plunged out into the early morning light, aiming for the intimidatingly large manor house three doors down. She rapped on the door knocker, a thousand insults flashing through her mind. But when the door was opened, those insults died on her tongue. An elderly butler stood in the doorway in his night shirt, holding up a candle and looking as surprised to see her as she was to see him.

Drat it all, of *course* Westmore wouldn't open his own

front door at half past five in the morning. He likely hadn't even come home from the night before.

She pulled her wrapper more tightly about her. "Is Mr. Westmore home?" she asked in a tight, small voice. She lifted her hand, with its crumpled paper. "I need a word with him."

The servant opened the door wider. "What has Master Geoffrey done this time?" the man said, shaking his balding head. He motioned her forward. "Please, do come in, miss. If nothing else, you can wait in the drawing room until he stumbles his way home from whatever gutter is occupying his attention at present."

To WEST'S MIND, the early morning sun peeking over Grosvenor Square seemed clearer than usual. Or perhaps that clarity was owed to his unfortunate sobriety?

After seeing Mary home, he'd made his way to White's, keeping the earlier promise he'd made to Grant. He'd spent several hours with an untouched drink in one hand, ears tuned to the room's surrounding conversation, watching his friend fall ever deeper into his cups. When Grant had suggested a visit to Madame Xavier's, he'd declined.

What would be the point? Vivian was gone, and there were more important matters holding his attention at present. Scarlet and her dubious charms were not chief among them.

As Grant had staggered off in search of a splendid frolic, he'd pulled out Mary's list of dukes, running through each one in his mind. Most were far too old—the whispered voice in his head almost certainly belonged to someone young and arrogant. But there were enough possibilities to leave him stumped. It looked like Mary was right, in her approach, if not her enthusiasm. He needed a more methodical way of sorting through the list than lurking in shadows and trying to match voices to the one in his memory.

Not that he would ever admit such a thing to her.

Finally, when the staff at White's began straightening the chairs and collecting empty glasses, he'd picked himself up and headed home, the need for sleep muddying his thoughts. But even as he fit his key to the lock, West dreaded the thought of finding his bed and the nightmares he knew would await him there. His gaze drifted down the street, three houses to the left. No. 29 Grosvenor Square. Perhaps he ought to find *her* bed instead.

He suspected his dreams would be more pleasant, at any rate.

Unexpectedly, the front door jerked open, carrying his key with it. "Nice of you to finally come home this evening, Master Geoffrey." Wilson loomed in the doorway, his wrinkled face seemingly more in focus than usual. Of course, there was no whisky involved to take off the sting of the servant's disapproval this morning. "Though, evening no longer seems the appropriate term."

West pushed past the butler, the idea of sneaking into Mary's room withering to nothing but a twitch of want. More than likely, she'd greet him by whacking a bloody book over his head, and then produce a list she'd written of all the reasons why their continued flirtation was a very poor idea. "Not now, Wilson, I've had a hell of a night." He pulled a weary hand across his face. "I am not in the mood for another one of your lectures."

"Though it appears you are in the mood for a visitor," Wilson replied calmly. "I've placed her in the drawing room. Though, given her state of undress, I suppose your bedroom might have been just as appropriate."

West stared at the old servant. He'd never, not once in his life, brought a woman home to Cardwell House. This was where his demons lived, where his nightmares stalked him. "Who on earth are you talking about?" he demanded.

"Your paramour did not provide her name. I took the liberty of *not* informing your parents."

"But I don't have a—" West's protest that he didn't have a paramour trailed away. In fact, he hadn't had a single woman since that mouse of a virgin had snuck her way into his life.

Which meant it could be only one woman who was waiting for him.

He pushed open the door to the drawing room, his heart thumping its eagerness, though just a few hours before he'd berated himself for touching her. She was standing by the front window, her hands clutching the thin white muslin of her night wrapper. Seeing her virginal image, so at odds with the siren she had been in his coach last night, he felt a bit as if someone had kicked him in the stomach.

Or the very stones she had accused him of lacking.

"Miss Channing," he said, deciding that formality was as good a defense as any. "To what do I owe the pleasure this morning?" Though, it might be more correct to say she owed him the pleasure, after last night.

She regarded him with an intensity he couldn't quite define. "I watched you come up the steps. You seem quite steady. You . . . ah . . . haven't been out drinking?"

"No." He shook his head. *More's the pity.*

She hesitated. "Have you been to see Scarlet?"

"No. I haven't seen Scarlet since our visit to the brothel last Sunday." He took a step toward her, shattering his resolve to keep his distance. "You should know that Wilson is under the impression that *you* are my chosen diversion for the evening." He loosened a low chuckle. "Or the morning, as the case may be."

Her eyes widened. "But . . . why would he think that of me?"

"Probably because he would believe it of *me*." West stepped closer, until she was standing within an arm's length. He gave his eyes permission to drift over her body. "And you dressed the part." The gentle scent of lemons tickled his nose. He shook his head, trying to clear the buzz she always seemed to cause out of his brain. "What do you want, Mouse?" he asked, abandoning both his stiff formality and his predatory march. "It's been a long, tiring night and I need to find my bed." And, if he was lucky, a dreamless sort of sleep.

Her hand pushed forward, a piece of crumpled paper clasped in it. "Not so long or tiring you couldn't find the time to do *this*, it seems."

He eyed the bit of paper in her hand, wondering why her voice sounded so strained. "Another list?" He took it from her hand. "You might wait until I've had a chance to finish investigating your first three lists."

"It's not a list," she said, her voice a hard knot. "As you well know."

He unfolded it and stared down at the paper. His gut clenched as he read the words. "Where did you get this?" he demanded, finding it hard to breathe.

"You placed it in my journal."

"No. I didn't. Why would you think I would do such a thing?"

"And after you lectured me last night about the danger in asking questions, I thought . . . perhaps . . . you were trying to teach me a lesson." Her voice trailed off, and her chin started to tremble a bit. "It *has* to have been you, West. You are joking with me now."

"You just received it? Last night?" The blood pounded in his ears, very near the same feeling he'd once felt in battle. A battle where men had died, in spite of his best efforts.

He wasn't properly armed. Not for this.

"It can't have been me," he said tersely. "You saw me come in. When would I have had time to do such a thing?"

"I . . . that is . . ." She trailed off, uncertain.

To hammer home this point—and because God knew he had a trickster's reputation to overcome—he strode to the writing desk on the far side of the drawing room. Opening a drawer with an angry rattle, he pulled out a sheet of paper, scribbled something on it, and then stalked back, shoving it at her. "*This* is my handwriting. See? It doesn't match."

The color drained from her face. "But if not you," she whispered, "then—"

"You said you found it in your journal?" he snarled, grateful that at last she was starting to believe him. "Where do you keep it?"

"By my bed!" she cried, losing her composure now. "I wrote a journal entry before I went to bed last night, and I know it wasn't there then. That meant someone came into my room while I was sleeping." She swallowed. "My *locked* room, West." She began to pant, small beads of perspiration shining against her forehead. "The window was locked, too."

West crushed the paper in his hand. "That means someone used a key." He hesitated. "Or else picked the lock."

"What am I going to do?" she cried.

West wanted to smash a fist against the wall. Instead, he pulled her into the cage of his arms, determined to protect her, even from herself. He'd told her she was behaving dangerously, but the warning had come too late. He burrowed his nose in the citrus scent of her hair, and his gut clenched with the need to keep her safe. He thought back to last night, how he'd watched her from the hallway, envy making his skin itch. He'd watched her speak to a dozen different people before he'd whisked her home. The traitor must have been one of them.

"I think the more appropriate question," he said, worry thickening his voice, "is what are *we* going to do? I would not leave you to face this alone." He held her tightly, unwilling to loosen his grip, though his body was responding to such closeness in a very instinctive way, no matter the danger lurking outside their door.

He wanted her.

But wanting her and having her were not the same thing. And the thought he might lose her to an assassin's bullet made him break out in a cold sweat.

THROUGH THE POUNDING of her ears, it occurred to Mary that her face was pressed against an evening jacket that smelled faintly of smoke and spirits.

The scent reminded her he was a scoundrel.

Not to be trusted. And yet, somehow, with his arms around her, she felt . . . safer.

Though she wanted to burrow closer, climb inside him and curl into a ball, she forced herself to pull back. "I am so, so sorry, West," she said, wiping her eyes. "I imagined you were just playing another prank. But you were right all along. If I hadn't barged about the ballroom last night, asking those awful questions—"

"Stop," he interrupted, his face darker than she'd ever seen it. In a book, a man who looked like that . . . well, a heroine ought to run fast and furious in the other direction. But the knowledge that his anger was not directed toward her made her want to dive back into the shelter of his arms.

"It is done," he ground out, "and so now we need to focus on removing you from harm's way. Someone within Ashington's household staff must have placed that note, which means you cannot stay there, not anymore." He looked toward the door, as if mulling over a decision. "You will stay here at Cardwell House until I can sort out who sent this note."

It was not posed as a question.

But no matter the impropriety of it, his words brought an awareness that heretofore had been lacking. "Eleanor!" Mary gasped. She lifted a fist to her mouth, thinking of Dr. Merial's warnings and servants sneaking into locked rooms to leave threatening notes. "Oh, West . . . my sister. She is not in the best health, and Lord Ashington isn't due back for two more weeks." Her knees threatened to buckle. "I will never forgive myself if I have brought harm to her or the baby."

His jaw tightened. "Then Lady Ashington will stay here as well."

Mary's heart lurched. He was promising her the impossible. Safety. Shelter. "But—"

"No buts, Mary. I need to know you are safe, in order to focus my efforts to track down the traitors. I can't do that with you there, unprotected."

"You . . . are trying to track them down?" She gulped, trying to understand. "But last night, at the ball, you said . . . that you didn't care any longer. That we should forget what we heard in the library."

"I only said that because I didn't want you to do anything rash," he growled. "I've been working this trail as hard as I can, trying to get enough evidence that Scotland Yard would *have* to believe me. For God's sake, I even visited Bedlam! And in the evenings, I have been attending every possible social event where a duke might be present, listening for that whisper of a voice I can't get out of my head." He exhaled slowly. "Why else do you think I have been out so late at night?"

"I had thought, perhaps, you'd been visiting Madame Xavier's."

"No. What would be the point of returning to the brothel when the trail there has gone cold?" He reached toward the bell rope. "There is no time to waste. I will send Wilson over to collect your sister."

"Wait!" she cried out, panicked. She clutched at his arm, pulling him away. "We can't stay *here*."

"Well, you aren't staying there, not with a lunatic on staff in that house."

"We don't know he is a lunatic." She offered him a tremulous smile. "After all, it could still be the Fenians."

"Be serious," he barked down at her.

"All right. Let's be serious, then. The rumors are already rife thanks to our unfortunate incident at the literary salon, and if this morning's gossip rags really do include mention of our dance, it will be even worse. My sister doesn't trust you, West. She will never agree to let me stay here."

"Tell her the truth, then."

She heaved out a frustrated breath. It was all too tangled, too complicated, and—as her sister grew ever larger—too dangerous. "I wasn't lying in the coach last night. Telling Eleanor about the plot we overheard and the fact that some-one on her staff is involved might well send her into a di-sastrous, early labor. Dr. Merial said she is to avoid undue excitement." She pressed her hand against her throat, know-ing that whatever she did, she was posing a danger to her sister. The only question was, which was the least dangerous course? "I would do anything to protect her, to shield her from that."

"Even die?"

She sucked in a startled breath. "I . . . that is . . ."

"This isn't a prank, Mary. It is a threat, and a very explicit one at that. You can't stay there, not until we uncover the traitors and link them to whoever left this."

IT WAS HARD to understand why this was even a discussion they were having.

Mary was in danger, and she needed to find a safer place to stay.

Why was she being so bleeding obstinate about this?

"Would you consider returning home to Yorkshire?" West asked, though he was beginning to think anywhere other than Cardwell House was too dangerous.

"It would be too dangerous for Eleanor to travel all the way to Yorkshire in her advanced state, and I can't leave my sister behind, not when whoever did this is still in the house."

She rubbed a finger against her forehead, looking distraught. "Could I stay at your sister's house? Dr. Merial was my family's physician when I was younger. Surely they would be willing to take me in, and while not strictly proper—"

"We cannot ask them." West shook his head. "They have three small children, and I don't want to put my niece and nephews in harm's way." He tossed about for other possibilities. His sister Lucy's London house was similarly bursting with children, the youngest not yet even six months old, and Lydia lived in Lincolnshire now, a similarly impossible journey. "Is there some reason you are afraid to stay at Cardwell House? Beyond the issue of what people may say or think? Because truly, they already think the worst of us."

"Can't you see?" She looked close to crying. "I can't stay here with you, not with your reputation. And my . . . weakness." She buried her face in her hands.

He stared down at her, agape. *Weakness?* She was quite possibly the strongest woman he'd ever met—that single, uncharacteristic fainting spell notwithstanding. But at least now he understood the reasons for her hesitancy. She was afraid of whoever placed that note, but she was also afraid to stay here.

With him.

This thing between them . . . it *was* dangerous. But not as dangerous as leaving her to fend for herself. Almost two weeks ago, he'd had to drag himself up the steps of No. 29 Grosvenor Square to offer for her, feeling as if he was staring down the barrel of a loaded rifle. But things were different now. She'd received a note threatening her life, and she was worried more about her sister's health than her own life. He respected that.

And he would not do this in a way that marred her reputation any further.

He reached in his jacket pocket and pulled out a piece of paper. "I imagine this would help your sister come around.

She couldn't say 'no' to the notion of you staying here, at any rate."

She gasped, looking down. "But . . . this is a special license!"

He nodded. It was the very one he'd obtained the morning after the literary salon. He'd taken to carrying it around in his pocket as a reminder to stay far away from her, though the reminder had gotten harder and harder as the days had dragged by. "A wedding ceremony would permit us to place an announcement in the *Times*, let the world know you have my protection. That should send a stern message to whoever did this."

"Surely there is another way," she protested, her voice close to a squeak.

"I cannot see one." And he wanted to make her lean *this* way, with a ferocity that had only partly to do with the danger. Whatever the reasons, the direction felt right. Little else did at the moment. "I swear, Mary, I will do everything in my power to protect you." He stepped closer, taking up her hand. "You did say you would do anything to keep your sister safe."

"But . . . that is . . . I would be nothing but a burden to you." Her eyes searched his. "You don't *want* to marry me." She swallowed. "Do you?"

He stepped toward her. "Don't I?" He turned himself over to the truth he'd been running from since that moment when she'd first told him "no". "Even if there wasn't an assassin's plot, or the danger to your sister . . . I would want this." He lowered his head, until his lips were brushing against her temple. "I would want *you*," he murmured against her skin.

"Oh," she breathed, and as he pulled back, he could see that his gesture had brought a welcome bit of color to her cheeks. But had it convinced her?

"I . . . that is . . ." Her brow pinched, and he didn't—couldn't—say anything, even though his breath was close to bursting from his chest as he waited for her answer. "I suppose," she said, her chin lifting up and then down, "my answer would be yes, then."

West wanted to pull her into his arms, to kiss her senseless and make short work of the thin cotton that lay between them. Instead, he yanked on the bell pull.

There was no time to waste, and a dozen things to do.

"But what if Eleanor still refuses to come here?" she asked, wrapping her slender arms about her body. "She thinks you are a degenerate."

"Well then, we can invent a reason. Something unlikely to cause her harm, but dire enough to force her to seek temporary shelter here at Cardwell House."

"I suppose we might let loose a few rats in the foyer?"

Though it was a brilliant suggestion, a shudder worked its way down West's spine. "God, no," he choked out. "Not rats. Perhaps an infestation of fleas instead. If she is worried about the health of her unborn child, she will do what she must." He grabbed her hand and pulled her toward Wilson, who had materialized at the drawing room door.

If he could keep her close, he could keep her safe.

She would not die, not on his watch.

And he would willingly kill any man—or woman—who thought otherwise.

From the Diary of Miss Mary Channing
June 13, 1858

It seems I am to be married.

I know . . . I can scarcely believe it myself. The entire thing feels like a torrid novel, where in order to escape a villain, the heroine is forced to marry against her will, the circumstances spiraling beyond her control. But it isn't <u>exactly</u> against my will. It's something I brought upon myself, and West is being exceedingly chivalrous to sacrifice himself in this way.

I know I would never be his first choice for a wife. But truth be told, even if the circumstances were different, I would have been tempted to say "Yes."

And that has me worried for a different set of reasons.

Chapter 15

"*E*leanor, for heaven's sake, *you* are the one who told me I needed to stop reading unrealistic novels and find a husband. My present circumstances have imperiled any future chance for a good match, and so I've decided to do something to erase the scandal hanging over me by the only means possible. What does it matter whom I marry, as long as it is done?"

But even as she shaped the lie, Mary anxiously watched Eleanor's face for signs of distress, worried that this unwelcome news, while better than word of a possible assassin on the household staff, might still be enough to send her sister into labor. God knew she was already doubting her own agreement to this crazy plan.

What was she *thinking*, agreeing to marry West?

The armed footman hovering in the hallway did little to settle her fears, though she was grateful that West had reluctantly agreed to her demand that he not accompany her himself. It was hard enough to have this conversation with Eleanor without giving it all away. The last thing she needed was a handsome blond scoundrel glowering over her shoulder.

Thankfully, her sister seemed more interested in doubting her capacity for rational thought than succumbing to panic. "While I can concede it is important for you to marry someone, and rather quickly at that, whom you marry matters a good deal when the man in question is that damned Westmore!" Eleanor retorted.

"Well, he is the only one who has asked me," Mary pointed out.

Eleanor waved a fist, clutching the scandal sheets—which had indeed printed the news of Mary's eventful night out. "A fact which would not have happened again if you hadn't snuck out last night to dance with the scoundrel!"

Mary spread her hands. "I can admit Westmore isn't the optimum choice for a husband. He's rude and crude and a bit too handsome for his own good. But the point is, I doubt I will receive another offer, particularly now that I've made the scandal sheets a second time. And I *do* so want to be a wife. A mother. Like you." She smiled, hoping she looked at least a little besotted with the man. "I cannot help but feel this is my only chance for happiness."

A lie, that. Because beneath such a flimsy, fabricated argument ran a ribbon of solid steel. In the end, Mary hadn't hesitated to say yes. Hadn't considered whether her answer might be based more on want than need. It might be unfathomable to her sister, but deep in her heart, in a place she didn't care to unlock for further dissection, she *wanted* to be Mrs. Geoffrey Westmore.

Good heavens. No wonder her sister doubted her sanity.

Eleanor began to look uncertain. "You really . . . like him?" she asked dubiously. "You do not mind his . . . er . . . significant reputation?"

The blush that claimed Mary's cheeks did not have to be manufactured. Did she like him? She was afraid she might feel more for him than such a bland, simple emotion.

But she was terrified, too. He was a man of a certain reputation. He made her feel things. *Deeply*. And as worried as he seemed to be for her safety, she was equally worried for his. They were tracking potential killers, one of them the most powerful of peers. History had taught her that love, whether for a father, a brother—or, she feared, a future husband—could be lost in the space of a moment. And in spite of his assurances that he wanted to marry her, in spite of her own desires, she couldn't shake the feeling she was agreeing to a future heartache.

"I know he is a bit of a rogue, but perhaps I might yet shape him into a better man," she said softly, wondering if perhaps she was giving too much rein to her imagination once again. After all, heroines might change the men they loved in books, but as she was discovering, things were a bit more difficult when experienced in the flesh.

In response to such nonsense, Eleanor gave a soft cry, swatting at her arm.

Mary looked down as something pinched her wrist as well. She could see a half dozen fleas, jumping across the lace edging of her sleeve, and hid a relieved smile to see her future husband was a man who kept his promises, even when they were of the "vermin-producing" variety.

"Fleas!" she cried, leaping to her feet.

"Fleas?" Eleanor echoed, looking dazed.

"There must be an infestation."

"But . . . we don't even have a dog! Or a cat . . ."

Inspiration seized Mary. "Well, you probably ought to get one, don't you think?"

"Why would you say that?"

"Because if you had a dog, or a cat you probably wouldn't have rats, which is no doubt where the fleas are coming from." As Eleanor turned pale, Mary pulled her sister to her feet. "Come on, then, you can't stay here. We'll need to call an expert in to deal with it." She all but dragged Eleanor from the bedroom. "But do not worry, you can stay with me tonight."

"Stay with you?" Eleanor asked in confusion. "Where?"

"At Cardwell House. After all, where else would I spend my wedding night?"

"TODAY?" WEST'S MOTHER asked, her hand fluttering about her high lace collar. She looked around the drawing room in horror. "*Here?*"

"This evening," he affirmed. "Six o'clock."

"But . . . we've no flowers!" his mother protested. "And I'll have to send cook to the market if we are to arrange a wedding luncheon—"

"We do not require flowers." It wasn't as if this was a joyous celebration. Someone had threatened Mary's life. The more planning that was put into this furtive ceremony, the more delay that was introduced, the more chance there was for something to go wrong. "Or a wedding luncheon," he added, seeing his mother's forehead wrinkle in objection. "We wish to keep everything simple."

To have Mary gone so long from sight made his fingers twitch with worry. He'd accompanied her home, but had been forbidden to stand guard while she spoke with her sister. She'd insisted she needed privacy to convince her sister of this plan, and that his presence would only make things more difficult. Still, he'd dispatched his own footman to stand guard—he didn't trust any of Ashington's staff—and pressed his pistol into the man's hand, warning him to be on guard. He'd dutifully loosened the fleas on his way out.

And he'd been on edge, every moment since.

His father laid a hand on his shoulder. "Geoffrey. I can see you are eager to have this done, but could we not even wait until tomorrow? Why such hurry? For heaven's sake, it's a Sunday. And we need time to send an invitation to your sisters."

"I already sent a footman to Lucy's house a half hour ago," West countered, "and Wilson is delivering an invitation to

Clare as we speak. I am afraid it is too late to summon Lydia from Lincolnshire, but I will simply have to beg her forgiveness when we see her at Christmas. I've sent a note to Grant, although I suspect it will be a miracle if he wakes in time to read it. They have all been instructed to be here by six o'clock this evening. Never fear, there will be the appropriate number of witnesses."

His father took off his glasses, and peered myopically at West, as if trying to see his son for the very first time. "For God's sake, Geoffrey, it isn't only about witnesses. We've not yet even *met* Miss Channing. I know you intended to marry the girl after that business with the gossip rags, but I thought she had refused you, to our great relief."

West bristled. Why should his parents be relieved Mary had initially refused him? And why would they hesitate to wish him well now? "When you meet her, you will think she is wonderful, as I do. I'll have you know I feel fortunate to be marrying this woman."

At their matching shocked expressions, he realized, then, how odd such a thing sounded coming from him. And how odd it felt to realize that it wasn't even a lie.

He *did* think she was wonderful. He *was* fortunate. The threats delivered by that note may have provided the means to this marriage, but he was by no means averse to the outcome.

"It isn't that we object to Miss Channing," his mother protested. "It's that we haven't had a chance to meet her. You've never shown the slightest interest in a woman before, at least not seriously." She hesitated a telling moment. "Does she know what she is getting in you?"

West realized, then, that perhaps they weren't worried about him so much as they were worried about her. He was glad, perhaps, that their doubts were of the more familiar variety, a disappointment in him, rather than a disapproval of her. "I think she has a fair notion. And in spite of it, I vow to do my best to make her a good husband." He turned on his heel. "I will leave the preparations to you then, Mother." He aimed for the door. "No flowers. No luncheon. No guests beyond family and Grant."

"But Geoffrey!" his mother's voice tugged at him. "Where are you going?"

"I need to buy a wedding gift." And given his future wife, he knew just the one.

BY HALF PAST six, it was done.

The vows were mumbled, the rings exchanged. The sure, quick pressure of West's lips against her own told the small audience of family and friends that she now belonged to him, but the gesture sent confusion cascading through her.

No matter his earlier claims to the contrary, he'd well proven himself a hero this evening, marrying her, giving up his future for her protection. They'd put on a proper show, but did he mean for this to be a real marriage? And what did *she* want out of it, beyond an assurance of Eleanor's safety? All good questions in need of answers.

But first, she had a small gauntlet of guests to survive.

Dr. and Mrs. Merial stepped forward to offer their congratulations, followed by Lady and Lord Cardwell. They welcomed her warmly, though they all seemed a bit dazed by the suddenness of it all. Eleanor drifted away on Mrs. Merial's arm, murmuring something about "needing to find her bed and lie down for a nap." Mary knew Eleanor wasn't happy about the marriage. But no matter how angry or confused she might be, her sister was at least safe.

Mary could not bring herself to apologize, or regret the lengths she'd taken to ensure it.

The stooped, smiling butler who'd opened the door that morning materialized in front of them, clearly as much a part of the family as anyone else in the room. "Mrs. Westmore," the man said with a delighted smile, bowing formally in greeting. "I am so pleased to meet you."

"And I you." Mary smiled, appreciating the kindness she could see on his wrinkled face.

"This is Wilson, our family's butler," West explained. "Enforcer of manners and all around meddler in things that ought not to concern him."

"Whatever you wish, Mrs. Westmore, you have only to ask," Wilson said, chasing it with a small wink. "Especially if it's a proper prank we might play on Master Geoffrey together."

"Oh?" She glanced up at West, who was glaring down at the servant with a mixture of affection and annoyance. "A *proper* prank? I am afraid only the improper ones come to immediate mind. I shall have to wrap my head around that."

"I shall eagerly await your ideas." Wilson bowed again before taking his exit.

"He seems nice," Mary giggled.

"You might wish to reserve judgment until you get to know him better," came her husband's dry reply. "Because if you let him, Wilson will harangue you within an inch of your life."

A sullen, dark-haired gentleman stepped forward next, and the laughter died on Mary's lips. She had noticed the man's belated arrival, which had come nearly at the end of the brief ceremony. How could she not? He was impossible to miss—bleary-eyed, unshaven, two buttons undone on his wrinkled jacket.

And most importantly, glowering at her from the back of the room.

"Grant!" West exclaimed, slapping the man on the back. "So glad you finally deigned to make an appearance at my nuptials."

"Yes, well, it seems I arrived too late," the man growled.

"Well, late or no, I am still glad you cared enough to get out of bed."

"Yes, well, if only I'd done so five minutes earlier, I might have had a hope of changing your course. Now it seems I must pray for an annulment."

West tensed beside her. "Careful, my friend," he said, his voice edged with a warning. "There is no cause for a lack of civility."

"No cause for any of this, near as I can tell. Friends forever, eh?" The man snorted. "What a crock. I can't believe I saved your life, only for you to throw it away like this."

As he pulled a flask from his trouser pocket and tipped it to his lips, Mary felt a frisson of worry. So this was Mr. Grant, West's friend and partner in infamy. Somehow, she felt as though she ought to try to make a good impression, though he clearly had no intention of doing the same. "It is nice to meet you, Mr. Grant," she said softly.

"I wish I could say the same." He scowled at her. "Not that I hold it against you personally, but you've managed to trap a good man with your charms."

"I suspect charm had less to do with it than fate." Mary looped her arm through West's, knowing this performance would set the stage for how they meant to go on. "However I've acquired him, I am grateful. He *is* a good man." Or at least, she wanted to believe he had the potential to be a good man—opera boxes and prostitutes aside. "And I intend to be a good wife," she added, tightening her grip.

"Well, the best wives permit their husbands a certain amount of freedom. I suppose it remains to be seen which category you will fall under." Grant's gaze narrowed toward West. "As a start, will I see you at White's later tonight?"

West shook his head. "I'll be a bit busy, as I am sure you can imagine."

"Oh, I can imagine. You forget, I've spent many an hour with you at Madame Xavier's." Grant snorted, then made a lewd gesture with one hand. "Tomorrow, then?"

Mary could feel West's arm tense beneath her fingers.

"I've only been married ten minutes, Grant. We shall have to see how it all goes."

Grant shook his head. "I hope to God you know what you are doing." And then he made for the door, his flask still fisted in his hand.

"Your friend doesn't seem very . . . friendly," Mary said, low under her breath.

West sighed. "Give him time. He just needs to come to terms with the change in my situation." He pressed a quick kiss to her temple. "And understand that I might prefer to spend time with you on my wedding night instead of him."

Mary nodded, though she couldn't help but suspect there was trouble brewing there.

Finally, there was only one more person left in the drawing room, a blond woman who had earlier been introduced as West's sister, Lady Lucy Branston. She stepped up to have her turn at them. "Couldn't do this the usual way, could you, Geoffrey?" She gave her brother a playful tap on the arm. "Four hours' notice for a wedding invitation? I didn't even have time to fetch Branston from Westminster. I always knew you would crash spectacularly when love finally found you."

"Yes, it's been quite the whirl," West said, not contradicting her in the least.

Mary felt like fidgeting when he didn't do anything to correct his sister's presumption. So, he meant for people to imagine this was a love match? Well, she'd read enough books with happy endings to pretend she knew how to do this.

She only hoped her acting skills were up to the challenge.

"And as for you, I hope you know what you've fallen into." Lady Branston smiled down at Mary. "My brother is a terrible prankster."

"Perhaps I can reform him." Mary beamed at her new sister-in-law, hoping she didn't look like a loon. Or perhaps she ought to look like a loon—if her sister and Lord Ashington were any indication, one turned a bit silly over it all. "Love has a way of changing the staunchest of scoundrels to responsible citizens."

Lucy snorted. "I see you are fond of fairy tales." She leaned in to kiss Mary's cheek. "And you are far too lovely for the likes of my debauched brother." When Mary gaped at her, she laughed. "Oh, but you must pay my teasing no mind. Geoffrey deserves his comeuppance for the ribbing he gave me on my wedding day."

"Also done by special license, if my memory serves," West pointed out.

"Yes, but I believe I gave *you* four days' notice," she retorted, then blew her brother a saucy kiss as she sailed away.

As the room's sudden emptiness pressed in, Mary cut a curious glance at her new husband. He was staring down at her with a smirk on his face that could only be interpreted as . . . *anticipatory*. And then he took her hand and led her out of the drawing room, heading toward the huge, spiraling staircase that led to the upper floors of the house.

"Well, Mrs. Westmore," he said, tugging on her hand. "It is time for the next phase of this mad adventure."

"Do you mean you wish to plan our next steps?" she asked, thinking that by mad adventure he meant the assassination plot. "I haven't had time to work on another list, but if you could find me a pen and paper I could list the gentlemen I spoke with last night—"

"Mary." He pulled her up onto the first step. "You won't need a pen for a solid few hours." His easy smile shifted to something more wolfish. "You must trust me when I say your hands will be too occupied for lists."

Mary swallowed. It was still quite early, not even dark outside yet—surely too soon to be retiring abovestairs. "Do you mean . . . they will be occupied with a fork?" she asked. "Because we've not yet eaten and I do think I could use a—"

The Perks of Loving a Scoundrel   199

"If you are hungry we can have a tray sent up to my bedroom."

She tripped on the bottom stair. He'd said bedroom. *Oh, good heavens.* He wanted to do this *now*? Her free hand gripped the banister. "Wait!" she gasped, scrambling after him, but then her foot hit a place on the stairs that unleashed a loud, spluttering sound.

She froze, her cheeks burning as he looked over his shoulder.

"That is quite a wedding gift you've just given me." His smile curled the edges of his mouth. "Fortunately, I have one for you, too."

She shrank backward. Oh, but how could he think she would do such a thing? It hadn't been her breaking wind, surely he knew that! But that didn't make it any less mortifying.

"Don't look so pained," he chuckled. "It was a joke, and one not even intended for you." He bent down and pulled a flattened object from beneath the step. "See? A windmaker. I like to tease Wilson, every now and again. The man likes to lecture me in return. Somchow, we reach an equilibrium."

Her breath caught in her throat, her own equilibrium anything but reached. She stared at this man who was now for better or worse her husband. He had placed that . . . that . . . *thing* beneath the stairs on purpose? *Good heavens.* Eleanor and Lady Branston had both warned her he was a prankster, but somehow, in the terror of the morning and the need to ensure her sister's safety and the fluttering anticipation of saying "yes", she'd forgotten what this man was capable of.

She was well-reminded now.

"Well then, no wonder Wilson wants to play a proper prank on you," she frowned.

Unrepentant, he tugged her upward until she fell into his arms. She tried to hold tight to her annoyance, but her stomach slid somewhere to her knees as his lips met hers in a kiss far more steeped in promise than the perfunctory wedding kiss he'd given her below. His tongue traced the seam of her closed mouth, urging her to open until finally she did so with a small sigh of surrender. But that, of course, was when he pulled back, drat the man.

"Do not faint on me now." He smirked. "Not until I've got you up the stairs and undressed, at any rate." He tugged at her hand again. "Then you can faint at your leisure."

As he urged her up the last few steps, she forced herself to breathe. Her new husband was a scoundrel of the highest order, and by his own words he meant to undress her. The conversation she'd had with Eleanor nearly two weeks ago flashed through her mind in bits and pieces. He'd had intimate relations with the household governess. Four woman at once.

And oh, good heavens, that bit about the corpse . . .

She'd quite forgotten about that in the chaos of the morning.

Too soon, she found herself pulled into his bedroom. She breathed in deeply, trying to force away the nervousness that plagued her. But that lungful of air only made the fluttering of her stomach intensify. His bedroom didn't *smell* like a den of depravity, which she imagined would smell something like brimstone and opium. No, it smelled like him. Spiced rum and soap. Things that made her muscles clench in pleasant anticipation, not fear.

"If you are wondering where your things are, I suspect the footmen will bring your trunks up later," he said.

"I . . . that is . . ." Her voice trailed off. How to articulate that when asked her preferences earlier, she had instructed the footman to place her trunks and things in the bedroom next door? She'd thought she was being brave at the time, even selfless, giving West his privacy. But now she only felt foolish.

She heard the door shut behind her and the key turn in the lock. She closed her eyes, slivers of doubt scratching at her. This was a man who could have any woman he wanted. He'd married her to protect her, not to ravish her. But then came the creak of rope, the sound of a mattress settling. As she scrunched her eyes tighter, mortified, she heard him chuckle.

"Frightened to watch me undress, Miss Mouse?"

Her eyes flew open. He was sitting on the edge of his bed now, one hand loosening his necktie with slow, lascivious intent.

"No," she choked out, not willing to admit it if she was. She willed herself to be brave. Or at the very least, pretend to be. "And shouldn't it be *Mrs.* Mouse now?" She hesitated, then gave voice to the fear that would not quite let her be. "Or is this just a ruse we shall maintain in public so others don't suspect this is a farce of a marriage?"

"Hardly a farce." He pulled his necktie free of his collar. "It's as proper a marriage as it can be." He placed the necktie to one side. "Or at least it will be, as soon as we divest you of your clothing." He reached into his trouser pocket.

"What . . . are you doing?" she gulped.

He tossed her a bemused smile. Pulled out his revolver, checked the chamber, and placed it on top of the bedside table. "I felt I should disarm myself first." He shrugged out of his jacket, tossing it over the back of a nearby chair. "Don't want to go off half-cocked."

She stared at his face, not wanting to see the silver gleam of the barrel. Too many bad memories there, memories that would only serve to make it all worse, if she gave her imagination permission to drift there. But it seemed, though, by the grin on his face, that he was no longer talking about a gun. "No?" she breathed.

He stepped toward her. "Oh, no. Fully cocked is the only way to do this. And trust me when I say I am already there."

Chapter 16

West reached for his new wife's hand.

Felt the pounding of her pulse through her trembling fingers.

He pulled her down until she was sitting beside him on the mattress, her spine a determined knot. He'd only meant to tease her a little, but it seemed his words had taken them backward, not forward to where he wanted them to be.

"Why are you wound so tightly?" he asked gently. "Surely you aren't frightened of me."

"We did not discuss . . . that is . . ." She stared down at her hands. "I am not . . . proficient in these matters. You say so many things, and I don't . . . I don't even know what you mean when you say half-cocked. Or fully cocked." Her gaze shifted to a distant point on the carpet. "I understand, however," she said, her voice slowing, "that you are *very* experienced."

"Yes." He grinned at her. If there was one good thing he could say of his vast experience on the matter, it was that he knew quite well how to take care of the intimate needs of his new wife, thank you very much.

"*How* experienced?"

Her question caught him off guard. "Experienced enough to make this pleasurable for you. Do you have questions for me about . . . er . . . it?" Because truth be told, he'd rather show her what it was all about. It was arguably one of the things he did best.

Better, even, than practical jokes.

She peeked up at him, worrying her lower lip. "Did you really have relations with your sister's governess?" she blurted out, the words all but tumbling from her.

Bloody hell. So, Mary had questions about his past sexual exploits, did she? She really shouldn't ask questions when it was clear she feared the answers. "Yes," he admitted. "Their former governess, mind you. I was in my first year at university, and came home to London to find she had . . ." He hesitated, but there was no sugar-coating it, was there? "She had aged well," he finished lamely.

"Oh." Mary seemed to mull over that a moment. "I suppose that isn't *so* bad, if you were old enough to be at university. I'd imagined a lad of twelve or so, trying to toss up the governess's skirts."

"I would have probably tried to do such a thing at that age, if I'd thought I would meet with success," he chuckled. "Only, my sisters didn't think twice about boxing my ears when I misbehaved. And they dearly loved their governess."

"That isn't funny, West." A moment passed, where he could almost swear he could hear the cogs turning inside her head. "I had heard . . . that you engaged in intimate relations in public view. With Scarlet at the opera. Is it true?"

West stared at her. "What on earth are you are talking about?"

"Don't try to deny it, West. My sister saw you herself."

He searched his mind. Came up empty. He hadn't done anything of the sort with Scarlet at the opera—though she'd made it clear he could have had her there, if he wanted. He'd left, gone out to have a smoke, annoyed by it all. He'd left her, in fact . . . with Grant.

"That was actually my friend Grant with Scarlet in the box," he answered carefully, the truth clicking into place. He wondered why he didn't feel angrier about it. Probably because Scarlet hadn't meant much to him. Not the way this woman did. "Not me."

"Oh." There was a moment of heavy silence. And then Mary's gaze slid sideways, hot across his skin. "It is said you had four women at once."

"Well, that is simply not true." West's legend was not nearly as large as the gossip implied. His prick, on the other hand . . . well, some rumors one encouraged, especially when there were plenty of whispers to the contrary.

She closed her eyes. "Oh, thank heavens."

"It was only three other women," he clarified. As her eyes flew open, he added, "There is no need to look so shocked. It is not as unusual as you think."

"Did you . . . *enjoy* it?" she asked, stumbling over the question.

"Not as much as I enjoy the full attentions of a single partner," he answered truthfully. There was something distracting about too many arms and legs, not to mention the expectations of too many women. "I like to linger over my lovemaking, and multiple partners don't permit such leisure," he told her, wishing he could somehow soften the slope of those stiff shoulders. Perhaps he should just kiss her. Chase away these doubts the best way he knew how.

"Were two of them . . . sisters?" she asked.

"Good God, no!" The very thought made him break out in a sweat. "How could you think that?" he asked indignantly.

"Eleanor heard about it from Lord Ashington, who must have heard it from someone." She blinked rapidly. "But if it isn't true, then how did such rumors gain a foothold?"

Annoyed now at anyone and everyone who had burned

his new wife's ears with such sordid tales, West leaned back onto the mattress, glaring up at the bed curtains above his head. He wrestled a moment with impatient memories of his past, of the various women who had shared his bed. He didn't regret those experiences, any more than he regretted marrying Mary. But while he didn't give a fig about what others thought of him, he didn't want her thinking so poorly of him. "I don't know how such rumors have persisted, but I am not as depraved as you have been led to believe, Mary." Though, he was depraved enough to want to pull her down beside him and kiss the pinch of uncertainty from her lips.

She gripped the coverlet with two fists. "Then you should know," she said miserably, "you are rumored to have had intimate relations with a corpse."

He chuckled. "Oh, that one is true."

"*What?*"

He let her stew for a moment. But after a second of watching her panicked breathing, he relented. "Mary, it isn't what you think. It was only a barmaid dressed as a corpse. White powder on her face, ragged clothing, chains. It was All Hallows' Eve and we were out guising, having a bit of fun, knocking on doors." He chuckled, which was his usual reaction when remembering that night.

How old had he been, sixteen? Seventeen?

The woman in question had been a local barmaid in Harrow, and well known to the more adventurous youths. She'd been as game for the adventure as he was, rattling her chains and moaning in a theatrical way. That she had chosen to indulge her fun with him instead of Peter Wetford, the now Duke of Southingham, had eventually led to the infamous standoff with the rats. "Well, an *actual* corpse would be beyond the pale, don't you think?" He reached out a finger and trailed it down his wife's wool-covered arm, trying to earn a smile. "I promise you she was very much alive."

Mary jerked away from his touch. "Even if the worst of the rumors aren't true, the parts you have admitted are bad enough. Surely you can see why I would hesitate to be intimate with someone like you."

West lifted himself onto one elbow. "No, darling, I can't."

"But you . . . you've been with so many women!"

"Shouldn't that make you curious?" He wrapped his fingers around her wrist and pulled her down, until she was lying beside him, stiff as . . . well . . . a corpse. "Shouldn't that make you want to jump into my bed?" He lowered his voice, turning on his side to face her. "See what all the fuss is about?"

"No," she whispered, her eyes fluttering half-closed.

There it was, her favorite word again. But she hadn't said "no" below stairs, when she'd recited her vows. And in spite of the tension in her limbs, she didn't sound convinced of her refusal on the matter now, either. "There is more to it than I showed you last night," he pointed out, knowing she had at least enjoyed that much.

"I know," she said, sounding unconvinced. "I have read about it."

"Ah. I see." His lifted his fingers to trail them across her cheek, counting the lack of a resultant flinch as a small victory. He suspected books were part of the problem here. The ones she had been reading had made her too nervous by far. But that only meant she was reading the wrong kind of books. "Well, I enjoy reading myself, on occasion. And if I'm reading you correctly, you want me, every bit as much as I want you."

Her shoulders twitched. "You . . . you want me?" she breathed.

"I do." His fingers danced across the fine curve of her chin.

She bit her lower lip, worrying it in a circle. "Well, *I* don't want the pox."

Good God. His finger stilled. "Is that one of the rumors?" He drew his finger away. "I am not pox-ridden, Mary. You may trust me on that."

"That is just what the villain *always* says." She pushed herself to a sitting position. "But then the heroine always dies at the end."

FOR A MOMENT, he gawped at her.

No doubt he was reconsidering the wisdom of marrying a woman who would accuse him of such a horrid thing. About such a delicate place.

But she'd read far too many books to take it back.

Unexpectedly, a low chuckle escaped his lips. "I suppose you could always examine me." He gestured to the upper area of his trousers, as if daring her to do her worst. "Confirm for yourself that I lack any symptoms. Or, I could provide a doctor's note certifying my good health."

She didn't quite know what to think of that, other than the fact that no hero in her reading memory had ever offered a heroine quite such a choice. "You would have a physician examine you before demanding your rights?" she asked, incredulous.

His smile faltered. "Let us be clear here, Mary, I do not intend to *demand* anything that passes between us. In fact, I plan to have you so thoroughly kissed and pleasured you will beg me to indulge you." He leaned forward, and she held her breath, not at all sure what he was about in this moment. After all, she had just more or less accused him of having the pox.

Slowly, purposefully, he pressed a kiss against her cheek, a featherlight promise of what might come. She could feel his breath, fanning out against her skin, rippling through her like a wave on water. "Pleasure is meant to be shared," he said, his voice low and husky, "not commanded." He pulled back. Met her eye. "I would never want anything but an eager partner in my bed."

Heat flooded her cheeks. *Good heavens*, even her ears felt warm. She was knocked off-kilter by the dark promise in those words, and even more by the wicked hope they inspired. None of the heroes in her precious books had ever said anything like *that*.

She looked down at her hands, knotted in her skirts. She recalled how he had touched her last night, so thoroughly. She had no doubts that he could kiss her until she forgot about the pox and the pretend corpse and the scores of women who had come before her.

Drat it all, he could probably make her forget her own name.

"Unfortunately, pleasure isn't the only thing that can be shared," she said, shaking her head slowly. Oh, how she wished they could just go on with beautiful kisses, and pretend the other pieces of it didn't matter. But her imagination had settled over her like a cold, wet blanket, and it wasn't so easy to pull it off, now that the worst of it had been said.

"Then let me show you this." He pushed up to a sitting position and reached for a drawer in the bedside table.

Mary tried not to notice the way the muscles of his back rippled beneath his silk waistcoat and shirt. Tried, too, to analyze the quiver of her own nerves. Pox-ridden or no, after last night's misadventure in the coach, she could admit he possessed talents that could unlock an immense sort of pleasure. He wasn't the sort of husband she would have chosen from the pages of a book, but he *was* her husband. He could legally demand this of her, whether she hesitated or not.

Why was she acting like such a ninny about it?

He pulled something out of the drawer and turned back around holding a silver case. As he opened it, she saw three objects lying in a nest of blue velvet. They were long, nearly transparent, and had delicate pink ribbons threaded through the tops.

"For you." He held the case out.

She reached out a finger, tracing the outline of one. "What are they?"

"French letters. A brand-new set."

When she snatched her hand away as though touching a snake, he laughed out loud, then laid the box on the bedside table, next to the revolver. "I have always used one faithfully, in all of my exploits. When my brother-in-law Dr. Merial realized my . . . er . . . early proclivities, he encouraged me in their use. They protect the user against the risk of the pox, as well as one's partner from a possible pregnancy."

"I . . . see," she stammered. Though she didn't really.

"If you wish," he said, cocking his head, "we can continue to use one until you are ready to trust me." His eyes softened, and for the first time in this entire conversation, he looked pensive. "Until you can accept my past, and understand that you, alone are my future. I would not hurt you, Mary. Not purposefully."

"Oh." She felt very foolish now. He was putting this choice in her hands.

If she asked him to, he would put one of those on his . . . and she would tie it about his . . . and then they would . . . heat suffused her cheeks.

Well, now she *did* see, thank you very much.

And the part he'd said about she alone being his future . . . the thought made her chest tighten in what felt like hope. She wanted to believe this marriage—while necessary and rushed and somewhat contrived—could evolve into a future happiness. But it was hard to imagine that a man of his legend might be satisfied with only one woman—and a wife, at that—in his bed.

Harder, still, to expect him to keep such a promise, knowing so little as she did about the matters shared between a husband and a wife.

"Thank you. For telling me the truth about your past." At least, she *hoped* it was the truth. There was still so much about this man she felt she did not know. Every layer she peeled back only raised more questions. "And thank you for my wedding gift," she added weakly.

Though, it was surely the strangest gift ever given a bride on her wedding day.

"Oh, that is not your gift." He chuckled, then reached back into the drawer and withdrew a slim novel, presenting it to her with a flourish. "*This* is your wedding gift. I had to go to three different bookstores before I found one who would sell it."

"You are giving me a book?" Tears welled up in her eyes, and her breath grew tight in her throat. She ran a finger over the gold embossed letters of the title, trying to make it out through the sudden shimmer of tears. "*The . . . Lovely . . . Turk?*" She'd never heard of it, but it didn't matter if the author was obscure, or if the writing was terrible.

It was a *book*. Its very existence meant West had thought of her, considered what she might enjoy, and then gone out to purchase it.

Unexpectedly, she felt the press of his thumb against her cheek, wiping away tears. "Not exactly. Look again."

She blinked away the moisture. The letters swam into view. "*The . . . Lustful Turk?*"

"And perhaps, once you've read it, it will prove a gift for both of us."

Chapter 17

He waited to see what she would do.

What she would say.

Given her obsession with books, he'd known immediately what he wanted to get her as a wedding gift, but something of the devil had seized him in the choice of it.

The book had been published nearly three decades before, too salacious for the author to even affix a false name to it. West had only seen one other copy, a much-tattered and snickered-over version that was handed down through the hallways of Harrow like a rite of passage. The bookseller had extracted it from a secret shelf beneath a desk and then handed it over with the hushed authority of someone delivering an opium pipe.

Of course, it had been purchased *before* she'd so prudishly questioned him about his sexual exploits. Before he'd realized she might have qualms about their wedding night. Surely now was when she would burst into a spate of tears, to see the reading preferences of the degenerate she had married.

But once again, she surprised him.

"Should I read it . . . now?" she asked, brushing the remnants of tears from her eyes.

West felt a smile begin to spread across his face. He began to unbutton his waistcoat, anticipation making his fingers feel clumsy. "Out loud, I should think."

As he shrugged out of his braces, she settled her shoulders against his pillow. "*Scenes in the Harem of an Eastern Potentate*," she began, then hesitated, her eyes widening. "*Faithfully and vividly depicting in a series of letters from a young and beautiful English lady to her friend in England the full particulars of her ravishment and of her complete abandonment to all the salacious tastes of the Turks.*" A vivid flush stained her cheeks, spreading downward toward her décolletage. "This sounds . . . ah . . . interesting."

"Quite," he chuckled, pulling off his shoes and socks.

"Should I read on?"

"As you wish."

She eyed his progress warily, but nodded. "*Dearest Sylvia . . . We arrived here early this morning after a most melancholy journey. Time alone can remove the painful impressions which the appearance of poor Henry created as we parted.*" The gaze she leveled at him then was nearly reproachful. "This doesn't sound nearly as interesting as before."

"Oh, poor Henry is not the hero of this tale." West lowered himself onto the bed, leaving his shirt and trousers in place for the moment, then propped himself up on one elbow. "It starts slowly," he admitted, lifting his hand to begin exploring the damnable mystery of the fastenings of her bodice, "but trust me, it gets much better."

She turned her attention back to the pages and West took advantage of her distraction to begin to slide free the brass eyes hidden beneath the brown wool, each inch of progress an agonizing triumph. He had a set path in mind: get her undressed while she was distracted, and then kiss her until she forgot her fear.

But as her voice settled into the story, it became difficult to concentrate on her seduction.

Because he was the one being seduced.

God, but she had the loveliest voice. He could nearly imagine that *she* was the one captured by the fearsome Turk, the way her breathing hitched at key parts, the way her lip quivered in anticipation. The temptation to hurry made his hands curl to fists, but he forced himself to go slowly. He had but one chance to introduce Mary to the pleasures of a wedding bed. He was determined to get something right, for once in his life.

By the time the narrative began to shift into something more interesting, he had gotten her skirts off and unlaced her corset—which was every bit as plain and utilitarian as he had once feared. As he slid the last of the laces free, his hands hesitated over the dilemma of her chemise.

How to remove it without interrupting such a sweet, sinful oration?

"*Nature,*" she breathed, hardly noticing his snagged progress, so engrossed was she now in the unfolding tale, "*had become aroused and assisted his lascivious proceedings, conveying his kisses, brutal as they were, to the inmost recesses of my heart.*"

Abandoning the idea of removing it, West lowered his head, tracing his tongue across her chemise until the fabric grew damp and he could see the dark temptation of her nipple beneath. God, but she had perfect breasts, small and round and shaped for his tongue.

He blew across them, his thumb caressing the pert tip.

A small hitch of pleasured surprise escaped her lips—though whether from his touch or from the direction the story had suddenly gone, it was difficult to be sure. "*I felt his hand rapidly divide my thighs,*" she went on, her voice growing hoarse. "*And quickly one of his fingers penetrated that place which, God knows, no male hand had ever before touched*." Her voice trailed away, and he knew she was re-membering how he had touched her last night.

West reached out and lifted the book from her hands. "That's enough for now, I think. Perhaps we might continue reading later." *Much* later. There were parts of this book not for the faint of heart. In fact, later passages contained lots of plundering and tearing asunder of virgins, including one memorable bit with a specially designed couch that fastened a lover's arms immobile and lifted her bum high in the air, readied to receive . . .

West drew a deep breath as he placed the book on the bedside table. He could not—would not—think of such things. At least . . . not yet. But who knew how adventurous his new wife might yet prove to be?

He turned back, his mouth going dry at the sight of her. She was close to naked and propped on his bed—the only woman to ever have graced his coverlet, dressed or otherwise. The small bit of text she'd read out loud had unmoored him. He wanted to hear her voice say *his* name in that same hoarse quiver, feel the heat of her body close against his cock.

It occurred to him that he probably ought to kiss her, now that she was no longer using those delectable lips for reading. He stretched out a hand toward her coiled hair and began to pull out pin after pin, until that thick, fragrant warmth spilled down into his hands and draped across her slim shoulders like a wave of temptation.

And then—*then*, she looked at him, almost shyly, and lifted her arms.

He growled his approval and skimmed the lingering bit of cotton over her head, then fell upon her bared breasts, pressing kisses across their rosy surface, drowning in the simple taste of her. He knew a surge of relief to hear the small sob of a sound she made as his mouth closed over her nipple, felt her hands flutter about his ears, not stopping him. In fact, urging him on.

Lust roared through him to realize she was every bit as aroused as he was.

Slowly, he cautioned himself.

But then she placed her hands against his face, and pulled him to her to press her lips against his, no longer waiting quietly. And just like that, his good intentions were ripped free of the promise of control he'd made to himself, and his senses spun in a new direction where slow, steady seductions had no place.

MARY GASPED AS his mouth finally met hers, her blood stirred to eager acceptance by the flavor of the erotic pages. A groan escaped him as her tongue tangled with his, and she felt a curl of possession to know that in spite of his very vast experience in the matter, *she* was the one he wanted in this moment. The contact of his body against her bare skin was searing, the gentle scrape of his clothing too much. Not enough.

Anything and everything in between.

She arched against him, wanting something she couldn't even name, but she knew a moment's confusion as he pulled away, panting.

Had he changed his mind?

But no . . . he was fumbling at his wrists. "Bloody . . . frigging . . . cufflinks . . ."

She stifled a giggle that her very experienced husband could be stymied by something so simple, then helped tug his shirttails free and up and over his head. Only then did she pause, lifting her hand to press it against the startling mat of blond hair scattered across this chest. She breathed in, a bit overwhelmed by it all, then lowered her hand, exploring.

It seemed the books she had read only skimmed the surface of it all. Not one of the books she had read had ever described the complex thrill of running one's hand over a flat, ridged abdomen and feeling the muscles contract against her touch.

Or the way her own stomach would quiver in the exploration of another's skin.

She aimed higher, tracing a faint circular scar she saw on his left shoulder. It was no bigger than a ha'penny, but the ruined surface hinted at some violence in his past. She felt a sudden chill to see it so close to his heart. She slid her palm against the healed whorl of skin. "You've been shot at some point. What happened?"

"A tale for another time."

She opened her mouth, intending to ask more, but he pressed his palm against hers and then guided her palm lower, down past the waistband of his trousers. She sucked in a surprised breath as her fingers curved slowly around the wool-covered length of him.

Oh, good heavens. He'd teased her about the size of his body, and while she had no notion of comparison save a few drawings in an old anatomy text, he certainly *felt* impressive, swelling to attention beneath her palm. As she contemplated what lurked beneath, he pushed the wool down over his hips, kicking his trousers and small clothes free, and she gasped as he spilled into her hands. She swallowed to realize that this was what would bludgeon its way through her virginity. "I don't think—" she began, only to be silenced by another searing kiss.

He loomed over her, pressing her down into the mattress, that concerning part of him pushing rudely against her hip. "Don't think, Mary," he murmured against her mouth. "*Feel.*"

"But logically—" she started, only to find her objection silenced in the depths of another scalding kiss. His hands swept down her arms, working some kind of sinful magic, making her forget to breathe, much less question how they would fit.

"Focus on the sensations, not the facts." He licked his way up her neck, making her gasp and arch against the bed-clothes. "It defies whatever bit of logic you want to throw at it."

He moved further afield to blaze a trail down the length of her body, his tongue swirling a heady promise. She gasped as he rounded the curve of one hip, and felt the slide of his hands beneath her derriere. And then he was settling between her quivering thighs, his breath warm and dangerous. "West . . ." she gasped, suddenly anticipating what he was about.

The tenor of his kisses shifted to something unimaginable, and then he was well and truly proving himself a scoundrel, placing his mouth against the seam of her, his tongue swirling hot circles of need. Her hips arched upward from the mattress, aided by the press of his hands, and she could do nothing but turn herself over to the maelstrom he commanded.

Good heavens, how the man could kiss. And in unexpected places, but in wonderful ways. It wreaked havoc on her very sanity, the way he made her feel, the things he knew to do.

She'd never imagined lovemaking was so . . . *feral*.

There was no other word for it. The books she had read implied a refined exchange, elegant and polite, sometimes coercive. But this was raw and sweaty and altogether too much. The pleasure building in her—in her mind, in her limbs, in her womb—had nothing of a civilized nature to it. "West!" she cried again, sensing that moment of crisis bearing down on her, and not yet ready to give herself over to it, for then surely she would die too soon. But it seemed dying was her due, because she skidded into it, hung on the edge, and then plunged into sensation. She broke apart, ten thousand pieces, each of them gasping his name.

Still breathing hard, she slumped back against the bed-clothes, stunned.

He had just done something unthinkable to her.

And yet . . . when her breathing quieted and coherent thought resumed, she had a notion she wasn't going to be able to stop thinking about it.

With boneless fingers, she lifted him toward her. Brought him back to her lips for a more proper sort of kiss, not even caring that his mouth had just been on her in other more stunning places. "That was . . . that is . . ." She sighed against his mouth, abandoning the effort to articulate her thoughts, because she wasn't even sure she understood them. "Inventive."

He chuckled, shifting his lips to press a kiss to her temple. "Well, I've been called many things, wife, but that is a new one."

She blushed. "I just never imagined . . ." Her voice trailed off as she realized he was looming over her, holding his necktie in his hands. A shiver coursed through her. Did he mean to tie her up? Did she mean to *want* him to tie her up?

But no . . . he was handing the necktie to her.

"What are you doing?" she asked in confusion.

"Proving my inventiveness knows no bounds." He flashed her a grin. "I would promise to behave without it, but we both know I'm not to be trusted."

WEST SETTLED DOWN onto the mattress and held out his wrists.

It was the only thing he could think of that might prolong the moment, slow down the mad pace they were setting. The taste of her was still warm on his tongue, the sight of her, disheveled and shattered against his sheets, a beautiful memory he wanted to repeat.

He wanted to go further, faster with her. He very nearly frightened himself with how much he wanted her. She tested his restraint at every turn, and he was beginning to doubt his capacity to be as careful as she needed this first crucial time.

He halfway expected her to refuse. This was a woman who had once fainted on him, after all. But it was also a woman who had bravely borne a kiss from a brothel owner. A woman who had just read aloud from a salacious book, lingering over the filthy parts.

Who knew what she would decide to do in this moment?

She lifted the necktie. Pulled it through her fingers.

Looped the necktie loosely around his proffered wrists.

He thought she might leave it at that. Or, at best, give him a half-hearted sort of tie, something he would have to pretend held him fast. The necktie might prove nothing more than a symbolic restraint in the end, but it would remind him of the need to go slowly. But she surprised him by suddenly moving, twisting the ends with deft hands. Before he could blink, he found his wrists bound in a perfect, immovable Highwayman's Hitch.

"Good Christ." He stared at his hands. "Where did you learn to do that?"

"*The Seaman's Manual.*" She tested the strength of the knot, then lifted his hands over his head to secure them to a bed-post.

"You mean . . . you read more than novels and newspaper accounts?" He stared at her bare, rounded breasts, which were currently hovering a tantalizing inch or so from his mouth, shifting as she worked. "I thought you favored gothic novels."

"I've read every book in my brother's library." She leaned back, regarding him with what might be characterized as a smug smile. "*The Seaman's Manual* had excellent illustrations."

West tugged against his restraints. Realized he was well and truly tied. And that he, a former officer in the Royal British Navy who ought to know how to tie a knot with the best of them, had no idea how to undo the damage.

"Well then," he said slowly, wondering just what sort of

derangement he'd just invited upon himself. Clearly, one ought to not tease bookish women. "I . . . ah . . . hope you haven't read anything about castration techniques."

"Oh, *English Agriculture*, by Sir James Caird, also had a series of excellent illustrations." She raised a dark brow. "I've read it twice, so you might want to behave."

He nodded, praying she was teasing. "Yes, ma'am."

For a moment, she stared down at him, her gaze roaming with a shy intensity. "So, this is my chance to . . . touch *you*?"

"Yes." It scarcely sounded like his own voice uttering the hoarse word.

She ran the backs of her fingers along his ribcage, pulling a coarse, involuntary shiver from him. "However I want?"

"I haven't a way to stop you," he pointed out. And even if he had, even if she had tied him up with nothing more complicated than a half-loop, he wouldn't have. Because she was rising up over him like a goddess, her hair tumbling over her shoulders, her breasts peeking out through the dark strands. She was glorious. Uncertain. Brave.

His.

He held his breath as her fingers moved lower, across the terrain of his lower abdomen. In spite of the faint edge of worry that he was incapable of escape, his cock was fully engaged in whatever game she was playing. It jerked, throbbing against his skin, wanting her touch. Her fingers curled over it, squeezing, testing, making him hiss out through his teeth. "Just have a care with how far you tease me, Mary," he groaned hoarsely. "I'm apt to spill in your hands."

She hesitated, her touch lightening against his skin to something akin to agony. "I hadn't imagined I might . . . be in control of this."

"No?" he asked, trying in vain to pull away from her endless, innocent touch, his cockstand so painful as to cause him to grit his teeth. "You can be in control whenever you want," he panted. "Just promise to untie me when you are done."

Her smile turned saucy. "You probably should have extracted that promise before you let me tie you up." She leaned over to press a kiss against his upper thigh, too close to the sun for comfort. Her tongue, so small and perfect, reached out to lave him in small circles, but her nerve seemed to fail her at the thought of going higher.

No matter. They had a lifetime to discover such things.

She ran her questing hands down his limbs, each curious touch of her fingers making him want to leap off the sheets. He'd started this game, but it was clear now that she was the one playing it. Her mouth pressed here and there, her tongue swirling hot against his skin. She lingered in places he'd never imagined as all that interesting: the side of one knee, the lower curve of his calf muscle. She seemed to find each spot on him fascinating, a thing to unravel. He was panting beneath her ministrations, writhing against the restraints he'd so stupidly offered. But he'd committed to this course, and so he bore it: breathlessly, if not bravely.

Finally, she kissed her way back up to land on his mouth. He welcomed her there with an almost-anguished groan. "Have you seen enough yet?" he murmured against her lips, praying that now, perhaps, she might untie him.

She drew back, then reached over to fumble at the bedside table, returning with one of the French letters. "Can you guide me?"

He stilled. His body wanted to sink into her, skin against skin, no hint of ugly beneath. He'd meant what he had said: she, alone was his future, and in a perfect world, they would have no need to ever use the French letters again. But he'd made the promise she could use them as long as she wanted, and he was determined to be a man who kept his word.

"Not with my hands. Not unless you untie me." His wrists were already straining against her very skilled knot. He exhaled, cursing his inventiveness. How could he help her enjoy this properly if he couldn't use his hands?

"With your words, then," she suggested, blushing deeply.

"Slide the open part over the tip," he instructed, his voice a hoarse caricature of its usual confident self. She complied, and he arched in vain against the fumbling perfection of her inexperienced touch. "Now, slide it down and tie the ribbon near the base." As she began to fix the ends, he added, "Not *too* tight." He forced a laugh, though he was half-terrified of what sort of knot she might be capable of in this instant. "This isn't ship's rigging."

"Like this?"

He nodded. As her nails scraped pleasurably against him, he shuddered, sure he was going to embarrass himself.

"What comes next?"

He unclenched his jaw, willing his body to stay the course until she'd done whatever it was she had in mind. "Whatever you wish, Mouse. Just promise you will be gentle with me."

SHE HAD A notion of it all, the mechanics of what went where.

But Mary's understanding of the act—framed by the hurried notations in the books she had read—was of a technical variety.

Now that she was here, on the cusp of discovery, with West tied up in the bed and clothing strewn here and about, she found herself uncertain of what to do next.

She raised herself up, positioning herself over the covered tip of him. Slowly, she joined their bodies together. Settled lower, letting her weight pull her down, then stopped as she felt a bit of pain. She tensed. Retreated. Tried once more, only to draw in a sharp breath as the pressure became too much. She'd imagined it might pinch the first time, of course, but this was something more. Though, surely they were done now.

No need to drag it on.

She climbed off and lay down beside him, resting her head upon his chest. She felt a dull ache in places that just minutes before had felt such an astonishing sort of pleasure. It was nearly disappointing to realize there hadn't been more to it than that. "Well, I suppose that wasn't *so* bad," she breathed.

There was a moment of silence. She felt an odd, fluttering movement beneath her cheek, as if he was trying not to laugh. "Mary." He pulled against the knot binding his hands. "If you are . . . er . . . finished, do you think you might untie me now?"

"Oh." She blushed, pulling the ends of the hitch and releasing his hands. "I am sorry. I did not mean to leave it on so long."

But the moment his hands were free, she found herself flipped onto her back, and he was looming over her, his handsome face lowering toward her. He kissed her, his hands framing her face, lifting her to meet the demands of his mouth.

"Now it's *my* turn," he told her, his lips moving against hers. "And I intend to banish the words 'not so bad' from your otherwise impressive vocabulary." His hands swept down her body, as if they'd spent an eternity planning the course they would take when finally granted permission to roam. They lingered on her breasts, kneading them to heady awareness, then moved lower, two fingers slipping inside her. They moved gently, in and out, a building promise of something yet to come. And all the while he kissed her, his tongue sweeping inside her in nearly the same rhythm.

"God, Mary. You are so ready for me," he murmured against her lips.

"We are going to do it *again*?" she asked, tensing in anticipation of the pain.

He chuckled, shaking his head slightly. "We've not even started." He shifted. She felt him push against her, less pinch now, and more pleasure. A surprised squeak escaped her lips as he seated himself deeply inside her, far more deeply than her first fumbled attempt. She lay still, stunned by the completeness of their joining, her body adjusting to accommodate the invasion. All the while, his mouth still played against hers, a welcome distraction to whatever was happening *down there*.

Finally, he began to move, the slide of his body inside hers a strange, wonderful thing. Whatever discomfort there had been faded. Or rather, she soon forgot it existed. Every movement was an epiphany, every inch of her skin consumed by this fever. She felt that coiling inside her, a quickening in her abdomen that fanned outward like a flame. More intense than before, and more centered inside her. And all the while, with every thrust, every gasp, every murmured word of encouragement, his mouth wreaked tender havoc against her lips.

Oh, the stupid, stupid simplicity of books. She wanted to cry, she'd been so wrong about this. Last night, West had told her the right friction could create the most delicious kind of pleasure, but she'd thought his words hyperbole, the rhetoric of a practiced scoundrel to talk her into wanting more than she'd been willing to give.

But his explanation in the dark coach last night hadn't even come close to what they were doing, what she was feeling now. The slide of his body over hers, the burning beneath her skin . . . she closed her eyes, lost in the cacophony of sensations. She'd never imagined the intensity of the emotion, how she'd feel connected to him, from the inside out. It was a joining of souls, and she was falling in a direction she'd never anticipated.

Too soon, she found herself tossed upward, once again, to that place he'd taken her before, where the world receded in one large rush and she was suspended in time, breaking apart, reformed as something beautiful. He thrust once again inside her, gasping his own release into her mouth, his big body going tense above her.

She realized, dimly, that he'd found his own crisis, as brilliant as her own.

And that contrary to her initial thoughts on the topic, the stick she'd been given with this man wasn't short at all.

Chapter 18

Mary awoke with a start and sat up, blinking into the gray light.

Five o'clock then. Odd how her body kept to such a staid routine, even when her world had been shaken inside out. She stretched, feeling sore in strange, new places. Embarrassment rose as her nudity registered. But as she turned her head to see West's rumpled blond head, lying on the pillow they'd shared during the night, the embarrassment receded.

This was her *husband*.

And she was now well and truly a wife.

West seemed dead to the world, snoring in a soft, gentle patter. She smiled to think she now knew such an intimate thing about him. She filed the small fact away, tucking it tenderly beside the dreadfully short list of things she knew about her husband.

But . . . hadn't he once told her he was plagued by nightmares? At the moment he looked peaceful in slumber, the planes of his face relaxed and unguarded. The sheet had slipped down to his waist, and she was able to see the muscled ridge of his chest muscles, the gold dusting of hair that wanted to catch the morning light. The scar on his shoulder.

She reached out a hand to touch it. Yesterday, he'd refused to divulge its origins when she had asked. A product, perhaps, of the duel he was rumored to have had?

Or something more sinister?

After all, the man carried a pistol around in his pocket like it was a pocket watch.

Old, cold fears tried to creep back in, whispers of what she feared might still come, but she forced those withering thoughts to one side. She couldn't go into this marriage paralyzed by the fear she was going to lose him. Each day, each breath, was a new start, and she needed to cast off her fear of the past and concentrate on the present. It didn't matter if he'd had a dozen duels, or how many women had come before her. She was here now. She was the one in West's bed. *She* was the one he had kissed last night.

The one he had called his future.

The least she could do was trust the man he was proving himself to be.

And at the moment, he was proving himself to be a solid sleeper instead of a gun-wielding philanderer, and so Mary set her bare feet on the plush carpet and pondered her next steps. She had no books to read, no journal to write in. Her trunks with her things had been put in the room next door, when she had foolishly still imagined this might be a marriage of convenience. That meant that she lacked a wrapper or even a nightrail to pull over her head.

But perhaps, given the early hour, she might have a chance at fetching a few things before any of the servants began to stir.

She slipped from the bed. Taking the top sheet with her, she wrapped it around her body as best she could, tripping over the long, dragging trail of it. But as she passed the bureau, she caught a glimpse of herself in the mirror. Her hair stood out in a wild halo about her face, and there was a pink, fresh-scraped look to her cheeks. But worse—far worse—there was a distinctive reddened mark on her neck where West had laid his claim last night. She stepped closer to the mirror and peered at it, rubbing with a frantic finger.

It didn't come off.

She began to tug her fingers through her hair, wishing she looked less like a demented hedgehog and more like a radiant, well-pleasured wife. She began to hunt for a comb amidst the items that littered West's bureau top, pushing aside a silver case with West's initials engraved on the top. But instead of finding a comb, she stilled as she saw something else entirely.

Clutching the sheet to her chest with one hand, she lifted the medal up with the other, gasping in awareness. Even in the early light of morning, its distinctive blue ribbon and square points were unmistakable. *A Victoria Cross.* She'd seen a likeness of it printed in the *London Gazette*, had read about the men who had been given this newly created honor, just last year, for the most heroic deeds performed at the Crimean front.

She swung around to stare at his sleeping form. West had spent time in Crimea?

Just who *was* this man she had married?

But like a puzzle, the missing pieces slid into place. The lines of his body were muscled, hinting at hours spent doing something more than drinking with friends or playing at future viscount. Her gaze pulled to the glint of the revolver on the bedside table. She'd seen him wield it with precision, checking the chamber as though it was long-standing habit. She remembered how at the cathedral he'd asked about her opinion of the war, even as he'd withheld his own.

He was a soldier. Or had *been* a soldier.

Her fingers tightened around the Victoria Cross. It was

Britain's highest honor, newly created by the queen. Why was he so reticent to talk about it?

A noise from the bed jerked her gaze away from the revolver and back to West. He gave a low moan, a sound of anguish, and she darted toward him as he began to thrash about the bed.

"West," she hissed, suddenly afraid.

She'd suffered from an occasional nightmare herself as a child, especially in those terrible months after her brother and father had died, but she had never seen someone caught in the grips of a nightmare like this. West was trapped in something terrible and unseen, his eyes a flutter of motion beneath his eyelids.

Kneeling on the bed, she tried to wake him, but finding a handhold proved difficult in the flurry of motion. Dodging a flailing hand, she added her voice to the mix. "West." She placed a gentle hand against his chest, startled by the rapidity of the pulse she could feel there. "West," she said again, more firmly. "Wake up."

He gasped, followed by a long inhalation. His eyes opened. Tossed about. Settled on her. "Mary?" he breathed out. "You are here?"

"Yes," she said simply, placing a hand against his damp brow.

Without warning, she found herself crushed against his bare, muscled chest, her ear pressed too close to the scar on his shoulder. She let herself go limp, knowing he needed something of comfort from her but not entirely sure how to give it.

She felt him smooth a hand over the top of her hair. "I dreamed . . ." His voice was hoarse. "Well, I dreamed you *weren't* here. Not anymore."

She shifted, pressing her lips against the salty tang of his skin. "I am here. I am safe." She hesitated, pushing up and away from him and holding up her hand. "Thanks to you. My hero." She smiled, almost shyly, then held up the medal she'd carried with her from the bureau. "You were a soldier. Why did you never tell me?"

His demeanor abruptly changed. The look of relief on his face was kicked aside, and resolve settled into the line of his jaw. "You've got it wrong." She could feel him stiffening. Retreating. "I wasn't a soldier. And I certainly wasn't a hero."

Confusion swept through her. The whispers of who Eleanor thought he was poked at her. "Did you steal this then?" she asked, confused. "As one of your jokes?"

"No." There was a moment's hesitation. "I was a sailor, not a soldier. Rank of lieutenant. But only because I bought the honor, not because it was a position I properly earned." He made a rueful sound. "And I didn't earn the medal, either, so you can cease with the starry-eyed debutante routine. I am not a national hero. I am a national joke."

She bit her lip, unsure of why his words sounded so bitter. He'd shown dramatic flashes of heroism, to her, at least. He'd plunged into the shadows of St. Paul's Cathedral, chasing a possible traitor. He'd married her to save her from an assassin's threats. If she was honest with herself, he'd even tried to save her from her own stupidity that night in the library, trying to shield her from the ruin she'd so naively stumbled her way into.

"Someone must have thought you were a hero," she murmured. "The queen, most especially. Won't you tell me what happened?"

CHRIST ABOVE, SHE wanted to talk.

West wanted to do something entirely different. He'd awakened in the grip of a ferocious nightmare, and was only now settling into the reality that his new wife hadn't died at the hands of an assassin's bullet. He wanted to sink inside her, bury his nose in the fragrant mass of her hair. Convince himself she was real, something more than a dream.

And Crimea was . . . best forgotten. The medal was ridiculous.

Nearly a prank in and of itself, to be suspected of such bravery.

"West?" She loosened his name like a question, stumbling into the silence.

"You don't understand," he ground out, not wanting to talk about it. In fact, he'd rather move on to more enjoyable tasks. Such as tipping her onto her back and tying *her* up this time.

"I would like to understand." She clutched the edges of the white sheet to her throat. "I promise you, I am a very good listener."

That made his teeth clench. He didn't deserve her patience, any more than he'd deserved the damned Victoria Cross. But if a brief explanation would help them move onto more pleasurable things, so be it.

"My time in the navy was nothing more than a lark. Grant and I left university when we were twenty, seeking a bit of adventure, the same as many of the men who signed on." He reached out a hand to tug against her clutched fingers. The sheet slid down a promising inch or two. "We spent our service aboard the *HMS Arrogant*, with little enough action to impress anyone," he murmured, focused only on the business of uncovering her, one delectable inch at a time. "We didn't even see the front lines. Sevastopol was where most of the action was. We were sent to Fort Viborg instead."

She frowned. "One doesn't receive a Victoria Cross for unimpressive actions." She batted his hand away, her brow furrowed in concentration. "There was vigorous fighting at Viborg, too. I read the accounts in the papers."

West's hand fell away. Of *course* she would have read the details of the war. The woman never met a paragraph she didn't like. He knew her well enough by now to know she would not leave off until she had what she imagined was the truth out of him.

Still, he hesitated.

He wasn't even sure he knew what the truth was.

"It was all a misunderstanding. Something about a bomb and the ship." He still felt too close to the clench of his nightmare, and her gentle probing was making the dark edges peel back on a day he preferred to forget. He could nearly hear the sound of the live shell, rolling across the wooden planks of the lower deck. The laughter of the sailors, thinking it was just another one of his pranks. He'd reacted on instinct, tossed it overboard just in time.

"I am no hero," he repeated gruffly, opening his eyes to face her. He'd never told anyone—not even his family— what had happened. Some pieces were buried too deeply to explain. "I was fortunate, that is all." That fact, at least, was indisputable. Two seconds' hesitation, and the shell would have gone off in his hands.

He saw the carnage that should have been nearly every time he closed his eyes.

But she was looking at him strangely now, as if she didn't quite believe his dismissal of the events in his past.

"I didn't deserve the medal, Mary," he insisted. And he didn't deserve her either. He felt dismantled by her questions, the look of pride he'd seen shining in her eyes when she'd waved that medal about. He was more comfortable, perhaps, with the confusion he saw flitting across her features now.

She bit her lip, her eyes lowering. And then her hand reached out to take up his own fingers. "In due time, then. I can understand being hesitant to talk about the darker things in one's past. But you shouldn't be ashamed of the medal, West."

"If you like it, then you should keep it," he said, trying to soften the gruffness that wanted to linger in his voice. God knew it ought to be kept by someone who appreciated it. He wanted to push back against her presumption that he would eventually offer her a better explanation for what had happened that day, but he held his tongue, not wanting to talk about it anymore. Better to let it lie. She was so damnably innocent . . . what did she know of darker things?

But her fingers felt warm and reassuring, curled into his, and he knew—because he was no gentleman—that he would take this empathy she'd allotted him and twist it to whatever advantage he could. He drew a breath. Repositioned his thoughts.

Time to seduce his wife.

"I am sorry if I awakened you with my thrashing about this morning." He ran a questing finger up her pale, perfect arm. "I am afraid my nightmares aren't pretty, but I've never had to worry about someone else in my bed before. You are the first woman I've ever had here, and this is the only place I suffer them."

"Oh." She breathed out, almost shyly. "You didn't wake me. I was already awake. I am a dreadfully early riser."

"Dreadfully?" he teased, his finger moving higher, hovering against the reddened mark his teeth had left on her neck the night before. "How early do you usually wake?" he said, imagining the dreadful hour of seven. Or eight.

"At five o'clock every morning."

"Good God." He tried to imagine it, and the havoc such a schedule would wreak upon his life. "*Every* morning?"

"Like clockwork," she admitted. "I try not to disturb the household. At home, in Yorkshire, I usually go outside to the garden in the summer, read a book."

Understanding trickled into him. "Is that why you were out in the garden that first morning we met?"

"Yes. I was hoping my sister's garden might prove a similar retreat. In the winter, when the light comes late and the weather is foul, I am forced stay in my room, and those are long hours, indeed. I . . . that is, I am afraid my habit will disturb you. Eventually." She bit her lip. "That's why I put my trunks in the room next door."

"There is no need to apologize." In fact, he ought to apologize to her. He felt suddenly ashamed of how he'd treated her that morning when she'd been standing in the garden. "And there is no need to keep your trunks next door, either." The idea of her sleeping somewhere other than his bed was appalling, and not only because he needed to make sure she was safe. "This dreadful habit of yours sounds promising."

Her eyes met his, wide and questioning. "It does?"

He cupped her chin and lifted her face toward him for a tender kiss. "More time to spend with each other, I should say."

"Oh," she breathed, and he could feel her smile against his lips. "But, what shall we do that early every morning?"

With a grin, he flipped her onto her back and pulled away the sheet. "You've got a vivid imagination, Mouse. I am sure you can think of something."

From the Diary of Miss Mary Channing
June 14, 1858

I may not have felt changed following the occasion of my ruin, but there is no doubt I feel changed after the occasion of my marriage. Last night was revelatory. All the time I spent reading about it, believing I knew what life was about, and yet the actual beauty of the act astonished me. Perhaps it is because I have married a man of some experience, but I no longer see this as merely a marriage of convenience.

I see it as a marriage of great potential.

Still, there is a good deal I do not know about the man I have married. He clearly carries wounds from Crimea not easily seen. And however it happened, the scar on his shoulder is a reminder that there is more than my own safety at risk here. Danger follows him, and now it is following me as well. But it isn't fear for my own safety that makes my throat swell tight. This man means something to me. In my life, I've lost too many people who meant something to me to accept such an emotion without worry.

What if I lose him, too?

Chapter 19

The line of household servants snaking down the hallway outside Lord Ashington's study at ten o'clock on
that Monday morning was long. Restless. *Nervous.*
And well they ought to be.

Because when West found the person who placed the note
in Mary's journal, there was going to be hell to pay.

He'd left his new wife sitting in the drawing room at
Cardwell House, reading some Dickens novel out loud to
her sister. He might have liked to have plopped down into
a chair, listened to his new wife's voice for a few minutes.
Tossed aside the dull book they were reading and livened
things up with *The Lustful Turk*. Instead, he'd taken advantage of her devotion to her sister and slipped away without
her knowing to walk three doors down.

Though he truly had no right to be here in Ashington's
study, conducting interviews with the man's staff, the
housekeeper, Mrs. Greaves had not objected. Though West
had not divulged the reasons for his demands, the woman
had seemed nearly relieved to see him. Was it any wonder
Mary had been able to slip away from the poor woman so

easily? The household staff ran slipshod circles around the aging housekeeper. He decided he ought to introduce Mrs. Greaves to his butler. If anyone could force a bit of starch into a person, it was Wilson.

"Next!" he called out, waving away the gardener who'd just stood in front of him, hat in hand, to confess to a dalliance with a somewhat promiscuous scullery maid. Which was all well and good for the gardener, but as the man appeared to have no idea who Mary was, much less where her room abovestairs might have been, West dismissed him and moved on to the next worried soul. He interviewed upstairs maids. Downstairs maids. A cook, a butler, and a handful of kitchen maids. There were two unimpressive footmen, a gardener's apprentice, and a groomsman who saw to the horses in the mews. Most of the staff appeared to think he was interviewing them about a piece of silver that had disappeared from a locked cabinet last week.

One of them even produced said piece of missing silver.

None confessed to an association with terrorists, or appeared capable of anything more sinister than picking a lock on the silver cabinet or lusting after someone they oughtn't.

Two hours into the interrogations, Mrs. Greaves popped her head through the door. "That is the last of them, Mr. Westmore. I trust your inquiry went well?"

West held up the previously missing piece of silver, which Mrs. Greaves accepted with a relieved "thank you". But he himself frowned. How could that be everyone? There was no valet, though it made sense the man was traveling with Lord Ashington. But in reviewing the frightened faces, he could not recall speaking with anyone who professed to be a ladies' maid.

And as there were two ladies who had been residing in the house . . .

"What about Lady Ashington's personal maid?" he asked gruffly.

"O'Brien?" Mrs. Greaves looked startled. "Did no one tell you? She followed Lady Ashington to Cardwell House."

West lurched to his feet, panic slamming through him. The missing maid was at Cardwell House? And named *O'Brien*?

It was a distinctly Irish name, and thoughts of Fenian rebels urged him onward. His feet flew out of Ashington's study and through the front door. *Bloody, bloody hell.* How could he have been so stupid? To be sure, he'd left a well-armed footman discreetly guarding the drawing room door, but even so, he raced down the street and burst through the doors of Cardwell House without even a greeting for poor Wilson. He skidded past the drawing room to see that his new wife and her sister were still calmly—and safely—reading aloud, then took the stairs two at a time.

He didn't even bother to knock, just threw open the door of Lady Ashington's room.

A pretty woman in a plain gown looked up, startled. "Mr. Westmore!" she exclaimed indignantly, lowering her needlework to her lap. "You may *not* be in Lady Ashington's room."

"O'Brien, I presume?" At her uncertain nod, he stalked into the room. "Surely you don't think I am here to proposition Lady Ashington," he scoffed, trying to rein in his temper to something that might have a hope of producing a proper interrogation. "For heaven's sake, I've just married her sister."

Her eyes widened at his approach. "I truly don't know what you might do." A faint pink bloomed on her cheeks. "I've heard plenty of rumors regarding your behavior."

West clenched his teeth. "I know you left the note in Miss Channing's journal." At her gasp of surprise, he circled her chair, making her twist to watch him with fear-filled eyes. "What I want to know is *why*." He forced his voice to stay even, given that the girl looked about as sturdy as a feather in the wind. "Who put you up to it?"

She squirmed in her chair, her hands knotting in her needlework. "Please, Mr. Westmore. Do not tell anyone. It was just a little fun. What harm was there in it?"

"What harm?" West gave in to a growl of frustration. "Are you *kidding* me?"

The maid frowned. "I only passed the note on as a favor for a friend. I do not even know what it said!"

"You passed on a note from your friend." West circled back around to glare down at her from in front of the chair. "And delivered it to an unmarried, wellborn woman. But you did not stop to think about whether the contents might prove harmful to the person receiving it? Did you not wonder, O'Brien? Were you not tempted to take a little peek?"

"No." She began to look panicked now. "I . . . I presumed it must be a note requesting an assignation."

"An assignation?" West began to feel murderous. He placed his hands on the arms of the chair and leaned in, until he was eye-to-eye with the frightened maid. "And why, pray tell, would you think Miss Channing might be receptive to such an offer?"

"It was just . . . after the gossip rags . . ." O'Brien began to tremble, her voice trailing off. "Well, I thought she must enjoy such things."

West balled his fists. With the maid's unmistakably Irish surname, he'd presumed this interview would lead directly to information about a Fenian cause, Irish rebels bent on recognition. But instead, he'd stumbled into a conversation leading to nowhere, and with a girl whose accent told him she'd actually been born in London's Cheapside, not Cork.

And he couldn't quite contain the rage he felt at the notion that everyone—this maid, included—presumed his new wife to be of such loose morals she would gladly accept notes from strangers asking to meet in darkened corners. Particularly when he'd had to work so hard to take off her corset last night.

"I will have your friend's name, O'Brien."

Her face went white. "I meant no disrespect. If the note hurt Miss Channing's feelings, it was not my intention. I thought she might *want* such a note, after that business with the scandal sheets. You must help me make her understand. I cannot afford to lose my position."

"You should have thought of that before you set Miss Channing up to become a plaything for your lover. His name, please."

She gasped, her eyes growing wider still. "No, you have it all wrong! He isn't my lover. I only just met him, really," she cried, wringing her hands now. "His name is George. George Carlson. And it wasn't a note from him. He said he was only paid to see it delivered, by his employer."

West glared down at her, his instincts sharpening. This didn't feel like a woman feeding him a lie. O'Brien wasn't trying to dodge out. Not trying to run, the way Vivian had. A woman with so much to lose would be unlikely to face her accuser so meekly. He wasn't quite sure what to think. Either she was a very good actress . . .

Or she was telling the truth.

His gut told him it was the latter, and he was inclined to trust his gut, given that he'd had several excellent actresses in his day.

"Who employs your friend?" he demanded.

"H-he's a gardener." She shrank into her seat, tears welling in her eyes. "For the Duke of Southingham."

West reared back. The room felt as if it was spinning. Memories pushed in, knocking against the roar in West's ears. *Southingham.* Could it really be so simple? A duke, and one he had known for over a decade? He thought he'd recognized the voice, of course, but this was a connection he'd not considered.

"Describe your friend," he said gruffly, needing to be sure.

Tears filled O'Brien's eyes. "He's . . . ah . . . not so tall as you, sir. Brown hair, tied in a queue."

"Does Carlson have a scar here?" West traced the line of his jaw, remembering the man he'd seen in St. Paul's Cathedral, the one who'd brought Vivian the money.

O'Brien nodded, the tears falling in earnest now. "But . . . oh, please. Do not say anything to his Grace, nor to Lady Ashington either. I am so, so embarrassed. I couldn't bear it if they knew I had done this, when the note was unwanted!"

West gritted his teeth. *Good Christ.* If the man who had bribed the maid to deliver the note worked for the Duke of Southingham, it was nearly assured that Southingham was the peer behind the plot. The thought of it filled him with a righteous sort of rage. Southingham had always been a bully, even when he'd just been Peter Wetford. He'd used his superior title to prey upon boys who couldn't raise a hand in defense without fear of repercussion. An easy man to hate . . .

But could he really be a traitor, too?

And as much as West wanted to shout his suspicions from the rooftops—especially given the rumors the man in question had spread about him through the years—one couldn't just claim such a thing of a man as powerful as Southingham.

West needed proof. *In hand.*

The fact that it was Southingham's purported gardener who'd arranged the note on Mary's pillow wasn't enough to prove to Scotland Yard the duke was involved in the plot. But as he considered whether or not it could be Southingham, his anger swelled with surety. Even if no one else believed him, he at least had a name to investigate more closely now. West's experience with Southingham suggested the duke preyed upon those he considered weak.

Unprotected. When he'd threatened Mary, he must have

presumed he was dealing with an innocent, someone he could push around.

West needed to make sure Mary wasn't so innocent anymore.

But first, he needed to ensure the maid's silence.

"I can see how this . . . misunderstanding may have occurred, O'Brien," he said slowly, letting a practiced smile drift over his mouth. "But if you value your position, you mustn't ever do anything like it again. Lady Ashington is most protective of her sister." He raised a brow, hoping he looked threatening. "If she ever knew you'd done something like this . . . I feel sure you'd be sacked without a second thought."

The maid knotted her hands vigorously. "Oh, no, sir. I wouldn't dream of doing anything like that, ever again." She looked up at him through tear-filled eyes. "Please. I . . . I need this job, sir. I'll do anything you want. You see, I've eight siblings, still at home, and I send money to my family, every month."

West leaned closer, knowing that keeping the girl silent was of paramount importance. "Then it seems you've a good reason to do as I ask." He hesitated. "You said you've heard rumors about me, O'Brien. What have you heard?"

She blushed, her eyes landing on his mouth. "They . . . ah . . . say you are fond of a good joke." Her lips parted. "And that you are a dreadful rake." She drew a deep breath, her blush deepening. "And if you want something from me, in exchange for my silence . . ." Her voice trailed off, nearly ashamed. "You have only to ask. Sir."

West shook his head, more than a little disturbed by her offer and her tear-filled eyes. *Good Christ*. Did she really think he would do such a thing? He had a wife to protect. To honor. And the thought of taking advantage of a woman like O'Brien, who was so desperate to keep her position she was offering to do anything he wanted, made him more than a little uneasy.

He took a step away from her, as disgusted with himself for putting her in the position as he was with the notion that he might be considered a man who might want such a thing. Really, perhaps he needed to pay more attention to the sort of rumors that trailed him.

"That won't be necessary, O'Brien. But on the matter of jokes . . . have you heard about the time I dressed as a chamber maid to sneak into the Duchess of Southingham's bedchamber?" At the maid's ready nod, he inclined his head. "This time it seems the Duke of Southingham has tried to play a joke on me. He was aware of my interest in Miss Channing, you see, and wanted to see if she would stay true."

She nodded again, apparently keen to believe any explanation that might relieve her of some responsibility.

"I am going to play a joke on him in return, one he won't be able to stop laughing about for years." He lifted a finger to his lips. "And I need you to keep my secret, or my surprise will be ruined. Mum's the word, O'Brien. You can't let anyone know, especially your friend, Mr. Carlson."

"Oh, no, Mr. Westmore." She shook her head vigorously, swiping at the tears that still stained her cheeks. "I won't see him again, anyway. Seems like he tried to steer me wrong."

"Good girl, then. If you stay silent on this, your position will be safe. It will be our small secret." He hesitated. "And my wife must not know any of this."

MARY STOOD OUTSIDE her sister's open door, clutching the book she'd intended to return to Eleanor's bedside table. She'd caught only the last piece of the conversation, but it was enough.

Her husband's voice, coming from her sister's room, speaking with the maid.

It will be our small secret. My wife must not know any of this.

Her always-eager imagination leaped to the inevitable, shards of doubt burrowing beneath her skin. She lifted a hand to her mouth to catch the horrified gasp that wanted to escape.

Just last night, West had told her that she, alone, was his future. He'd made her feel like the only woman in the world. Little could she have imagined that world might only extend to his bedroom door, and that the future he'd described expired at dawn.

Embarrassed and heartsick, she hurried away, her thoughts racing, the book clutched against her chest like a shield. Somehow, she made her way to West's room. Or rather, to *their* room. Standing in the doorway, she could see her trunk had been moved in this morning. But its new, hopeful position at the foot of the bed didn't make this her room, any more than the wedding ring on her finger ensured West belonged only to her.

Through a blur of tears, she eyed the open trunk, with its neatly folded linens. Further afield, she could see a trio of brown wool dresses hanging beside dark, masculine jackets in West's wardrobe, an intermingling of textures and fabrics that might have seemed romantic a quarter hour ago, but instead seemed hopelessly naive. She stepped inside and placed the book on the bedside table, beside the silver case of French letters.

The sight of them made her blink back tears.

She would need to insist on their use for a while longer, it seemed. Possibly a lifetime.

She swiped angrily at her eyes. Honestly, what good would crying do? It wasn't as if tears could fix any of this. She'd spun a fanciful lie for Eleanor, told her sister she imagined making West a better man. Somehow, she had foolishly come to believe in the possibility of it.

But she shouldn't be surprised—obstinate asses did not

become strapping, well-trained steeds, just because their rider wished it so.

She began to pace, needing to focus her energy on something productive. She could write in her journal. Writing down her thoughts always seemed to help. But as she glanced down at her ink-stained fingers, she hesitated. Those stains were fresh, a product of this morning's journal entry. If she opened her journal now, she'd see the thoughts she'd written about her wedding night, so hopeful and giddy and stupid. She couldn't bear to think of it.

So instead, she reached into her trunk and snatched up her small jar of lemon paste, then unleashed her frustrations on her hands, scrubbing at the ink marks as though she could similarly scrub away her doubts. This marriage, she told herself firmly as she scrubbed, was not meant to be a love match. It had taken place only out of necessity, and she had no right to expect fidelity from West, not when he'd given up so much on her behalf.

But oh . . . the things he had said last night . . . the things they had *done* last night. And this morning, as well. She thought of him doing those things with someone else.

Had she so badly misjudged the situation? The man?

Or was it only herself she had misjudged?

Perhaps this was yet another casualty of her active imagination. She'd only seen what she'd wanted to see in him, a hero from the pages of one of her books, a champion come to rescue her. She'd seen the Victoria Cross on his bureau top and imagined him as strong and capable and caring, and perhaps he *was* those things, beneath his easy smile and his flirtatious ways. But the hesitancy to talk about his past, the things she had just heard from the hallway . . . those things argued trouble ahead. She didn't know anything about him, other than the way he made her feel.

What if this was simply who he was? Had she any right to

expect more of West than he was capable of delivering? She slowed her scrubbing, feeling sick to her stomach. One ought not to presume that heroes existed only to save the day. They were people, too, with faults and secrets of their own.

And she really needed to stop reading so many books.

The sound of a throat clearing scattered her focus. She whirled around, gasping in surprise, the pot of lemon paste shattering on the floor. The very man she'd been trying to scrub from her heart stood in the doorway, one shoulder casually leaned against the door frame.

She willed herself not to react to the sight of his smile, the strong hands that could wreak such beautiful havoc on her body. She *ordered* her fingers to uncurl, told her heart to stop hammering away in her chest. Her body, however, refused to listen. She wanted him, even with the imagined knowledge of what he'd just been up to.

Even knowing how he would hurt her, in the end.

Because when this business with tracking the traitors was finished, when their task was complete and the queen was safe from harm, they'd still be married. And if she complained about his liaisons, demanded his undying devotion, he would only grow to resent her.

For now, at least, he was smiling at her.

She straightened, embarrassed by her own weakness, by the helpless direction of her thoughts. Her past had taught her to fear. To anticipate loss. Seeing that scar on his shoulder this morning, imagining him in battle, she'd feared losing him, of course.

She simply hadn't imagined fearing loving him.

He sniffed the air, a predator spotting its prey. Moving forward, his feet crunching on salt and glass from the broken pot, he picked up her hand and pressed a simple, seductive kiss against the back of it. His smile deepened as he inhaled. "Lemons." The word sounded almost reverent as it fell from his lips. "Always lemons, with you."

In spite of her resolve to harden her heart, she felt a liquid beat of pleasure in her stomach, the heady sensation that came from simply being near him. Her cheeks heated as she lifted her other hand, showing him the faint smudge of black still lingering on her fingers. "Ink stains, from writing in my journal. I scrub them with lemon juice and salt."

"Thank God for ink stains then." His smile was nearly to be believed. So, too, was the press of his lips, moving higher now to her cheek. "Because lemons are my new favorite scent."

She wanted to trust him. Wanted to lean into him as those sinful lips began to nibble on her ear, sending coarse shivers cascading through her. "Really? You wouldn't prefer something less . . . ordinary?" She swallowed as his lips moved next to her temple, his breath feathering soft against her skin. "It seems a man of your appetites might grow bored with lemons every day."

"A man of my appetites?" He pulled back. "Why would I grow bored with lemons?"

"It just seems you might want more . . . variety." She shrugged. "Perhaps you might like vanilla one day instead. Oranges." She cast about. "Bergamot."

"*Bergamot?*" He met her eyes. "Mary." He said her name gently. "I've given you no cause to doubt me, and I won't." His finger cupped her chin. Lifted it until her eyes met his and she could see the darker blue ring about his irises. "You have my word on that."

His soft command nearly convinced her. Perhaps . . . perhaps she had misheard just now, standing in the hallway. Misunderstood. But even if the worst of her fears weren't true—even if he *wasn't* seducing her sister's maid, which was an awfully big leap of faith—by his own words, he was still keeping things from her, secrets he was sharing with others.

She wanted to close her eyes and go back to where they'd

been this morning, when he'd learned the secrets of her body as she had begun to learn his. But the memory of what she'd just heard in the hallway cast a shadow over that want.

"Did you want something from me?" she asked miserably, wanting only to change the subject.

"I will *always* want something from you, Mouse." His hand fell away. "But yes, I came in here looking for you for a particular reason." He studied her a moment. "Have you ever fired a gun?"

"No." She shook her head, the very notion of it sounding ten kinds of wrong. "I do not like guns." A hopeless euphemism, given that her oldest brother had been killed by one. She swallowed her rising fear at the thought of such a thing. "My family doesn't even keep hunting rifles inside the house." *Not anymore.* "I've never held one."

"Well, we are going to change that today."

In spite of her fears, she blushed as she imagined what he might want her to do with a gun. "I . . . that is . . . the necktie was one thing, but this—"

"Not for *that*." He chuckled. "Not that I wouldn't try it if you wanted to, but being held at gunpoint tends to have the opposite effect on a man." He reached under the bed and pulled forth a wooden case, placing it on top of the bed. "I wanted to show you this for another reason."

He lifted the lid. Inside lay two long-nosed pistols with identical, gleaming wood barrels.

Mary gasped. "Why do you own a set of dueling pistols?"

"So you at least know what they are."

She shuddered. "I've seen engravings in books."

"I should have known you would have read about them." He chuckled. "For a shy little mouse, you have a frightening degree of knowledge shored away. Grant purchased the set for me for my twentieth birthday. These are made by the finest gunmaker in London. Grant said every gentleman with a proper reputation ought to own a set of dueling pistols."

"Your friend Mr. Grant seems to have a very odd view of gentlemen's reputations." She looked up, remembering all the things her sister had told her. *He's already caused one duel, thanks to his philandering nature.* Her thoughts leaned toward the scar on West's shoulder. "Have you ever had need to use these?"

"No. Nothing beyond a bit of target practice."

"Eleanor told me you had been in a duel."

"Yes, well, your sister also said I had been intimate with an actual corpse." He grinned. "You might have cause to question the veracity of her claims."

Mary pressed her lips together. "Yes, well, your reputation makes it somewhat hard to sort out the truth at times."

His smile turned grim. "It is true that I *was* called out once. But I issued a formal apology before it came to pistols at dawn."

She nodded, fitting the pieces together. *Nearly* a duel then. She supposed she ought to be grateful that his legend was larger than life. "Who called you out?"

"The Duke of Southingham was very angry after that business with his new wife's bedchamber. A challenge was issued, and I nearly accepted it. But then my brother-in-law, Daniel Merial, suggested that perhaps I ought to do something more useful with my life than dying of stupidity. So I offered Southingham an apology." He lifted the two pistols from their velvet-lined case and placed them on the bed. "I've avoided him ever since. Figured it was best to avoid opening old wounds."

Mary felt nervous at the sight of the firearms, lying atop the coverlet where just this morning, West had made love to her. "Then why are you showing me these now?"

Blue eyes slid to meet hers. Held, making her lungs contract. "There is a ball we might attend, on June 19th. It will be our first opportunity to be presented publically as husband and wife. The notice of our marriage will come out this week in the *Times*, but not everyone will see it. It is important that everyone sees you are under my protection." He hesitated. "And a good number of dukes will be there."

"Including Southingham?"

"Probably." His jaw hardened. "But that is not why I am showing you this." He peeled back the velvet lining, reaching deeper into the case. "We've your list to investigate, and while I may have once thought it a poor idea, I am inclined to think your idea of speaking with each of our suspects, asking the right questions, is the only option we have left. There may come a time when I won't be by your side. I need to know you can protect yourself, whatever happens."

Understanding jolted through her. "You expect me to learn how to shoot one of those?" she asked incredulously, staring down at the monstrously sized dueling pistols.

"No, these are smooth bore caplock pistols. Inaccurate, unwieldy, useless in a proper fight. I've a theory they are fashioned that way so gentlemen with murder on their minds haven't a prayer in hell of hitting anything." He pulled out a derringer from a hidden chamber beneath the velvet lining, a glint of silver and polished wood. "No, *this* is what I expect you to learn how to shoot. And we are going to start with target practice today."

Mary looked down at the small, snub-nosed weapon he held out, her heart knocking around in her chest. It fit tightly in his palm, and if he curled his fingers about it, she imagined it would be nearly hidden. Its diminutive stature made it seem close to harmless. Certainly nothing like the hunting rifles of her nightmares. But that didn't make it any less dangerous.

"It's awfully tiny," she said dubiously.

His chuckle swam up her skin. "If there's one thing I've learned since I met you, it is that surprising things come in petite packages."

"Still," she breathed, knowing her limits for bravery only went so far. "I am not overly fond of firearms. I think I'd rather learn how to use a knife." She raised a brow as his mouth opened in surprise. "And it doesn't have to be small at all."

From the Diary of Miss Mary Channing
June 18, 1858

We are running out of time.

The end of June, the traitors whispered that night in the library. June is marching by, and we still have no idea who the traitors may be, which makes tomorrow night's ball all the more critical. West returned my list of dukes, neatly divided in half, and suggested we split our efforts. He even underlined several on my half of the list, suggesting that when I speak with them, I should keep my inquiries more subtle this time.

In truth, West is acting very strange. Generous, trusting, and attentive. He provides instruction with the knife every afternoon, and then kisses me senseless every night.

But are his attentions because he has decided to treat me as an equal in this mad chase?

Or because he feels guilty about the secrets he keeps?

Chapter 20

*M*ary sat with her gloved hands resting softly in
her lap.

Hands that now knew how to use a knife to
slice a man's diaphragm, fingers that knew how to gouge
a man's eyes. Her new husband had odd ideas for the sort
of knowledge a wife ought to possess, and they went a bit
further than how to tie a man up.

They were hardly the sort of hands that ought to be wearing gloves, but one needed gloves with a ball gown, and the
gold brocade confection she was wearing—another one of
Eleanor's too-small memories—demanded the proper ac-
coutrements, even if it pinched at the seams and itched at
the neckline. She thought longingly of her brown wool day
dresses, hanging safely in West's wardrobe, but one did not
wear ordinary wool gowns to speak with dukes.

Or so she kept reminding herself.

As her sister's maid hovered over her wielding a dangerous-
looking pair of curling tongs, Eleanor barked directions
from where she lounged upon the bed. "Put more curls near
her forehead, O'Brien. We want Mary to look *stunning* to-

night. Everyone who sees her must know immediately why Westmore fell in love with her."

"Yes, Lady Ashington," the maid murmured, then wrapped another finger's length of hair onto the heated tongs.

Mary closed her eyes. As if an hour of primping and some well-placed curls could turn her into a raving beauty. Being thought something less than beautiful was the least of her worries tonight. She had a vicious little dagger tucked in her reticule, and a carefully rehearsed plan to speak to every duke on her half of the list. She ought to feel brave. Excited.

So why did she feel close to wilting instead?

She opened her eyes, sneaking a peek at the maid through the mirror. Probably because the last hour of sitting so still while the maid had hovered over her had freshly stirred the doubts she'd tried to suppress. O'Brien, her sister's maid, had blond hair and soft, round features to match her ample curves. Was this the sort of woman her husband was attracted to? Someone uncomplicated, a pretty distraction? Or was it more that any willing woman would do?

Mary willed her thoughts not to stray in that direction. The first week of her marriage had been the most gloriously confusing of her life. If West was already straying, he was showing no signs of it with her. He sought her out at every opportunity. Kissed her in corners. Held her hand beneath the dinner table, and whisked her abovestairs for dessert. Just two hours ago, he had pulled her from her bath and then proceeded to play upon her damp body as if it were a beautiful instrument.

His attentions made her feel . . . hopeful. Her doubts had been nearly drowned out by the rhythm of so many deliciously decadent days of love-making, days where he scarcely let her out of his sight. She must have misheard, that day in the hallway. Or perhaps, West had changed his mind and decided he was happy with her after all.

But now that she was face-to-face with the pretty servant

she suspected of snaring his attentions, she was no longer so sure.

A pounding at the door pulled her attention in a new direction. Mary jerked against the insistent pull of the curling tongs. "Ow!" she exclaimed, forcing herself to sit still until the maid was done with her torture.

"Your new husband seems anxious to see you," Eleanor observed, shifting to a sitting position on the bed and arranging her skirts about her.

"He is just excited about tonight. It's our first ball as husband and wife, you know." Mary forced a light laugh. Everyone—Eleanor especially—was supposed to believe this was a love match. If only she could so easily convince herself. "Either that, or he's come to confess his undying love again," she added, reminding herself to smile. As the last curl slid from the tongs and the loud knocking came again, Mary motioned for the maid to answer the door, then turned in her chair to face her sister. "I believe he hopes to meet friends at the ball tonight. I understand Mr. Grant will likely be there."

And with any luck, a traitorous duke.

Eleanor smiled—just a little. "I well remember those days when Ashington was so anxious to see me he couldn't wait a decent hour before sweeping me away for a kiss." She ruefully gestured to her enormous middle. "Now it seems he cannot wait to escape on business."

It was the first time Mary had heard her sister utter a cross word about her husband. "I am sure Lord Ashington will be back soon," she soothed.

"Even if he returns tomorrow, he will not want to stay long," Eleanor said bitterly, "with me growing larger by the second."

"I promise you, it will soon be over." Mary didn't like the strain she saw on her sister's face, wished she could ease her sister's discomfort. Though, she prayed it would not be *too* soon. Dr. Merial had said the baby could come as early as July, but as it was still June, she couldn't help but remain worried about Eleanor's health.

Though Mary had fully expected to see West at the door, as O'Brien opened it a very large, unshaven man burst into the room. "Eleanor?" he shouted, stumbling past the startled servant, his bloodshot eyes landing on the woman in the bed.

Eleanor gave a shriek, her hands immediately flying to her unkempt hair. "Ashington!"

He rushed to the bedside. "I received your note." He fell to his knees and clutched at Eleanor's hand. "But you gave no indication of the problem, and so I rode all night, like the very devil, to get here. Is everything all right? The baby is well?"

"The baby is fine." Eleanor twisted her hand from her husband's. "But no, everything is not all right, you insensitive clod. I . . . I've *needed* you here. How could you leave me for so long? In the weeks you've been gone, I've become the size of a draft horse, I'm not sleeping well, and I've ruined my sister's life!"

"Not sleeping well?" He reared back, as if trying to discern whether the woman railing at him from the bed held any resemblance to the woman he had married. "Is , . . ah . . . that why you are sleeping here?" he asked in confusion. "At Cardwell House?"

"Are you even listening to me? Do you want to know why I am here, at Cardwell House?" she demanded, agitation setting her diamond earbobs swinging. "There are *fleas* in our house, Ashington. *Thousands* of them."

"Fleas?" Ashington echoed uncertainly.

"We need a dog," Eleanor commanded. "On account of the rats."

"A dog? You've called me back about a *dog*?" Ashington's head swiveled, and his befuddled gaze swept past Mary at the dressing table, to the open-mouthed maid still standing by the door. "And what is this about rats?"

"There are no rats." Mary quickly shook her head.

"If there are no rats," Ashington said, sitting back on his heels, "and this has nothing to do with the baby, will somebody please tell me what in the deuces is going on?"

WEST HANDED ASHINGTON a glass of brandy, though the man looked as though he could really use a bottle of whisky.

"Sit." West pointed toward a chair in front of the low-burning fire, though why his father's study needed a fire in this summer heat was anyone's guess. It was probably demanded in some obscure servant's handbook, a list of instructions that ensured butlers frowned at all times and that a fire was kept burning in dark studies regardless of need.

In spite of the gravity of the situation, his lips twitched.

No doubt Mary would have read that book, too.

As soon as this business was over, he would look for a home where he and Mary could settle, start a proper life together, whether it be in Yorkshire or London. Let *her* decide when and where fires should be kept, how many servants to hire, how many children to come. His bright, rosy view of this hoped-for future depended on getting through tonight, however, and finding once and for all the sort of evidence that might properly prove Southingham was the traitor.

He felt guilty for not having told Mary what he had learned, but then, she had a habit of pursuing things blindly, without giving proper thought to all the potential outcomes. It was almost like she was determined to turn the page too quickly, write her own ending. But this wasn't a book. A happy ending was anything but assured. He couldn't afford to take any chances. Not with the queen's life.

And not with his wife's life, either.

West corked the decanter and left his own glass empty, wanting to keep a clear head for the coming night. "Er . . . Mary asked me to explain a few things to you, while she tries to calm your wife down."

"Mary? Do you mean Miss Channing? Eleanor's sister?" West nodded.

Ashington eyed him suspiciously, then tossed the glass back, staring up at him through bleary, bloodshot eyes. "You've my undying thanks, Westmore, letting my wife stay here like this. I can't pretend to know what's going on. I am afraid she's come unhinged, babbling about fleas and wanting a dog, and some nonsense about ruining her sister's life."

"She didn't ruin her sister's life," West said firmly. He couldn't let anyone else take that blame—he'd taken care of that job neatly himself.

Ashington stared morosely into the fire. "I never would have left to see to this business at my country estate if I'd known how this pregnancy would affect her. I swear to you, she seemed fine when I left."

West poured the man a second glass, not even bothering to replace the stopper this time. This could take a while, and he wasn't yet sure of how much he wanted to say. "If there is one thing I have learned in the short course of my own marriage, it is that you can't predict what a wife will or will not do."

Ashington's gaze jerked toward him. "I beg your pardon?"

"Miss Channing and I were married. Six days ago, by special license."

"But . . . why?" Ashington looked stunned. "*How?*"

"The usual way, I assure you. Well, the usual way for *me*. We formed an attraction and the gossip rags noticed." He shrugged, as if it really didn't matter, when in truth, the woman they were discussing held his entire world in her ink-stained hands. "The fates demanded a sacrifice."

Ashington stood up, bristling. "You compromised my wife's sister?"

"Calm yourself. There is no need for anger." West shoved the second full glass toward the man. "I didn't compromise her, not really. But the gossip rags went on a rant, and it seemed best to silence the chatter. I promise you, I hold your sister-in-law in the highest regard."

Ashington snatched up the glass, his knuckles white against the crystal glass. "Come now, Westmore, what really happened? Everyone knows *your* reputation, but Eleanor's sister is a quiet thing, withdrawn. She's never even been to London before now. When Eleanor asked her sister to serve as a companion during her confinement, I thought it was a ripping good idea. My wife needs a quieting influence in her life." He snorted ruefully. "As you can well see."

"A *quieting* influence?" West rolled his eyes. "*Mary?*" Since he'd met her, he had sprinted through St. Paul's Cathedral brandishing a loaded pistol and visited the finest brothel in London without even wanting to sample the wares. And her endless lists, her unexpected bravery—he'd never met a less quiet female in his life. "She is like a spring rainstorm," he said, wondering if he ought to just pour a glass of brandy for himself. "She charms you into believing she's a quiet, gentle sort, while all the while she's hiding a bolt of lightning."

Ashington stared at him as if his head had grown two sizes. "Honestly, a spring rainstorm? Bolts of lightning? Does she inspire you to sing about daffodils and baby birds, as well?" He raised his hands, making the brandy tilt in the glass. "Your reputation for pranks and philandering is one thing, Westmore, but a poet you are not. Tell me the truth about why my wife is here, at Cardwell House, and why you really married Miss Channing." He took a swig from his glass. "She isn't even the pretty sister."

West bristled. No wonder the man had imagined his wife would be fine left home alone in the last two months of a difficult pregnancy. He was oblivious. Had he even noticed the two women were identical twins? Although, not *so* identical.

Given the choice, West knew who he would marry again.

But if Ashington wanted the truth, West would give it to

him. It was nearly a relief to have someone demand it, someone in a position to help fix it. Despite being something of
an arse where his pregnant wife was concerned, Ashington
was generally well-respected, someone who might even be
able to convince Scotland Yard to take action. "It is true that
Mary and I were caught in a compromising situation, but
that isn't why we married. We overheard a plot to kill Queen
Victoria. One of the men involved is a duke, and as Scotland
Yard refuses to believe me, we have been left with no choice
but to try to stop them ourselves."

Ashington tilted his head. "Queen Victoria, you say?"

"We've been making inquiries, a bit at a time, trying to
track them down. But six days ago, Mary received a threatening note from someone on your household staff, and so I
married her to keep her close and ensure her protection. She
wouldn't agree to the plan without her sister coming, too,
and so we unleashed a vial of fleas on your hallway carpet."

Ashington cleared his throat. "You are claiming—let me
see if I have this straight—that someone on my household
staff is plotting to kill Queen Victoria, and that a vial of fleas
is the only reason you married my wife's sister."

"Yes. *No.*" West felt an impotent rage building. "That is
not the point."

Ashington's brow rose. "Then what *is* the point?"

"That Mary is *clearly* every bit as attractive as your wife!"
West snarled, well recognizing the disbelief on Ashington's
face. It perfectly matched the sneer he'd seen on the face of
the constable at Scotland Yard.

Instead of taking offense, Ashington burst out laughing,
the brandy sloshing over the sides of his glass. He stepped
forward and slapped West on the back. "Christ, Westmore,
your reputation is well-earned, I'd say. You'll do anything to
get a woman in your bed."

"I didn't . . ." West checked himself. Why did he feel the
need to defend himself to this man? Ashington was a bum-

bling idiot who had left his new wife alone for far longer than was prudent when she was in such a delicate state. He himself would *never* make such an imprudent decision.

The thought drew him up short. *Well*. The thought of even having to make that choice seemed impossible, at the moment. He might be thinking of a buying a home where they could raise a family, but was his wife? Mary was wildly willing in his bed, sweetly inventive, her enthusiasm and innocence inspiring ever higher levels of lust and appreciation. But she had insisted on continuing to use the French letters.

Questioned his faithfulness with her timid little speech about the tedium of lemons.

It seemed no one was bound to trust his word.

"Well, no matter what rig you've pulled this time, if you've been forced to marry her for all of it, I'd say you've paid your dues," Ashington snorted, his face a jovial shade of red. "So I won't call you out. Your reputation for dueling aside, it won't do to go about killing new family members." His smile turned rueful. "And I *really* don't want to make my wife any angrier than she already is."

"Oh, stuff it, Ashington." West turned on his heel in disgust. "Take your wife home," he shouted over his shoulder. "We took care of the fleas days ago. But you should know Lady Ashington has been ordered by the doctor to avoid undue upset until the baby comes. So if she wants a damn dog, I'd suggest you get her one."

Chapter 21

As they stepped down into the crowded ballroom, Mary gripped West's arm.

The announcement of their names—Mr. and Mrs. Geoffrey Westmore—had pulled two hundred pairs of eyes their way, and sent up a din of murmured speculations rippling through the room. "They are all staring," she told him, concentrating on not tripping over her feet as they descended into the mass of curious people.

"They all want a peek at the woman who took me off the marriage mart." West's hand closed reassuringly over hers as he led her toward the waiting crowd. "They are only staring at you because they are wondering."

"Wondering what on earth you were thinking," she retorted. Not even the importance of tackling her half of the list, which was tucked discreetly inside her glove, could ease the strain in her lungs.

West's lips brushed her ears. "No, they are wondering what they missed before. You might look like a mouse, but they can't help but wonder what sort of a minx you must be in bed, to have so successfully snared this infamous bachelor."

Heat flooded her cheeks. "I am not a minx!"

"Well, perhaps an innocent minx." He chuckled, and then drew her into the thick of the crowd. "And I am looking forward to debauching you in the most wicked way possible later tonight," he added in a low whisper of a promise. "But first, we've a traitor to catch." He looked up, his voice returning to its usual timbre. "Oh, good evening. May I introduce my new wife, Mrs. Westmore, formerly Miss Channing of Yorkshire?"

And so it began. The crowd pushed in and West greeted them all, smiling like he'd come into a great fortune. By the time they made it to the refreshments table, Mary was nearly convinced herself that theirs was a love match for the ages.

"Good gracious," she gasped, bracing herself against the punch table. "That was . . ."

"Crucial." West poured a ladle of punch into a cup and handed it to her. "We needed to be seen together, our heads held high. It is important that everyone realizes you are under my protection."

Mary nodded, taking a sip of the cool beverage. She glanced back across the ballroom, at the long gauntlet they'd just navigated. "It helped you were with me." She offered him a smile. A month ago, she couldn't have done it, would have curled into a ball and rocked herself into denial. "Truly, it wasn't as terrible as I'd feared."

"Well, it was as terrible as *I'd* feared," came a masculine drawl. Mary turned to see Mr. Grant glowering at them from the far end of the punch table. "My first sighting of you in days, and it's to see you presented to the crowd like a stuffed and married pheasant." His eyes narrowed as he moved toward them. "Where have you been, West? The new Mrs. Westmore keeps you on a tight chain."

"Willingly, I assure you." West poured his friend a glass of punch. "I was hoping to see you here tonight."

"You were?" Grant accepted the glass, then immediately

added to it from a flask he produced from his jacket pocket. "Any why, pray tell, would you be hoping to see me, when you haven't even deigned to make an appearance at White's in the last six nights?"

"To apologize, of course. I should have given you more than a few hours' notice about my nuptials. You are my oldest, dearest friend, and you deserved better."

Grant held the flask out, presumably for West to help himself to its contents. "Does this mean you will come with me later to White's?"

West shook his head. "No, but that doesn't mean I don't hope my best friend and my wife will find a way to get along, somehow. I do not want you to blame her, for any of this."

"Oh, I do not blame *her*." Mr. Grant lowered his hand. "I blame you, you silly sod. For leaving me alone in bachelorhood, and at such a tender age." He took a gulp of his laced punch, and then offered Mary a conciliatory smile. "I hold your new wife in the highest esteem. Truly."

West beamed. "Excellent. Then will you help introduce her to the Duke of Rothesay and perhaps the Duke of Harrington? Because believe it or not, I already need to use the necessary."

"Oh, I believe it." Grant winked at Mary. "Although, if you are planning to loosen a capful of spiders in there again, give me a heads-up this time, would you? I still can't sit down in a lavatory without looking for the nasty creatures."

In spite of it all, Mary giggled. In this, at least, she and Mr. Grant could find some common ground—being on the receiving end of her husband's jokes. "Oh, I think we are safe enough tonight," she told him. "I've made him leave his spiders and his wind-maker at home, you see."

Grant grinned down at her. "*Touché*, Mrs. Westmore! I see West has married a woman with a sense of humor." He held out his flask. "Would you like to make things more interesting tonight?"

"Er . . . no thank you." Things were proving interesting enough as it was. She eyed West's retreating back, and realized with a start that instead of moving purposefully, he was drifting through the crowd, searching to the left and the right.

Not, it seemed, a man with his mind on the necessary.

"Will you excuse me, for just a moment?" she murmured. "I just want a quick word with my husband, and I will be right back."

Grant chuckled. "And so the nagging begins." He lifted his glass in salute. "Carry on, Mrs. Westmore. Carry on."

Lifting her skirts, Mary hurried after her husband, her chest feeling tight for reasons that had nothing to do with the swirling, bright, perfumed crowd. "West," she called out, making him turn. "Where are you going?"

"The necessary, as I said." He stopped and offered her a wink. "Or do you want to follow me there and see what pranks we can get up to together?"

"No." Her cheeks heated. She may be a new bride, but she'd already been granted a rather thorough education, and she could well imagine what sort of mischief they could generate in a room with a locked door. "You said you had already ruled out the Duke of Rothesay and the Duke of Harrington. Why should Mr. Grant have need to introduce me to them?"

"It doesn't have to be one of them." He shrugged. "Pick anyone else on your list."

She bit her lip. "Truly?"

"I only suggested those two as a start because I thought you might wish to begin with easy targets, ask questions of those we think are safe first, hone your approach. Although it occurs to me we may have been hasty dismissing Rothesay. I've heard his wife has relatives in Ireland. There could be a Fenian connection, you know."

"Oh." Her irritation lessened slightly. "So you truly want me to speak with the men on my half of the list?"

"Absolutely." He waved her on with his fingers. "The sooner the better."

But as she watched him disappear into the crowd, a lingering doubt remained. His about-face on the matter of her involvement in such a dangerous undertaking seemed out of character for a man who'd married her to save her from harm. Was he trying to shift her in a safer direction, freeing his time up to pursue the more likely list of traitors? Why, then, had he felt a need to teach her how to handle the knife sitting so precariously in her small bag?

And she couldn't help but notice that the Duke of Southingham—a man who seemed far more dangerous than not— was on West's half of the list, not hers.

As WEST THREADED his way through the crowd, he risked a peek back over his shoulder and sent up a silent prayer of thanks to see Mary returning to stand next to Grant. He'd left her in Grant's dubious company because it was safer by far than having her with him. Grant was battle tested, as scarred inside as he was. He would protect Mary, no questions asked.

Which was a good thing because West had no answers for those questions, *Yet*

He felt guilty as hell for telling Mary the lie he'd spun about Rothesay's wife. Yet, he was also resolved to suffer his guilt in silence. He had to be sure Southingham was their man before telling her of his suspicions. He was more than a little worried about what would happen when they yanked the cover off this secret and exposed such a powerful man as a traitor.

The urge to protect Mary from the repercussions of a wrong move was a powerful enough incentive to keep her in the dark. But the repercussions of involving her in a right move?

Far more terrifying to contemplate.

He caught sight of the Duke of Southingham on the periphery of the ballroom, and aimed for the man, contemplating how to best orchestrate this confrontation. But as West drew closer, he recognized the duke's pale, pretty wife standing meekly to one side.

His feet slowed. Damn it, he hadn't imagined speaking to the duke with an audience. Perhaps it would be better to do this another time, another place. But then Southingham spied him and the matter was taken out of his hands.

"Mr. Westmore," the duke said, looking none too pleased to see him.

"Your Grace." West's hands curled to fists. "It's been a while."

"Never long enough, where you're concerned."

West paused. Not at the insult, but at the hopeless task of trying to sort out whether Southingham's voice matched the whisper he'd heard from the library. It was frustratingly difficult. The duke had the sort of perforating voice that moved through walls, and he was projecting it loudly now, as if to call attention to their interaction. It was nearly impossible to compare to a whisper he'd overheard in the library.

But oh, how he wanted to imagine they were one and the same.

West offered Southingham's wife a more gracious smile. "It is good to see you again, Duchess. How long has it been? A year?"

The duke's eyes narrowed. "Have a care, Westmore," he warned.

"Oh, surely you aren't still upset about that?" West forced a laugh. "It was simply a joke, no harm done. But if it helps, I would again offer the duchess my most sincere apologies. I am truly sorry for any confusion." Although, West felt more sorry for the woman, who appeared hesitant to speak up for herself. And was that a hint of a blackened eye he spied beneath the duchess's carefully powdered face? Anger needled him with sharp teeth.

Southingham had always enjoyed using his fists.

"To make up for my former boorish behavior," he said slowly, thinking to possibly get a closer look at the faint bruise, and to ask her some questions about her husband's political leanings, "would the duchess do me the honor of a dance later?"

The Duchess of Southingham stared up at her husband, her eyes wide, as if waiting for his answer. Southingham nudged his wife in the opposite direction, toward the refreshments table. "Alas, my wife's dance card is already full," he growled. "And didn't you say you could use a glass of punch, dear?" He jerked his chin. "Go on, quickly now."

She did as she was told. West watched her retreat, noting the hunched shoulders and bowed head. If he ever treated Mary that way, he suspected his new wife would pull out her knife and show off her newly honed skills—and rightly so. Still, he suspected he'd just found Southingham's weakness. The man was overly protective of his wife.

"Whatever does she see in a brute like you?" he observed, hoping to prod Southingham into saying something imprudent—preferably a threat delivered in a terse whisper that could be compared to the one in his memory, "Especially when she could have had me?"

Southingham bristled. "She would never want you."

"No?" West shrugged. "It is so hard to know what women want."

The duke's jaw twitched. "And what does *your* new wife want? I'd ask her if the rats did any permanent damage, but then, I wouldn't want to embarrass her if you are less than whole."

West rolled his eyes in spite of the anger that spiked through him. Following the incident at Harrow, Southingham had gleefully embellished the tale. With every retelling, the rats had gotten larger, the damage from their teeth more permanent. "I think my exploits about town ought to have laid that rumor well enough to rest by now. Then again, you could always ask your wife what *she* thinks about it. If memory serves, she caught an eyeful on your wedding night."

Southingham's face darkened. "How does your wife even stand you, Westmore? I would feel sorry for the woman, but I suppose it doesn't matter anyway. She won't have to suffer you long."

In spite of the heated exchange, a chill rippled through West. After all, this was the man he suspected of sending a threatening note to Mary. A man who was very likely involved in a plot to assassinate Queen Victoria. "Why would you say that?" he said slowly.

Southingham offered him a nasty smile. "You should check the betting book at White's. Your friend Grant laid a wager for how long it will take you to stray from the marital bed. He gave you a month, but I've got three hundred in you won't last two weeks."

The blood pounded in West's ears, given that he had every intention of this marriage lasting a lifetime. *Damn Grant to hell and back.*

If this was his friend's idea of a joke, it wasn't very funny. *And God forbid Mary ever hear of it.*

"Have a care," West warned. "I am much devoted to my wife."

"Do you imagine you will last longer?" Southingham sounded surprised. "Need I remind you the gossip rags have given us all an unobstructed peek at the assets to which you now lay claim? Your new wife is a slight, ordinary little thing, isn't she?" The duke raised a mocking brow. "Perhaps I should have said you would only last one week. If I recall, you always liked women with big tits who lay there as if they are dead."

The reference to that fateful All Hallows' Eve was easy enough to ignore, but the insult to Mary proved significantly less so. The urge to plant a fist in Southingham's face hissed like a lit fuse, but as he'd learned so long ago at Harrow, one didn't strike a duke without repercussions, and this time they were in a crowded ballroom with two hundred pairs of eyes.

Instead, he let his words serve as weapons. "Do you mean, like *your* wife?"

The duke reared back, his face turning nearly purple. "I ought to call you out for that."

"If you do, don't expect an apology from me this time," West warned. "And know that you will almost certainly leave your pretty wife a widow, ripe for the picking. I didn't survive Crimea by being a terrible shot, you know."

For a moment, West thought he might have pushed the man too far. Southingham looked ready to pick West apart with bare hands. It was just like Harrow again, only magnified tenfold.

This time, though, West had more to lose.

Southingham finally spun on his heel, the crowd parting against his angry charge. "Stay away from my wife, Westmore!" he shouted over his shoulder.

"As long as you stay away from mine," West muttered more quietly, glaring at the duke's retreating frame. What had he been *thinking*, goading the man like that? He knew he wouldn't have forgiven such an insult lobbed at his own wife. It was a miracle he hadn't been called out.

Again.

He wanted to smash something. Pound something. Shoot something. Or *someone*. Because while Southingham's personal weakness might be obvious, it seemed all too clear that his nemesis now knew he had a weakness as well. "God *damn* it," he exploded, hitting a marble column with his fist. Which of course, did about as much good as striking Southingham.

He reeled, his hand feeling as if he'd taken a hammer to it.

Realized everyone was watching.

A steadying hand met his shoulder. "Are you all right?"

West turned to see Grant's concerned face peering at him. He shook out his throbbing hand. Was he bloody all right? He'd just punched a marble column in front of everyone, and missed his opportunity to match the duke's voice to the whispers in his head. He'd pretended to be interested in Southingham's wife, when his own seemed to already suspect him of a wandering eye. And the knowledge that Grant had wagered against him made him want to strike the column again.

"I am fine," West muttered. He cradled his bruised hand. "Where is my wife?"

"Don't get yourself in a lather." Grant held up his hands. "I left her in Harrington's capable hands, and he offered an introduction to the Duke of Rothesay after. She's out on the dance floor somewhere, so I figured my usefulness was at an end."

"Thank you." In spite of his simmering anger, West gave Grant a stiff nod.

"Why were you arguing with Southingham?" Grant asked curiously.

"He was needling me. About you, actually." West met his friend's eye. Held it longer than was comfortable. "I hope you didn't put too much money on that wager you laid in the betting book at White's," he warned, "because you are going to lose every bit of it."

"Don't tell me you are angry about that?" Grant rolled his eyes. "And here I thought you were a sensible sort."

West narrowly held back the urge to take his friend by the neck. It hurt to know that Grant would do such a thing, but then, was it any wonder? West had a reputation he'd worked hard to earn, and Grant had been with him, every step of the way. His friend likely *did* believe Mary was little more than a passing curiosity.

But that simply meant he needed to be proven wrong.

From the Diary of Miss Mary Channing
June 19, 1858

It was quite a night.

When we returned from the ball, I told West every detail of my evening. How the Duke of Harrington had missed the literary salon because that was the night he'd asked his new fiancée to marry him—in Gunter's Tea Shop, no less, to the approval of three dozen witnesses. How Rothesay's wife was actually Welsh, not Irish, and how I was able to exclude three other dukes from our list, one way or another.

To give him credit, West listened. Even asked some questions, and nodded at my assessment of each man. But through it all, he said not a word of his own night's discoveries.

And I can't help but worry he is keeping something important from me.

Chapter 22

The moment he was sure Mary was asleep, West extracted himself from the bed and hurried into his clothes. Slipping the pistol into his jacket pocket, he leaned over his wife's sleeping form. Smoothed his hand over her soft, dark hair.

God, what this woman did to him. A part of him envied her such easy, uncomplicated sleep. He knew her well enough now to know she would slumber on for hours, as if caught in a laudanum-induced dream, until five o'clock in the morning when she would sit up, blinking in awareness. That gave him five hours to find the evidence he needed.

Not nearly enough time, given where he had to go to look for it.

He moved down the stairs, trying to be quiet. He'd been unsuccessful in his attempt to match Southingham's shouts to the voice in his memory, but that didn't mean he could so easily let go the possibility. Somehow, the duke was connected to the note Mary had received. If there was even the smallest bit of evidence to be found implicating the Duke of

Southingham in this assassination plot, West was resolved to leave no stone unturned in his quest to uncover it.

Even if it meant returning to the scene of a past crime.

As he reached the bottom of the stairs, a light loomed up from the shadows, stopping him in his tracks. "Master Geoffrey?" Wilson held up a candle. "Are you going out for the night? 'Tis past midnight." The reproof in his voice echoed through the dark foyer.

"Not now, Wilson," West warned, reaching a hand toward the front door. "I've . . . somewhere to be."

"I admit some disappointment. I had thought, perhaps, that you had changed." The butler's gray, rheumy eyes fixed on him, disapproving. "If you don't mind me saying, you have seemed happier of late. As it happens, I quite approve of your bride and the changes she has wrought in your life. Would *she* approve of your late night activity?"

West gritted his teeth. No, Mary would not approve, but he wasn't going to admit that out loud. And hopefully, by the end of this long night, he'd have some bit of evidence in hand that confirmed his suspicions, something to properly share with her. "Save your disappointment for my windmakers, Wilson," he growled. "You don't even know where I am going."

The old servant straightened his shoulders. "I could hazard a guess."

"Well then, guess away." West tipped a finger to his forehead in a sort of salute. "And I'll raise a toast when I get there."

Irritation continued to poke at him as he stepped out of the front door and swung south toward St. Audley Street. It stung, a bit, that Wilson had presumed the worst of him. But there were more important things at hand than correcting the old servant's presumptions. If he was being honest with himself, he was disappointed by the events of the night, and not only the exchange with Wilson just now. The conversation he'd suffered with Southingham tonight in the ball-room had opened old wounds, raw slices of his past that still rankled. But as incendiary as it had been, it had also been painfully unilluminating.

He'd *wanted* Southingham's voice to match the voice in his memory. But it hadn't seemed to, at least in the course of a heated conversation.

Which meant none of this made sense.

Was it because a man's voice changed at a whisper, became something less discernible? Or perhaps Lady Ashington's maid had lied about that business with the note. Or perhaps . . .

Perhaps West was losing his mind. Perhaps there were a dozen people involved in this plot, all of them dukes, and the joke was really on him.

The Duke of Southingham's home was a white brick behemoth built in the most fashionable part of Mayfair. To the inexperienced bystander, it would appear to be an impenetrable fortress, a Queen Anne-style manor four stories tall.

But West wasn't anything close to an inexperienced bystander. Thanks to his now-infamous prank, he had an intimate knowledge of the household and its various vulnerabilities. The gate to the inner courtyard could be breached with a running start, and the window at the far side of the scullery still boasted an insecure latch. He jiggled the frame until he heard the latch fall away, then opened the window and climbed inside.

Straightening, he took in the shaded shape of the kitchen. One year ago, he and Grant had navigated this space wearing skirts and smirks, then climbed the stairs with a bit of a drunken swagger. Only, he had fallen prey to the wrong pretty smile.

This time, however, his destination wasn't the duchess's bedroom, and his self-appointed task for the evening wasn't a stolen kiss or two.

He crept along a pitch-dark hallway, feeling his way with a hand on the wall, looking for Southingham's study. But when he found it, the muted glow of candlelight leaked from below the closed door. He stared down at that strip of light, hardly daring to breathe.

What the devil? It was close to one o'clock in the morning. Hardly the time of night to be going over household ledgers and accounts.

Carefully, he pressed an ear against the door. Caught the low murmur of voices.

The hairs on the back of West's neck stood at attention.

Because the whispered voices were all too familiar.

"Keep your voice down," he heard a man say from inside the room. "What did you need to speak with me about so urgently? It's dangerous for us to meet here like this."

"I didn't know what else to do. It's Westmore," a woman's voice answered, miraculously matching the one from his memory. "He's married that girl who was asking questions about us. I am worried that he knows something."

"Don't worry about Westmore. He may *think* he knows something. But the man isn't as smart as he seems." Though the voice was muffled, something about the way the man said his name rang warning bells of familiarity again in West's head. The whisper matched the memory from the library. Holding his breath, he reached out a hand to gingerly try the door handle.

It didn't budge.

He lowered his ear to the locked door again, holding his breath.

"I told you," he heard the man say, "no one will believe either of them. I'm more worried about our friends in Scotland. How goes our business there?"

"There's a problem." The woman's voice lowered. "Vivian has disappeared, the money with her. Carlson says the money was never delivered. I knew we shouldn't have trusted her."

A frustrated growl echoed through the door. "There's no time to fix it. The date is set. It was in the papers just today. June 24th. There won't be a better chance." There was a furious silence. "If they can't be brought to heel, I'll have to do it myself."

The woman gasped. "That was never part of the plan."

"Don't worry, darling. They'll bear the blame, regardless."

West caught a soft moan, and then other sounds that told him something beyond a little negotiating was going on in the room. He pushed away from the door, even as his mind cartwheeled around the bits he had overheard.

June 24th. It wasn't much time.

And Scotland? That scarcely made sense. To be sure there was a good deal of nationalist pride in the Highlands, but it was the sort to inspire festivals, not murder.

Without warning, the light beneath the door snuffed out. West's instincts screamed at him to go. But he couldn't leave, not yet.

Not without some proof in hand.

West scrambled sideways as he heard a key turn in the lock, pinning himself into the shadows beside the door. He held his breath as the door began to creak open, and pulled his pistol from his jacket, just in case. His finger hovered ready on the trigger, but he would not, *could* not, shoot, not unless his own life was threatened. Because while he'd heard enough things to want to shoot the man about to walk through that door, *he* was the one skulking about Southingham's hallway. The one who had broken into the man's house.

The one the authorities would presume was in the wrong.

"Not that way," he heard the woman hiss from inside the room. "Someone could see us. We should use the other door. Quietly, now."

The door swung shut again. The footsteps grew fainter. West took a deep breath over the too-loud pounding of his heart. Reached out a hand to carefully open the study door. Nudged it open with his shoe and then crept soundlessly inside, his pistol raised.

But he was too late.

A door on the opposite end of the room yawned open.

The instinct to give chase nudged him in that imprudent direction. But what was he thinking to do? Stalk Southingham down in his own home and shoot the man in what would appear to be cold blood? If he shot Southingham tonight, he might disarm one of the traitors, but he would leave others on the loose. Worse, it would ensure his own arrest, and leave Mary vulnerable and unprotected. Because he had no proof of Southingham's perfidy, no word against the man beyond his own.

And in the eyes of the authorities, his word was about as useful as a three-legged horse.

Instead of giving chase, as the blood in his veins demanded, he invested that burning energy into quickly searching Southingham's desk. He pulled out his case of matches and struck one after the other, using the meager light to rifle wordlessly through drawers, looking for some piece of paper, some irrefutable proof of the duke's involvement, something that might convince Scotland Yard to take the threat more seriously.

There was maddeningly little to be found, no notes outlining murder plans, no receipts for bullets or the like. He found a single scrap of paper, a note scribbled to some London modiste providing direction for a delivery.

Anger burned through him as he stared down at the note. It was in a handwriting that perfectly matched the writing he'd seen on Mary's note.

Well. If he'd had any doubts before, they were well and truly buried now. He was more convinced than ever that Southingham was one of the traitors, and the one who'd sent Mary the note. But while it was a damning bit of evidence for *him* to see, it was still not enough to convince anyone in a position to act.

He could only imagine the sniggers of the Scotland Yard officials when he produced a note to a modiste and claimed it was a clue to a traitorous plot.

Finally, as he came down to his last, flickering match, West picked up the only other thing he could find, a much-folded copy of *The London Times*. As the last flame died, he shoved the pages into his jacket pocket. But even as he climbed out of the scullery window and vaulted over the courtyard gate, West couldn't help but worry. Based on what he'd seen and heard tonight, Southingham was *definitely* plotting to kill the queen.

And he suspected he was going to need more than a few dozen rats to make this right.

Chapter 23

Though he knew Mary would be waking in only a few hours, West's feet did not seem to want to turn toward home. He felt the burn of nervous energy, the impossibility of sleep.

He needed to talk to someone, someone he could trust.

And although his first instinct was to talk to Mary, she was still asleep in their bed, oblivious to what he had just uncovered.

So his feet turned south, carrying him toward St. James Street and the friendship he'd neglected for the past few weeks. Though it was now past two o'clock in the morning, White's was still open, as he'd known it would be. West settled into his usual chair at his usual table, then looked about, hoping to find Grant. But when he spied his friend holding court by the betting book, West was reminded, then, of the wager that had placed against him.

Bugger it all. Perhaps this wasn't such a good idea after all.

He looked away, irritated, only to see Lord Ashington sitting at a nearby table, nursing a glass of brandy. There would be no help from that quarter either—his new brother-in-law had already refused to believe him once tonight. In point of fact, *no one* believed him.

No one, that was, but Mary.

He fumbled in his jacket for a cigarette and his matches, only to find the bloody matches had gone missing. He frowned in irritation, wondering where the case had disappeared to.

Not that it mattered.

Not that *any* of this mattered.

He stood up. Pushed back his chair, feeling out of sorts, out of place, and nearly out of time. For Christ's sake, what was he *doing* here? White's and whisky and the occasional defiant cigarette might have once defined who he was, but he had more to live for now. And the ear he really wanted to bend, the ear he *needed*, would be waking up in—West impatiently checked his pocket watch—exactly two hours and thirteen minutes.

As he slipped the watch back in his pocket, the door to White's flew open. Southingham staggered into the room, his chest heaving, spittle flying. "Westmore!" the man roared, looking around with wild eyes, then aiming directly for him.

West stood up and faced his old enemy with an almost preternatural calm. "Was there something you wanted, Your Grace?"

"It seems there's something *you* want!" Southingham slapped a hand down on West's table. "And I'll see you in hell for it!"

West inhaled sharply as he saw the glove Southingham had just thrown down. "Is this about what I said earlier tonight?" he asked, recognizing the wide eyes crowding in around the scene, anticipating the wagers that were no doubt already being placed in the bloody book.

"It's not about what you said. It's about what you've done."

Southingham flung something at him then, a flash of silver, end over end. "And I demand satisfaction."

West caught it. Turned it over in his fingers. It was the small case that held his matches. He didn't need to look down to know what he would see the initials engraved on it.

G. W.

Damn it all to hell. West closed his fingers over the silver case. He must have forgotten it earlier, when he was rifling through Southingham's desk. The duke had clearly misinterpreted things, and seemed to believe he'd left it behind as a bragging point after a midnight visit to the Duchess of Southingham. Either that, or the man was seeking to remove the threat he posed to the plot in a very public way, one no one would question.

As West studied the man seething in front of him, an idea unfurled like a banner, borne as much from necessity as helplessness. He'd found no evidence tonight linking Southingham to the plot to kill the queen, nothing tangible he could hold in his hand or show someone. But perhaps . . . if he was very lucky . . . and very, very careful . . . he might take this opportunity to defuse the threat Southingham posed without worry of a murder charge.

He forced his hands to stay loose by his side, neither defending himself nor contradicting the presumption. He only prayed the duke hadn't taken his anger out on the duchess. She was truly innocent in all of this. "Very well then," he said slowly. "I accept your challenge."

"Choose your weapon," the duke snarled.

West nodded, turning himself over to the inevitability of it. "Pistols. What distance?"

The duke's eyes narrowed. "Twenty paces."

"Hyde Park," West shot back. "Dawn."

"Name your second, Westmore."

West hesitated. He didn't want to drag someone else into

this mess if he could help it. And as he was still rather angry with Grant for placing that gut-terrible wager . . .

"I'll stand up as Westmore's second."

West turned his head to see Grant standing beside him. "No," he protested, shaking his head. "This isn't your fight, Grant." Or at least, it wasn't a fight Grant had chosen to believe in.

"Save your breath, West." He shrugged. "It's what friends do for each other. We save each others' lives, be it from war or stupidity." Grant's forehead wrinkled in thought. "But tomorrow is too soon. You both need time to calm down and get your affairs in order. Shall we say the morning of June 26th?"

"*No.*" Panic became a drum beat in West's ears. By the established rules of etiquette, one's second chose the time and date for the dual, and it was customary to allow time for both parties to cool down, contemplate an apology. At least, that was the way it had gone the last time Southingham had challenged him. But for God's sake, the date Grant was suggesting was impossible. "It must be sooner," he insisted.

Southingham's eyes narrowed. "Eager to meet your maker, Westmore?"

"Perhaps I am just eager to make your wife a widow," West shot back.

Instead of enraging the duke to imprudence, as he'd hoped, his words seemed to have the opposite effect. "Well you know, I do think the 26th shall do nicely," Southingham sneered. "Especially as I know it doesn't particularly suit you."

West clenched his hands. "I suppose you need the time to brush up on your target skills?" A ripple of laughter spun through the room, confirming they had a wide and interested audience.

"I could kill you with my eyes shut," Southinghman countered. "In the dark!"

West was desperate enough to unleash his tongue, though it was a foregone conclusion he was going to say something stupid. But truly, stupid was about all he had left. He needed to push Southingham beyond reason if he was going to have any chance in hell of saving the queen from whatever was going to happen on June 24th.

"Everyone knows I do my best work in the dark." He hesitated, but the man already believed it of him. "Just ask your wife," he added, hoping it would be the final nail he needed.

The buzz of the room became a roar, and from the corner of his eye, West saw several gentlemen gleefully exchanging money—no doubt over the apparent end to Grant's unholy wager. He felt Grant's hand on his shoulder, gently pulling him back.

"What in God's name are you doing?" his friend protested. "Are you trying to get him to pull out a pistol here and now?"

"He's a coward to insist on a date so far into the future!" West glared at Grant. "And you're a bloody fool to suggest it."

"Don't be rash," Grant said firmly. "Give me a chance to do my job as your second, and pull an apology out of your stupid arse, as I did last time. Regardless of whether you both end up splattering each other's brains on the ground, you owe it to yourself to ensure a bit of time to return to rationality first." He straightened his jacket, tugging at the ends. "I didn't save your life at Viborg only to have you squander it now," he warned. "And if either one of us are going to die for this, I'd suggest we ought to take a few days to enjoy ourselves first. Visit Madame Xavier's one last time. Indulge in Vivian's lovely feet."

"Vivian isn't even there anymore," West ground out. Which Grant would have known if he had ever listened to a single word West had tried to tell him.

"Someone else's feet then." Grant shrugged. "And while *you* might be quite confident in your shooting abilities,

I don't mind saying that I could use some target practice myself."

"There won't be a need for you to shoot anyone, because I'm going to finish him off." West tossed a simmering glare in the duke's direction. "And if Southingham is truly as confident a shot as he claims to be," he taunted, trying one last time to send the man over the edge, "it shouldn't matter when we meet."

Southingham bristled. "I should have killed you last year, when you first tried to steal what was mine. Saved us all a bunch of trouble."

"It isn't stealing when you don't 'own' it," West pointed out. "The duchess is a person, not a thing." And that, perhaps, was at the heart of all of it. Southingham had never understood that women were more than objects designed for his personal amusement. Perhaps that was why he had reacted so poorly that memorable All Hallows' Eve night.

The man had never once, in his wildest dreams, imagined the woman in question might have made her own choice in the matter.

"Damn it, Westmore." Southingham looked ready to explode, but alas not, it seemed, on the side of brevity. "It shall be the 26th, and not a day before." He picked up his glove and turned on his heel, but shouted over his shoulder as he left. "And this time, I'd advise you to bring something other than rats to the fight."

DARKNESS SWIRLED. ROUGH hands shook her from her dreams.

"Mary, wake *up*."

Sleep was yanked from her like a curtain pulled from its moorings, and Mary opened her eyes to the confusing combination of darkness and the bright, searing light of a nearby lamp. Not yet five o'clock then. Her mind pinwheeled against the unaccustomed intrusion, wanting only to return to sleep. But then her gaze swam upward to see her sister's pale face looming over her.

"Eleanor," she gasped, pushing off her covers. "Is something wrong?" The last dregs of sleep slid away, and a ribbon of fear spiraled through her. "Is it the baby?"

"Get your things," Eleanor said firmly. "You are coming home with me."

Confusion crushed down on her. "But . . . I *am* home." Mary reeled, trying to make sense of it all. Behind her sister, she could see Lord Ashington standing silent, a lamp in one hand. Mary reached out beside her, intending to shake West awake, only to realize that his side of the bed was empty, the sheets cold to the touch. She cringed, realizing that while she might be home, her husband clearly was not. "What on earth is going on?"

"Ashington came home from White's bearing the news." Eleanor's voice was pinched with anger. "And it's simply not to be borne. Perhaps we can have your marriage annulled, somehow, given that Westmore seems to regard it as a joke."

"*Annulled?*" Mary gawped at her sister. "Joke? Eleanor, what are you talking about?"

"Ashington saw all of it." Eleanor glanced back at her husband. "Tell her. Tell her what he has done this time."

Ashington cleared his throat, looking uncomfortable. "Westmore has taken up with the Duchess of Southingham. The duke discovered their affair and called him out this evening."

Mary gasped. "*What?*"

Eleanor nodded. "There's going to be a duel in Hyde Park, and his friend Mr. Grant will stand up as his second." She laid a hand around her swollen middle, though the expression on her face looked the opposite of motherly. "And if Southingham doesn't kill him," she added fiercely, "I'll tear him apart myself, for treating you this way."

Through the haze of disbelief that threatened to swamp

her, Mary shook her head. "You should not be up," she protested. "Surely it wasn't good for you to be this upset. You could force the baby to come early." Then again, it was nearly July now, closer to Dr. Merial's prediction for a delivery date. And in truth, Eleanor looked fine, her eyes flashing, her chin held high. She was stirred up, to be sure, but not courting the edge of a crisis.

If only Mary's own reaction were so measured.

Her thoughts raced in the direction of denial. It was all a misunderstanding—West wouldn't do such a thing to her. Perhaps he had just stepped out for a moment, gone to the washroom, or to the kitchen for a bite to eat—

A movement at the bedroom door pinned her doubts to a spot where they could neither shift nor slide out of reach. West stepped inside, fully dressed, his hat in his hands. His gaze roamed the room. "What's all this about?" he asked slowly.

"My sister could ask you the same thing," Eleanor retorted. "Come, Mary. You don't need to stay here with him."

Mary hesitated, her eyes afraid to settle on her husband. Instead, they drifted toward Lord Ashington. "You saw it yourself?" she asked in a small voice. "It isn't just a rumor you heard?"

Ashington nodded. "I saw it unfold. There's already a round of wagers in the betting book as to who will emerge the victor."

Mary pulled her knees up tight, disbelief and disappointment clashing in her chest. It wasn't possible. West was standing in the doorway, his handsome face unreadable for the moment. But just a few hours ago, he'd been in bed with her, her head on his shoulder.

It couldn't be true. It *couldn't*.

But what if it was?

Hadn't she imagined tonight he was keeping something from her? Hiding some important detail, some crucial fact?

And in spite of the way he could make her feel, hadn't she feared he would never be happy with nothing but a mousy wife in his bed?

Her gaze settled on her husband. Standing there in his street clothes, he looked windblown and cautious and guilty as hell.

And for once, she was determined to have the truth out of him.

"Eleanor," she said, not taking her eyes off West, "please go home now. I will speak with you in the morning, but for now I would have a word with my husband in private."

"I really don't think—"

"Eleanor!" Her voice came out more sharply than she intended, but she couldn't soften it, not now. Her gaze finally swung from West's guilty face to her sister's shocked one. "I am a grown woman, and this is *my* life, and I would appreciate it if you would let me manage things myself for once!"

Her sister's lips flattened into a line. "Very well then. But know you've a place to stay with us." Eleanor shot West a poisonous glare. "A home where you are wanted and loved." She reached out a hand and beckoned to her husband. "Come, Ashington."

As they filed out of the room, Mary sat, waiting. Hurting. How inconvenient an organ the heart was, a stone about one's neck, pulling one down, suffocating. And how persistent the mind, sifting through evidence while wanting to pretend none of it mattered. She reached out a hand to turn up the lamp burning low on the bedside table. Not that she expected it to help her see more clearly. There were shadows in this marriage, shadows purposefully created by her husband. She felt abraded on the inside, the fragile trust that had been starting to take shape in her marriage toppling into a pile of rubble. She'd feared losing him, of course.

Imagined all the terrible ways this affair might end.

But this was something else entirely.

"MARY, I CAN explain." At least, he *hoped* he could explain.

West was really rather afraid he couldn't even explain it to himself.

No matter his earlier conviction that he had the power to fix this, he was only now beginning to realize that the cost of this misguided attempt to save the queen might yet be his wife. He feared he was going to lose her. If not by gunshot, then by stupidity.

Because she'd never before looked at him with such profound disappointment, not even when she'd imagined he'd slept with a corpse.

She lifted her hands, as if trying to shield herself from his words. "Is it true, then?" The doubt in her voice told him all too clearly that she already suspected the answer, and it came close to breaking his heart. "There is to be a duel with Southingham?"

He took a tentative step forward. "Southingham called me out tonight," he admitted. "That part's true enough."

"And the rest?"

He moved toward her then, wanting desperately to make her see. "No. My association with the duchess is just a misunderstanding."

"Is this one of your infamous jokes, then?" she asked sharply.

He stopped as though she had struck him, her words twisting like the very knife he'd shown her how to use. "No. This is not a joke. Mary, I wouldn't do that to you. Not on purpose." Though, given his significant reputation on the matter of jokes, he probably couldn't blame her if she believed such a thing.

"Then *why*." She didn't ask it as a question.

He moved again, stopping in front of her. "Ashington should not have rushed back to tell your sister," he growled, pulling a hand through his hair. "The man's a proper idiot. I thought Dr. Merial had strictly warned him against agitating your sister."

"I do not dispute the claim of Ashington's idiocy, but you cannot blame my sister's agitation solely on her husband," she snapped. "Eleanor has never liked you, and she would have found out about this, one way or another. I imagine the gossip rags are already printing the news of your evening's adventures, and she most assuredly will see those on the morrow."

West lowered himself to sit beside her on the bed. Caught the scent of lemons, rising off her heated skin. "I suspect Southingham is one of our traitors, Mary. I had planned to tell you myself, tonight." Regret tugged at him, knowing he had delayed this reckoning. Perhaps even caused it, with his careful attempts to shield her from the emerging truth. But much like Crimea, he was proving ill-equipped to save those who insisted on leaping into the fray. "As soon as you woke."

"When I *woke*?" she choked out, and he could hear the anger splinter through the earlier doubt in her words. "Why didn't you tell me before I fell *asleep*?"

He hesitated, knowing she wasn't going to like his answer. "I wasn't sure yet that it was Southingham when you were falling asleep," he said, though the explanation sounded lame, even to him.

"But you could have told me you suspected him. I told you everything I had discovered tonight, every piece of every conversation, and you sat there and said *nothing*. I suppose you think it is better for a wife to be kept in the dark as her husband goes about flirting with duchesses and dueling with dukes?"

In spite of the anger rolling off her, West found his lips twitching. Whether she realized it or not, her choice of words was illuminating. He was beginning to understand that beneath her anger lay something . . . interesting. "Are your objections more to a perceived flirtation," he asked, cocking a brow, "or the threatened duel with Southingham?"

"Don't try to distract me with that scoundrel's smile. In

fact, never mind." She swung her legs over the opposite side of the bed. "Perhaps it is best if I go to stay with my sister after all," she muttered, reaching for her wrapper. "It is clear you are not the sort of man I thought you were, to do something like this as a lark."

"Mary." He reached out a hand, curling his fingers against her arm. "It wasn't done for a lark. That is not why I was smiling. And I don't want you to go."

She looked back at him, her hands clenched to fists. "Give me one good reason why I should stay and listen to another word you say."

He bowed his head. "I will give you the truth. It is up to you to decide if it's a good enough reason."

SLOWLY, SHE SHIFTED back onto the bed. At least he was talking to her now, and not avoiding the topic. Promising her the truth, instead of trying to distract her with a practiced seduction.

Whether or not he was capable of delivering it, however, was another thing entirely.

"Tell me, then," she asked warily. "Why were you smiling just now?"

"Because it is clear you are jealous of the thought that it *might* be true."

She opened her mouth to protest. Closed it again. Drat it all, but he was right. The man really could read her like a book. "What if I am? It seems I've a right to be, given that you have been tupping the Duchess of Southingham!"

"Tupping, is it? You seem to have lapsed a bit in your vocabulary since marrying me."

"For heaven's sake, can you not be serious for two seconds?" she snapped.

"All right. I've not tupped the Duchess of Southingham. Tupping requires touching, and I swear to you, I've never even touched her. Not now, and not last year, either."

"Then why does the Duke of Southingham believe you have?"

He exhaled loudly. "I'll admit that I permitted the misunderstanding to persist tonight, but only because it was necessary."

"Necessary? For *revenge*?" She threw up her hands. "I know there is a good deal of sour history between you and the duke, but this is scarcely a harmless prank. Did you think about those who would be hurt by it? For heaven's sake, you have very likely destroyed the duchess's reputation. Perhaps the duke might even blame her for this. Divorce her over it."

"He is far too possessive a man for that." His jaw hardened. "But if he does, I say she is better off without the bastard. The man has a heavy hand."

"Be that as it may, that ought to be her decision, not yours. And duels are nothing to trifle with. Neither are they strictly legal, West. If you kill Southingham, you could very well be charged with murder." She swallowed, unable to give voice to the rest of it.

And I could be left alone.

"Mary. This wasn't about revenge, or even a good joke. It was about justice." He hesitated. "And while not legal, duels are still somewhat tolerated. Meeting Southingham on a field of honor would afford me at least some protection against a proper murder charge. But I never planned to kill the man." He hesitated. "I only intended to take out his shooting arm."

"What? *Why*?" She glared at him, none of it making sense. He'd promised her the truth, but she couldn't see anything of it in the fits and pieces he was handing her. "If you expect me to make sense of any of this, I think you better start at the beginning."

"The beginning, hmm?" There was a slight upturn to his handsome mouth. "Very well then, once upon a time, a man met a woman in a garden—"

"West!" she shrieked. "This isn't one of your silly jokes!"

"I know." He reached out. Threaded his fingers into hers. "Very well then. From the beginning. Earlier this week, I interviewed Ashington's staff and discovered who had left the note, and at whose request. That information made me suspect the identity of our duke. Tonight I snuck into Southingham's study and confirmed it." At her resulting gasp, his fingers tightened against hers. "There can be no doubt he's the duke we overheard the night of the literary salon. Tonight, I overheard him making new plans with the woman from the library."

"Are you absolutely sure?" she asked, stunned.

"His handwriting matches the note that was left in your journal. His voice has always seemed familiar, and now I know why. I heard him, in his house, making these plans. And I did not agree to this duel out of some twisted sense of revenge. I did it because it afforded me an opportunity to disarm him." He met her gaze. "Before he destroyed the queen."

The room spun around her. They had a name. An identity. This changed *everything*. For weeks, they'd been searching for a single, guttering candle in a sea of lights.

But now, the candle had a name. A face.

She listened as he told her about interviewing Eleanor's maid, and the girl's roundabout connection to Southingham. He told her about the mention of Scotland and June 24th and Vivian's escape with the money, as well as the fact that the duke now planned to carry out the assassination himself. He told her about searching Southingham's desk, picking up the newspaper, and accidentally leaving behind his case of matches.

"When he burst into White's shouting for blood, I could think only of defusing the threat, so I agreed to the duel, thinking that if I could injure him, prevent him from carrying out the plan on June 24th, I might at least buy a little time to sort the rest of it out."

Mary sank back onto the pillows, finding it hard to breathe. "But . . . Southingham could just as easily kill you."

"Do not worry." His hand tightened over hers. "I am a decent shot, Mary."

Her thoughts pulled to the scar West bore, just above his heart. Being a fair shot didn't save someone from death if their opponent was also a fair shot. Nor did it excuse the idiocy of presuming there was no other way to go about this. "Bollocks to that," she huffed.

In spite of the gravity of the moment, his lips twitched. "Mrs. Westmore." He tilted his handsome head. "Did you just say 'bollocks'?"

"I did, and I will say it again," she said impatiently. "*Bollocks* to you trying to disarm Southingham in a duel. You told me yourself that dueling pistols have terrible accuracy, that they are designed to ensure gentlemen bent on killing each other haven't a prayer of hitting where they aim. And bollocks as well to the notion that *we* have no other options to pursue."

His smile faltered. "There are no other options, Mary. I swear, I have told you everything I know."

"I believe you are telling me the truth," she breathed. But neither could she trust he would continue to do so. Even if what he said was true, even if this started as a misunderstanding and evolved into a plan for him to play the reluctant hero, he was apparently willing to let everyone else in London believe he would do such a thing, her sister included.

Which meant he had no notion about how such a thing might hurt her.

"It just seems clear you didn't believe in *me*. You interrogated Lord Ashington's staff without telling me your plans, and then you pursued the lead with Southingham without giving me any clue you suspected him." Her voice hitched, though she tried in vain to steady it. "You didn't care enough about me to have been honest with me from the start."

"Good God, Mary," he said, his voice sounding raw. "How can you think that? I believe you are brave, and smart, and too full of good ideas. But the thought of involving you in this terrifies the hell out of me." He shook his head. "I used to have nightmares about Crimea, but now my dreams are tangled with you and the danger I cannot defuse." His eyes met hers, pleading. "Can't you see? I care about you, too much. And the notion that I might be unable to save you . . . I don't think I could live with myself if anything happened to you."

"Live with yourself?" Mary snorted, though her heart had thawed several degrees to hear him say he cared about her. It wasn't a confession of love, but it was something more than she'd feared several minutes ago. "For heaven's sake, tonight you goaded a man into a duel." In spite of her resolve, her voice wavered. "You may not *live*."

He bowed his head. "I should have told you before now, but I was afraid . . ." She heard him swallow. "I was afraid of losing you."

"You might still," she warned. "Because while I can forgive the deception this time, I can't help but fear you will just break my heart again and again." She choked on the last piece of it, but somehow got it out. "And I am not sure I want to spend the rest of my life with someone I cannot trust."

He winced. "You deserve better than me, Mary, God knows you do. I've been a scoundrel and a rake and more than a bit of a hothead. But that just means I need to become the man you deserve. When this is all over, I vow I will fight to earn your trust."

Mary allowed herself a slow nod of agreement. *When this is all over.* It was a reminder that the path to this happy ending was far from assured, and that the fate of her marriage took a second place, at present, to the fate of the queen.

"When do you meet the duke?" she asked.

He sagged visibly. "That's the worst part of it. Southingham has insisted on June 26th. Too late to do any good."

A chill ran through her, but she pushed it from her mind. If nothing else, the delayed date gave her time to think. "Of *course* Southingham didn't want to meet you before the 26th. He has something important to do first." She held out her hand. "May I see the newspaper you took from the duke's study tonight?"

He pulled it from his jacket pocket and handed it over to her.

The answer was on the first page, the headlines all but screaming it out loud. "The foundation stone is to be laid for the new Freemason's Hall in Edinburgh on June 24th." Mary tapped a finger against the newsprint. "There is to be a grand procession of Freemasons from Holyrood Palace, with thousands in attendance. Look."

He stared down at the paper she held in her hands. Took a moment to take in the details. "Good God." His jaw hardened. "Southingham plans to blame it on the Freemasons."

"That night, in the library, when they mentioned the word constitution, they must have been referring to the new Grand Lodge, and the Scottish Constitution of Freemasons," Mary said, her mind connecting all the puzzle pieces, seeing, at last, how they fit. Dread sent her stomach churning, though the sensation warred with the relief she felt to have finally figured it out, "And according to this newspaper account, the queen plans to attend the laying of the foundation stone."

West looked up. Met her gaze for a smoldering second of indecision, where she feared he might once again prove himself an overprotective oaf.

But then he nodded once, as if coming to an important decision. "You are right. The only question is, what are *we* going to do about this?"

From the Diary of Miss Mary Channing
June 23, 1858

The motion of the train makes it difficult to write, but the distraction of my journal is far preferable to the distraction of my husband. He sits beside me, brooding and distant, not voicing his objections to my presence, but not voicing his encouragement, either.

What does he think of all of this? Of me?

I still do not feel as if I really know him. And while I am not so silly or naive to imagine a husband must necessarily profess love and devotion for a wife, shouldn't a wife at least feel as though she knows her husband? The fragile truce that has been formed between us strains at the seams, and when I look up to see him watching me, doubts crowd too close. And yet, just ahead, still out of reach, I have the sense that this marriage might yet prove worthy of saving.

But first we must save the queen.

And that is why I pray that at least one of my plans works.

Chapter 24

To Mary, Edinburgh was a city of startling smells and contrasts.

Hewn from damp, gray stone, the city boasted teeming, unwashed masses and tall tenement buildings. Some four stories below their hotel room, the squalor spilled forth onto Cowgate, rivers of waste running beneath carriage wheels, ragged clothes flapping from lines crisscrossing the cobblestone streets.

And yet, just ahead, through the hotel window, Mary could see the shine of the newer part of the city, the streets widening to accommodate the deeper pockets of Edinburgh's wealthier citizens. Further on ahead, on a bluff of dark granite and green moss, Edinburgh Castle rose like a phoenix against spinning, dark clouds.

"Looks like rain tonight," West remarked as he came to stand behind her, his body not even touching hers, but nonetheless sending electric sparks singing beneath her skin. She crossed her arms, trying in vain to ignore the way her body reacted to him. They'd not been intimate since the night of the ball, and she wasn't at all sure how she felt about the idea of being intimate now. Somewhere in this city, traitors were plotting the death of the queen.

And trust in her husband was proving a difficult thing to regain.

He'd been nothing but a gentleman the entire journey. At her request, he had ensured that their hotel room—small though it may be, thanks to their late arrival and the burgeoning population in town—had separate beds. His patient accommodation of her every request boggled the mind. This was a man who could have anyone he wanted. Before their marriage, he'd garnered an immense reputation for enjoying a variety of women—and not all one at a time.

And yet, he seemed willing to sleep alone tonight, because that was what *she* said she wanted. Even if she was no longer sure of her own feelings on the matter.

Drawing a deep breath against the treacherous leanings of her heart, Mary peered out the window onto the early evening cityscape. The clouds *did* look ominous, boiling on the horizon. "Hopefully the rain will hold off until tomorrow, when it would do us some actual good. A damp day might discourage such wide attendance during the procession." She looked down, feeling again that sense of dread to see how many people clogged the narrow street below. "Although, the threat of rain doesn't seem to be thwarting any of their enthusiasm at present. The streets are absolutely mobbed."

"Yes, tomorrow's event has drawn crowds from the surrounding countryside, hoping for a glimpse of their queen." She felt the gentle brush of his lips against the nape of her neck, the small scrape of unshaven whiskers against her skin.

Shivering against the unwelcome feelings he could pull from her, she turned to face him, placing a hand against his chest, pushing gently. "You need to shave." A lie, that. In truth, she liked him like this, slightly unkempt, a bit of a rogue. But she needed her wits about her for what was coming, and unfortunately, proximity to this man made her head spin in unfortunate circles.

She needed a moment to breathe, to think.

He yielded, though he looked none too happy to do so. She saw him rub a hand across the stubble on his chin, knowing he was wishing for his valet. But they'd travelled light and fast, eschewing the accompaniment of servants in favor of time and stealth. No one at home even knew where they were, thanks to West's story about taking a brief wedding trip to the Lake District, a tale everyone seemed to believe.

"I could go and see about a barber," he offered, working his jaw.

Mary sighed. He was trying so hard, but it only forced her to sidestep him at every turn. "The fate of the entire country could be hanging in the balance," she told him, though she prayed things weren't as dire as that. "Instead of a barber, we might first start with a visit to the Edinburgh authorities. Perhaps they would believe us, if we just went to them and explained—"

"Impossible," he interrupted with an impatient shake of his head. "I am on their list, too. Grant and I attended the University of Edinburgh, and there was that time when we—"

"*West.*" She wrapped her arms around her, feeling sick. *Good heavens.* She hadn't known he'd lived for a time in Edinburgh. It was yet another reminder there was so much about him she didn't know, and she was beginning to despair she would ever learn half of it, especially given their current predicament. "For heaven's sake, this isn't a joke!"

"No," he agreed. "It isn't a joke. It is a bloody dangerous mission, and I am not entirely sure what we are doing here, but it seems we have a better chance to do something here, in Edinburgh, than pacing the streets of London."

Mary hesitated. "I just . . . that is . . ." She wrapped her arms more tightly about herself, half-wishing they were her husband's instead. This forced separation, the stiffened shoulders—none of it was helping. But she'd made her preferences on the matter of his proximity all too clear, and his arms stayed firmly by his side. "There are times," she breathed out, frustrated, "when it just doesn't seem fair that we must be the only heroes in this."

"I know." He looked down at her, shaking his head. "I've got a bloody Victoria Cross gathering dust on my bureau, but I don't feel like a hero, not even close. But fate has a way of forcing one's feet into the fray, making heroes of the worst of us. Some may say we made this bed ourselves, me with my reputation for pranks and you with your wild imagination. But regardless of how it came about, it seems we are the ones meant to do this."

She drew a deep breath. "You are right." She nodded. "But how can we stop it if we don't know what Southingham is planning?"

WEST DIDN'T HAVE a proper answer to that.

It would definitely help to know Southingham's plans, where the man planned to do it, and more importantly, how. But they lacked those crucial pieces of the puzzle.

Worse, West didn't know what his wife was planning either. Something about the slant of her brow told him her mind was working hard, and he wasn't to be privy to the entirety of it. It hurt, that she distrusted him enough to hold something of herself back.

Hurt, too, to know that perhaps he had earned the new doubt in her eyes.

"I know. I am worried, too," he admitted. His gaze pulled to something beyond Mary's slim shoulders, a movement through the window, down on the street. He stepped around her and peered down through the glass. Relief skittered through him, to finally have something to do other than wait for whatever it was that would happen on the morrow. Because outside the window, four stories down, he caught the profile of someone he recognized.

"But we might yet find out what they plan," he muttered.

"What do you see?" she asked, stepping up to stare out the window beside him.

"There." He pointed, guiding her gaze. "The man there, walking down Stevenlaw's Close. It's difficult to see from here, but he's got a scar on along his jaw. That is George Carlson, the Duke of Southingham's man. I recognize him from the day I chased him in St. Paul's Cathedral. When Queen Victoria arrives on the morrow, the royal route will surely take her over South Bridge, on her way to Holyrood. Perhaps he is scouting locations nearby."

Beside him, Mary gave a small gasp. "Oh, but that is perfect! We can follow him."

"I can trail him," West agreed grimly, "but I think you ought to keep watch from the window." But his thoughts fell into empty air. He heard the click of the door latch, the creak on a hinge. Turned his head to see Mary's skirts, disappearing into the hallway. "Oh, bugger me blue," West groaned, dashing after her. "Mary, *wait*!"

She whirled to face him, having nearly made it to the stairwell, a belligerent pinch to her mouth. "You aren't going to leave me out of this," she warned. "Not this time."

As if he had a prayer in hell of stopping her.

"I only wanted to ask . . . do you have your dagger?" She lifted her wrist, showing him the reticule that dangled from it. "Better to keep it in a pocket," he advised. "Stuffed in your reticule like that, it's a bit useless as anything more than a bludgeon."

She nodded, pulled the sheathed knife from her reticule, and shoved it into a pocket of her skirts. Then, turning on her heel, she hurried down the stairs.

He could do nothing but try to keep up.

They plunged outside into the sour-smelling alley. Just ahead, West could see Carlson greet a man who was jumping down from a wagon.

"West," Mary hissed, poking him in the side with her elbow. "Do you see?"

"I see." And what he was seeing was money being exchanged, a good deal of it, from Carlson's hands to the driver. The two men stood a moment, their heads bent in conversation. The wagon rumbled off in the direction of High Street, a lumpy oilcloth draped over its bed.

As Carlson set off, his hands in his pockets, Mary tossed West a triumphant look, her eyes shining with excitement. "We nearly missed our chance to follow him." She pushed forward.

West grabbed her arm. "What are you doing?"

"Following him."

"*Which* him?"

She paused. "Oh. There are two of them now, aren't there?" She bit her lip. "Very well then, I will follow Southingham's man. You should track the wagon and see where it is going."

"I think *I* should follow Carlson," he protested. He *knew* Carlson posed a danger. The tarp over the bed of the wagon could be covering anything. China dolls. Rotting turnips.

Cages full of rats.

"You are doing it again," she accused, craning her neck in the direction her quarry had gone. "Carlson may very well know your face now, after the chase you gave in the cathedral. I have a better chance of following him undetected."

"It's too dangerous," he protested, shaking his head.

She twisted against his grip. "The longer we stand here and argue about it, the greater the chance that he is *getting away*."

Which was, unfortunately, true. Even now, their one clue to follow in the city could be disappearing into the throngs of people lining the streets. Damn it all, but it was too much of a risk to *not* let her go. West released her arm, cursing the situation, fate, Mary's stubbornness, and any other number of things that had led them to this impossible crossroad.

"Go then," he agreed reluctantly. "But please be very, very careful. Do nothing more than watch him from a distance, Mary. See where he goes, and take note of anyone he speaks with."

She nodded, her face brightening. He was reminded of the way her eyes had shone that day when she had appeared in St. Paul's Cathedral. It was only when he tried to hold her back that the brightness ebbed. Well, no more holding back. If this was the man she needed him to be, so be it. He only hoped he survived the uncertainty.

"Be inconspicuous." He grinned suddenly. "Like a mouse."

"A role I've been training for my entire life," she shot back with an answering smile, then tore off in the direction Carlson had gone.

And West headed toward High Street to follow the wagon, praying he hadn't just made a terrible mistake.

CALLING ON EVERY skill in every book she'd ever read, Mary followed Carlson to the edge of Old Town. She paused, on occasion, to peer through the odd storefront, trying to give the appearance of being a woman intent on window shopping. In her plain, ordinary dress she imagined she could have been a woman of nearly any mediocre station in life, out running an errand, shopping at the milliner's. But her mission was something more critical than purchasing a pretty set of ribbons or buying a lovely new hat.

And with each block, her confidence grew.

Carlson initially proved easy to follow through the old city, even though the dark clouds and encroaching evening promised to obscure him soon. But as they tumbled into New Town, she lost sight of him as she stepped around a busy corner. She stood for a moment, searching for the man's battered hat, his distinctive slouch of a walk. Against the more fashionable crowd, it ought to be easier to pick him out, not harder.

Which meant, she realized with a pang of worry, he was trying to disappear.

She peered through the nearest storefront window. Inside she could see a tea shop, well-dressed men and women sitting at tables, hear the hum of distant conversation and the delicate ring of silver against porcelain. The scent of tea and biscuits wafting onto the street made her stomach rumble, but she couldn't take the time to eat when there was an assassin on the loose. "Where have you gotten to, Carlson?" she muttered beneath her breath.

"Right behind you," an unexpected growl rang in her ear.

Mary turned. Gasped at the dark eyes glaring down at her. She drew her hands up, though her reticule proved a hopeless shield between them. "Please," she gasped, even as his hand came up to snatch at the bit of fabric, the ribbons close to breaking. "If you want money, I can get it—" She tried to reach inside, only to realize with a sinking feeling that her dagger was no longer there.

"What do you 'ave in there?" The man's eyes narrowed. "A weapon?" He snatched the reticule from her wrist and tossed it to one side.

As she watched the bit of fabric fly through the air to land in a foul puddle, her dreamy adventure came skidding to a halt, along with every bit of her confidence. Oh, but what was she doing? West had warned her that she was to watch the man. Keep her distance. And she had tried, truly she had. In the books she had read, the heroines were *never* caught spying on the villain. She was beginning to suspect someone ought to write a more accurate book.

Carlson grabbed her hand, his fingers cruel against her

wrist, and pulled her around a corner, into a narrow alley, her feet grappling uselessly on the cobblestones.

"Please, sir," she gasped. "I am just an ordinary woman, looking for an ordinary cup of tea." She tried to step around him, dash back out to the relative safety of the street.

He grabbed her arm and pushed her against the wall, and the hard pressure of his fingers against her arm made her cry out in pain. But he'd chosen this moment and this location well: no one could see them, or come to rescue her.

"'ardly ordinary," he growled. You know my name. I 'eard you, I did. And I know yours as well." His mouth opened in a terrible grimace, and she could smell his sour breath. "You're that bitch, Miss Channing. The one I arranged to send the note to."

Oh, God. He knew who she was after all.

Against his punishing grip, Mary's free hand reached through the folds of her cloak into the pocket of her skirts. Closed in relief over the dagger West had ensured she knew how to use. Untangling it from her skirt pocket, she pulled it out of its sheath and pressed the tip of it carefully into the man's groin. "That's *Mrs.* Westmore, thank you very much," she somehow found the courage to say, though her heart was tearing a hole in her chest.

"What in the—"

"And next time you take a woman's reticule, you might want to make sure that's where she's stored her knife."

"Whoa, there. Easy, luv." The man released her arm and held up his hands, his eyes wide with fear. "No need to get so excited."

"I'm not the one whose future excitement is in jeopardy." She pressed the point home a quarter inch further, making him grunt in alarm. "Now, we can do this the easy way, or the messy way. But either way, you are going to stop calling me 'luv'." She lifted her chin. "Where is the Duke of Southingham? We know he's behind the plot."

White-rimmed eyes goggled down at her. "I don't know what you are talking about, luv—" She wiggled the tip of the knife, earning a squeak from the man. "That is, Mrs. Westmore," he amended. "The duke's got nothing to do with this."

"No?" She tsked in disappointment. "Such loyalty. I do hope he's paying you well, given that you could swing from the gallows for him. Move out." She jerked her chin toward the street, trying to keep the hand gripping the knife steady. "Quickly, please."

As Carlson stepped reluctantly in the direction she indicated, Mary moved the knife to his back, urging him on. In spite of the danger, a thread of breathless excitement bubbled through her. She had captured a villain and saved herself, no need for a hero after all. A new plan tumbled about in her head. She'd march him back to the hotel, tie him up using a Blackwall hitch knot, and have West interrogate him when he returned.

They'd find out what the plan was, and then the queen would be—

A shot rang out, just as they stepped into the main street.

Carlson sagged in front of her, crumpling onto the cobblestones, a scarlet bloom spreading from his chest. Horrified, Mary gaped at him, then fell to her knees, fumbling at the man's neck, searching for a pulse. Her hands grew slick with blood as she came to the sickening realization there was no longer a pulse to be found. She felt a howling frustration at losing the opportunity to interrogate the man. And then her thoughts flew further.

What if the bullet hadn't been intended for Carlson?

The bullet could have come from anywhere.

Been meant for anyone.

Her lungs clawing for air, Mary leaped to her feet. Hands reached out toward her, hands that no doubt meant to detain her, question her. Panicked, she dashed toward the tea shop and plunged through the front door. At the sight of her blood-covered hands, chairs tumbled back, men bellowed, women screamed.

A surprised waiter gaped at her, his hands full with a tray and tea service.

"Is there a back door?" she asked desperately.

The waiter inclined his head toward the back of the room, and Mary darted in that direction, tripping over knocked-over chairs. All the while she held her breath, terrified of hearing another shot with so many innocent people at risk.

She dashed through a bustling kitchen and skidded out a back entrance.

Then, her hands still slippery with a dead man's blood, she lifted her skirts and ran as hard as she could toward the relative safety of the hotel. One thought beat through her mind.

She shouldn't have insisted on doing this alone.

She needed to remember that her husband had rather more experience in matters of life and death than she did. And, like her dagger, she needed to remember that a living, breathing hero wasn't necessarily such a terrible thing to keep in one's pocket.

Chapter 25

s West stepped inside the hotel room, he saw Mary standing over the hotel room's washbasin. She was stripped down to her corset and chemise, her hands soapy.

He didn't ask permission, didn't wait for her to even dry her hands, just strode toward her, turned her around and clutched her to his chest, welcoming the dampness soaking through his jacket and shirt. It told him she was real. Whole. *Safe*.

It had taken a good deal of restraint to refrain from shouting his objections out on the street, to follow the wagon even as she followed Carlson. He would take a moment and appreciate the fact that she'd survived.

"You cannot imagine," he said, his voice hoarse, "how happy I am to see you."

He closed his eyes, savoring the feel, the sound, the scent of her. But as he held her, he became aware of another scent, too, hovering in the background, a coppery tang of violence that did not belong in this moment. Startled, he opened his eyes and forced his gaze further afield. Her dress lay bunched upon the fraying carpet, scarlet smears across the front of her bodice. He glanced toward the washbasin and his hands tightened around her.

The water was tinged pink, with blood.

The walls of the room seemed to swim around him. Blood. *Too much of it*. The sort of blood one didn't get from a paper cut, turning the pages of a book.

The only question was, *whose* blood?

He set her away from him. Noticed, for the first time, her obvious pallor. He could see no bullet wound, no obvious damage, but that didn't mean she wasn't hurt. "Are you shot?" he demanded. "Injured in some way?"

She shook her head dully. "No." It was a whisper of a word.

Hardly a reassuring sound.

He picked up her hand, turned it over. Instead of ink stains, remnants of blood rimmed her fingernails. Panic thumped in his ears at the sight of it. He felt yanked straight back to that lower deck on the *HMS Arrogant*, the blood of innocents spreading around him.

"What happened?" he snarled. "I swear to God, I'll *kill* the bastard."

"I am afraid someone's already done that for you." She shuddered, staring down at her hands. He recognized the vacant, glassy look in her eyes, knew what an unwilling battle did to a soul. Knew, too, that he needed to find out what had happened without shoving her back into the thick of whatever memory was causing her to sway like that on her feet.

Leaning over her, he picked up the soap, dipped her hands back in the water, and then began to rub them slowly, working the fine bones and delicate skin with his fingers, as if he could strip the memory away as easily as the blood. "Won't you tell me what happened?" he asked in a lower voice. "What occured after we separated?"

She stood still, letting him wash her hands like a child. "I . . . I thought I was following the man from a safe enough distance. But Carlson must have realized it. He circled behind me and threatened me." She shuddered. "I pulled my knife, thinking to bring him back for you to question, but then someone shot him, right in front of me." She stood immobile as he lifted her hands from the basin and began to towel them dry. "It happened out on the main street." Her eyes lifted to meet his. "There were innocent bystanders." She swallowed, and the sound was jagged to his ears. "And I am not entirely sure the bullet wasn't intended for me."

"Good Christ," he breathed, dropping the towel to the floor. She could have been killed. Very nearly *had* been killed. The knowledge that whoever was caught up in this may have taken a shot at his wife made his blood boil hot. "Did Carlson say anything before he died?"

"He claimed to not know anything about the duke's involvement. I didn't believe him, and imagined if I could just get him back here, you might be able to get more out of him, but now . . ." She buried her face in her newly washed hands, hands that West knew from personal experience would take a very long time to feel clean again. "I've ruined our chance to find out what they were planning."

"Mary, you can't think that way," he countered. "Carlson was surely shot by Southingham. Perhaps it was part of the duke's plan to do away with the man all along. He'd not want to leave witnesses lying about."

Though, that statement was hardly as reassuring as he'd intended.

Because what were he and Mary, if not more witnesses?

She didn't look at him, just began to breathe rapidly into her hands. "I shouldn't have pushed him out on the main street. I should have been more careful. . ." Her hands clenched over her face. "I don't think I realized the full extent of the danger. In books . . ." She hesitated, then breathed out, lowering her hands. "Well. This real-life business of hunting traitors isn't much like books, is it?"

West resisted the urge to answer. His agreement here wasn't needed. Judging by the look on her face, her prior naïveté was a fact she now well understood.

He scooped her up, settled onto the lumpy mattress. Holding her on his lap, he rocked her gently. "Yes, this is a dangerous business. That's why I have wanted you to be careful, why I made sure you knew how to protect yourself. But you didn't ruin anything. I don't know that I would have done anything differently, Mouse."

And truly, he didn't. There were no wrong or right choices in those moments—you just went with your gut and hoped for the best.

"But this danger, this uncertainty, is why I don't like being separated from you," he told her, brushing his lips across the top of her hair. "Not because I do not think you are brave enough, or capable enough to try to manage things yourself. You've proven you are, time and time again. Truly, you are one of the most courageous people I have ever met. But when things go to shite, it helps to have a hand you trust there at the ready. Someone to look out for the person aiming at your back." He sighed. "If nothing else, Crimea taught me that."

He felt her tremble in his arms. Knew she was thinking of the man who had just died in front of her, the man whose blood he'd just washed off her hands. "Did you see men die in Crimea?" she asked in a small voice.

"Mary, I *killed* men in Crimea." He hesitated. "War is a messy, unpredictable thing, and things go to hell in a hurry when you are trapped on a ship. But thankfully, Grant was there, watching my back." His arms tightened around her, and his thoughts spun away from that dark time, not wanting to remember. "That is why we need to stick together. Watch out for each other." His voice cracked. "We need each other to do this properly. Because if you are killed, I swear to God the queen's health and safety will be the last thing on my mind. I need to know you are whole and standing beside me, helping to do the job before us."

"*Us?*" She pulled back, her eyes filled with a sheen of tears. "You mean . . . you still imagine I can help?"

He offered her a grim smile. "Well. You didn't faint out there today, did you?"

She shook her head.

"You've seen and done some things you wish you could forget?" At her nod he lifted a hand and smoothed the dark strands of hair off her forehead. "Well then, I'd say you've more than proven your stones." That brought some of the color back to her cheeks. "There's no one else I'd want to do this with. In fact, I'd say you are ready for a Victoria Cross of your own."

That, finally, pulled a small laugh from her. "Well, you *did* already give me yours."

They sat for an almost-comfortable moment, the soft feeling of her in his arms nearly heaven. Now that the difficult part of the conversation was over, now that she was returning to some semblance of her normal pattern of breathing, his body reacted with predictable interest.

The soft inward rise and fall of her chest settled her bum more firmly against his lap and reminded him of other things. But as his body hardened—something she could almost certainly feel, with so little clothing separating them—he felt a shift in her posture, a tightening of her spine. Her mind was turning in another direction.

And unfortunately, not the direction his had turned.

Her hands pushed lightly against his chest. "I forgot to ask . . . were you able to find out anything about the wagon?"

He let her slide off him, her bum settling onto the mattress. Watched her dawning self-awareness, the way her hands tugged down the hem of her rucked-up chemise. She looked a bit flushed, truth be told. As if she might be easily convinced to return to his lap. But he didn't permit himself that thought. He was willing to reach deep inside his well of patience if it meant an eventual return of her faith in him.

Nothing else had ever felt quite so necessary.

"I did not discover much," he admitted. "The wagon didn't go far, perhaps a block or two. It stopped in the middle of South Bridge. The oilskin on the back was covering a load of barrels, which the driver carried underground, one by one."

"I don't understand. If he stopped on the bridge, how could he carry the barrels underground?"

"The lower arches of the bridge were walled in some time ago, and form a series of vaults below. It's cool and dark down there, and some of the merchants use them for storage, though you couldn't pay me to go down in there. Years ago, when the burkers were stealing bodies for the medical school, it is rumored they stored some of the bodies in the vaults. A good many Edinburgh residents think they are haunted."

"Haunted?" She gave him an odd look. "Surely you don't believe such a thing. And how do you know so much about the bridge?"

"I studied its architecture when I attended university here. The vaulted arches support the bridge, and without them the bridge would come down. But the city decided to wall them in, thinking to make more usable space for commerce. Unfortunately, walling them in rendered them nearly unusable. They leak terribly from whatever is flowing across the top." He shrugged. "Rainwater, sewage, it all filters down into the vaults."

She pulled a face, and he was at least glad to see she was no longer looking at him as if he might have sprouted an extra limb.

"So, the driver carried the barrels down into one of the vaults," she said, frowning. "What do you think they contained?"

"The shop on the top of the bridge belonged to a wine merchant, and the barrels had the name of an Italian vineyard stamped on the barrels. I presume they contain wine."

"An *Italian* vineyard?"

"Yes," he admitted, "but we no longer suspect the Orsinians anymore, remember? It is the Freemasons who are involved."

"But we don't think the Freemasons are at the heart of the plot. They are simply the face the assassins planned to pin it on. Southingham *has* to have a political or personal reason to want to kill the queen. Perhaps we've overlooked an Orsinian connection there." She slid off the bed and began to pace. "You have to admit, it is an odd thing to imagine a wine shop might receive such a large delivery of unbottled wine. Wine is most often bottled at the site of the vineyard, or at the port, where it is unloaded."

Once again, she surprised him. He realized, then, that he'd only been watching the wagon and cataloging its contents, not thinking properly about what either could mean. "How do you know that?" he asked, shaking his head in awe.

She waved a dismissive hand in the air, her brow scrunched in thought. "Oh, I once read a book featuring a vintner as the villain. He stuffed his victims into empty wine barrels, then shipped them overseas." She turned toward him, the hem of her chemise swishing about her calves. She looked fierce in her musings, well-recovered from her earlier brush with terror. "If the barrels contained something other than wine . . . guns, for example. Ammunition."

"Southgate Bridge would be a convenient staging place," West agreed, still trying to catch up with racing thoughts.

"They could be thinking to arm a makeshift army on the morrow. Or . . ." She stopped. Gasped. Rummaged through her valise and yanked out a clean dress, pulling it over her head.

"Mary, what is it?" he asked, concerned.

"Can't you see?" Her hands began to fly over the buttons marching up to her throat. "The plot is larger than a single assassin, and larger, even, than the queen, it seems."

"What do you mean?"

"Whatever is in those barrels, they are stored under Southgate Bridge. The Queen will cross over it on her way to Holyrood Palace, where the Freemason procession will start."

Understanding dawned. "You think they plan something with the bridge?"

"I don't know." She frowned. "But I think we need to find out what is in those barrels."

A RUMBLE OF thunder greeted them as they stepped outside the hotel.

The air smelled of coming rain, which was preferable to the less palatable undertones of Edinburgh's streets. Night had fallen, an inky darkness. The threatening weather had driven most of the earlier revelers indoors, and the streets had an eerie, deserted feel. She was reminded of West's terrible description of the vaults, of the dank, dark space and the bodies that had once been stored in them.

She shivered against the thought. *We need to stick together*, he'd told her.

And for the rest of this adventure, she intended to be a bur by his side.

As they hurried down the city's narrow cobblestone streets, the darkness seemed nearly overwhelming. In Mayfair, the gaslights lent some warmth to the night, but here, in Edinburgh's back alleys, there was no more light to be found beyond the occasional streak of lamplight, filtering through a shuttered window.

And in truth, there was nothing warm about a night that might see a monarch dead with the sunrise.

Somewhere above her head, she heard the scrape of a

shutter opening. A shout of "Gardyloo!" sang out, several stories up. Mary leaped forward just as something was tossed out, splashing out onto the streets behind her. She plastered herself against West's strong back, crying out in surprise. "What was that?"

"Mouse," she heard him chuckle, his voice low and warm. "It's just a pot of piss. Nothing you haven't seen before. In fact, I seem to recall something of that sort on the day we met."

Slowly, she peeled herself off him. "Well, I certainly don't recall seeing a chamber pot that morning," she shot back. But the small joke helped to dispel the tension. "How much farther?"

"Nearly there now," he said, threading his fingers into hers. "Are you ready?"

It was then she realized his other hand was holding his pistol, raised and at the ready. She nodded, unable to speak. She couldn't exactly admit she was frightened when this was all but her idea. Or that the sight of his pistol terrified her nearly as much as their mission. He called her courageous and brave, but in this moment, she felt anything but.

As they turned onto South Bridge, she could see the shops on each side had already been completely shuttered and locked up for the night. He stopped beside an unpainted door, then cocked his head, listening a long moment. "I do not think anyone is here," he finally said, putting his gun away.

She loosened a breath she hadn't even realized she was holding. Heard him fiddle with the latch on the door, the creak of rusty hinges. Felt the first cold drops of rain pelting her face. And then he was lacing his fingers into hers, tugging her inside.

Immediately, she was enveloped by smells.

Musty and dank, with an echo of something sharper, hanging on the edge of each breath.

As West pushed the door shut behind them, the darkness inside covered her like an immense, unmovable blanket. "Oh," she gasped, her heart galloping up another few degrees. Had she thought it dark outside, in their mad dash through the dimly lit streets? She would have given anything to have that meager light now.

She had never seen or felt anything so complete.

"West . . . do you have a match?" she whispered.

She heard soft noises, clothing rustling. A muttered curse, delivered into the darkness. "There are none left," she heard him say. "I used them all the night I snuck into Southingham's study. Besides, I don't think an open flame is a particularly good idea in here. We don't know what we are dealing with yet." She felt his hand bump into her arm, then trail down to curl over her hand. "So, no light then. Down we go. Stay close."

She followed him blindly down what seemed like an endless set of stairs, her free hand braced against the cold stone wall. It felt as if they were descending into hell itself—if hell were made of stone walls three feet thick, and composed of a silence nearly as complete as the darkness. She couldn't see anything beyond her imaginings, couldn't hear so much as a peep from the outside, though the storm must certainly be close over the top of them now.

Finally, they emerged into a more open space. They stood a moment, hand in hand, ears cocked toward the open darkness. Mary heard nothing beyond the labored sound of their own breathing, but her imagination was helpfully supplying some terrifying ideas about what awaited in the looming darkness.

Bodies. Ghosts.

Guns.

"Perhaps we should split up," she offered in a small, terrified voice.

"Mouse," she heard him sigh. "I hope you are joking."

She felt the punishing but welcome grip of his fingers, knew the relief of his pulse, steady, if a bit fast, there through his fingers. "We stick together, no matter what."

"Agreed," she breathed.

Together, they stumbled along the perimeter of what turned out to be a small room, feeling their way, using the wall as a guide. In spite of his admonishment to stay together, once they'd made a circuit of the small room and found nothing more interesting than cold stone walls, they aimed toward the center of the room, until her questing fingers dragged across a bit of rough wood and metal. "Barrels," she called out. "Here, in the center."

She fanned her fingers out to see the shape and scope of her discovery, imagining what might be inside. The scent she had noticed abovestairs was stronger here, clearly emanating from the barrels themselves.

She sniffed, trying to place the sharp, acrid scent. "Definitely not wine."

"No," he agreed, just to the right in the darkness. She felt the air move. Heard him grunt, and then a mighty crash made her nearly jump out of her skin.

"Bloody hell," she heard him snarl as bottles spilled out of the knocked-over barrel, some rolling loudly across the stone floor, one or two breaking in sharp, tinkling notes.

Mary stooped down and rubbed a finger against the liquid now soaking the floor. "Well." She sniffed her finger, recognizing the scent. "Unless they plan to pelt the queen with whisky bottles in the morning, I would say we have dodged a catastrophe."

A low chuckle rose somewhere above her head. "If Grant were here, he'd complain about such a bloody waste of whisky. Still, we ought to check the others."

Working together this time, they carefully opened the other barrels. Reaching inside, her hands met a surprisingly fine powder. She sneezed as it puffed up into the air, choking on the invisible assault. "What . . . *is* that?" she gasped, trying in vain to see something other than the black curtain that currently enveloped them.

"Gunpowder." West sounded grim. "And a good lot of it."

They checked another barrel, and then another, all full of the same powder. She realized, then, why West had wisely refrained from her suggestion to light a match.

The entire place might have gone up in flames.

"Oh, good heavens." She stared into the blackness, wishing she could see West's face, imagining it bore the same look of horror that was surely claiming her own. The realization of where they were and what eleven barrels of gunpowder might achieve in this location sent a chill rippling through her. "They are going to blow up the bridge."

"With a crowd of hundreds and the queen's entourage on top," he agreed grimly.

Mary stared into the darkness, her thoughts sifting through the pieces. "We have to do something. This is *finally* the evidence we've been needing. Surely the authorities would believe us now, if we lead them here so they can see for themselves."

There was a moment's hesitation. "Or else they might arrest us," West said slowly, "and presume we had a hand in all of this."

"We have to at least try," Mary pointed out. "I won't have the deaths of innocents on my conscience. I'd rather be charged with treason than live with the knowledge I didn't prevent a tragedy when I had the chance."

"I know." His hand looped against hers. "And for once, I agree with your plan. But I will take the blame if it comes to it. It was all my idea, and you knew nothing about it. Agreed?"

"No." It was a word he'd once teased her about using, but it had never been more appropriate. "You yourself said we need to stick together. Whatever happens, we will face it together." Still, his offer unmoored her. She leaned toward him, into the darkness, her throat tight. He had already sacrificed his freedom, to marry her. Now he was offering to sacrifice his very life, his family's reputation, to protect her? He might not be fashioned like the heroes from the pages of her books, but he was indubitably a hero.

Her hero.

Somehow, through the darkness, her lips found his. His hands came up to frame her face, demanding, desperate, and she hung there, lost in the moment. It was tempting to imagine sliding back into his arms, letting him push her against the stone wall, dispensing with three days of doubt in a moment of pleasure. But instead, she reluctantly pulled away, her lips moist, her heart tipping toward truth. They couldn't do this, not with so much at stake.

Still, she turned her face into his palm, trembling. "I wish . . ." she sighed, but then stopped the trajectory of that hope. She wished theirs was an ordinary marriage. She wished West was an ordinary man, and she was an ordinary woman, and they were here to do ordinary things, like make love to each other in the darkness.

"I do, too, Mouse." His voice sounded hoarse. "And perhaps we can figure out how to make that wish come true, once we've dispensed with our assassin." His hand fell away from her face. She let his fingers curl into her hand, tightening protectively.

And then she followed him up the stairs as fast as their lightless path permitted.

As they reached the small landing where they had come in, she girded herself to step out into what must by now be a raging storm. But instead of rain and thunder, they were met with a door that wouldn't budge. "What in the devil?" she heard him growl.

She heard the rattle of a latch. "If the wind's blown it shut—"

"It wasn't the wind. It's bloody locked." She heard him hurl himself against the stubborn wood, his shoulder landing with solid whumps, three in all, each more painful to hear than the last. "God *damn* it."

"What are you saying?" she asked, her heart twisting in fear.

"I am saying"—she heard him snarl through the darkness—"that someone has come back and locked the place up for the night. We are trapped in here until morning."

Chapter 26

They sat side-by-side in the darkness, West's jacket spread out beneath them, shivering on the cold stone floor.

It was a terrifying predicament. They were trapped in the vaults below Southgate Bridge with a room full of explosives. If they survived the rumored ghosts, they would be stuck in here until morning, when Southingham would return, almost certainly armed and none too happy to deal with them.

And worse—if there could be a worse—now they would never be able to alert the authorities in time to stop the plot.

Shivering against the direction of her thoughts as much as the chilled air, Mary stared out at an invisible black landscape she knew contained eleven barrels of gunpowder and one tipped-over barrel of whisky bottles. Just an ordinary Wednesday night, she tried to tell herself.

That is, an ordinary night if one were the heroine of a tragic novel, *literally* facing one's darkest hour.

The blackness began to seep into her very pores until she felt as dark as their surroundings. All around her, she could hear the faint drips of water, the sounds telling her that the storm outside—the storm she still couldn't hear, in spite of straining her ears to catch some vital sound beyond her own breathing—was intensifying. She listened in vain for a rumble of thunder, tried to imagine she could see a flash of lightning. There was nothing beyond the relentless drip of water and her own labored breathing.

Clearly, screaming for help would be a waste of time.

"Do you think Southingham locked us down here on purpose?" she whispered, finally giving voice to the fear that had plagued her from the moment she realized they were trapped. "That he heard us, and knows we are down here?"

"No. I think he must have simply checked the door one last time and realized it was unlocked," came West's firm reply. "No one from the street could have heard us so far down here. And if he had a suspicion we were here, I doubt he would have left us here, mucking about in his barrels. He would have just shot us, don't you think?"

Mary wanted to believe West's matter-of-fact cataloging of their predicament, his simple explanation for the reason they were likely still alive. But fear had hold of her now. "How can you be so calm?" she choked out. The thought that they were trapped here, like animals in a cage, ghosts and bodies and barrels lurking in the darkness, made her want to claw her way to freedom, even if it meant tunneling ever deeper beneath the earth, or scratching through three feet of stone.

Through the darkness, she felt West's hand bump into hers. "Here," he said gruffly. "I can feel you shaking. Have a bit of this. It will warm you up, if nothing else."

She felt the cool press of glass against her palm. Realized he was passing her one of the unbroken bottles of whisky. She hesitated a moment, then bolted down her first swig of something more interesting than punch.

The burn of it caught her off guard. It tasted like a smoky

peat fire—not the sort of thing one willingly swallowed. She choked a moment, then found her words swimming drunkenly somewhere near the bottom of her throat. "*This* is what you and Grant are so fond of drinking? How on earth do you stand it? It is the most vile thing I've ever tasted!"

He chuckled, and she felt the warm press of his shoulder, leaning into hers. "In truth, it's generally regarded as an acquired taste."

"And just how does one 'acquire' this horrid taste?" she sputtered, still trying to clear her head from the unexpected burn of the stuff.

"By taking another sip, and then another, until oblivion and pleasure take over and you no longer care what it tastes like." He hesitated, then added wickedly, "Just like me, Mouse."

Well. He had a point there. So she lifted the bottle again. Sniffed at it, then sipped, more gingerly this time, handling it far better now that she knew what to expect. The third and fourth gulps were even better, but then she felt West's fingers reaching through the blackness to lift the bottle from her hands, spilling a bit down her chin in the process.

"That's a bit more than a sip." She heard him chuckle.

"Well, given that we are locked down in here in a room about to explode, oblivion sounds like a good alternative." She wiped her sleeve across her mouth. "I feel helpless, with no way to fix this." She felt the moisture from the spilled drink soak through the thin wool of her sleeve, giving her a small shadow of an idea. "Although . . . could we dampen the gunpowder with the whisky?"

"I don't think so. This particular variety tastes like the sort Grant likes to smuggle down from the north, strong enough to take paint off a wall. A much more potent brew than the sort they sell at White's. If we dampen the gunpowder with this, it's liable to make the place go up even brighter."

"Oh." She looked down in the area where her lap would

be, if only she could see anything in the blackness. "Well then, bugger me blue."

He burst out laughing. "Clearly, your vocabulary has taken a turn for the worse since marrying me."

"Well." Her lips twitched. "I've been taking notes." She wanted to dive into the sound of his laughter. Sighed heavily instead. "Isn't there anything we can do besides drink the rest of the bottles and wait for morning?"

She felt his hand fumble through the darkness to land on her arm, where it settled softly, a whisper of promise. "I have a few ideas."

She sucked in a breath. Already, the whisky was doing strange things to her head. Or perhaps that was owed to the touch of her husband's hand. She leaned toward him, the whisky stripping away the last of her doubts, the promise of a different kind of oblivion urging her on. But before her lips could find his, she stopped as she caught the sound of something new.

Tiny nails on stone, skittering through the darkness.

He apparently heard it, too. "Good *Christ*, what was that?"

She reached out a hand, seeking his. "West . . . are . . . you afraid of ghosts?"

"Hardly." She could hear him panting in the darkness. "Ghosts don't bite."

She smothered a laugh. It hardly made sense. This was her large, strapping husband, the man who plunged after criminals brandishing a gun, the man who kept a Victoria Cross lying about the top of his dresser bureau. The skittering came again, this time to their right, and he jerked beneath her palm, kicking at imaginary things.

"Are you . . . afraid of mice?" she asked, understanding dawning. "But you call *me* Mouse!"

"I know." She heard him gasp through the darkness. "And that's because you've been terrifying me since the very first moment I saw you."

SHE BURST OUT laughing, and he supposed he couldn't really blame her.

He felt a bit like laughing himself.

Oh, but the universe had a terrible sense of whimsy, to trap him down here—at Southingham's hand, no less—with a room full of what he could only imagine were a horde of beady-eyed, sharp-toothed creatures. Even if he could only hear the one.

He supposed he could just tell her. Explain all of this. His instincts always pushed him toward tight-lipped silence when it came to managing his demons, but it was clear that silence was not going to be useful around his new wife.

And truly, what else did they have to do here to pass the time, sitting in the darkness, vermin closing in on every side?

"And it isn't mice as much as rats," he admitted, staring up into the cavernous darkness. "Do you remember the corpse?"

"Please don't call her that," he heard Mary say tightly, her laughter dying.

"Very well, the barmaid, then. Southingham wanted her, too, and he wouldn't let it go. The barmaid preferred me, you see, and his ego was quite smashed over it. So he took every opportunity to harass me afterward." West winced as he said it. A euphemism, that. He could still remember the day Southingham had cornered him, the broken ribs, the week he'd spent in Harrow's infirmary. He recalled how difficult it had been not to unleash his fury, knowing that he—not his bully—would risk expulsion if he struck out in defense.

"But there's a code amongst gentleman, you see. Future viscounts don't go about pummeling future dukes, even if those dukes deserve a thrashing. Retaliation was a bit tricky. So one night, I filled his room with rats. Only, they didn't stay in his room. Some of them found their way back to mine, chewing their way through the walls." He shuddered, even as his ears strained for more unwelcome skitters. "Southingham told everyone who would listen the rats had chewed my prick to a nubbin. And of course, a proper gentleman could not go around showing everyone the part in question, just to prove a rumor wrong. So for a time there, half of London imagined I was . . . lacking."

"You? *Lacking?*" This time, her laugh was welcome. "Good heavens, West. Judging by my sister's utter horror when I married you, there's not a woman in London who believes such a thing anymore."

"Well, I may have worked hard to disprove it." His lips twitched. "And that prank with Southingham's duchess last year . . . it was intended to ensure the one woman who mattered would know my prick was intact, thank you very much." He leaned his head back against the wall, feeling better to have told her this piece of his life. He wouldn't have imagined that unburdening himself would feel right, but with her, somehow, it did. "Your turn now," he said softly into the darkness. "I've told you one of my truths. I'd ask a question of you. Why are you so afraid of guns, Mary?"

He could hear her exhale, the rattle of her nerves. "I . . . don't know what you mean."

He shook his head, recognizing with a skill borne of experience that she was trying to evade some pertinent truth. "It may not be obvious to everyone, but I watch you. I *know* you, Mary. You refused to learn how to fire the derringer I offered you, even though it is far safer for you to handle than a knife, and you grow pale and quiet every time you see a gun in my hands. Why?"

"It . . . that is, it isn't precisely a secret," she stuttered. "Just memories." There was a moment of silence, and he could feel her tremble through the darkness. "When I was nine years old, my oldest brother was killed by a hunting rifle, and most people believed my brother Patrick killed him, in order to inherit the title."

"Good God." West tried to remember if he had heard anything of that sort. Came up blank. Then again, a decade and a half ago, he'd still been playing with toy soldiers, not focusing on mysterious murder plots. But she had borne it. And it seemed she was bearing it still. "But your brother is now the Earl of Haversham," West said. "He was acquitted, I take it?"

"Yes, but only because"—her voice broke—"because then my father was killed, and there was no way Patrick could have done it, given that he was hiding in Scotland at the time. And so suspicions began to take root, and they finally uncovered the real killer . . ." Her voice trailed off, and he could hear the anguish in her sigh. "I nearly lost Patrick, too, even though he'd done nothing wrong. The point is, I've lost so many people in my life, West. It seemed safest to stay in Yorkshire all these years, my nose buried in books. And it isn't so much guns that I'm afraid of, as the reminder of what they can do. It is losing the people I love that terrifies me the most."

West's heart clenched for the shy, scared girl she must have been. He remembered how she had seemed to know, to understand, the source of his nightmares. She had her own demons to fight, it seemed, though she was doing an admirable job stepping out of that shell and standing on the edge of courage now. Only . . .

He sucked in a breath, realizing, then, what lay at the heart of some of this. Damn it all . . . he'd badgered Southingham into a duel, a fight to the death.

With pistols.

A duel he might yet lose.

Good Christ. No wonder she was finding it so difficult to trust him.

The skittering came again, farther away now, and this time he didn't jump. Perhaps it was because he could feel her hand in his, small but reassuring.

Or perhaps it was because he was more concerned about her.

"Your turn again," she said, her fingers tightening over his. "Would you tell me what happened in Crimea?"

She was holding her breath, waiting for his answer—he could hear it. Or rather, he *couldn't* hear it. But the small telltale sign told him this was important to her.

And for once, it was easier to face this confession in total darkness.

"I told you some pieces of it," he said gruffly. "How we were sent to Viborg instead of the front lines. There wasn't expected to be any fighting there." He could still remember how young and naive he and Grant had been, how the adventure—not the fight—had been the point.

And how quickly it all went to shite.

"But you were wrong," she prompted, and he remembered, then, how she had followed the accounts of the war in the newspaper.

"It started with an explosive shell," he said, feeling the sharp edges of the various pieces of that day, the shattered remains of the memory he had tried so hard to forget. "It rolled right up to our feet on the lower deck. Most of the men were laughing over it." He swallowed. "They assumed it was a prank, you see. But I knew it wasn't. Or at least, I knew it wasn't one of *my* pranks. I could see it was the sort of shell that had a delayed charge, and so I seized it and threw it overboard. It exploded outside the ship, where no damage was done." He shook his head. "Hardly a brave act, it was simply a matter of survival."

He could feel her mind working through the tightening of her hand. "Who placed a shell in such a place? I have to imagine it was a calculated act."

"There was a saboteur on board. A traitor who was willing to sacrifice himself for such a prize as sinking the *Arrogant*." He closed his eyes, though the gesture scarcely made a difference in the darkness. "There was a fight afterward. Shots were fired."

What came next was mostly a haze of fury, flashes of memory. He couldn't remember the feel of the bullet entering his shoulder, but he could still feel the roar of vengeance pounding in his ears, the solid crunch of his fist striking bone, the way his feet had scrabbled on the deck slick with blood. Too much blood, and not only his own.

He felt the crawl of her hand, reaching toward him, working its way up to land just above his heart. "Is . . . that how you got this?"

"Yes." He opened his eyes, and stared hard into the darkness that swallowed her. "I was injured wrestling the gun from the traitor's hand. But honestly, Mouse, I was the lucky one. Three of my men were killed that day, sailors whose only sins were throwing themselves into the fray, trying to help me subdue the threat." He shook his head, remembering those slow-motion moments all too well, no matter how long and hard he'd tried to forget them. "Afterward, Grant held his shirt over my wound, even pulling out his flask to clean it out. He saved my bloody life. The others weren't so lucky. One man died there, on deck. The others died later, when their wounds festered."

He stopped. Swallowed. Gave his tongue permission to go on.

"William Breech. Danny O'Shea. Pete Thompson." The men's names came out in whispers, the first time he'd spoken them out loud since that day. "They were sailors for whom I was responsible." he said hoarsely. "And I didn't react in time to save them."

There was a moment of silence, though her hand did not loosen from his, despite the damning confession. "You were credited with saving the ship," she said softly. "And that is why you were awarded the Victoria Cross."

"I told you, it was a joke. I didn't know it was a live shell."

Although, in truth, he hadn't known it *wasn't* live, either.

Her hand tightened over his chest. "I think that your instincts very likely saved the day."

"Saved the day?" An aching part of him wanted to believe her words, but his own snarling objections were too great. "Good Christ. Can't you see? It's *my fault*, Mary. The traitor was one of my own sailors, and I should have known, should have been able to stop it before anything happened. I was the bloody officer in charge of that deck that day. And the men who deserve a Victoria Cross are the ones who never made it home."

SHE COULD HEAR the anguish in his voice. Knew all too well the heartbreak that came from looking back on a tragedy and wishing you had seen something, *done* something differently.

Her own life had been shaped by similarly violent forces—her brother's death, her father's murder, those dual tragedies had consumed her spinning, chaotic adolescence. She had wished, on so many occasions, that she might have been in a position to stop it, to change things. And she knew all too well how such imaginings could eat at you, change who you were.

"I understand," she whispered, her heart twisting in her chest.

"How can you understand?" His voice was sharp in the darkness, a rooting tip of a knife. "Grant doesn't even understand, not entirely, and he was bloody *there*. No one understands why I can't just move on from it, least of all me. There has been no one I can talk to about this, not the families of the men who died, not Wilson, not even my best friend."

"You have *me* to talk to," she told him gently. She lowered her hand to curl into his again. "And I understand more than you might imagine." She turned her hand over in his, staring down into the darkness where they were joined, even if she couldn't see it. Hers was not a fierce battle, perhaps. The balance of a nation's power had not sat so heavily on her young shoulders. But the endless nightmares, the punishing memories, the questions that she could not seem to stop asking herself—those things she knew all too well.

According to her own sister, those events of her childhood had caused her to lose the vivaciousness that had once defined her, turning her into someone who panicked in crowds and hid away in Yorkshire.

And West's past had turned him into . . .

She stopped, suddenly fitting it all into neat pieces, a puzzle she'd not previously understood. Her husband's scandalous reputation, the terrible pranks, the drunken antics, the line of women eager for a chance in his bed—relics of a youthful exuberance, perhaps, but also something more.

He'd been traumatized, looking for an escape.

And she imagined, now that she could see it, that she could understand a bit of what had been driving him since his return from Crimea.

"I believe in you." Her hand pulled out of his, searching through the darkness until it landed on his chest again, her fingers curling deep. "If you hadn't reacted so quickly that day, how many more of your men might have died at the hands of that madman? And if the ship had been damaged by that shell, would the *Arrogant* have gone on to win that day?"

Beneath her fingers, she could feel him suck in a breath. "But—"

"I know you feel terrible about the men who died." Her fingers pressed into a point over his heart. "I can hear it in your voice, in the tightness of your chest, just here. But they died fighting for something important, and you don't have the right to take that honor away from them, any more than you have the right to determine who Queen Victoria chooses to bestow the honor of the Victoria Cross upon. What about those men who lived only because you'd had the wherewithal to act in their moment of indecision, those men who eventually went home to their wives and families? Do *they* mean nothing?"

"No," he choked out. "They mean everything. But they didn't realize—"

"No, *you* don't realize. You've been trying to find a distraction to help you forget what happened. To forget the names of those men who died. But what if remembering them, talking to their families, honoring them in some way, is the real path to healing?"

"I . . . I hadn't thought . . ."

"It sounds to me," she said gently, her hand pressing more firmly against his body, "as though you are the only one who thinks this honor that has been bestowed upon you is a joke." She curled against him, her head somehow finding the shelf of his chest in the darkness. "When I am reading a book, do you know who my favorite sort of hero has always been?"

He didn't answer.

She told him anyway. "I've never really much liked the strutting peacock heroes. They tend to beat their chests and belittle the heroine and generally get too many people killed. No, I'd rather find myself in love with a reluctant hero." She turned her head. Pressed her lips against the cotton of his shirt, right above his heart. "Someone who shuns the honor, but steps up when the circumstances demand it."

His breath whooshed out of him, and she could feel his arms come up to cradle her gently. "Are you saying . . . you could love me?"

"Can't you see?" She turned herself over to it, the truth she'd been trying to avoid, ever since he'd given her cause to doubt him. "I already do."

Chapter 27

*S*he . . . *loved him?*

West tightened his arms around this woman who was his wife, his confidante, his partner. If this damp, dark vault was their confessional, she had just confessed a miracle, one he'd not ever imagined earning. Somehow, beyond all reason, she'd looked inside him, seen his faults and his demons, and still found something to love.

He felt gutted by the wonder of it.

He pulled her up the length of his body until their noses bumped in the dark. A tricky business, navigating such blindness, but his other senses filled in the holes. He could hear her softly indrawn breath of anticipation, taste the whisky on her lower lip from where she had spilled a few drops. He could *feel*, against his hands, the quickening of her heart beneath all those maddening but necessary layers of clothing.

There would be no undressing tonight, not in the damp chill of this place.

Not that he needed such a luxury to show her how much she meant to him.

Somehow, his lips found hers, the sort of kiss that bespoke everything he was feeling inside, a kiss that stirred the blood and made other parts sit up and take notice.

"I love you, too, Mouse," he murmured against her softly parted lips. His hands lifted, cradling her face, feeling the warm wet tears on her cheeks. He'd never confessed a more potent truth. He couldn't point to precisely where or when it had happened, but it had. From the moment she'd first kissed him back in that library, he'd not been able to get her out of his head *or* his heart.

"I don't know why," she gasped, but it was a happy sound, one that told him she was as moved as he was. "I've been very difficult about all of this."

He rubbed a thumb along the wetness of her cheek. "Ah, but I love that about you, too."

She pulled away. "How could you possibly love the fact I am difficult?"

He let her go, not because he thought it was good idea, but because he had an idea to put his hands to a better use. "Mouse," he told her. "I love *everything* about you." He ran his fingers up her arm until they found the front of her bodice. Found the hidden brass eyes and opened them with a practiced flick. "Number One, I love the way you argue with me, and the way you make your endless lists. Number Two, I love the way you look in the morning, with your hair sticking out in twenty directions."

She made a strangled sound. "That is actually three items. You don't have any idea how to make a proper list."

His hand slipped inside her bodice to flirt with the edge of her corset and the thin, worn cotton of her chemise. Even in the darkness he knew they were plain, white, unadorned— and he no longer imagined ever wanting them any other way. "Well then, Number Four, I love the fact there are always ink stains on your right hand, from writing God knows what. Probably from making lists about why marrying me was a very bad idea. Or perhaps you are writing your own salacious novel," he teased. "*The Lustful Librarian*."

"I write nearly every day in my journal, if you must know." But it was clear from the slight hitch of her voice she was trying not to laugh now.

"Well then, I love that about you, too. There isn't a thing you could do or say that I wouldn't find perfect. I love the way you know the oddest things, from all the obscure books you've ever read." He paused, his hand stilling, then added, "I even love the way you are scrunching your nose right now."

MARY LIFTED A hand to her face. "How did you know I was scrunching my nose?" she asked in wonder. To know that he knew such a thing about her was one thing, but to hear him make a list . . . to actually catalog those things about herself she so often doubted, to tell her they were the very reasons he loved her . . . it boggled the mind.

"Because you *always* scrunch your nose when I say things that made you squirm." She felt his hand slip deeper, beneath her chemise. Moaned as his fingers found the berry of her nipple and rolled it gently between his fingers. "But when I *do* things that make you squirm," he added wickedly, "oh, that is a different look you give me all together."

"And . . . ah . . . what look is that?" She felt breathless.

"Well, it has been a while, but if memory serves, your eyes go a little unfocused." She felt the swoop of his finger over her mouth, testing, lingering. "Your lips part slightly, all but inviting me to take advantage. And then . . . *then* you usually do something unexpected."

Her hand reached out through the darkness to cup his straining length. "Like this?"

"Oh, God, Mary, just so," he said hoarsely.

His words sounded raw. Driven from an inner need that matched the aching echoes of her own body. She wanted to stoke that fire, push him over the edge, the way he always seemed to push her. And so her fingers found the buttons of his trousers, working at them until he sprang free into her hands. Her mouth found him in the darkness, the feel of his skin against her lips impossibly warm, impossibly right. She ran her tongue up the length of him, tasting salt and musk. As her tongue swirled warm circles on him, his visceral groan told her more than any list how she pleased him.

But then he reached down to loop his hands beneath her arms, hauling her to his mouth, turning the tables. He kissed her until she was moaning, writhing against him. Until she was climbing onto his lap, straddling his body's erection, her hands tangling in his hair and pulling him into her mouth, and then, finally, to the entrance of her ready body.

"Good *Christ*," he gasped, as if he was only just realizing what she was about. "Mary, wait . . . we don't have the French letters—"

"I know," she whispered, her mouth flush against his own, turning herself over to the truth of it. "We don't need them anymore."

WEST GROANED HIS acquiescence, sinking into the blinding comfort she offered him, the act as primal as any he had ever known. He gripped her hips, guiding, steadying.

Gritted his teeth against the urge to spill instantly into her heat.

He discovered, then, that it was an entirely different act, loving a woman with no barriers between them. It was a joining of far more than bodies: it was a joining of trust. No one had ever put so much faith in him.

He turned his fractured thoughts to a different task, straining toward her, his teeth nipping against the soft skin of her neck as she leaned over him. The motion ripped a whimper from her, echoing off the stone ceiling, bouncing off the walls. She began to twist over top of him, her hands gripping his hair, gasping out loud.

I love you. The words had already been offered, but still they echoed like a drum beat through his head. So he said them, blowing softly across her skin, nibbling between syllables.

"I. Love. You."

"I love you, too." She choked out a cry, and then he felt her hands pulling his mouth up and into hers, her tongue reaching, searching against his own. He kissed her back, putting everything he had into her pleasure. But while his voice might now be curtailed, each thrust, each moan, repeated the improbable, unavoidable refrain. He loved this woman.

She was voracious. Perfect. *His.*

And she loved him back. He could hear it in her panting sighs, feel it in the way she moved on top of him, every secret stripped away. More importantly, he could accept it now without pushing the idea of it away. She knew the worst pieces of him, and chose to love him anyway.

And he would spend his life showing her how grateful he was for that trust.

He reached a hand down to where they were joined, searching through the slick darkness, seeking the place that would make her fall apart. But she was in total control of this moment and she twisted away from him, leaning forward and bracing her hands on his shoulders, finding her own rhythm. He lay back and let her go, willing to go wherever she wanted.

And while he couldn't see her release, he could feel it building, the rippling tightness of her quim, the lovely, stuttered breaths. He turned himself over to ensuring her pleasure, holding himself back as well as a man might, given the extraordinary circumstances, waiting until he knew she was there, hanging on that precious edge. He pulled her down tight onto him, gripping her hips, and then she gasped his name, the perfection of her release upon her.

And then, only then, did he pour himself inside her.

Chapter 28

$\mathcal{M}$ary sat up, the darkness pressing down on her. For a moment, her sleep-addled thoughts swirled, the brush with whisky still limping slowly through her veins. Her eyes tried to unpeel the darkness, searching for a hint of gray light, something to guide her. But even without it, she knew what time it was.

Five o'clock.

They'd found a few hours of sleep, at any rate.

She reached a hand through the darkness. Gasped as her hand skidded into a cold puddle of water that had not been there the night before. She cocked her head, listening. The steady *drip, drip, drip* of water along the walls had dissipated several hours ago, but the remnants of last night's storm seemed spread all around them. She tried again, reaching through the black, inky space, and this time felt relief as her fingers settled over West's sleeping frame.

She splayed her palm against his chest, and in spite of the terrible date—June 24th—she smiled to herself to feel how soundly he slept. Exactly one month ago today, she had received the letter from her sister, asking her to come to London.

So much had changed since then, not the least of which was her.

But West had changed, too, it seemed. After their frenzied reunion, he'd slept soundly last night, in spite of the potential for vermin. No nightmares had invaded their idyll.

Unless you counted the nightmare of the coming day.

She shook him gently. "Wake up, West."

As he came awake, Mary climbed to her feet, the toe of her shoe kicking against the empty whisky bottle and sending it rolling and splashing away across the floor. A cold wetness seeped into the soles of her slippers, wrenching a shiver from her already-chilled body.

"We seem to have been invaded by water last night," she said dryly. "Although . . . perhaps the water has dampened the fuses?"

She heard rustling noises as West gained his own feet. Followed the sound of his movements toward the center of the room. Finally, his voice pierced the darkness. "The powder is still dry, damn it. The fuses as well. Smart bastard, to consider the possibility of rain and place them accordingly."

"Hardly a stroke of brilliance. It's Scotland," Mary pointed out. "It rains nearly every day." But unfortunately, it didn't appear to be raining anymore. She wished, in that moment, for the steady drips of water that had lulled her to sleep. She could see now they'd missed an opportunity last night to roll the barrels closer to the walls.

Not that she regretted the distraction that had prevented such strategic thinking, but panic was now swirling inside her at the thought of what daylight was posed to bring. All those people, standing on the bridge, hoping for a glimpse of their queen—so many lives were at risk, and not only royal ones. And yet, she felt helpless to do anything to stop the march of disaster.

"West," she whispered miserably. "What are we going to do?"

"Well, Number One, we are going to make a list," he said. "And then Number Two, we are going to try not to panic."

"I hope you have a Number Three in mind, because I lack pen and paper, and truth be known, I am already panicking a bit."

"Damn it, Mouse, I'd rather hoped *you* had a Number Three in mind."

She moved toward his voice, wanting to feel the strength of his arms around her in this miserable moment. Tripped over the empty bottle again, sending it splashing into a puddle. She stopped. Bent down. Picked it up. She could feel liquid sloshing in it, liquid that hadn't been there last night, when they'd finished the last of it off.

A thought whirred through her. She reached out a hand, feeling the depth of the puddle where last night's rainwater had collected. "Number Three," she said, excitement vibrating through her. "Empty more whisky bottles."

"I hope you aren't proposing we drink the rest of it," he said dryly. "Because we are going to need our wits about us when that door upstairs opens later this morning."

"No, I am proposing we empty a few bottles and fill them with water." She stood up, the bottle clutched in her hand. "Because while there might not be enough water in here to dampen the powder, surely there is enough to soak the fuse."

THEY DID WHAT they could with what they had, although West couldn't help but think Grant would have howled in outrage to see the loss of all that lovely whisky.

They used the empty bottles to collect the rainwater, carrying the precious drops through the darkness to soak the fuses. And now that it was done, now that they were standing by the door that would lead them to the street, West's gun drawn and waiting for whatever came through that door, his thoughts centered on something far more important than whether their morning's exertions had been enough to save the queen.

He needed to save *Mary*. His brilliant, passionate, maddening wife, whose idea to waste perfectly good whisky came close to mathematical brilliance, but who was still in the sort of danger that made his palms sweat around the barrel of his pistol.

If he pressed his ear hard against the door, he could just hear a distant din outside, suggesting the revelers along the bridge were gathering in earnest now. He felt the weight of that sound acutely, like a knife point in his chest. "When this door opens," he told her, his voice low, "wait for my signal. When I tap you on the shoulder, dash out through the door and run like your life depends on it. No matter what you hear, do not stay, do not wait for me. Go toward Holyrood, away from the bridge."

"Why are you telling me this?" she hissed back. "West, you cannot be thinking to stay behind. You told me yourself we need to stick together." He could hear the panic framing her words. "I am not going to leave you here."

His fingers tightened over the pistol, and he turned himself over to the truth of it. "If we are lucky, we may have been able to stop him today, but Southingham won't be thwarted for long, Mary. He'll find another way. If I've a chance to end it here, I should take it."

"No."

He peered into the darkness, wishing he could see her face. Bloody hell, there was that word again, and delivered as emphatically as the first time he'd heard it. He'd told her he loved how complicated she made things, but right now was not the time. Already, he was listening for the ominous scrape of a key in the lock, a sound he knew could come at any moment.

"Damn it," he growled, "we don't have time to argue about this."

"Then stop arguing." He felt her hand bump into his. "If

you kill him here, you could be charged with murder. Even worse, you said it yourself last night. The authorities could blame *you* for plotting to kill the queen. We can find another way to stop Southingham." Her fingers curled, tight. "But grappling with him down there in the dark, surrounded by barrels of gunpowder that may or may not go off, is not the way to do it." He could almost feel her shake her head in the darkness. "And I am *not* leaving here without you."

They fell silent, each fuming. And then West caught the sound he'd been dreading.

A key, inserted into the lock. Turning.

He pulled Mary behind him, flattening them both against the wall behind the door and sheltering her with his body. He tried to control the angry hammer of his heart. Failed utterly. The man unlocking this door was plotting to kill the queen, and had quite possibly tried to kill Mary on the street yesterday. He wanted to launch himself at shadows, choke the life out of the body coming through that door. But somehow, he held himself back.

The door swung open on a rusty creak of hinge. Sunlight flooded inside, nearly scalding in its intensity, rendering him unable to make out anything beyond an ominous shadow stepping inside. And then the man to whom that shadow belonged headed directly down the stairs, humming a tune, the sound trailing away as he disappeared into the vaults below.

West stared in the direction the man had gone, his mind racing to an importune suspicion. Even without the words, he *knew* that song. Had heard it roared drunkenly over billiards at White's, whistled on board ship in the Crimea.

"Ye Rakehells so jolly, who hate melancholy,
and love a full flask and a doxy!
Who ne'er from Love's feats, like a coward retreats,
Afraid that the harlot shall pox ye."

A damning suspicion began to take root, one born of instinct, rather than evidence. And yet, it scarcely made sense. He was looking for a duke. *Your Grace.* The words had been clearly uttered that night in the medical library. They *had* to be looking for a duke.

Nothing else made sense.

He felt the firm tap of Mary's hand on his shoulder. Looked down to see her face, rimmed by sunlight and smudged with dirt.

"Go," he mouthed silently, knowing that the man, whoever he was, would discover their treachery in a matter of seconds.

She shook her head.

West gritted his teeth. Because no matter how he wanted to dive down those stairs, getting her to safety was the most paramount piece of it.

And he couldn't do that if she refused to play along.

She could see the moment he gave in, felt the relief of his capitulation all the way to her marrow. He wasn't going to play the stupid sort of hero, then.

Thank goodness.

She'd always preferred the smart ones.

Gripping his hand tightly, she tugged him outside, and they tumbled into the shock of a blue-sky day. After the long hours spent in total darkness, the bright light felt like a branding iron to her eyes, but there was nothing to be done but grit one's teeth and plow on.

They stumbled hand-in-hand toward New Town, careening out into a throng of people, moving opposite the mob streaming toward the bridge. They reached High Street just as a great collective shout of disappointment went up, somewhere near the middle of South Bridge.

Mary craned her neck. "There's a happier sound than the one I was dreading," she said, trying to sort out what was happening.

"Actually, I was just thinking they don't sound very happy."

Mary cocked her head, tensed for an unholy explosion, terrified the plan—either of them—hadn't worked. But gradually, she came to realize nothing was happening.

Nothing was *going* to happen.

And the lack of something had never felt more crucial to a story's happy ending.

They watched as a carriage rolled slowly past—a plain, ordinary carriage, lacking the royal arms. The shades were open, no one inside. As it turned toward the Royal Mile, heading toward Holyrood Palace, groans began to echo around them, people frustrated to have their day's plans to gawk at royals so summarily foiled. But Mary felt only the burn of relief as the carriage rolled slowly past. "Perhaps," she said, "they are unhappy because they were hoping for a glimpse of their queen. Some of them have no doubt been waiting for hours."

She could feel West's gaze, hot against her skin. "Doesn't it seem odd," he asked slowly, "that the queen isn't here, given the newspaper very clearly said she would be attending today's event?"

"Perhaps she changed her mind." Mary permitted herself a secret smile of triumph, even as the people around them began to disperse. And even lacking a royal entourage, there was no doubt they had saved the lives of countless people standing on the bridge.

"What do you know about this?" West asked, sounding suspicious.

"Well . . . ah . . . that is . . ." Mary bit her lip. She felt a little guilty, given that she had lectured her husband quite sternly on the matter of keeping his plans from her, but honestly, she hadn't known this piece of it would work. It had been a wild, willful gamble, albeit one that had paid off. "The queen appears to listen to good advice."

"Listen to *whose* good advice?" West's hand on her arm

was gentle, but he still turned her toward him, demanding an answer. "I recognize that look on your face every bit as well as your other looks. You always bite your lip when you are thinking about some plot you've arranged. What have you done now, Mary?"

"I *might* have arranged to have a note of warning slipped to the Queen before we left London, in case it all went to shite," she admitted, smiling to think her alternative plan had actually worked. "Wilson helped me. He called it a proper prank, one worthy even of you."

West gaped at her, his eyes goggling. "But . . . how? *Why*? My reputation—"

Mary struggled to contain the smile that wanted to bloom on her face.

She did so enjoy surprising . . . well . . . the shite out of him.

"Scotland Yard might not have believed your claims of a treasonous plot, but the queen apparently did. It turns out your medal was good for something beyond gathering dust on top of your bureau. We sent the note pinned to your Victoria Cross, and even signed your name to the note." She touched his arm, wanting him to see himself the way she saw him, for once: brave, trustworthy, believable. "And her majesty wisely chose not to ignore a warning from one of her own decorated heroes," she finished softly.

From the Diary of Miss Mary Channing
June 25, 1858

We spent most of yesterday in Edinburgh, exploring the architecture of the Old City.

Among other more decadent things.

It felt nearly like a real wedding trip, to traipse these old streets on my husband's arm and admire the beautiful old buildings. To enjoy the pageantry of the Freemason's procession, experience the revelry of the crowd. We seem to have turned a new corner of trust. A new corner of understanding, as well. It turns out my husband is obsessed with Gothic spires and Palladian columns, something I never would have guessed even a week ago. His renewed interest in such things suggests a step forward in his recovery, and gives me strong hope for our future.

But beneath that hope lies a fear I cannot shake.

We leave this morning on the train for London, and what awaits us there is anyone's guess. West seems troubled, no doubt because the matter of our traitor is still unresolved.

And there is still the not-so-small matter of what to do about tomorrow's duel . . .

Chapter 29

The train pulled into the station just as darkness fell over London.

Dawn was a long way off, and yet not nearly long enough, given that Mary very much feared the morrow would bring pistols at dawn, drawn on a field of dubious honor.

She followed West up the stairs to the quiet sanctuary of his room. Or rather, *their* room now. She closed her eyes, breathing in the familiar scents, weariness crashing down on her. She wanted only to go to bed, pull her husband tight against her, breathing in tandem.

But the scrape of a latch, the lifting of a wooden lid, those things opened her eyes. West was standing beside the bed, staring down at the case that contained his dueling pistols. She started forward, a protest hovering on her lips.

Gasped to see the case was empty.

"Where are your dueling pistols?" she asked in surprise.

"I sent them to Grant for safekeeping, before we left for Edinburgh." He lifted the velvet liner from the bottom of the case, and then pulled out the small derringer he kept there. "He will bring them to Hyde Park in the morning."

The realization that her husband meant to go through with the duel after all sent fear lurching through her. "West," she pleaded. "For God's sake, let's talk about this. We can find another way. You can send Southingham an apology, buy us some time, and then together we can think about what else we might do to expose him for the traitor he is."

West placed the derringer on the mattress, the wide barrel pointed carefully toward the far wall, then pulled his usual pistol from his jacket pocket and placed it beside the smaller weapon. For once, Mary wasn't tempted to stare at the guns. Her gaze lingered instead on the tension so evident around the corners of her husband's eyes. Tired eyes, too tired for a man of his age and vigor. He'd not slept in days, but even with that obstacle aside, something was dreadfully wrong. Far more wrong, she feared, than the appointment at dawn.

He opened a small case and removed a series of bullets.

The sight of them made her blink. "I was not aware," she said slowly, "that you could use a revolving pistol during a duel."

"These aren't for the duel." He hesitated. "They are for what I fear may come after."

"*After?* What are you talking about?" When he didn't answer, she sat down on the mattress. "If this marriage is going to work, you must be honest with me. You must trust that I can handle it, no matter what it is."

A muscle ticked in his jaw. He began to load the firearms, first the derringer, then his pistol.

"West." She reached out her hand to cover his. "After all we have talked about, all we have shared, you must know that I can't have this conversation when you are doing that."

He breathed out, a ragged sound. "Mary," he said, placing the firearms down on the mattress once more. "I know you don't want me to do this," he said, his voice close to cracking, "but talking about it won't do any good." He turned to face her. "I can't—I *won't*—back out of this."

"Not even for me?" she demanded. "For *us*?"

His gaze met hers, anguished.

"I love you, West." Her breathing hitched, and she realized she was dangerously close to crying, but this piece of it needed to be said before she dissolved into hysterics. "I love you the way I never imagined loving anyone. But now that I am finally emerging from that dark period of my life, the thought I might yet lose you, too, and to something so stupid, something you had a hand in orchestrating, something you have the ability to stop—"

Her words fell away as he caught her up in his arms. She could feel his body shaking against hers. "Christ, I love you, too, Mouse. And that is why I have to see this through." She felt his breath, warm against the top of her hair, and she closed her eyes, wanting to burrow deep. "There is no choice, not for me. Whoever did this, they won't stop. They know you tried to interfere, saw your face that day in Edinburgh and possibly even took a shot at you." His tender words turned into a growl. "And I am not going to sit idly by and let that happen again."

She breathed in, the familiar wool and tobacco scent of his jacket something she didn't want to ever let go. But in spite of those comforting scents, she could feel the tension, vibrating inside him. "You are scared," she asked slowly, "for me?"

She felt him nod against the top her head.

She pulled away. "But . . . if we know it is Southingham, we can take precautions to ensure my safety." She picked up the small derringer. Hefted it in her hand. Though the feel of it against her palm sent her heart thumping in her chest, she imagined she could carry it, if she had to. Firing it, though . . . that was another thing entirely. She drew a deep breath. "I will even learn how to shoot this if need be. The point is, we can find another way—"

He shook his head, his gaze probing, insistent. "The man we saw going down into the vaults . . ." His body tensed. "I don't think it was Southingham."

Mary stared at him in shock. "But then . . . who?" But even as she asked the question, a sliver of selfish hope worked its way through her confusion. "If you no longer believe it is Southingham, there is no need to go through with this." Her imagination helpfully supplied a change in the unfolding plotline. "You must summon Grant," she insisted. "Have him issue the duke an apology on your behalf, and we can—"

He cut her off, shaking his head. "I *can't* summon Grant."

"But . . . that's the role of your second, isn't it?"

"I can't ask Grant to do that because I think . . ." He swallowed. "I think the man we saw going down into the vaults may have *been* Grant, Mary. And while it may not have been Southingham down in the vaults, the man is almost certainly still mixed up in this somehow."

The weight of what he was saying pressed down on Mary, making it hard to breathe. She placed the derringer in the pocket of her skirt, her thoughts swirling wildly. "You think . . . Grant and Southingham . . . are working together?"

"I don't know. But it was Southingham's study where I overheard the whispers about the Scotland plot. And the threatening note you received matched the handwriting on the receipt from Southingham's study."

"But . . . why would Grant do such a thing?" Mary gasped. "I thought he hated Southingham as much as you do?"

"I don't know. But if he's mad enough to be involved in a plot this dangerous, and carried it through to this point, one thing's bloody certain: he isn't going to issue an apology on my behalf. And I can't stop the duel because I need to remove at least *one* of them as a threat while I still have the chance."

IT WAS A glorious summer morning.

Glorious, that was, except for the question of his own mortality.

West squinted into the dawn, waiting for Southingham to arrive. The mist rising off the Serpentine lent a fairy-like quality to the scene, but the crowd of witnesses quite destroyed the effect. They joked and drank and jostled each other to get a frontline view for the gossip that would almost certainly dominate tomorrow's rags.

Mary stood to one side, her hands wrapped around her slim body, her eyes locked on him. She'd insisted on coming in spite of his objections, pointing out that his insistence on "sticking together" applied to duels every bit as much as dark, dangerous vaults. In the end, he'd been forced to give in or else tie her up. She was clearly better with a knot than he was, and so this morning he'd chosen the battle he was more likely to win.

But he wasn't happy about it. Not one bit.

A commotion in the crowd pulled his attention toward the left. He could see Southingham striding toward him through the mist, coattails flapping.

"He's here," Grant said beside him.

"Yes." West studied the man who was approaching them, looking for cracks in Southingham's armor. The man looked as pale as Mary did, and far less composed. "He doesn't look all that eager for a shot at me," West mused, which was a small blessing. Nervous men tended to have shaking hands. It was the stone-faced ones you needed to worry about.

And beside him, Grant's jaw looked chiseled from granite.

"Do you wish to issue an apology?" Grant asked, though he didn't sound enthusiastic about the prospect.

"No." West gritted his teeth. *Do you?* The unspoken question roared through his mind. Because God knew that he and Grant were sidestepping a very pointed conversation about just what, exactly, was going on.

Grant grunted. "I'll confer with Southingham's second, then."

West watched as his friend walked toward the man who was supposed to be their enemy. Doubt sizzled down the edges of his resolve. There were so many unanswered questions, not the least of which was *why*. To West's knowledge, Grant *hated* Southingham, nearly as much as West did. Grant, too, had suffered the man's fists during their days at Harrow. Christ, it had been Grant's desire for revenge to sneak into the man's house on his wedding night, every bit as much as it had been West's.

But none of this made any sense unless Southingham and Grant were working together.

And the sting of that imagined betrayal hurt worse than any future bullet.

Grant returned to stand beside him, holding out one of the dueling pistols. "I made sure he took the other one," he said, his face unreadable.

"Why?"

"Trust me on this."

West took it. Confirmed the pistol contained the requisite, single bullet. Checked the barrel. But something caught his eye. Scratches along the inside of the barrel, marks that hadn't been there before. "What is this?"

"I took the liberty of having the barrel rifled for you," Grant said, keeping his voice low.

"*What?*" West scowled at his friend. The point of dueling pistols was their marked inaccuracy, though he'd practiced enough with this pair to imagine he might be able to compensate for their shortcomings. Rifling the bore of a smooth barreled pistol provided the shooter a vastly improved aim. In a duel, it would nearly be considered murder. "Did you rifle the barrel of Southingham's pistol, too?" he demanded.

Grant snorted. "Christ, no."

"Grant. That is—"

"Ungentlemanly?" Grant shrugged. "You're my best friend, West." He reached out a hand, taking back the pistol and performing the same check West had just done. As he stared down the barrel, his face finally softened, a wistful smile tugging the corners of his mouth. "Friends forever, eh? And I can't have you dying on me this morning." He looked up, the smile falling away. "At least, not until we've had a proper chance to talk."

"If you want to talk, talk now," West said, clenching his teeth. Because when all was said and done, they might not get another chance. "Tell me where you were two days ago. Because I know for a fact you weren't here in London."

Grant's eyes narrowed. "You and your lovely new wife did not really go to the Lake District, did you?" Not that it needed to be said. Something in Grant's voice told West his friend already knew the answer to that particular question.

"We went to Edinburgh, actually, hoping to see the queen. The odd thing is, though, the queen didn't come." West raised a brow. "I imagine that must have come as a disappointment to some."

A muscle ticked beneath Grant's eye.

West took a step toward his friend, his fingers closing over the barrel of the pistol in his friend's hand. "Now why don't you tell me why *you* were in Edinburgh, damn it. The truth this time. What are you mixed up in, Grant? Whatever it is, it isn't too late to stop it."

Grant exhaled, a rough sound. "How did you know?"

"I saw you, the morning of the parade. You seemed to have a special interest in the vaults below Southgate Bridge."

"You are the one who dampened the fuse?"

"Mary and I did it. It was her idea to use the rainwater."

"She's a smart woman," Grant admitted, a bit grudgingly.

"Yes. The most brilliant woman I know. And if you tried to kill her in Edinburgh, I swear to God, Grant, it won't matter if you saved my life a half dozen times in Crimea. My hands will be tied as to the conclusion of this conversation."

Grant's eyes narrowed. Held a moment. "Christ. You're in love." He snorted. "I should have guessed. Deucedly inconvenient thing, that. Makes a man lose his very mind." His eyes hollowed, as if reaching a grim conclusion. "Very well, I'll tell you everything." He relinquished his hold on the gun. "But only after this is over."

West's fingers tightened over the handle of the dueling pistol. "Bloody hell, Grant, tell me now—" But his protest was cut short.

A call rang out, a summons to start.

"This isn't finished," West warned, and then strode, head down, toward an uncertain fate. Perhaps it was too late for explanations anyway. Grant had all but confessed his role in the plot to kill the queen, though he hadn't precisely said why he'd done it. Perhaps there wasn't any more to it than that. It was perhaps too late for regrets, as well.

But that didn't stop him from having them.

He regretted not guessing Grant's role sooner. Christ, he should have suspected the moment he'd realized the prostitute Vivian was involved. The moment Grant had pretended not to believe him, placing that bloody wager in the betting books to throw West off the trail.

He stood like a statue, seething, his pistol pointed firmly toward the ground. Just behind him stood Southingham, similarly arrayed. Somewhere to the right, the countdown began.

"One. Two. Three."

West counted off his paces, his heart thudding in his chest, hoping to God Mary would forgive him when this was all said and done.

"Seven, eight."

As he strode past Grant, West risked a look at his friend,

his finger slick on the trigger. Grant was watching South-ingham, his face an unreadable mask. The question arose as to just who the bullet in his pistol's chamber might best be reserved for.

"Eleven, twelve."

And no matter what was going on in his friend's head, West could not get past this one pertinent question: had Grant really tried to shoot Mary in Edinburgh? Because while he could forgive a great deal, there were some limits to friendship.

"Fifteen, sixteen."

As he walked, West caught sight of the Duchess of South-ingham in the crowd. He imagined making the woman a widow today. Felt sick to his stomach at the thought of it.

"Nineteen. Twenty."

West stopped. Turned.

Raised his pistol, his lungs working like a bellows. He could see Southingham in the distance, the man's hand similarly raised. They stood that way for several seconds, the silence of the watching crowd nearly deafening. He ought to be able to pull the trigger, no regrets. After all, the man staring at him from across the field was a man he hated.

But was it a man he could kill?

Southingham looked nervous. Hesitant. Not at all like a man with West's murder on his mind. He saw Southing-ham's gaze pull toward his duchess. Was he questioning it all now? He should be. After all, the Duchess of Southing-ham had presumably possessed the power to stop this duel. She could have told her husband he was wrong in his suspicions, that she and West were not having an affair. She could have begged him to stop.

But she hadn't, apparently. She was standing, her chin up, watching it all unfold with an almost preternatural calm.

The question of *why* flailed about in his mind.

And just like that, the facts settled into place.

Your Grace, the voices had whispered that night in the library. But dukes were not the only peer of the realm addressed as Your Grace. Duchesses, too, had that courtesy.

Oh, *good Christ.*

Had he and Mary been wrong, all these weeks, searching for a bloody duke?

Slowly—because, after all, he was no longer sure that Southingham was the man he needed to kill—West lifted the point of his gun into the air. A collective gasp rang through the crowd. He held his breath, ready to dive to one side if it came down to it, hoping his reflexes might be enough to save him if the duke decided to take advantage of his decision.

But then the barrel of Southingham's pistol swung wide, veering off course, aiming for the center of the path. West saw the smoke curl out of the barrel before he heard the retort. He heard a shout—not his own.

And then he saw Grant slump to the ground, a crimson hole in his friend's chest.

Dear God.

A woman's shrill scream arose from the crowd, and it gave chase at his heels as West raced toward his fallen friend, guilt and fear colliding in his chest, the unused pistol tight in his hands. He was skidding now in the wet grass, falling to his knees. In the back of his mind, he prayed that perhaps it was just a mistake. That Southingham hadn't really meant to shoot Grant, that the aim of the pistol had been too unpredictable to properly control. He prayed, too, that the gaping hole in his friend's chest might be nothing more than a bad dream.

But the grass was damp beneath his knees, soaking through his trousers, and the blood on his hands was slippery and warm.

No dream, this. A nightmare come to life.

Shrugging out of his jacket, he pressed the wool against the wound in his friend's chest, as Grant had once done for him, on the lower deck of the *HMS Arrogant*.

"For Christ's sake, don't die on me," he warned his friend. Not yet. Not without answers.

And not without a chance to make things right.

Grant coughed, an agonizing sound. "West?" he croaked, his eyes fluttering open.

"I am here," West told him, fighting back a snarl of frustration.

"I knew you would be." Grant closed his eyes again. "Friends forever, eh?"

"Damn it, Grant, why did you do it?" West choked out, trying in vain to stanch the endless flow of blood.

"Someone . . . had to . . ."

The words scarcely made sense. No one believed they had to kill the queen—not if they were of sound mind. West lifted Grant up and cradled him in his arms, a terrible weight pressing down on him. It occurred to him, then, that Grant might well and truly be mad.

Grant shivered in his arms, though it was scarcely a cold day. "I want you to know, though . . . I didn't try to kill Mary. Knew . . . you wouldn't forgive . . . that." The words rattled in his throat. "Killed Carlson. Before he told her anything."

"But *why*, damn it?"

"I did it . . ." Blood gurgled on Grant's lips. ". . . for Crimea. For them."

"*Them?*" West blinked, knowing instantly his friend meant their colleagues, the ones who had not made it home from the *HMS Arrogant*. The ones they never spoke of. He leaned over, straining to hear Grant's garbled words. "Why didn't you tell me what you were thinking? What was happening to you?" he said hoarsely. "I could have found you help, made sure you had someone to talk to. We should have talked about what happened more. We should have spoken their names, and talked to their families. If only I'd known—"

But it seemed speaking of them now was no longer an option.

Because Grant went limp in his arms.

"Grant!" West shouted, shaking his friend. Grant's head lolled back, the light in his eyes extinguished. "Damn it, *no*!" Unexpected tears clouded his eyes. In spite of it all, in spite of what Grant himself had just confirmed, there was still a swirl of guilt in West's mind. Hadn't he wrestled his own demons, those long months since their return from Crimea? He'd always thought he'd had the worst of it. But he could see, now, how wrong he had been.

In the distance, he could hear the shouts of a struggle as a group of men tackled the duke, wrestling him to the ground. West couldn't even summon any pleasure with the knowledge his former nemesis was being taken care of in such an undignified manner. Duels might be the gentleman's way to resolve a dispute, but Southingham had just killed someone in cold blood, to the horror of two dozen or more witnesses. One didn't need a room full of rats to bring down a duke after all. They'd manage it themselves, if you gave them enough rope.

Slowly, he picked up the pistol he'd tossed to one side.

And then slowly, regretfully, he climbed to his feet. He drew a deep breath.

Turned toward the silent crowd.

"Someone should notify the coroner," he said, shaking his head.

A woman's heart-wrenching sobs tore through the mist. "No!" The Duchess of Southingham broke out of the crowd, ran toward him, and fell to her knees beside Grant's still body. "Charles," she cried, leaning over him, shaking his still form. "Do not leave me here!"

"Your Grace . . ." he said, tugging on the distraught woman's arm. He pulled her free of the body. Helped her to her feet. "Grant's gone," he whispered.

And damn it all, his friend had taken his remaining secrets to the grave.

The duchess swiped at her eyes, leaving behind a smear of rice powder and revealing the extent of her horribly bruised face. She hugged her arms about her body, rocking back and forth. "My husband killed him," she spat, "because he knew I loved him."

West placed a hand on the duchess's shoulder, his other loosening about the pistol he still carried. "Won't you tell me what happened?" he asked softly.

"Southingham forced my confession last night," she choked out, tears spilling down her cheeks. And judging by what West could see of the duchess's bruised face, it was a confession that had not come easily. "I tried to warn Charles this morning. To tell him my husband knew. But Charles wouldn't listen. He said we needed to see this through. That you would kill Southingham. I'd hoped he would kill you as well, and then it would all be over."

"*Over?*" West blinked down at her. Good Christ, was the woman mad? The crowd was pressing closer, curious ears, chattering mouths. It would never be over, not once the gossip rags found out. "You expected me to die today?" he said tersely, keeping his voice low. As the duchess nodded, he thought of how Southingham had aimed. How the bullet had flown with such deadly accuracy.

And he knew, with a sickening sense of betrayal, that the barrel of Southingham's pistol had most certainly been altered as well.

"If your husband knew you were in love with Grant, why in the hell did Southingham come here to carry through with the duel this morning?"

"Because I told him you'd encouraged us." She looked down. Trailed a finger across the bodice of her pale yellow walking gown, now smeared with Grant's blood. "That you'd helped us, arranged our liaisons. I told him . . ." She shuddered. "I told him he'd been the butt of your joke for over a year."

Good Christ. No wonder Southingham had shown up this morning, pistol at the ready. He was probably even now wishing he had a second bullet. "How did you and Grant even know each other?" West demanded. "I never suspected anything."

"Do you remember that night you and Charles tried to sneak into my bedchamber?" the duchess said, spreading her hands.

"Yes. It was one of the few pranks that Grant and I pulled that failed spectacularly."

"It didn't fail." She shook her head. "You see, Charles made it to my chamber that night. We sent my maid to distract you, so we wouldn't be disturbed. We embarked on an affair. But eventually we became tired of hiding. Of lying to everyone."

"Not so tired of lying," West pointed out, "that Grant ever saw fit to tell me the truth." It stung, somehow. All those nights at White's, all those drunken conversations they had shared, and Grant had never once hinted at such a liaison. Then again, Grant had also hidden his plans to kill the queen from his best friend. Had worked, in fact, to throw West off the trail. Had never truly revealed the extent of how much Crimea had affected him.

Suffice it to say, he had not known his friend as well as he'd imagined.

"I can understand a desire to escape your husband," West said slowly. *Softly.* "He's a brutal man." He shook off the anger that wanted to creep into his voice, knowing that he needed more answers yet. "But none of that explains why you helped Grant plot to kill the queen."

The duchess lifted a trembling finger to her bruised cheek. "My husband wouldn't grant me a divorce, even after I told him I was in love with someone else. It was Charles's idea to kill the queen. He hated her, you see, for everything that happened in Crimea. He said it would be justice, not murder."

She looked back in the direction where Southingham was lying prone on the ground, struggling against his captors. She laughed, a close-to-maniacal sound. "But it was *my* idea to pin it on my husband." Her voice softened. "It was my idea to rifle the barrel of the pistol you carried this morning." Her eyes swung back to West. "And *I* am the one who altered the second gun, the one my husband carried."

West gaped at her. "*You* rifled the barrel?"

"Grant never knew I had done it. He thought only your pistol was altered. But you were too dangerous to let live, you see. I couldn't take the chance you would tell someone."

West took a step backward, his fingers tightening over the dueling pistol still grasped in his right hand. While he was relieved it hadn't been Grant who had plotted to have him killed, he was growing increasingly worried about the state of the duchess's mind.

He knew as well as anyone that trauma had a way of twisting the soul. Grant had been undone by the events of Crimea. The duchess's cross to bear was being married to a brute of a husband with no way out. "I rather think you'll be free of your husband a good long while now," he said carefully, "as Southingham will very likely hang for this."

"Hanging isn't good enough for him." She lifted a trembling hand to her ruined cheek again. "And can't you see? I will *never* be free. I will never be happy, not now that Charles is gone." Her gaze turned accusing. "You've ruined everything, Westmore. You were supposed to kill my husband this morning." Her voice grew strangled. "And he was supposed to kill *you*."

West took another step backward, thoroughly unsettled now. The duchess was placing the blame on him now? For not dying, as he was apparently supposed to have done? How could one argue against that? There was no logic there, no hope for rational discourse. He turned his head, searching the crowd, looking for Mary. He didn't see her. Hoped she'd gone home.

Knew, in his gut, that she hadn't.

His wife was too headstrong for her own good, and while it was one of the things he loved about her, he wanted her as far away from the duchess as possible, given the nasty turn in this conversation. No matter how much sympathy he might have for the Duchess of Southingham's position—and no matter how terrible her marriage, no matter how brutal her husband's fists—the fact remained that she and Grant had plotted to kill Queen Victoria.

And that was a crime punishable by death.

The duchess was advancing on him now, pushing him back toward Grant's lifeless body, into the milling crowd. "You were supposed to be his friend," she choked out. "He tried to protect you by throwing you off the trail. Wouldn't listen to my plans to have Carlson kill you when we had the chance." Her hands fisted and she twisted her head, staring at so many people close by. "And now you and your wife will tell everyone what we have done."

"I do not know that we will have to tell everyone," West said cautiously, holding up his hands, the dueling pistol pointing safely upward. Though, he rather thought he ought to tell *someone*—preferably someone who worked at Bedlam. "And if anyone does suspect," he said in a soothing voice, trying to sort out how to get her to the authorities— and get them to believe his explanation—without causing a ruckus, "we can pretend it was just a prank. Grant always liked a good prank."

"A *prank*?" The duchess looked up at him, her eyes wild. "My life is not a joke, Mr. Westmore. Charles's *death* was not a joke!" With a feral cry, she lunged forward, grabbing the dueling pistol from his hand. She swung the heavy barrel wildly, gesturing at the crowd. "Get back!"

she screamed at the open-mouthed onlookers. "Get back, or I'll shoot!"

And that was when West saw Mary. Charging toward them, white as a ghost, her hair streaming out behind her like a brilliant brown banner. Her mouth opened in a silent scream of protest, and then the sound of her panicked voice hit him like a wall of bricks.

"West! Watch out!"

Fear rode spurs up his spine as the duchess jerked the barrel of the gun toward Mary. "No!" he roared, leaping in front of the path of the pistol. He didn't feel the bullet slam into his shoulder as much as welcome it, knowing that if it was lodged in him, it was no longer a threat to the woman he loved. He looked down at the wound in his right shoulder, the edges of his vision going dark.

The duchess was standing before him, her eyes wide with fear. The pistol in her hand fell to the ground, useless now that its one bullet had been spent. She looked uncertain of her next move.

But that didn't mean she wasn't still bloody dangerous.

West tried to pull his own pistol from his pocket, determined to defend Mary to his last breath. But his hand—his arm—wouldn't work properly, and as he fumbled with it, the duchess snatched the gun from his hand and turned it back on him.

"Your Grace . . ." he started, raising his hands. From the corner of his eye, he saw Mary slide to a stop in the slick grass, one hand on the ground, the other tangling in her skirt pocket. Though his head was spinning now, West threw himself in front of her once more, blocking the duchess's shot, ready to take the second bullet, anything to keep it from firing in Mary's direction.

The Duchess of Southingham lifted the pistol, tears spilling down her cheeks. "There is no other way," she cried. "You both know too much." He heard a hammer cock.

And then the duchess flew backward, a bullet slamming into her heart.

Shocked, he turned. Mary stood like a white-faced statue, smoke still curling about the derringer clasped in her hand, her mouth fixed in a determined line.

And the last thought West had before he fell unconscious was that for a woman who was afraid of guns, his wife had remarkable aim.

Everyone knows that gunshot is but one of the ways a hero can meet his end.

There is also blood loss, fever, carriage accident, and the ever-popular festering wound.

Not to mention the fact that this hero's wife might yet strangle him for stupidity.

I fear that while our villain has been vanquished, our happy ending is not yet assured. West remains unconscious, fighting the threat of a fever. I worry his struggle is owed as much to shock as blood loss. After all, he was betrayed by his best friend, and a person doesn't recover easily from a loss like that. I have stuck close to his side, as I promised I would. And I have regularly doused his wound with whisky . . . just in case.

After all, if there is one thing I have learned from this mad adventure, it is that you don't sit back and wait for fate to decide what to do with you.

And a little bit of whisky can sometimes save the day.

Chapter 30

West awoke with a start, gasping in awareness.

He could see a thin gray light filtering in through the bedroom window. Beyond that, however, time remained uncertain. So, too, did the nature of his immediate circumstances. He could see he was in his bed, at Cardwell House, but beyond that lay a murky confusion.

He leaned back against his pillow, thinking hard, until the pieces clicked into place. Grant was dead. This was a painful truth, one he was forced to face anew at the start of each day.

With that recognition came the inevitable, accompanying guilt. If only he'd seen his friend's worsening derangement, recognized Grant's irrevocable descent into darkness . . .

But then, how could he have, when West had been so distracted by his own demons?

Nearly everyone associated with the plot to kill Queen Victoria was dead, and West rather thought the imaginative story his wife had concocted to explain Vivian's disappearance was likely not far off the mark. No doubt the woman was now living in the Mediterranean or some similarly far-off clime, enjoying the money with which she'd absconded.

And oh yes . . . speaking of his wife . . . there was this piece to his life.

A smile tugged at his mouth. He was married. Happily so.

To a proper heroine, who carried a snub-nosed derringer about in her skirt pocket and shot villains when she needed to, and who kissed like a bloody siren when she wasn't tracking down traitors.

He turned his head to see Mary sitting up in bed next to him, bathed in a soft glow. As it always did, the sweet, simple sight of her hit him like a pleasant punch to the gut. Her bedside lamp had been turned up, and she was staring down at a book clutched tightly in her hands, a brown braid over one shoulder, her brow furrowed in concentration.

Had he just been wondering the time? A bit after five o'clock in the morning, then.

It must be, if his wife was already awake.

He shifted, letting out a small groan as the bandage on his chest pulled tight against his wound. It was healing well, no more signs of infection, but he was growing impatient with the grand pageantry of being an invalid. Wilson checked in on him far too regularly, and his family filtered through his room at least once a day.

Mary had been a rock throughout all of it, soothing his grumpiness, making him laugh. He was grateful to have her, but here it was, a bit after five o'clock in the morning, and already he felt restless, restricted to his bed.

The noise he made pulled Mary from whatever story had her so engrossed. She looked down at him, a pinch of concern on her face. "Did you have a nightmare?" she asked, lowering the book to her lap.

West shook his head. No, nightmares had become a thing of his past. His dreams had been more of the pleasant variety of late, in part due to her.

And in part due to his acceptance—his ready remembrance—of his past.

He felt alive again. In fact, he felt so alive, he was presently considering pulling his wife onto his lap and divesting her of that nightrail, no matter Dr. Merial's orders to the contrary. The lamplight was turning parts of the thin cotton transparent, and he could see the lovely curve of a small, perfect breast as she reached a hand out to smooth the hair from his forehead.

He gritted his teeth, wanting far more than the nurse-like touch of her hand. A man ought not to have to suffer a beautiful woman in his bed if he wasn't permitted to touch her. Two weeks into this convalescence, and he was about ready to clock Dr. Merial over the head every time the man appeared with a fresh set of bandages.

Didn't people understand his life was marching by? There was architecture to study, a wife to pleasure . . . but resuming those things was hardly possible while he was under strict instructions to suffer a full month's bedrest.

And judging by his wife's careful adherence to Dr. Merial's instructions, he was going to have a devil of a time changing her mind.

"I FIND MYSELF bored," West complained. His fingers drifted toward the ties of Mary's nightrail. "It's after five o'clock in the morning," he said, a hint of wicked hope in his voice. "Surely there are more important things we can be doing than reading some obscure novel."

Mary smiled down at her handsome, disgruntled husband. Seeing his petulant frown was like seeing dawn break over the horizon. It meant he was agitated, and *that* meant he was healing, and not only in the physical sense.

She'd worried in those first few days after Grant's death that the loss of his friend might set West back, renew the lingering terror of Crimea.

Instead, it had proven a galvanizing force. He spoke of things now that would have shocked her a month ago: a return to his love of architecture, his enthusiasm for her suggestion to build a new wing of St. Bartholomew's Hospital dedicated to helping soldiers heal, his hopes for a family of their own. If nothing else, Grant's treachery had highlighted what could happen when a man was unable to pull himself back from an abyss.

And she was glad to see her husband had backed away from the edge on his own.

"Oh, you are bored, are you?" she asked unsympathetically, batting at his wandering hands. She regarded him with a raised brow. "I suppose you want to talk again?"

"Actually, I had a different cure for my boredom in mind."

"Well, perhaps *I* want to talk." She laid a hand on his bare chest, taking care to avoid the bandaged area, but enjoying the way her touch made his body stiffen in predictable places. "You see, I have a confession to make, Mr. Westmore. I've been keeping a list of secrets from you, things I haven't told you yet."

"Not another list," he groaned. "And no more secrets. We promised we would always be open and honest with each other."

She smiled, her heart twisting agreeably in her chest. Had she once despaired of ever having a husband who included her in his thoughts and plans? Who told her all his secrets, and listened patiently to hers? How much had changed in two weeks. During the time he'd been forced to stay in bed, there had been plenty of time to talk. She'd learned nearly his entire life's story and suffered through a cataloging of all his various transgressions (not nearly as dramatic or awful as the rumors implied), down to the time when, at thirteen years old, he'd electrified a doorknob at Eton, shocked the shite out of his headmaster, and promptly gotten expelled.

"Which is why I am telling you now," she agreed. "No

more secrets between us. I shall start with Number One on my list. This isn't some obscure novel." She lifted her book again, feeling a bit wicked. Using her most seductive voice, she began to read again, continuing right from where she had left off. "*Driving close into her, I for a moment stopped my furious thrusts to play with the soft silly hair which covered her mount of love; then slipping my hand over her ivory belly up to her breasts, I made her rosy nipples my next prey.*"

He held his hands over his ears, shaking his head. "I can't . . . that is you shouldn't . . . Good Christ, you are a cruel, uncaring woman. Are you really reading *The Lustful Turk* without me?"

"Yes." She shrugged. "Although . . . it doesn't have to be without you."

"But Dr. Merial said—"

She leaned down and kissed him, swiftly, on the mouth, silencing his protest. "Number Two," she breathed against his lips. "Staying abed may not be *such* a terrible thing. Dr. Merial said we might resume . . . er . . . well, if we are very, very careful and do not do anything strenuous to dislodge the bandages—"

Without warning, she found herself flipped over on her back, her blond and bandaged husband looming over her. "I swear to God, Mary, if you've kept that secret longer than five minutes, so help me . . ." His eyes narrowed.

"Only since last night." She held her breath. Lifted her hands. "I suppose," she added hopefully, "since I've been so naughty, you might have to . . . tie me up and punish me?"

He burst out laughing. Leaned over her to deliver a stinging, beautiful bruise of a kiss, and she moaned as she felt the sweep of his tongue inside her. But instead of pursuing the tumult of feelings he was kindling inside her, he broke off the kiss, smirking down at her. "Aye, my sweet English rose," he said, adopting a hideous Turkish accent. "I know how to punish you. But not with a rope. With my very hand." His hand slipped lower, beneath the hem of her nightrail, and she felt the sure, knowing sweep of his fingers, swirling softly against her seam.

"I am at your mercy, my fearsome sheik," she said back, in a throaty voice that promised more love play, should only he want it.

"Although, truth be told this comes closer to punishing me," he admitted with a groan. He leaned his head against the curve of her neck, breathing harder now, even as his fingers strummed a primal beat inside her. "I've gone two weeks without a proper release. I don't know how long I can hold out."

"Well, please don't hold out too long," she informed him, wrapping her arms carefully around him, being sure to avoid the bandages. She lightly scraped her nails down his back, shivering as the motion evoked a lovely growl of pleasure from him. "Ever since our little adventure saving the queen, reading books no longer brings me quite the same degree of enjoyment." She gasped as his perfect fingers found a place that made her hips lift off the mattress, begging for more. "I've changed, thanks to you," she panted, "And I've decided I need to create a bit of adventure, not just read about it."

"I see," he said gravely, not diverted from his path in the least. "And given that I must stay in bed, just who do you propose to have this adventure with?" he asked, even as he played her like a beautiful instrument.

"I didn't say I was going to have the adventure. I am going to create it." She drew a deep breath, closing her eyes, turning herself over to the last of her secrets, though this one felt as though she was baring her very soul. "I haven't yet told you Number Three on my list. You see, I've been thinking . . . about writing a book of my own."

His fingers stilled against her. There was a moment of profound silence. And then he was lifting his hand, pressing a kiss against her lips. "Good Christ, Mouse," he breathed. "That's the best idea you've had yet. You'd make a *brilliant* authoress."

Her eyes fluttered open. She stared up at him. Was he joking?

But no . . . he was smiling at her, his blue eyes shining with something that might have been pride. "You . . . really think so?" she asked, biting her lip. "It won't be easy. I've never written anything more than a journal entry."

"With your imagination? You'll be a far better authoress than those boring, blathering idiots from the night of the literary salon."

"Better than Dickens?" she squeaked, shaking her head. "You are mad."

"Not mad. Just selective in my reading preferences. That book *Bleak House* you once told me to read sounds so . . . bleak." He smirked at her again, then pulled her nightrail up and over her head. "And at the risk of pointing out the obvious, you already have the ink stains on your hand, the mark of a proper author. I'd say the only thing missing at this point is the actual book."

He fell upon her, kissing his way up her body, his tongue merciless against her skin, until she was trembling against him. "But promise me," he said as he rounded the curve of one breast, his breath hot against her quivering skin, "the first book you write will be based on your life. You can call it *The Lustful Mouse*."

"I don't know," she giggled, happily letting him do what he would. "Perhaps a book based on my life isn't such a good idea. The best heroines always die at the end. And I've heard the hero of that tale is an utter scoundrel."

"Not in this story," he said, nipping his way toward her

other breast. "In this story, the heroine lives to be a hundred years old, and the hero is a devoted husband, determined to bring his wife the utmost pleasure into her dotage. *This* story shall have the happiest of endings."

And then he set about proving it.

Epilogue

November 21, 1858

The smell should have been worse.

She expected something sour, a nappy fouled in the worst possible way. Just last week she'd read a book on motherhood, which had warned against taking little ones out in public so as not to risk undue embarrassment.

But as Mary felt the telltale dampness spreading through the blanket and onto her bodice, she felt anything but embarrassed.

She smiled down at the cherubic face, the wide, innocent eyes. "What have you done now?" she murmured, slipping a finger inside the blanket to check the flannel. Only damp. Nothing more ominous, and certainly nothing requiring an immediate return to his mother.

"Do you want to give him back?" Eleanor asked anxiously.

"No, it's just a little misplaced urine. Nothing I haven't seen before." Still, Mary leaned down and whispered in her nephew's ear. "Although be careful where you aim, or they'll be calling you that damned Ashington one day."

And in spite of the wet bodice, she wasn't quite ready to return the baby yet. She loved holding her nephew, even the less palatable pieces of the experience. Though it would not yet be obvious to the crowd in attendance today, she could feel the pleasant quickening in her abdomen, the secret evidence of her own impending motherhood. She did not fear her new condition, any more than she feared standing in this jostling crowd. Having come through so much, she knew there was nothing she couldn't handle.

"Even wet, you are a cute little nubbin," she said, tickling her nephew on the chin and earning a happy giggle from the baby.

"Can we please use another word?" came West's voice, pushing pleasantly over her shoulder. "That one brings back unfortunate memories."

Mary glanced up from the distraction of making her nephew laugh. She'd come here today with Eleanor, knowing West needed to arrive early to see to all the arrangements. She hadn't seen him for several hours at least, and she'd *never* seen him looking like this, wickedly handsome in full military regalia, the honor bestowed upon him for his role in today's event, even though he had long since sold his commission.

Mary returned the baby to his mother, then looped her arm through West's, half-wishing she might be able to drag him to a corner and enjoy his startling appearance in private.

But the day was too important for such distractions— even ones so delicious—so she settled for a quick kiss on his cheek instead. "Oh, I think we will soon lay that rumor about what you may or may not be lacking to rest once and for all, don't you?"

"NOT SOON ENOUGH for me," West chuckled, although in truth, he no longer gave the rumors that trailed him any real thought. He lived for the woman in front of him now.

And soon, he would live for the child she carried as well.

"What are you two talking about?" his sister-in-law asked suspiciously.

Mary shook her head. "Oh, nothing."

West held his own tongue as well. She'd told him the very day—the very *minute*—her courses were late, keeping the promise they'd made to be unfailingly honest with each other, and he would keep this promise as well.

Thank goodness Mary was handling the first few months of pregnancy well, with no outward signs of distress. He couldn't imagine having accomplished any of this without her. The idea to build the new wing of the hospital had initially been hers, and she'd encouraged him to apply his rusty architecture skills in its design. It had also been her idea to delay the timing of their happy announcement until after the cornerstone of the new wing of the hospital was laid.

He had agreed because the new ward had demanded a good deal of both West's and Dr. Merial's attention, but now that the cornerstone was being laid, there was no longer a need to wait. Tomorrow she would have a proper evaluation from Dr. Merial.

But for now, the secret was happily their own.

A familiar face emerged from the crowd, looking dapper in a dark jacket and top hat, his usual white gloves replaced by dark leather for a change. "I see you've decided to finally take my advice and make something of your life," Wilson said, his rheumy eyes shining, and his voice gruff with something that might have been emotion.

"Wilson!" West exclaimed in surprise, reaching out a hand to clasp the aging servant on the shoulder. After all, this was the man who had helped Mary with that note that had saved the queen's life. "I cannot believe you came today."

"I wouldn't miss this proud day for the world, Master Geoffrey."

West's gaze fell on a row of medals pinned to the man's

chest, tarnished but unmistakable. "What is this? You were . . . a solider?" he asked, stunned.

"I fought beside Wellington, once upon a time." The older man smiled at West. "Taught me a few things about being a proper butler."

West gaped at Wilson. "I . . . that is . . . you might have told me," he said, feeling a bit embarrassed. "For God's sake, I would never have subjected a proper military hero to my wind-maker under the stairs gag."

Wilson shook his head, chuckling. "Oh, I don't know. I suspect knowing about my past military experience might have earned me even more of your tricks, given the rough time you had adjusting after your return from Crimea. But you've come through it and victory is in sight. This hospital is a fine and honorable undertaking. Well done, Master Geoffrey."

The kindly old servant turned smartly on his heel. West watched him go, his mouth still open in surprise. "I never knew Wilson was former military," he muttered.

"You didn't suspect?" Mary asked, sounding surprised.

"No." Although, it made a good deal of sense in hindsight. Wilson's almost-painful interest in West's slow recovery after Crimea, the way the man ran Cardwell House with such military precision—but what a trick to have never said anything before. A grin split his face.

A trick worthy, perhaps, of West himself.

The sharp ring of a bugle pulled his attention toward the front, signaling the start of the afternoon's event. All around them, uniformed men snapped to attention, and West cupped his hand against Mary's elbow, guiding her to the place of honor in front of the milling crowd.

Just ahead, he could see the queen standing, surrounded by a small entourage of red-coated soldiers, four of whom were settling a cornerstone into place. When Queen Victoria laid a solemn hand on it and blessed it to a useful life, the crowd erupted in great cheers.

West felt like cheering, too. They were too far away to read the inscription on the stone, but he knew exactly what it said.

St. Bartholomew's Ward for Convalescing Sailors
For William Breech. For Danny
O'Shea. For Pete Thompson.
And for Charles Grant.

The building would be finished in the spring—not soon enough to correct the enormous social burden of so many soldiers and sailors returning from various foreign fronts, many stricken with malaria, some missing limbs—but sooner than he'd ever imagined.

So many men needed care, not all of which could be seen with one's eyes. Part of his architectural plans included a special ward dedicated to men whose minds were suffering the ravages of war, a place where they could receive help without the terrible permanency of Bedlam. And judging by the happy smiles of the military men around him, they were grateful for West's efforts to oversee the building of it. It turned out usefulness suited him.

Both as a man, a sailor, and a husband.

And Mary had been correct. Remembering the men who had died—even Grant, whose derangement had almost certainly been brought on by the circumstances of that brutal war—had helped him finally, properly heal.

A voice floated toward them, feminine and regal, pulling him from his self-absorbed distraction. "Mr. Westmore, I wanted to offer you my personal thanks."

West stiffened, at first seeing only a line of red wool,

frowning faces, and tall helmets. But then a woman stepped out of the circle of soldiers.

"*Your majesty*," Mary gasped beside him, then dipped into an inelegant curtsy.

West bowed from the waist, unaccountably nervous. He'd not seen the queen up close since she'd pinned his Victoria Cross on him in Hyde Park. "Your majesty," he said, his voice hoarse with emotion, "I assure you, no thanks are needed. We are happy to do what we can to help our country's returning soldiers, after all they have done for us."

The queen inclined her head. "Yes, I am thankful for your efforts to open this ward, especially given that my plans for the new military hospital in Southhampton have been delayed due to bitter politics. But there is this matter to thank you for as well." The queen held out her hand, and he could see his Victoria Cross, laying against a pristine white glove. "I believe this belongs to you, Mr. Westmore. And I believe the thanks I owe is for my life."

After a moment's hesitation, West stretched out a hand. The medal felt smooth and cool against his hand, but his cheeks warmed against the attention. "No thanks is necessary, your majesty," he said, his voice gruff with emotion.

"Oh, I beg to differ." The queen inclined her head. "You see, after receiving your note and deciding to delay my trip, I had Scotland Yard reach out to the Edinburgh authorities."

"Did they . . . er . . . say anything about me?" West asked weakly.

"Nothing I had not already heard, Mr. Westmore. Your reputation is legend among my chamber maids. They keep wishing you might try to sneak into *my* bedchamber."

Beside him, Mary let out a horrified gasp.

"But as this did not seem like one of your jokes, Mr. Westmore, at least none of the ones I had heard, I asked the authorities in Edinburgh to investigate the route I would have taken that day, leaving no stone unturned. They soon discovered something rather unusual beneath Southgate Bridge. A hidden vault, full of gunpowder. Do you know anything about it?"

West felt like squirming. "Very little, your majesty."

"Somehow, I doubt that very much. It seems you did more than save my life, Mr. Westmore." The queen raised a regal brow. "Though I have no proof it was you, or even who might have been behind such a nefarious plot, I suspect you also saved the lives of hundreds of innocent people that day."

"Not just me, your majesty." West exhaled as he looked down at Mary, knowing that without her, the outcome would have been very, very different. He cupped his arm around her shoulders and squeezed. "*We* did what we could."

At that, the queen smiled. "My Albert and I are also very much a team, you know. I only wish I had a medal for your wife then, as well." The queen gestured to the Victoria Cross, still resting against his open palm. "Will you wear yours today?"

For once, West didn't need to think about such a question. "With pride, your majesty." He reached up and pinned it to his jacket. "In honor of those who died at Viborg."

"And, I hope, for those who lived in Edinburgh," the queen added, "thanks to you both." She offered them both a last, grateful smile before turning away.

West glanced at his wife, only to realize she was staring at the queen's departing entourage with wide brown eyes. "Did that just really happen?" she whispered. "I just met the queen? Wearing a bodice soaked with urine?"

"Just so," West said, teasingly. Now that it was over, his breath returning to his lungs, he couldn't see what all the fuss was about. After all, the queen was just an extraordinary woman—no different than his wife, when it came down to it. "But perhaps I'd better pinch you, just to be sure."

Mary's eyes narrowed up at him, but her lips twitched upward. "The only question is *where* would you like to pinch me?" She stood on her toes to whisper in his ear. "You see, I've been doing some writing of my own, and on page 48 of *The Lustful Mouse* . . ."

And just like that, she had him standing at attention, and not in a proper military sort of way. West knew then that while the day was already off to a wonderful start, his night promised to be even better. And if he had anything to say about it, page 48 of *The Lustful Mouse* was going to be very interesting, indeed.

Author's Note

Queen Victoria was Britain's longest-living monarch, holding her title from 1837 until her death in 1901. Over the course of her life, she survived seven known assassination attempts and at least one notorious assassination plot, where, encouraged by the prime minister, Irish nationalists planned to blow up Westminster Abbey on the occasion of the queen's Golden Jubilee.

These are only the assassination attempts that were known: how many were thwarted by unsung heroes is anyone's guess.

At Avon Books, we know your passion for romance—once you finish one of our novels, you find yourself wanting more.

May we tempt you with . . .

- **Excerpts** from our upcoming releases.

- Entertaining **extras**, including authors' personal photo albums and book lists.

- Behind-the-scenes **scoop** on your favorite characters and series.

- **Sweepstakes** for the chance to win free books, romantic getaways, and other fun prizes.

- Writing **tips** from our authors and editors.

- **Blog** with our authors and find out why they love to write romance.

- **Exclusive content** that's not contained within the pages of our novels.

Join us at
www.avonbooks.com